Hyena Dawn

'This isn't about peace, laddie, it's about war. I'm asking you if you want to take part in perhaps the most important action of the whole war. A secret project. Something you'll never get public recognition for. A project so dangerous that no man in his right mind would have anything to do with it. In the long run it'll make a negotiated peace possible and stop Rhodesia heading into a bloodbath. And I need your decision now. No one else knows about this except a few men in high command. The whole operation is top secret.'

'Equipment?' Rayne could feel his pulse racing already.

'You'll get everything available – legally and illegally. And Rayne, you'll be in command.'

'You bastard, sir.'

'My pleasure, Captain Gall~~ach~~er. I ~~knew you~~ couldn't resist it.'

D0955069

CHRISTOPHER SHERLOCK

Hyena Dawn

A Mandarin Paperback

HYENA DAWN

First published in Great Britain 1990
by William Heinemann Ltd
This edition published 1991
by Mandarin Paperbacks
an imprints of Reed Consumer Books Ltd
Michelin House, 81 Fulham Road, London SW3 6RB
and Auckland, Melbourne, Singapore and Toronto

Reprinted 1991, 1994

Copyright © Christopher Sherlock 1990

A CIP catalogue record for this title
is available from the British Library

ISBN 0 7493 0564 9

Printed and bound in Great Britain
by HarperCollins Manufacturing, Glasgow

To Karen with all my love

Rayne

Mozambique 1978

The man walked out of the clearing. His face was black and his chin was covered by an enormous curling beard. He stank of four weeks' sweat. Hanging from his neck was an AK-47 assault rifle, and round his waist were pockets of ammunition. A torn French army parachute jacket covered his upper body and a filthy pair of jeans hid his legs. On his feet were thin black hockey boots caked with mud and dust.

Suddenly, amongst the sweet-smelling denseness of the bush the man sensed a different smell. The smell of other men. His hand moved easily across the breech of the rifle to make sure that the safety-catch had been released. His eyes scanned the trees, looking through them to the bush beyond. His finger rested close to the trigger and he moved silently towards denser cover.

Captain Rayne Gallagher had been operating this way for the last two months. His superiors had realised that he was better by himself, prepared to take more risks and able to move faster; but the loneliness of the work was itself a hazard. Now he felt very alone.

There was a shrill, high-pitched whistle. Rayne dropped to the ground and rolled over three times, coming to rest against the side of a tree. The whistle made his blood run cold. It was a call-sign, and it sounded familiar. For one crazy instant he was tempted to reply in English. He did not know if he was supposed to give a password. One word, one sound wrong, and he could

1

be dead. Death moved one step closer, too, in every second he hesitated.

The silence threatened. He had to reply. He shouted out in a language not his own – and shivered as he heard the metallic sound of a gun.

Who the hell was it? The sweat poured off his forehead. Every sensory organ in his body was strained to the limit of alertness. He had to try and keep the advantage.

Then he saw them, indistinct among the distant trees. Three of them. He raised himself upwards, his eyes surveying the bush around him, and in the middle distance he caught the glint he had been looking for. Four of them.

The voice of the man he could not see asked him where he had come from, speaking in the black language Rayne himself had used. He almost thought he recognised that voice. Momentarily his finger strayed from the trigger as his eyes strained to locate him. Where was the bastard? He couldn't be more than five metres away. He had to see him.

Something told Rayne to speak. He lied that he had been over the border and killed a headman who had been in the employ of the government forces.

There was a chuckle in the distance. He began to relax. He told the man he had laid mines which had killed a farmer and his wife on their way home. There was more laughter, then an unnerving silence. The man asked him the name of the farm.

Rayne gave it, and tensed for the reply. This time there was a new hostility in the man's voice. He said that the farm had been abandoned two years before.

Mistake. Now he knew he had to risk it – it was the only course left to him. Licking his dry lips Rayne said, 'Don't I know you?'

After he'd spoken, the words hung in the air and he sensed the moment of indecision. Is this the moment when you die, Captain Gallagher?

The movement of a gun barrel telegraphed the man's intention. Rayne moved forwards and sideways in a crouch, and heard the gunshot as the first bullet ripped across the folds of his jacket. He rolled over and brought his rifle round in a clear arc to where the man had been, the trigger flat as the rounds spat out on full automatic.

A man staggered out of the bush screaming, blood pouring

from his head and stomach. Rayne fired again as bullets sliced all around him, and the man's head exploded and he dropped to the ground noiselessly.

A second man revealed himself. Rayne put two bullets in the right shoulder-blade and his target pirouetted on his left foot and fell flat on his face. A third man came into view, ducked below Rayne's rake of fire, aimed and hit him in the leg as he ran out of ammunition.

Rayne screamed out as the pain shot up his thigh and he tried desperately to ram in another magazine. He saw the man rise, obviously realising Rayne was out of ammunition. Rayne slid his left hand to the pistol behind his back, rolled over and shot the man full in the mouth. The next instant he pulled a grenade from his pocket and lobbed it in the direction of the rest of the fire. There was a muffled explosion, then a scream. Mechanically he pulled out a second grenade and threw it after the first. He prayed he wouldn't pass out from the pain of the bullet wound in his leg.

The second man with the bullet in his shoulder staggered up from the ground. Rayne fired another shot, this time into the man's throat. The .45 calibre bullet mushroomed on contact and the man collapsed forwards, clutching at the sickening mess above his shoulders.

Suddenly, there was silence.

The tears were running out of Rayne's eyes. He was shaking with fear, and now he began helplessly to retch. The air stank of death.

He knew he must hide, crawl deep into the bush. If they came for him now, he was dead.

By the time night came, Rayne's right leg was numb and his lips were splitting for lack of water. He had crawled as far as a small thicket, but had not moved since. Four dead, but there might be more of them. They were hardened fighters; they could be waiting for him to fall asleep before they moved in for the kill. His only safety was in silence. His rifle lay next to him, reloaded, the selector switch on semi-automatic fire.

The night was well advanced when he heard the first sound of movement. It came from only one direction, and he guessed at once that the man who had been hit by the grenade had not been killed. He lay perfectly still in the moonless dark, sweating.

3

The sound came closer, then stopped. Rayne could hear someone breathing deeply. Then the sounds started again, moving away from him in the direction of the three men he had shot earlier. Rayne turned his head, but in the pitch dark he could see nothing. The noise stopped, and he could hear his own heart beating like a drum. The pain in his leg returned, agonising, unbearable.

He slowly began to lose consciousness, and in a few moments he had rolled over on his side, completely defenceless.

The hyena was cautious, even though he had not eaten for many days. Something bothered him, and he waited in the darkness before moving forwards. When he walked, it was still with a limp from the barbed wire trap that had nearly caught him in the last winter. Then he had been hungry too, but less cautious.

The smell of blood was strong and the saliva from his mouth ran into the short black hairs of his muzzle. He knew he was getting old; one day his leg would prevent him from scavenging altogether, and then he would starve and perhaps the men would get him. The sound of the gun was familiar to him, the sound that killed. All the men carried guns now, and they no longer kept to the paths. He had had to become more cunning to avoid them, and so he had left his group, preferring to scavenge alone. Once before he had tasted the flesh of man. Now he was about to taste that sweet meat again.

The body was under his front paw, waiting for him, and he knew he could not hold out any longer. He dropped his head and his teeth sank into the soft flesh and for a few minutes he ate ravenously. Then caution overcame him again and he pulled the meat away from the clearing and into the bushes.

He ate till he was bloated, then slunk away in the darkness. He would return the next evening, hopefully to find more human flesh. This was enough for now. This place made him nervous.

Rayne woke just before dawn.

The light came slowly, gradually revealing the outlines of the trees. It was beautiful to him, even though he was still on edge. He was alive, and that was what mattered; nobody was going to kill him now, and he was going to get up and get out of this hell-hole as soon as possible.

Rolling over onto all fours, he slowly raised himself to a

crouching position. His leg hurt badly, but to his relief he could still walk on it. He remembered his training: pain can be an advantage, it heightens your senses, keeps you awake.

He checked the pistol in his belt and then held the rifle firmly in both hands – his AK-47, the world's finest assault rifle. He doubled back quickly and skirted the edge of a clearing, making for a cluster of enormous boulders above it. The pain in his right leg dominated all other feelings. But no one fired at him. Nothing moved. Soon he was on the top of the boulders and able to survey the surrounding country as the light improved. He eased a grenade from his pocket and removed the pin. The explosion would give him the cover he needed if anyone tried anything now.

There was more light on the clearing now, and he realised that one of the bodies had moved. As he saw the marks in the sand, the cold edge of fear ran through him. That was the man he had shot in the face. It was just not possible that the man could have survived. It looked as though the body had been dragged . . . Others must have come stealthily in the night. But why had they only moved one body and not the other three?

Then he saw it lying beneath him in the bush. The face was gone, and most of the stomach and the intestines. The smell reached his nostrils and he retched, almost dropping the grenade. Hyena, bloody hyena, that was what he had heard. He eased the pin back into the grenade and pushed the grenade back into his pocket. Lying flat, he looked into the bush for any signs of movement. Nothing. He was alone.

Rayne dropped down from the rock and moved quickly towards the place where he had thrown the grenade the day before. Clinically he examined its victim. It had been a very lucky hit; the grenade had actually hit the man in the chest, exploding on impact; the body was mutilated beyond recognition. He circled the clearing once more and then walked to its centre. This was the place where all the shooting had taken place the day before. The bodies were lying to one side of him, all face down on the ground. One body had blood across the centre of the back where the fire from his rifle had entered the stomach. The other had a misshapen shoulder and the head was disfigured from the final shot he'd put into it.

He studied the corpses, mentally working out if he'd responded in the right way. God, he'd taken a risk shooting the one in the head. If he'd missed, he would have been finished. They'd always taught him to aim for the torso but instinct always took over when he was under fire.

He found a water flask in one of the men's packs and quenched his thirst. There was some food in the pack too, which he ate ravenously. What a place for breakfast! A clearing in Mozambique and four dead ZANLA terrorists for company! Rayne laughed so hard he thought his stomach would tear apart – a sick, mad laugh in the silence.

He pulled himself together. He must check the four bodies for identification, see if they carried any vital documents. Then he must move out of the area very quickly. This was what he had been taught.

The body of the man he had killed with the shot to the head was very heavy, and he had to struggle to turn it over. The face was unrecognisable because the bullet had imploded into the side of the skull, but he could see that beneath the dirt that was smeared over it, the skin was white. Perhaps the man was a Russian agent operating in the Mozambique theatre – unusual, but by no means impossible. Unfortunately he could find no identification on the man.

He rolled the second body over. The face seemed curiously familiar. His hand touched the closed eyelids and pulled them back.

He knew this man. Not as an enemy but as a close friend.

The cry rang out through the stark, silent beauty of the early morning landscape. It rose and fell, sometimes fading away almost to nothing, then rising again with renewed force. Not a woman's cry. The cry of a man crouched over the body of his comrade.

The man got up and moved to another body. For a moment the horrified scream penetrated the silence again. The man rose and ran up the side of the incline. He pulled up another body from amongst the rocks. He turned the bloody face to his own and screamed again.

'No! No! No!'

He collapsed to the ground sobbing, and his tears ran into the dry earth.

*

Rayne dug with his bare hands, like an animal. As the day progressed he buried each of the four bodies and above each mound of soft earth he mounted a simple cross of two sticks bound together with cord.

When at last they were all buried, he staggered up the heap of boulders and hoisted himself on top of the rock that commanded the whole area. He sat on the rock, watching the setting sun, and sat there still as the darkness closed in around him. The first light of the new moon came up, as if to offer him a sign of hope.

In a single day his joy in the excitement of war had been replaced by a sense of its absolute futility. Africa, the continent he loved so much, had spoken to him in the most savage way possible. As he dug the graves, he had thought of turning his pistol on himself. But he would not take the easy way out. That was against his nature.

A faint wind blew up and pulled against the folds of his combat jacket. It seemed to clean the air around him, recharge his lungs, give him renewed energy, before it died as mysteriously as it had come, to be replaced by the familiar sounds of the African night.

After a while Rayne heard the sound which had so disturbed him the night before. Now he could recognise the pattern of breathing and put the hideous face to it; he could understand the strange shuffling noises and the long, pregnant silences. Grimly he waited on the top of the rock for his moment of revenge.

It was not a long wait. After the blackness of the previous night, the bright moonlight made the hyena bolder, and he came early, moving quickly across the clearing to the mound of earth. Without looking round, he unearthed the body, already becoming high with the stench of putrefaction.

He stopped and looked up to the new moon for a moment, as if to say a silent prayer before the feast that lay in store for him. He would live well for the next few weeks. There would be no need for travelling or taking risks; he would get stronger, perhaps his damaged leg would get a little better. His mouth tingled in anticipation of eating that flesh again; his dark red tongue ran across his lips.

Then he heard the noise that spelt death, and turned to spring away. The flash followed instantaneously from the rock above the clearing.

7

He let out a desperate yelp as the bullet tore through the soft fur of his chest and buried itself deep within. He fell on his side, his head flopping in the dust. The struggle for survival was over . . .

Rayne felt the noise of the shot ring through his skull. He had killed again – this time to prevent the savage desecration of the body of his best friend.

He had known all four of these men, Selous Scouts like himself, members of one of the crack units of the Rhodesian Army – men to whom daring exploits were everyday events. At twenty-five, and though he was a South African volunteer, not a Rhodesian, Rayne had been made a captain. He had given these men orders, had fought and laughed alongside them. These men would have died to save his life.

They all knew the risks of the Pseudo Groups, of course. That was the risk you took when you became a Selous Scout. You disguised yourself as the enemy; you blackened your face and your hands, you grew a beard; you became a ZANLA freedom fighter. You moved into the bush, made contact with the men from ZANLA who accepted you as fellow warriors. And then you killed them.

Of course, if they saw through your disguise, you were dead. But apparently no one in high command had thought about what happened when Pseudo Groups confronted each other – when the disguise was so good that you each thought the other was the enemy, and then you shot at each other to kill and you killed your own men. That was when the logic of the thing fell away.

Rayne wished they'd thought of a password, or some other subtle means of communication. But as in all wars, at the moment of crisis it was every man for himself. You only thought about what you should have done after things had gone horribly wrong.

At least they would never know who had really killed them. They were better off than he was. He had to live with the fact that he'd killed four of his friends, his own men.

He had shot Ron in the mouth. Ron with the pretty, smiling wife and the two children. He had sawn through Mac's guts with an avalanche of bullets. Mac was the one who always made them laugh when things were bad. Mike had just got engaged. He'd blown away Mike's shoulder and then shot him in the throat. And he'd blown out Alan's guts with a grenade. Alan, with two brothers already dead in the bush war and his father a bitter old man.

How could he go back into Rhodesia? Tell Ron's wife that he'd killed her husband, and his three-year-old son that his dad wasn't coming home to the farm? They'd bloody understand. He w they'd accept it and that would be the hardest part of all, living with their understanding. In the last forty-eight hours he'd leapt an abyss and landed a different man on the other side.

For some bizarre reason he remembered a piece of poetry he'd learnt at boarding school in Natal. He recited it aloud, hoping to regain some sanity.

> He clasps the crag with crooked hands;
> Close to the sun in lonely lands,
> Ringed with the azure world, he stands.
>
> The wrinkled sea beneath him crawls;
> He watches from his mountain walls,
> And like a thunderbolt he falls.

After that he fell silent, listening to the sounds that came from the darkness of Africa. Eventually he fell asleep, a solitary body on a piece of stone in the hell-hole that was Mozambique.

He woke up sweating, the sun burning down on him. The rifle lay under his right hand, so hot it almost scorched his skin. He climbed down from the rock and back into the clearing below. His leg was murderously painful.

Rayne moved swiftly, taking one of their packs and most of their ammunition. Then he disappeared into the bush, moving in a zig-zag pattern and covering his tracks constantly. He was close to collapse; the wound in his thigh was still oozing blood, and it made him sick to look at it. But the fear that, in this weakened state, he might run into a genuine ZANLA group, pushed him on. He had to get out of Mozambique, and fast.

Five days later Rayne swam painfully across the Gairezi River, north of Ruda in the Honda Valley. He had covered some eighty-five kilometres, mostly at night, avoiding any contact with local people.

He had been in constant danger. There were ZANLA forces scattered over the entire area and also frequent patrols by Mozambique's own armed force FRELIMO. Either of these groups would shoot him on sight or worse, capture him and subject him to the horrors of interrogation. Several times, in fact, he had almost walked into a party of soldiers but years of experience had taught him how to melt into the bush at the first sight of the enemy.

The days had passed in a blur. The evenings and nights he had spent staggering wearily onward, the mornings and afternoons had been spent 'resting' – lying wide awake, listening for the sounds of enemy patrols. These were the worst times, for over and over again his mind replayed the ambush.

For Rayne, killing had always been something he'd done to the enemy. Its justification was that the enemy would otherwise kill him; he never thought about the men he killed. But now he had killed his friends, murdered them in cold blood. The guilt of it would never leave him. He felt sick to the depths of his soul. And how would he ever explain what had happened? Would one believe him? They would think he was out of his mind.

Rayne shivered, his clothes and his body still wet from his swim across the river. It was very dark; the moon was hidden by the trees, making it hard for him to see ahead. Above the usual sounds of the bush at night he strove to listen for the slightest noise that was out of the ordinary. He knew he should move off the path but he was just too tired, his eyelids would droop, stay closed for a fraction of a second too long . . . Only will-power kept him lifting one leg after the other along the narrow path.

He heard a noise in front of him, but his arms refused to respond. He held up his rifle ineffectually. Before he realised it a man was facing him, pointing a rifle directly at him. Then something struck him from behind and he keeled over, crashing to the man's feet.

They had been lying in wait since dusk. The path was a favourite route used by ZANLA terrorists coming in from Mozambique – terrorists determined to make an attack in the Thrasher operational area on the eastern border of Rhodesia.

It was thirteen long war-weary years since Ian Smith had signed Rhodesia's historic Unilateral Declaration of Independence. In so doing he had severed all Rhodesia's links with the British Crown, thus ending an eighty-year association that had begun when Cecil Rhodes' famous Pioneer Column hoisted the British flag in Salisbury in 1890.

The reason for the Declaration was simple. Rhodesia wanted Independence based on her 1961 constitution, which entrenched the rights of the white minority. This was unacceptable to the British government, and so Ian Smith had taken the decision to go it alone.

In 1966 the United Nations applied selective sanctions to Rhodesia in an effort to force the white government to make moves towards handing over power to the black majority. Four years later, in retaliation, the white government of Rhodesia declared the country a Republic. To black Rhodesians this seemed the appalling culmination of years of political frustration – but then came the offer of assistance. Two countries, China and Russia, were ready to provide military equipment, money and training. With this help, black terrorist groups began to make an impact. To the west were the ZIPRA forces based in Zambia and Botswana and attacking the western flank of Rhodesia in the operational areas designated Tangent and Splinter. The ZIPRA freedom fighters came mostly from the Matabele tribe. To the east were the ZANLA forces, primarily of the Mashona tribe, based in Mozambique and attacking the eastern side of Rhodesia in the operational areas known as Thrasher and Hurricane. Rhodesia was effectively surrounded except for a small area to the south, the border with South Africa. Apart from the air routes, this was her only lifeline.

What Rayne had walked into was an ambush laid for ZANLA terrorists by the Rhodesian Light Infantry, a crack battalion that was rated by international military experts to be amongst the finest in the world. In this instance the object of the ambush was to capture rather than kill. If a terr talked he would provide vital information about compatriots operating in the area.

The terr they'd caught coming up the path in the early hours of this morning was obviously pretty badly hurt. He had a serious leg wound, and a stab wound in one shoulder. That would give them plenty to work on during the interrogation. He must have lost his sense of direction, too. Why else would he be staggering across the Rhodesian border instead of returning to Mozambique? They could tell he was in a bad way because he had heard them coming but had been unable to retaliate.

They had disarmed him and tied his hands behind his back.

He was carrying a Browning pistol that he must have taken from a soldier or a farmer. He was white, not black as they had first thought. A white disguised as a black. Maybe a Russian or a Cuban. If he was Russian it would be a rare capture; the Russians usually only took high-command positions in the cities.

The terr opened his eyes and smiled at them.

'I've made it.'

The words had hardly left Rayne's mouth when he received a savage blow across the face. He muttered his name and regiment as the blood trickled down from his mouth.

'Captain Rayne Gallagher. Selous Scouts. Get Major Martin Long. He'll know me.'

They tied him to a tree and left two men to guard him, not taking any chances. The rest disappeared into the bush.

He didn't say anything more. He didn't want to antagonise them. They thought he was lying to save his skin. He kept his eyes closed.

The time began to drag. He wondered if they had just gone off to fetch more supplies. Perhaps they were just trying to faze him before they started the interrogation. He shook his head at the thought; he knew about interrogations; he'd conducted many himself.

After about two hours the commanding officer returned. He walked up to him. Rayne looked him square in the face.

Lieutenant Roy Brown RLI examined his captive closely. He had just spoken to Major Long of the Selous Scouts on the radio, and now he had to check out the visual description he had been given. He didn't like the look in the penetrating blue eyes that were staring at him. It was the look of a killer.

He pulled the man's hair back and saw that the roots were blond beneath the dye and the muck. The face was covered by a thick, dark beard. He felt the line of the man's jaw – firm and hardset. The eyes were positioned well back behind the eyebrows. Everything about the face projected strength. The neck was made up of cords of hard muscle and sat squarely on powerful shoulders. The body was superb. Well over six foot, he thought. He tore open the `battle smock to reveal rippling stomach muscles. Only a diagonal scar going right across the belly-button marred an otherwise perfect torso. The skin was dark and deeply tanned. When Brown slammed his fist hard into the man's stomach, it was like hitting a wet sand-bag. The man didn't even register the blow, just looked at him.

'Welcome home, Captain Gallagh – '

He didn't get to complete the sentence. The man's good leg shot out and hit him hard in the pit of the stomach. He collapsed on the ground, gasping for breath.

'Untie me, you bastards.'

The two guards quickly released Rayne from the tree he was haltered to. He staggered towards the prostrate form of Lieutenant Roy Brown, then he blacked out.

Once again he felt the early morning sunlight on his face. He didn't know where he was, but he remembered all too vividly the faces of the terrs who had nearly killed him. He tried to strike out with his left arm but got nowhere because it was strapped firmly to his side.

'Oh fuck.'

'Easy there, Captain Gallagher. You're going to be all right. You were given a shot of morphine to put you out. Lieutenant Roy Brown has two broken ribs which'll teach him not to throw his weight around in future. A helicopter should be here any moment. Please relax. You'll be back in Salisbury soon. You'll be OK. I've checked your leg, the bullet will come out easy. There's no infection. Bloody miracle you didn't lose it.'

The man was interrupted by a shadow falling across them both. The helicopter roared down from the sky, a dirty green K-car bristling with armaments, a troop-carrier that struck fear into the heart of every terrorist. Rayne was securely strapped on a metal stretcher and then hoisted carefully into the K-car. He saw Lieutenant Roy Brown follow him into the hold. He felt no remorse; the man should never have hit him in the stomach. The helicopter began to rise above the thick green bush that lay like a giant mat across the Thrasher operational area.

Rayne smelt something familiar – a perfume that roused him from the morphine-induced stupor that had taken over his body. He turned over, and saw a female face beneath a tin helmet. Her body was hidden beneath an unflattering camouflage uniform. He must be dreaming . . .

She leant down and kissed him on the lips.

'Samantha.'

He could see the other soldiers in the hold grinning. He shot

13

them an angry glance and they immediately turned away. Captain Gallagher was not a man to be treated lightly.

'Rayne, they thought you were finished. What the hell happened to you?'

'It's too bloody terrible.'

'Don't worry about it now, then. Relax.'

Relax, he thought, with that body leaning over him? Even her voice turned him on. He looked at the Nikon hanging from her neck. Samantha Elliot, war photographer extraordinary.

'How did you know they'd found me?'

She lifted up the Nikon, focused it on his face and pushed the shutter-release. The motor-drive sounded alien amidst the noise of the propeller blades whirling above them.

'Thanks,' he said mirthlessly.

'You might just make the next issue of *Time*.'

'Pervert.'

'You can talk.'

He smiled and lay back, knowing that for the next few weeks he wasn't going to have to worry every second about his chances of surviving. He would be in the hospital where the aim was to preserve life, not to take it away. It is one of the great absurdities of war, he thought to himself, that everyone tries to maim or kill as many of the enemy as possible, and then a dedicated band of men and women put the torn bodies together, knowing full well that they will be back fighting again as soon as they are repaired. At least he'd made it home. Not like the others who lay buried in the veld, food for carnivores.

The white man was in the minority in this war – the white man with his stupid bloody ideals hammered into him since birth. Do it for king and country; do it because it's right; do it because it's romantic. What was he, Rayne Gallagher, a volunteer from another country, doing it for?

The Rhodesian army was undoubtedly the finest of its kind in the world, but then it had been founded on a military tradition that had won two world wars. Most Rhodesian soldiers were professionals when it came to fighting to the death, just like their Australian and New Zealand counterparts. He had always been proud to be one of their number, proud to serve with the best. Now he wasn't so sure.

He turned and looked at the beautiful woman who was staring out of the helicopter, down into the bush. Her long blonde hair, the colour of golden corn in the evening sun, was partly hidden under the ugly tin helmet on her head. There was a mischievous twinkle in her green eyes that spoke of the fire beneath the ice. Her complexion was smooth and soft, giving no indication that she was in her mid-thirties. The full dark eyebrows perhaps suggested her tomboy spirit, the courage with which she faced whatever problems life put in front of her.

He mentally undressed her. The breasts were full and firm with big brown nipples. Beneath them was a tiny waist that both of his hands could fit round with ease as she sat astride him during their love-making. It was nearly two months since they'd last done that. He found himself becoming erect at the thought of the hair that lay between her exquisite thighs and the long legs that would wrap themselves around his body as he thrust deep inside her. She would claw into his back with her fingers, and come in long shuddering orgasms.

He thought back to their first meeting, three and a half years before. One of those rare happenings that had changed the course of his life.

He'd just received his wings after passing the tough initiation course and making it into the crack SAS regiment. He'd rented a small cottage in a Salisbury suburb and was looking forward to a couple of relaxing weeks. The first morning, trying to enjoy a lie-in for the first time in months, he'd been woken by a tirade of swear words. She'd been out in the street, trying to start her car.

When he got outside, wearing nothing except his shorts, she was kicking the side of the car. She'd flooded the engine, so he held the accelerator flat and the car started.

Later, when she got back, she invited him over for a drink. They were in bed within half an hour and didn't get out of it for the next two days. By the time they did, they'd completely exhausted each other. And they were in love.

Her name was Samantha Elliot. She was a woman with a passion for action – violent action. In her early twenties she'd gone to Vietnam with her Nikon and her good looks and nothing else. She started going to places most journalists avoided and taking pictures that revealed a side of the war that only the men who were fighting in it knew about. She was on the cover of *Time* a year later, and after that she could pick any assignment she wanted. Quite why she had chosen to go to Rhodesia she

15

didn't know. At the time she'd been in love with an American Green Beret helicopter pilot who was hungry for action after Vietnam and had travelled to Rhodesia to find it. After that, once she was in Rhodesia, she was hooked.

She turned from the door of the helicopter and stared at Rayne. Her vivid green eyes flashed like emeralds beneath the long black lashes.

War was her passion. There was an honour in it, a striving, that fired her. She had discovered this thing that men enjoyed doing, and it stirred the core of her sensual being. Sometimes she was scared of this feeling, but she could never resist its pull upon her.

Most war photographers were obsessed with the spectacular gore of warfare, the vivid colours of blood, smoke and flame, but for her the fascination lay in the men – in faces caught when they could not hide emotion: the look of horror on seeing a wounded enemy; the lust for blood in the heat of action.

Rayne had become the embodiment of this vision of hers. He was bigger than any man who had ever taken her, and his love-making had a dark ferocity about it. She could never have enough of it.

She looked down at him and shivered. His leg was roughly bandaged, blood already seeping through the white material; there was a deep cut in his neck, and his face was a mass of dirty wounds. Yet when she looked into the depths of the intense blue eyes she saw a deeper hurt. He had changed. Something had happened to him out there, and whatever it was had struck at the very core of him. He was hanging onto his sanity by a slender thread.

As she looked at him, she saw his eyes lose their focus, the lids fall. The drugs, and the shattering experience he had lived through, were at last taking their toll of him. He was blacking out; forgetting Samantha, forgetting where he was, forgetting everything.

Rayne came round much later. He seemed to be in a hospital bed. He must have been captured by the enemy. He knew he had no friends left; they had all been killed. A strange chill crept up and down his body. Deep down in the oldest section of his brain a voice was urging him to fight, to remember his old cunning and wait for the moment when he could burst out of the bed and surprise them.

He eyed the woman who stood by the bed. Yes, she should be afraid of him, all right.

'Rayne,' whispered Samantha. 'What's wrong? Don't look at me like that.'

His left hand shot out from beneath the sheets and pulled her down savagely. For a fraction of a second the grip eased, and then he whipped his forearm and bicep around her head like a vicious pincer. The grip hardened, his bicep pushing against her ear, and she screamed out as the crook of his elbow closed into her windpipe. She lashed out wildly but ineffectively. Then two male nurses were on him, prizing her out of his grip, binding him down with straps. He heard her screaming as they dragged her down the passage. He reached for his gun but could not find it.

When, later, a man came up to him and leant over him, pulling one of his eyelids back and shining a light into his eyeball, Rayne spat in the man's face. Then he reared up and bit the man's arm. The man jumped back with a look of horror on his face. After that Rayne felt a painful jab in his left thigh and he slipped away into another place that felt a lot safer than the one he'd been in.

It was a pleasant day. Rayne was glad to be outside in the open air. He was in a wheelchair, which was uncomfortable, and he still couldn't understand why they kept his arms and legs strapped up; he could have pushed himself around instead of having to rely on a nurse.

Nurse Maureen Thrush was careful with her charge. Captain Rayne Gallagher was a man they'd heard much of over the past few years. Not that they'd ever seen him until a week ago – and, she'd never imagined he'd be so good-looking, even after they'd shaved off his beard.

She remembered the first time she'd heard of him. Her boyfriend in the SAS had told her about it. Gallagher had apparently been put through the tough selection programme that all the men had to undergo, and one of the tests was unarmed combat. The instructor, Sergeant Rourke, had a habit of picking the toughest of the new recruits and working them over. Rourke tipped the scales at over two hundred pounds of solid muscle, and had never been dropped in a fight. Most of the men feared him, and he knew it.

Rourke had started by slapping Gallagher around and then giving him a kick in the groin. That was usually when it stopped; by that time Rourke would have earned the grudging respect of all the new recruits. Except that Gallagher was different. He got up and came back for more.

Rourke then started to hit Gallagher hard. He wanted to hurt him, to teach him a lesson. Gallagher came in close and brought his skull crashing into Rourke's face. Rourke staggered back and Gallagher hit him in the centre of the face with a hard left, then a right.

Rourke put the boot in. Gallagher gripped his outstretched leg and snapped it savagely upwards. There was a splintering sound, and Rourke keeled over as Gallagher kicked him in the side of the skull.

Gallagher was given a warning. Six weeks later Rourke was still in hospital and Gallagher was one of the twenty-three men who passed the selection committee out of the original one hundred and sixty-seven who had started the course. No one ever picked a fight with him after that.

Nurse Maureen Thrush was glad that Captain Rayne Gallagher was well again. This young man did not deserve to go to the institution. She had seen it so many times before – soldiers who had gone over the edge, driven beyond the limit of endurance.

Rayne had told the doctor that there was no need for him to be strapped down, but the doctor had just smiled and said it was good that his limbs should stay in one place for a time. Rayne respected the doctor's opinion but couldn't quite fathom the inscrutable look on his face when the latter talked to him.

Samantha came across the hospital lawn. He was pleased to see her. Her neck was covered by an enormous plaster cast – her luck in escaping injury in combat must have run out just as his had done.

'So the terrs finally got you, Sam.'

'I suppose they did, honey.'

Her soft American accent was as sensual as ever. But why was she looking at him in that strange way, just as the doctor had? He said, 'I don't understand why they're keeping me in here for so long. I'm sure I could easily get around on a pair of crutches.

There are plenty of men who need to be in this place more than I do.'

'Honey, you must give your leg a chance.'

He could always see when she was irritated, but then she must be in a lot of pain. He said gently, 'It's good to see you, Sam. I'm so glad you came with them in the K-car to get me. I needed to see someone I knew after what I'd been through out there.'

She bent over him and said quietly, 'They want to know if you can shed any light on where the rest of your men are, honey.'

'They want to know? I suppose they have a bloody right to know, but not right now.'

The tight, closed expression on his face made her do something she normally never did – she began to cry. He tried to lift his arm to comfort her but the straps held it down.

'How did you hurt your neck, Sam?'

She told him, told him how he'd tried to kill her. Then it was his turn to go silent.

'I've seen it before,' she said at last. 'It comes with the combination of the drugs, the shock and the strain.' She paused. 'Rayne, I still don't completely understand what happened to you out there.'

He was quiet. What more could he tell her? Sam lit him a cigarette, placed it in his mouth and watched him take a long, deep drag. Beneath his pyjamas, the muscled outline of his body was evident. Even though he was strapped down and still sedated, he sat erect in the wheelchair, and his sapphire-blue eyes were very bright below the blond fringe that needed cutting. He could have been a movie star.

'War is savage,' he said. 'There are no rules.'

'You're an undercover killer.' Sam never minced words. It wasn't her way to avoid an issue.

'By becoming the enemy you destroy their soul, sap their morale. The hunter and the hunted become blurred.'

'And if you fluff your lines you get your brains blown out.'

Rayne stared out of the door and through into another room. A soldier lay on a bed, bandages over both his eyes. He'd lost them in an ambush. His girlfriend was with him. Rayne wondered how long it would be before the real resentment would set in.

Then he told Samantha how he'd killed his own men. This time she understood the closed expression.

Rayne stared up at the old-fashioned fan on the ceiling as it rotated above his head in hypnotic circles. 'You see,' he said, 'I became the enemy.'

Outside the Livingstone Hospital the air was warm and sweet with the smell of summer flowers. Everywhere in Salisbury, trees and shrubs were in full bloom; scarlet trees lined the streets, their vivid red leaves sprouting from long black trunks into the blue sky; in every garden, hazy mauve jacarandas and the beautiful bauhinias in pink and white, white and purple, created a stunning display of natural colour. The air was full of birdsong and the hum of bees. Not for nothing was Salisbury known as the city of flowering trees.

The atmosphere was calm and relaxing in the way it can be only in Africa. Peace and war, she took them both in her stride. And war, now, was gathering apace all round Rhodesia. With ZANLA to the east and ZIPRA to the west she was virtually at war on every front. In the east particularly, with the withdrawal of all Portuguese forces from Mozambique in 1974, hostilities had taken on a new ferocity. And though Ian Smith had had to agree to the formation of a transitional government that would gradually transfer power to the black majority, both Joshua Nkomo, leader of ZIPRA, and Robert Mugabe, leader of ZANU, had vowed to destroy such a government.

The gruesome terror tactics of the black freedom fighters were accelerating. In June 1978 a massacre at the Elim Mission horrified the Rhodesian public in its barbaric intensity. The butchery of eight white missionaries and their children, and the rape of the women, achieved its goal of shocking a war-weary nation.

In September 1978, ZIPRA shot down an Air Rhodesia passenger plane, the Viscount Hunyani, just after it had taken off on a scheduled flight from Kariba to Salisbury. The plane was hit by a Soviet Sam-7 ground-to-air missile fired from the Matusadona mountain range on the Zambesi Escarpment. Thirty of the fifty-eight passengers died as the plane crashed to the ground. Another ten, women, men and children, were rounded up by ZIPRA ground forces and bayonetted to death. The rest of the world officially condemned the raid, but most people seemed to feel that the Rhodesians had it coming to them.

Then, that evening, late in the summer months of 1978, as

Rayne lay asleep in the Livingstone Hospital, Rhodesia's largest fuel depot exploded in a mountain of flame. Millions of dollars-worth of fuel lit up the Salisbury evening sky in a *danse macabre* of light and explosions – fuel that was beleagured Rhodesia's most precious resource, paid for with hard-earned foreign currency.

Looking at the newspaper the next morning, Rayne itched to be in action again. Whatever happened, the country could not be allowed to fall into a state of anarchy. Most Rhodesians had already reaped a bitter harvest from the conflict. Sons, fathers, brothers, lovers, husbands killed in action or maimed by land-mines. The women were sick of a war that never seemed to end.

Rayne was sure Ian Smith had realised that a negotiated settlement was the only answer to the problem. The objective must now be no longer to preserve white majority rule but rather to find a way to protect white rights in a black democracy. Rayne wondered how the soldiers on both sides would manage to make the difficult transition from war to peace.

He turned round to see Major Martin Long walking towards him. A military man in his late thirties, Long had made his name in the SAS and then the Selous Scouts. He was a front-line man. The black hair, hard face and Scots accent caused many people to mistake him for the film actor Sean Connery. He had a magnetic quality, an intensity that radiated from his probing dark eyes.

'Good to see you, sir.' Rayne extended his right hand, relishing the freedom of movement now that the straps had been removed. Long's iron-hard grip matched his own.

'Cut the regimental crap, Rayne. How the hell are you, you desperate bugger?'

'Well, they've cut me loose.'

'Yes, I heard you were a wee bother at the start. You're well, though?'

Long was sizing him up for something, he was sure of it.

'Well as a man can be who's been kept in hospital against his will. I'll be out next week, even if I have to take on Nurse Thrash hand-to-hand. But enough of that. The fuel depot going up, that must have hit us pretty badly?'

'The crafty sons of bitches. It was a masterstroke, a Soviet-backed operation. Excellent penetration of security. Minimum loss of life, maximum effect on our morale. Yes, it's bad, laddie. We keep telling everyone we can keep them out of Salisbury, but the terrs have shown us up. We are the guerillas now in our own guerilla war.' He sighed. 'The average bloke isn't looking for anarchy. He's looking to win this war, and from where I sit that looks pretty bloody impossible.'

Rayne could sense the tiredness in Long's voice. Only someone who knew him well would have noticed it. The words etched themselves into Rayne's brain: 'We are the guerillas in our own guerilla war'. It echoed his own thoughts. He had become the enemy.

'Och, Rayne. Don't look at me like that. I'm sorry about what happened to you, but it proves I was right to believe in you. You'd never have got the captain's rank unless they thought you could handle a situation like that. Death is something you deal with personally. Each of us will walk away from this with something we didn't want, and we'll have to live with it.

'My father's an army man, a good Scot. He was in the infantry in the Second World War. He once told me that the saddest part of the war was coming home victorious. He saw the jubilation in the eyes of my mother, the looks of adulation from the women who knew he'd been decorated for bravery – and who could blame them? But he and his men carried a sadness in their souls; the thought of their friends who wouldn't be coming back. The paradox is, they'd have gone back to fight for the same cause again. That's what being a good soldier is all about.'

'This is a bit different from the Second World War, though, sir.'

'Hear me out, you impetuous bastard. You survived against the most incredible odds. A lot of these doctors say you're off your rocker, but that's a load of crap. Certainly you've got a basic level of survival brutality that most men couldn't muster, but there's nothing wrong with that. What you did to Sam the other day was a result of all the drugs they pumped into you. Forget that business.'

'I already have.'

'Back to the army, then. There's a lot to be done.'

'I'm not a peacemaker, sir – whatever peace there ever will be between the Matabele and the Mashona.'

'This isn't about peace, laddie, it's about war. I'm asking you if you want to take part in perhaps the most important action of

22

the whole war. A secret project. Something you'll never get public recognition for. A project so dangerous that no man in his right mind would have anything to do with it. In the long run it'll make a negotiated peace possible and stop Rhodesia heading into a bloodbath. And I need your decision now. No one else knows about this except a few men in high command. The whole operation is top secret.'

'Equipment?' Rayne could feel his pulse racing already.

'You'll get everything available – legally and illegally. And Rayne, you'll be in command.'

'You bastard, sir.'

'My pleasure, Captain Gallagher. I knew you couldn't resist it.'

Major Martin Long walked down the long gravel drive that led from the hospital buildings to the road. He hated himself. He shouldn't have done it, but then who the hell else was there that he could have used? If Sam found out, she'd never forgive him.

The approaches made to him had been subtle. The Americans had obviously been looking for the right man for a long time, and then the CIA must have seen the intelligence reports on Gallagher. Rayne was an incredible fighter; he was also the only white man Long knew who could disguise himself as a black man and convince another black – his mastery of black languages was that good.

Who could really know what had gone on, out there in Mozambique? Rayne had started operating on his own a month before. Sheer suicide, they'd all thought, but he'd survived, and he had led the army into some of the biggest terrorist camps they'd found for a long time.

Now the Americans wanted to use him for their crazy mission. It had to be done, of course, the Russians had to be stopped. The timing was perfect: mentally speaking, Rayne was a total mess.

The door of the car was opened for Long by his army driver. He paused for a moment before getting in, and looked back at the hospital. There was still time. He could go back and tell Rayne they felt he wasn't well enough to do the job.

The car door slammed as he got in. The driver jumped in the front and pulled away. Sometimes, Major Martin Long thought, it was better not to think at all.

*

23

Rayne lay back in the wheelchair, thinking about the rollercoaster of events that had got him where he was. It had all started four and a half years ago, in May 1974. His mind drifted back to that time, helped by the effects of the drugs. He had been a different person then, with different goals. He had just turned twenty-one. He already had his BA in law, passed with straight As, and was in his final year of the LLB degree. He wanted to become a civil rights lawyer, like his father. Like Bruce Gallagher too, he wanted to win the coveted Rhodes scholarship and go on to Oxford University.

At school Rayne had been a *victor ludorum*, gaining colours in rugby, athletics and cricket. Now at university he had concentrated single-mindedly on rugby. He knew it was only a matter of time before he was selected for the Transvaal provincial team. More importantly, sport was a major part of the selection process for the Rhodes scholarship.

The match was an inter-varsity one between his own side, 'Wits', which he captained, and Stellenbosch, the 'Maties'. Stellenbosch was the home of the Afrikaner rugby elite, schooled by the legendary Dr Danie Craven. It was the best side in the country and unbeaten that year. Rayne was determined to change all that.

The match was referred to as a friendly. Really, he thought, that was a stupid description of any event that held up a challenge. You won or you lost, and there was nothing nice about losing.

It was the second half, and his team was losing by three points because of an unfair decision that had awarded the Maties a penalty in the first half.

The ball came into the Maties' hands after a rough scrum, and they passed the ball easily from one back to another as they shot down the sunburnt grass of the playing field. It was a try in the making. Rayne's mind had raced into overdrive. There was no way they were going to score a try if he could help it.

His legs forced their way into the dry, brown turf as he sprinted at electrifying speed down the pitch, his whole body focused on the Matie back who was dangerously close to the line. Almost upon him, Rayne saw the back grab the ball. He launched himself into the air and crashed down against the back's thighs in an expert flying tackle.

The man crashed to the ground and Rayne heard a muffled

crack. The crowd roared with approval and his own team-mates rushed to congratulate him on a brilliant tackle. The back was on the ground and still not moving. 'Still stunned,' Rayne had thought to himself.

The referee ran over to the slumped body and eased it over. A deathly hush came over the ground. The ref looked up into Rayne's steel-blue eyes and shivered.

'You've killed him,' he said very quietly.

Rayne went completely cold. The people, the ground, seemed to recede into the distance. He felt himself speaking. 'I didn't kill him. It was a fair tackle.' The words that came out of his mouth were without emotion.

Next day in the *Rand Daily Mail* the headline spelt out the words that were to haunt him for the rest of his life. *Death tackle kills mine magnate's son. Gallagher on the line.* The article continued in the same sensationalist style:

> Yesterday, in a so-called 'friendly' intervarsity match, Rayne Gallagher, Wits' star player and the captain of the team, killed Tom Rudd, son of Tony Rudd the mine magnate, in a flying tackle. Gallagher is said to have reacted to the news calmly.
>
> Rudd was rushed to the Johannesburg General Hospital for a full autopsy. Distinguished pathologist Dr Max Scheider made a short statement to this reporter later. He said that Rudd's neck had broken after being tackled by Gallagher.
>
> Tony Rudd said he would demand a full inquest into his son's untimely death and Gallagher's rough standard of play. Mrs Rudd is currently under sedation in a Pretoria hospital.
>
> This incident confirms criticism of the rough standard of play by the Wits team. It is believed that Gallagher had already been previously suspended from the Wits team for rough play.
>
> Neither Gallagher nor his father, the distinguished advocate Mr Bruce Gallagher SC, were available for comment. The Vice-Chancellor of the University of the Witwatersrand, Dr Bozzoli, said that he regarded the death as a tragic incident, and the matter would be fully investigated.
>
> The spectacular picture of the death tackle, exclusive to the *Rand Daily Mail*, was taken by Wits photographer Aaron Golding.

Rayne remembered the interview with his father that had followed. He remembered Bruce Gallagher's deep voice bellowing through the many rooms of the family's exclusive home on Johannesburg's prestigious Westcliff Ridge. Rayne had always known who he'd inherited his hot temper from. They were in the study. Through its large windows you could see as far as Pretoria.

'It was an accident, and they've branded you a murderer! And now this talk of a university inquest! It's farcical. That photograph should never have seen the light of day.'

'Forget it, Dad. You're wasting your breath, save it for the courtroom. The damage is done. I'm not going to get the Rhodes scholarship after that.'

Bruce Gallagher stared across at his son's hardened face. Not a boy any longer, but a man he was proud of. The keen blue eyes missed nothing. How would he take this?

'I've started clearing out my flat, Dad. I'll bring the furniture back in the morning. I have to get away from here.'

'Go away? Where? You've still got another six months to go before you get your LLB!'

'I've had enough. That was a good, clean tackle. I didn't come down on him that hard, any fool could see that. No. Enough of the charade. I've decided I want to join the Rhodesian SAS. I've studied enough. I want to be with some real people, men not wimps.'

'You're crazy, Rayne, you're over-reacting. How can you talk about joining the Rhodesian army? Think what you'll be fighting for, the supremacy of the white man and the entrenchment of his rights. Everything I've struggled against in my legal career!'

'Come off it, Father. Show me a black state with better justice than ours.'

'If you join the Rhodesian army, you can consider yourself a stranger in this house.'

Without realising it, Bruce had put Rayne in a corner. He regretted the words as soon as he said them, but it was too late.

'So be it. I'm going. I'll say goodbye to Mother.'

'Rayne, you bloody fool!'

'Goodbye, Father.'

Two weeks later he had been on the train, headed towards Bulawayo, the capital of Matabeleland. When they crossed the

South African border, Rayne had felt as though a weight had been lifted from his shoulders.

He remembered his first sight of this new land, Rhodesia, less inhabited and developed than the South African landscape he had been travelling across earlier in the day. He had no idea that the area of Matabeleland he was passing through would soon be known to him by the operational name of Repulse. Already he could feel the increase in temperature and see the landscape changing subtly. More green trees, and increasingly lush vegetation that clung to the sides of the rolling hills and rock outcrops.

The area was no stranger to violence, or to the changing procession of peoples who chose to live amongst its massive granite domes and rocky outcrops. First the peaceful bushmen were displaced by the Rozvi people, who developed a sophisticated civilisation mining iron and gold. Then in the nineteenth century the Zulu chiefs, Mzilikazi and Shaka, teamed up and seized the Rozvi people's land. Mzilikazi and his followers became known as the Matabele. But they in their turn, impressive warriors though they were, fell prey to the firepower of Rhodes' Pioneer Column in the quest to colonise. Thus Rhodesia had been born, and the seeds were sown of decades of future conflict between black and white . . .

'Sir, please be seated. Major Long will see you at eleven hundred hours. He would like you to fill out your curriculum vitae.'

Rayne vividly remembered the immaculately dressed junior officer who had handed him an anonymous-looking buff form and a black ballpoint pen. He had sat down on one of the cheap metal and plastic chairs that filled the tiny office. The place was hot and oppressive. He had thought that joining the army would be simple. He was beginning to find out that there was a lot of red tape to be gone through. Most of the questions on the form were similar to those on an application form for an ordinary job, but there were others that were more unusual. There was a section asking about his knowledge of black languages and tribal customs. Another section dealt with previous injuries and disabilities, and a third section had questions relating to the types of activity the applicant might be interested in. Rayne favoured joining the airborne regiment, the legendary SAS.

By the time he had answered all the questions it was nearly eleven o'clock. One of the phones on the reception desk rang and the immaculate-looking officer answered it. Then he put the phone down delicately and stared across at Rayne. 'Major Long will see you now, sir. Please take the form with you.'

Major Long had been standing up and staring at something through the window of his office. At first Rayne wondered if he had noticed him come in.

'Sit down.'

The accent had a Scottish flavour and was very precise. Major Long turned and faced him. The expression on his face was severe, the dark eyes running over Rayne carefully.

'So you want to fight in our stupid bloody war, laddie?'

He took the buff form from Rayne's hand and walked behind his desk. He sat down and scrutinised the paper carefully. 'Very interesting, Mr Gallagher. It doesn't tell me what I want to know. Why the hell are you in this office volunteering to fight in someone else's war?'

In as few words as possible, Rayne gave the story of his decision to join the Rhodesian army. The more he spoke, the more uneasy he felt. He began to realise how trivial his own problems must sound to a man who had seen soldiers die in action. He finished his explanation and there was a lengthy silence as Major Long continued to stare at him. Eventually he spoke.

'Mr Gallagher, you are not a Rhodesian. My father emigrated here from Scotland, he fought in the Second World War for Rhodesia – and that's why I'm here, fighting for something I believe in. I think you've made a rash decision. You must realise how much it costs to train and equip a fighting man. Having heard what you have told me, I cannot accept you for the Rhodesian Light Infantry.'

Rayne felt his face going purple with anger.

'Don't lose your temper with me, laddie. Now please leave. I have more important matters to attend to.'

Rayne had walked out of the office, slamming the door behind him. As he came into the waiting room he noted that the immaculate officer was grinning from ear to ear. He walked out of the building and sat on a bench outside.

A few moments later he heard someone behind him and the same officer sat down beside him. He offered Rayne a cigarette. Rayne took it and the man offered him a light.

'Major Long has a reputation,' the officer said, 'and he always lives up to it.'

'I thought you needed volunteers!'

'We do. But you came in expecting to be given the red carpet treatment.'

'How the hell *do* I join your bloody army?'

'The recruiting office is in Meikles Street. The Rhodesian Regiment is always looking for recruits. Any able-bodied man is welcome to join up.'

'Thanks. I will!'

It all felt like a hundred years ago, not just four and a half. Rayne looked round cautiously to see that there were no nurses in the vicinity, then eased himself out of the wheelchair and put his weight on his right leg. The pain was bad, but he was determined to walk.

He hobbled along for some hundred metres before he began to feel uneasy. The drugs had still not worn off. He felt as if he were going to pass out. Then he felt a hand clamp on his shoulder and steady him.

'You should be taking it easy, sir.'

The voice was a deep bellow. Rayne knew who it was in an instant. He turned to face the man who had stopped him from falling over. A big man, nearly six and a half feet tall, dressed in the uniform of a helicopter pilot.

'Thanks, Lois. I think I'd better be getting back to my wheelchair.'

The hand was released from his shoulder. Lois Kruger knew better than to try and help him walk back.

Lois was a good friend, and Rayne appreciated the fact that he'd come to visit him in hospital. A strange man, he had always thought, but an incredible soldier. Behind the haunted face with the fascinating green eyes lay a very complex human being. He'd known Lois at school. He'd been there when Lois had been expelled after being found in bed with one of the masters. None of them had known before that. For Rayne it didn't make any difference, Lois was still the tough Afrikaner to him, the one who excelled at karate and rugby.

After that, Rayne had lost track of him, only to meet him again in the harrowing selection process for the Rhodesian

Special Air Services regiment. By that time Lois had changed a lot. He was even harder. And he never talked about his past.

Lois stood back as Captain Gallagher staggered to his wheelchair. Already the man was walking normally. Lois knew that Rayne would be on his feet again the next day.

He was glad he'd come to the hospital to see how Rayne was, even though the place brought back so many unpleasant memories. He owed Gallagher a lot. He'd been flying choppers as part of a fire force when his machine had been shot down, and the terrs had got him. They were busy carving tattoos on his stomach when Gallagher came out of the bush with a machine-gun and mowed them down. How Captain Rayne Gallagher of the Selous Scouts had ever tracked him down, he never knew. Why he'd done it also eluded him; after all, Gallagher knew he was a homosexual . . . What he did know, was that he owed him his life.

Lois had always told himself that Gallagher might be the one man he could talk to about his past – the guilt that lay deep inside him. The hospital reminded him of that time, five years ago . . .

Lois knocked against the door covered with paint once white, now yellow with age. A faint voice told him to enter, and there was Dr Forsyth seated at a giant desk strewn with papers and reports. He looked over seventy, though in attitude he seemed as alert as a much younger man. He gestured for Lois to sit down.

'What can I do for you, Mr . . . ?' He squinted at the card. 'Kruger?'

'I had a fight in a bar. Really stupid . . . My groin, it's hurting badly.'

'All right, if you will take your clothes off, please. Behind the screen over there.'

Lois got undressed behind the screen and sat painfully on the high white table. Dr Forsyth came in and asked him to lie flat, then examined him carefully. Lois shouted out as the doctor gently raised each of his testicles. Having completed his examination, the doctor asked Lois to sit up on the edge of the bed. He checked his reflexes and his blood pressure. Then he asked Lois to get dressed.

Lois had the feeling that all was not well. Dr Forsyth smiled at him good-naturedly.

'I would like to book you into the hospital immediately. Fortunately we have a first-rate surgeon who can do the operation. Unfortunately, however, you will have to lose both testicles. They are severely damaged. It must have been a very direct blow to the scrotum. I'm sorry, Mr Kruger.'

Lois felt that the world was spinning about him. The doctor carried on speaking but Lois hardly heard him.

'. . . this does not, necessarily, mean the end of your sex life. You could still have children . . .' That was a joke. '. . . there are numerous documented case-histories of men who have been able to carry on an almost normal sex life with both testes removed . . .'

The sympathetic voice receded into the background as Lois thought deeper into his past. . .

He had been an only child, and his father had died of lung cancer before Lois was two years old. He had become very attached to his mother, while hating his father for having abandoned them. He had been a bright child and had attended one of South Africa's most exclusive schools on a scholarship. In his final year it looked certain that he would win the engineering scholarship he wanted. Then he had been found in bed with his maths master, a young man in his thirties. They had both been expelled.

So Lois became an air steward with South African Airways. The personnel manager had been perceptive enough to see that he was very bright and had suggested a course as an aircraft mechanic. By the time Lois completed his apprenticeship he had learnt to fly, and had also regained some of his lost confidence. All this time he lived with his mother.

He got a job at Lanseria airport outside Johannesburg, a small air terminal that handled light planes and private business jets. Then, in the autumn of 1973, the pictures started arriving. Explicit pictures of him and one of his lovers which the sender threatened to show to Lois' mother.

Lois met the blackmailer, a Lebanese runt who smelt of stale sweat and cheap cigars. The Lebanese told him that if he would sabotage a plane, they would destroy the pictures. Lois capitulated. There was another meeting, with a different man.

31

The night after he'd fixed the plane, he drank himself sick in a bar and staggered home. That was when they tried to finish him off. They'd sent in a hit-man who attacked Lois as he was drunkenly wending his way up a side street. They obviously hadn't done any research, or they'd have known he had a 2nd Dan black belt in JKA-style karate. At six five in his stockinged feet he weighed in at a lean 200 pounds. The paid assassin had badly underestimated his strength. But Lois had received a savage kick in the balls – a very bad blow – before he'd killed the hitman.

Lois had packed his bags, given his mother his considerable life-savings, and then driven for the Rhodesian border. He'd seen the news of the plane accident on a television at the Beitbridge Motel on the border. The plane had crashed in the Transkei, killing the pilot but not the two passengers – the son of prominent Johannesburg advocate Bruce Gallagher, and the daughter of multi-millionaire mining magnate Sir George O'Keefe.

Lois had made it to Livingstone Hospital the next day . . .

'Mr Kruger, are you listening to me?'

Lois had stared at Dr Forsyth.

'And if I don't have them removed?'

'Quite simply, the pain that you are experiencing now will get worse. You will have difficulty in moving at all. Then the same operation will have to be performed or you will be a cripple. Believe me, Mr Kruger, your wisest course is to have the operation as soon as possible.'

'All right. I take your word for it.'

Lois had decided then and there that he would make sure whoever had done this to him paid for it. First he would need money and time to get better after the operation. He would have to lie low for a few years; the South African police would be after him for sabotaging the plane, and there might be more hit-men waiting to have a go at him. But whatever happened, he would get his revenge.

The operation had taken place some four hours later.

'What's on your mind, Lois?' Gallagher's voice brought him back to reality. 'Listen to what I'm saying. I might need you for something soon. Something big.'

'You're not going back into the bush again?'

'No. This is different, Lois. I can't tell you any more now, but you'll hear from me soon.'

'Whatever it is, sir, I owe you.'

Rayne was discharged from Livingstone Hospital after another week. He moved into Sam's studio cottage in Salisbury and waited for Major Long to contact him. He told Sam nothing about this. He knew she wouldn't want him to go into action again, especially not into something that promised to be so dangerous.

The cottage Sam lived in was a single huge room with a kitchen in the far corner and a bathroom to one side. The whole of one wall consisted of giant panes of glass set in wooden frames. In a corner of the room an enormous table held scattered papers and a portable typewriter.

All across the wall at the back of the room were photographs, some black and white, some in colour. Most of them were of a war that Rayne had heard about but never known – Vietnam. Many of the pictures were horrifying – men lying mutilated, close-ups of faces in agony – pictures that captured the very essence of war. They sent a shiver up Rayne's spine. There was no doubt that Sam had a unique gift. No other photographer in the world had achieved the same understanding of violence and exceptional danger. Rayne thought that that understanding was probably what drew him and Sam together.

Sam was on an assignment in Matabeleland for a week, so Rayne was alone in the cottage. It was late on the Wednesday evening when he received the phone call. He picked up the receiver and glanced at his watch. Past midnight.

'Major Long here.' The voice sounded strangely detached. 'Meet me on foot at the corner of Jameson and Victoria Roads in five minutes. Tell no one.'

Rayne put the phone down and found he was sweating. The car picked him up as he arrived at the street corner. Major Long was sitting in the back, a driver in civvies at the front. Once the car had pulled off, the Major began to talk.

'You'll be leaving here very soon. You will effectively disappear.'

'You'll tell Sam?'

'Nothing. I'm sorry. That is one of the conditions of the operation – complete secrecy. Even I'm not fully in the picture.'

We're going to the rendezvous point now, where you'll get an initial briefing.'

'Dammit, you could have given me some warning.'

'We waited till Sam was away. It's your decision. We could call it off now. You must understand that this operation means making sacrifices. Mine was giving up the opportunity of leading it in favour of yourself.'

Rayne saw the grim look on Long's face. He realised what that decision must have cost. 'You're better suited for this operation than I am,' Long continued. 'You're younger. You're a natural fighter. You know the territory and your Shona is fluent. You also speak Portuguese.'

Rayne was taken aback. He had told no one that he spoke Portuguese, which he'd picked up on long fishing holidays in Mozambique with his father. He preferred to keep his knowledge, and his past, to himself.

The Major correctly interpreted the look on Rayne's face. 'We know because you interrogated a FRELIMO soldier in Portuguese. You're a dark horse, Gallagher, and that's another reason why you've been chosen.'

That was it, then. The operation, or Sam. As he figured it, he might have a chance of making it up to Sam – but he'd never have another chance to do something like this again.

'OK. I'm in.'

'Och, I guessed you would be.'

They continued the journey in silence till they arrived at an old farmhouse some distance outside Salisbury. The car pulled up outside the drive, and they got out.

'Good luck, Gallagher.'

They shook hands, and Rayne walked down the dirt drive without looking back. Moments later he heard the car drive off.

Martin Long looked out through the back window of the car at the house in the darkness. God, what had he come to? It was sheer suicide, what they'd proposed; he'd refused it point-blank. Then the pressure had started. If he wouldn't do it, then he had to find someone who could.

Rayne Gallagher had been the only possible choice. But what condition was he in to handle the pressure he was going to be under?

Martin Long turned and looked out of the front window,

concentrating on the dirt road curving ahead of him into the distance. How had John Fry found out about his father, about the disgrace and the cowardice? Fry was a bastard, threatening to unearth the whole story, feed it to the press. The price of his silence was a man who could lead his crazy mission.

He shivered. Had he been a coward? He tried to ease his conscience by telling himself that the release of the story would destroy his father, an old man in his eighties with nothing but his past to keep him going.

'Good evening, Captain Gallagher, I'm pleased you have agreed to lead this operation. My name is John Fry.'

From his accent, Rayne knew at once that he was an American. CIA? But why the hell were the Americans involved in this? He was in his early forties, in good physical shape and around five foot ten tall, with a clean-cut boyish face and dark hair. He would have been at home in the first class compartment of an aircraft or in the *salon privé* of a casino. He was dressed in a dark blue suit and pale blue shirt with a button-down collar. He looked out of place in the deserted farmhouse.

Fry walked over to a map that had been stuck on the wall with masking tape. The map was of the Mozambique area to the east of Rhodesia.

'Captain Gallagher, you are familiar with the location of enemy forces within Mozambique? The public believes that this is a territory receiving Chinese aid and military assistance. This is a naive assumption, and we wouldn't want to change it. The reality is that the majority of aid and assistance is of Soviet origin. Nothing startling about that.

'Now, my own government, together with the British government, has accepted that the Rhodesian War of Independence is entering – how shall I say it? – its final phase. Our intelligence reveals the existence of many bases within Mozambique for the supply and control of terrorist operations. Your forces have successfully eliminated some of these in the past. However, the major source of supply and control we have never, until now, been able to identify.

'Now, recently the CIA infiltrated this base. It has provided us with the most disturbing information. In short, we have discovered that a major attack on Rhodesia is to be launched very soon. The operation's code name is Salisbury. The intention, to decimate the capital city of this country and achieve immediate power for the ZANLA, Mashona faction. In short, it will be a Soviet take-over.'

Rayne whistled under his breath. Up to now, the war had stayed out of the capital city. This would bring it to the heart of their fragile society; it would be a bloodbath – something they had all feared but never believed would happen.

'They will utilise the very latest Russian fighter-bombers and helicopter gunships. The whole operation will be under Soviet control. Once under way, your army will never be able to stop it.

'Many men have died gleaning this intelligence information, now I must utilise it, and that requires both stealth and secrecy.'

'But I thought that this was a Rhodesian operation?' Rayne was perplexed by the absence of any Rhodesian officials. His guard was up.

'Relax, Captain. You were recommended to me by the Rhodesians. I needed a man who could operate in Mozambique, and they selected you. It is you, Captain Gallagher, on whom the success or failure of this operation depends.

'Your mission is simple. You are to leave this country and to recruit an elite band of mercenary soldiers. You will infiltrate the enemy position, destroy their aircraft and helicopters, and then get the hell out. The rest of the base must be left intact, the fuel storage depot and other secondary installations are on no account to be destroyed.

'This mission must not be seen as Rhodesian. The Soviets are waiting for an excuse for invasion – a Rhodesian-inspired attack would give them that excuse. For your operation to succeed, it has to be seen as a mercenary action.

'For the Russians, of course, Rhodesia is merely a pawn so that they can then advance on South Africa. That is quite clear, I think.

'This mission has the backing of both the CIA and MI6. The governments of the United States and Great Britain want the election process to take place unhindered in Rhodesia. They want the world to know that democracy can succeed in Africa.

'Now, do you have any questions, Captain?'

'Why?'

Fry looked momentarily disconcerted. Then he smiled good-naturedly. 'Ah, Captain Gallagher. I am not used to a military man asking such a question. You see, the objective for the moment is to achieve some kind of stability in this part of Africa. We have come to realise that black governments do not trust the superpowers. However if Russia were to help ZANLA get into power, they would then have a considerable hold over them. You see, we don't need a Soviet government in Southern Africa.'

Rayne got to his feet and walked over to the map. He wasn't thinking of the politics, just of the task in hand.

'Getting into Mozambique with a band of armed men won't be easy. The targets will have to be clearly identified. The speed with which we eliminate them will be all-important. A successful escape route needs to be well planned – one mistake and my force could be annihilated. Remember that in the Selous Scouts I've been up against ZANLA and FRELIMO, not a sophisticated Soviet force.'

John Fry smiled. 'You assess the difficulties well, Captain Gallagher. However, you will have every military resource at your disposal, and unlimited financial backing. It is a challenge, of course, but you were chosen for your unique leadership abilities and your fighting spirit.'

'So where is the target, Mr Fry?'

'The target is Beira.'

The harbour of Beira, on the east coast of Mozambique, had at one time been linked by railway all the way to Salisbury. The war had put paid to that; Rayne had even blown up some sections of the Beira line himself.

'Can you now understand why you were selected, Captain Gallagher?'

Rayne ignored the question. 'How much accurate information do you have on this Soviet build-up? Do you know how they propose to attack Salisbury?'

'An airborne assault will be mounted. After initial heavy bombing, fighter planes will move in and strafe designated areas. Then taskforce units will be airlifted in by helicopter. They will be briefed to shoot on sight, no hostages are to be taken.'

Rayne shivered. It was a brilliant, savage plan.

'We'll be able to give you a very detailed plan of the Beira airport. That's your target.'

'Mr Fry, I suppose that while I attack the airport, the Russian and Mozambique forces will miraculously stand back and not interfere?'

'Witty. You will have to operate under cover – get in there without being noticed, strike, and then get out as quickly as you can.'

Rayne's mind immediately went to work on the problem. He and his men would have to be flown in; there was no way they could make a ground-based attack if they were not coming from Rhodesia.

'Suppose I'm caught alive?'

'Another reason why you were selected. You are not the sort to talk. If they did break you, by that time they'd have to question whether you were telling the truth or lying to stop the pain.'

A frown appeared on Fry's face as he said this. Suddenly he seemed much older. Rayne noticed. 'You talk from experience, Mr Fry?'

'They got me in Korea. It changes one. I was lucky, I escaped.'

'I don't intend to get caught.'

John Fry got up from his chair and extended his hand.

'You'll be supplied with a contact number and a bank account in any country where you want to start recruiting – we'll take care of getting you in and out. Good luck, Captain Gallagher.'

'Thanks, but I don't believe in luck.'

Rayne's first priority was recruitment. Major Long told him he could recruit men from the army as long as they didn't hold rank, and within a fortnight he'd interviewed seventy and chosen fifteen, including Lois. There'd been a big argument over Lois, but eventually the Major had agreed to let him go.

Next, Rayne and Lois flew to Durban. Rayne planned to launch his force into Mozambique from South Africa, and north of Durban, on the east coast, he knew of the ideal place in which to establish a base. While the other fourteen men flew into Durban on random commercial flights, drove into the base and began a stiff training programme, Rayne and Lois organised stocks of weapons and explosives. Rayne also did some interviewing, but he found no one suitable. He was beginning to be worried; he still needed four more men, men who had proven ability with explosives, and also the ability to lead. Obviously, they weren't going to be easy to find.

There'd been plenty of candidates, of course, men who were just after a fast buck. But Rayne was looking for that rare breed, the hardened professional soldier, a man who would readily accept discipline but who could also act on his own in a difficult situation. He needed four of them, to complete his full complement of twenty.

Rayne knew of one person who could find him the men he needed, but that person was on the other side of the world.

The jumbo touched down on the slippery, wet landing strip of Heathrow and drew to a halt in the inevitable drizzle. For a few moments it sounded as though the engines were about to shut down, but instead the plane taxied a little further towards the terminal buildings before juddering into silence.

Outside the grey sky offered a bleak greeting after a twelve-hour flight from the heat of the South African summer. There were few passengers on board this mid-week SAA Boeing 747 flight from Jan Smuts, Johannesburg's main airport. Most of them did not look particularly pleased to be leaving the warmth of the plane.

In the crowded arrivals hall a man waited, slightly to the side of the main concourse. He was looking for a particular person. His instincts did not let him down. Almost the first person through customs, Captain Gallagher stood out in contrast to the rest of the passengers, and it was evident that he had immediately detected his watcher.

Yes, Michael Strong said to himself, this one would be fine. The hardness and the intelligence marked him as a fighting man. Definitely a man worth knowing. He moved forward to greet his foreign guest.

'Captain Gallagher, welcome to Britain.'

Strong could sense that he, too, was being assessed. 'Colonel Strong? I didn't expect to be met at the airport.' The tone in which Rayne spoke the words of the call-sign was suspicious.

'You'll enjoy our beer.'

'I prefer tea.'

Why were these call-signs always so stupid? Rayne supposed it was because people figured that that way, no one could come up with the correct answer by accident.

'I've booked you a room at the Dorchester, Captain Gallagher. I thought we might eat first at my club. That is, if you're not too tired?'

The car, a white Aston Martin DBS Vantage, moved effortlessly along the M4 motorway in the fading daylight. The brute power of the engine was just audible through the angry burble of the exhausts.

Rayne watched the Colonel as he drove. He was a big man with a wide craggy face topped by an unruly mane of dark hair. His mouth seemed bent in a perpetual sardonic smile, and the keen brown eyes gave the impression of missing nothing. His nose, slightly hooked at the tip, had the predatory air of a falcon. Colonel Strong, he thought, was a man he could get along with.

They dropped Rayne's cases off at the Dorchester, and then dined excellently at the Colonel's club. After that, Colonel Strong suggested entertainment. They walked down a narrow alley into a small square dominated by an elegant Georgian-style townhouse with an enormous black door. In front of the door stood a man who looked like a cross between a maitre d'hotel and a prize-fighter. He recognised the Colonel and swung open a wrought-iron gate to the left of the front door; Rayne looked down a line of steps that led to the basement.

'Evening, Colonel Strong, sir.'

'Good evening, Sylvester, how's business?'

'Typical for a weekday. Couple of drunk public school chaps. Some rather dour-looking Saudis. And then there are the regulars like yourself, sir.'

'Let me introduce you to Captain Gallagher, Sylvester.'

'Always a pleasure to meet your friends, sir.'

They walked down the steps and through a narrow side-door. Inside the air was thick with tobacco smoke, and the sound of a jazz quartet energised the atmosphere. As they walked into the room Sylvester vanished and they were met by another man in evening dress – a thin, debauched face with an aristocratic line to it.

'Good to see you, Michael. Ah, you have company. Your favourite table is available. Let me get you a drink.'

'Thanks, Richard. This is Captain Gallagher.'

'My pleasure, Captain Gallagher. I'm sure that you'll enjoy yourself. The Mandrake always endeavours to please.'

Rayne was impressed with the Colonel's natural air of authority. Even the owner of the club was clearly intimidated by the big man. They were led to a table that was close enough to the jazz quartet for them to enjoy the music but not so close as to kill conversation. Their drinks arrived a few minutes later, a neat double Scotch for Rayne and a gin and tonic for the Colonel.

Rayne was surprised at how full the club was. There were some very attractive women in the room, obviously high society; and then there were others of more dubious background . . . Many of the men were clearly in business, but others looked like actors, musicians, sportsmen and soldiers. This was obviously a night club that didn't care too much about the social standing of its members, more about their ability to pay their membership fees and enjoy themselves. No one had paid the slightest attention to the Colonel or himself. That was obviously part of the etiquette.

The quartet rounded off the number. The applause was muffled but appreciative. The Colonel had been in a meditative mood while the music was playing but now he became more expansive.

'You can really relax in this place. I've never been much of a man for words. Can't stand heavy books. Poetry leaves me cold. But music, music I've always liked. Especially jazz.' He took another sip at his drink and then continued, 'Jazz is non-aggressive. I can imagine going into a fire fight listening to rock music. Mind you, I don't think about music when I'm in action. All I think about is staying alive.

'Take a look at the lady who's about to sing. I've been after her for the last six months. She's still giving me a hard time.'

A very dark-skinned woman came up to the microphone and smiled at the tables. Rayne noticed that there was scarcely a man in the room who was not watching her. She waited for the quartet to settle down. The opening note came from the keyboard player and the other instruments moved in to create a driving rhythm.

She started to sing. Her voice was deep and sensual. Magical. Rayne was transfixed. She was not attractive in the conventional way, her figure was a little too full, her long legs a shade too muscular, and her face had a wanton look. But she radiated a

41

magnetic sexuality that could not be ignored. Her hair was long, raven black with dark russet streaks.

As she sang, the content and words of the song became irrelevant. It was the emotion in her voice that mattered. No man in the room was left unmoved by it – a voice more attractive than the female body itself.

Then the number was over, and only when it was clear that she was not going to continue, was there appreciative applause.

She left the stage and walked over to their table. The long black dress clung to her body. A slit that rose almost above her thigh revealed her legs as she walked towards them. She pulled up her chair and stared at Rayne. Dark, sultry eyes that were without embarrassment. She knew what she wanted. He could smell her now, a warm musky scent that caused him to come erect.

'Well, Michael. Your manners are appalling. If you won't introduce me then I'll introduce myself.' Her voice was not what he had expected. Deep, yes, but with a very English upper-class accent.

'Rayne.'

'An unusual name. I see you are surprised by my voice.'

'You haven't told me your name.'

'Priscilla. Priscilla St John.'

'Priscilla, you sing very beautifully.'

'Thank you. You are very flattering for a military man.'

'How do you know I'm a soldier?'

'Michael only mixes with fighting men.' She stared at Colonel Strong provocatively. 'Are you on holiday, Rayne?'

'Yes. I'm staying at the Dorchester. Just here to see London.'

'Oh, all Michael's foreign friends come here on holiday, don't they, Michael . . .'

At forty-seven, Michael Strong was wealthy and his business was successful, but he was a soldier at heart and longed for action. At first when he'd met Gallagher he'd summed him up as just another tough boy heading for an early death, but as the evening progressed he'd become aware of a sensitivity and a keen intelligence beneath the hardness. He found himself intrigued, too, by the operation – about which Gallagher refused to divulge details. It sounded dangerous but possible. He loved danger; without it he went into decline.

Michael Strong parked the Aston Martin in the garage of his South Kensington mews house and let himself in. Upstairs in the lounge he poured himself a last tot of Scotch and gazed round him at the pictures, medals and campaign memorabilia that decorated the walls. The men in most of the photographs had been friends. Very few of them were still alive. He himself had been lucky, or perhaps intelligent. It crossed his mind to offer Gallagher some friendly advice – but he was sure it would be construed as weakness.

He went up to sleep an hour later, alone, thinking of Priscilla.

Rayne woke up sweating. He had dreamed he was in Mozambique, in a clearing, alone, when he heard the sound of a rifle being loaded . . . He stared into the darkness of the London hotel room, wondering if he had really recovered from his ordeal a month before.

Then the door handle turned and the door opened very slowly. Someone moved into the darkness, came close. He grabbed an arm and twisted it up sharply. There was a high-pitched scream. He turned on the light and found himself looking at Priscilla St John.

'You're quite a man, Captain Gallagher.'

He had let her go and she was staring at his naked body.

'Didn't your mother tell you it was dangerous trying to get into men's bedrooms?'

'Yes. But I've never had much difficulty. I got your room number and a key from reception.'

'So much for the discretion of the Dorchester.'

'I told a lie. I said I was your wife.'

'Would you like a drink, Mrs Gallagher?'

'Later . . .'

He pulled her towards him and she did not resist. Her mouth locked over his and he felt himself swimming in her sensuality. She pulled him down on the bed and her hands began to work on him. He unfastened her dress and eased it off her body. Underneath she wore nothing but stockings and suspender belt.

She straddled him and lowered herself onto him. Beads of sweat broke out across her forehead and her nipples were hard with excitement. She stared into his eyes as he pushed himself up inside her and felt her body convulse as the orgasms began.

'Don't stop. Oh, don't stop.'

He pushed her over, sinking his face into her, and she screamed out with pleasure. He felt her lips teasing him, her hands fondling him, taking him to ever higher planes of excitement.

The alarm clock screamed in his ear and he buried it under the pillow. His whole body was still aching.

She was gone. But there was a message written with lipstick on the mirror above the dressing-table. 'Next time, you pay me a surprise visit. Love Priscilla.' Her phone number was underneath.

He smiled and went into the shower, turning the water on cold. Later he went across the road into Hyde Park and did a couple of quick circuits, sprinting hard. Then he jogged back to the hotel, ready to face what the day had to offer.

Again the room was plunged into darkness. Another face flashed before his eyes – one of the world's finest mercenary soldiers, another man from the exclusive files of Colonel Strong, ex SAS, known for his ability to supply quality.

Many of the men Rayne did not like the look of at all. Others he was indifferent to. He needed only four – but he wanted loyalty, intelligence and leadership ability, plus a highly specialised knowledge of explosives.

As the Colonel switched on the lights of the small viewing theatre, Rayne's mind was working in overdrive. These men were good, but were they what he wanted?

'It's not easy, Rayne, I know. No one can guarantee results. But these men are the best. Every one of them has been thoroughly checked out. They're hard, and you've got to be tough to command them.'

Strong looked at him with that predatory air of his, and Rayne wondered what was going through his mind. For him, this was a matter of life and death; for Strong, perhaps only another day's work.

'And the ones I want. When would I be able to get them to my take-off point?'

'All the men you've seen are immediately available. They all have valid passports.'

'Do you have any personal recommendations?'

'The magic question. I'd take the first three I showed you. As for the rest . . . your guess would be as good as mine.'

'Why the first three?'

He had to be sure. What if Strong was merely trying to get things in order as quickly as he could?

'Dammit, Rayne. You think I'm a bloody horse-trader!'

Rayne stared at him enigmatically. 'If they fail I die; you still make your commission.'

'You bastard!'

Strong picked up the file in front of him and closed it with an air of finality. Rayne remained seated. He had played his card, now he waited for the reaction.

Strong stood up. 'You can get out of this office right now, Captain Gallagher. I've always operated on the basis of trust. That's why the men you've seen put their lives in my hands. I don't supply people I don't like – and you fall into that category. Now get out.'

'No.'

Rayne felt himself being hoisted to his feet. He cannoned his right arm up and broke Strong's grip. Before he could make another move Strong drove his other fist into his stomach. Rayne staggered forwards and then swung, delivering a roundhouse into the Colonel's side. The big man crashed into the slide projector but stayed on his feet.

Then they were on each other, limbs flailing like fighting cats. Neither would give in to the other. After five minutes they staggered back from each other, bleeding and exhausted.

Rayne looked at Michael and began to laugh. The Colonel collapsed to the ground, laughing too.

'Deuce, Michael!'

'Well, I think we've earned a good lunch!'

Rayne looked out through the latticed windows of the old room to the branch of an oak tree waving in the wind. The noise of the raindrops on the windowpane was strangely soothing. After a lifetime in a climate where it rarely rained, he found the English weather a pleasant change.

He was waiting for the fourth of the men whom the Colonel had arranged for him to meet in this obscure little village hotel.

'Come in.' Rayne enunciated the words crisply as soon as he

heard the knock. He liked to project authority from the first moment of contact.

The door of the room opened. Rayne stared at the eyes that stared back into his. It was Michael Strong. He sat down opposite Rayne, in the chair the other interviewees had sat in. He spoke slowly.

'It's always tough for a soldier to answer questions. How much can you learn about a man during a five-minute conversation? Very little, except what your intuition tells you – and that's what you go by. I should be an expert at it after all these years, but I'm still never a hundred per cent accurate. I can give you a good picture of each man's background, and a good idea of his potential, but how he'll actually get on with you when the bullets start flying, that's something that only experience will show.'

The Colonel leaned forward, his forearms resting on his thighs. The brown eyes looked again into Rayne's, the craggy face was deadly serious.

'I'm the fourth man, Rayne. I'm with you. I have the explosives knowledge you want. I'm bored; I'm intrigued by your expedition. I'm divorced, my children are grown up. I want to get into the field.'

Rayne felt as if an enormous weight had been lifted from his shoulders. He now had a second-in-command – and he couldn't have wished for a better man.

Back at the Dorchester, Rayne packed the dossiers on each of the men into his attaché case. Now he had everything he needed. He had organised payment through the Swiss bank into which John Fry had deposited the funds. Now he and Strong were about to fly back to South Africa. He would be operational in less than a week's time.

He looked round the room one last time to make sure he'd forgotten nothing, and then carried his case towards the door – but before he got to it, Priscilla St John entered, wearing a vividly-coloured dress that stood out against her dark skin. The expression on her face, though, did not match the gay design of her dress.

'How did you know I was going?'

'I asked Michael.'

Rayne hadn't known how to say goodbye to her. He had been afraid to admit to himself that their relationship had become more than just a casual affair. The guilt was still there about Sam.

She sat down on the edge of the bed, and Rayne put down his case, took her in his arms and kissed her softly on the lips. The embrace went on. He felt scared of what had developed so quickly between them.

Eventually she pulled away and looked directly at him. 'You're so hard, yet underneath you're hurting. Tell me there's no one else.'

He shook his head. 'I have a duty . . .'

'A duty to live, not to die.'

She got up and went over to the mirror. Carefully she made up her mouth again. Then she turned to him.

'That woman, whoever she is, is very lucky. Don't let her down.' And before he could reply, she was gone.

Rayne was seated in the tourist-class compartment of a British Airways 747 flying direct from London to South Africa. Sitting next to him, thoughtfully sipping a glass of white wine, was Colonel Strong. Across the aisle were three hand-picked men. Rayne and his team were going on a long holiday to South Africa, and a rather interesting sight-seeing trip to Mozambique.

Bunty Mulbarton. Easily the most experienced; an ex-SAS man like Colonel Strong. Son of Major Mick Mulbarton, hero of the Somme and countless other actions. Heir to the Mulbarton Biscuit Company but preferring action to management. Active in the Arabian Peninsula with the SAS, particularly Aden and the Radfan Mountains. A weapons and explosives expert. Holder of the rank of major in the regular British army. Five foot nine of him in his stockinged feet. Blond hair, incongruous jet black eyebrows, over penetrating green eyes, sensual mouth, aquiline nose, old Etonian accent.

Guy Hauser. French national. A career soldier with the French Foreign Legion. Silent about his past before that. A first lieutenant with a violent temper who'd faced numerous assault charges but never been convicted. First-rate shot, hardened hand-to-hand fighter. Ruthless; also highly intelligent. A man who had seen action in Vietnam and anywhere else he could find a war and someone wanting to pay him to fight. Distinctive goatee beard, face deeply tanned, widow's peak. A tendency to raise the eyebrows and furrow the forehead when speaking.

Guy was the closest human equivalent to a bull terrier Rayne had ever seen. A good choice for mercenary action; a very intense and dangerous man.

Furthest away from Rayne sat Larry Preston. He was a very short, stocky man with long, straight blond hair, and he spoke with a Birmingham accent. Formerly an officer in the SAS, and now a full-time mercenary, Preston was a rough diamond with a penchant for the good life. He was expert with explosives, and claimed there wasn't a vault door he couldn't open.

Colonel Strong had provided Rayne with the very best. Now all he had to do was deploy them.

Mozambique at the end of 1978 was a wasteland. Outside the main towns any man who had a gun made his own laws.

The Marxist government headed by President Samora Machel had little long-term chance of success. It was merely a stumbling block for the forces intent on toppling the white regimes to the west and south.

The MNR, the Mozambique National Resistance, was gaining more and more members. Formed some five years before, it had been originally founded by the Rhodesians, but gained more local support as the people of Mozambique found the new independent regime little better than the Portuguese one which had preceded it. The South Africans also saw the numerous advantages of the MNR for the continued destabilisation of Mozambique. By 1978, the movement had a powerful leader, Andre Matangaidize. The Rhodesian SAS helped train the soldiers of the MNR and turned them into one of the most terrifying terrorist forces in Africa. They operated in ideal terrorist terrain – a subsistence economy. Many of the men in their ranks knew of no other way of life but fighting, and the MNR was their permanent employer. The state of Mozambique had little to offer those who wanted a peaceful life except pain, fear and poverty.

This then was the country that Rayne and his force would be entering. The MNR were fighting FRELIMO, the Mozambique people's army, for a new government in Mozambique; the Rhodesians were fighting Robert Mugabe's ZANLA forces, also based deep in Mozambique territory. President Samora Machel was having to rely more and more on Soviet aid. His crippled economy received no Western support because of his avowed communist sympathies. The formerly lucrative tourist trade with South Africa had come to a standstill after Independence, and seemed certain to stay that way.

Rhodesia had carried out over 350 raids into Mozambique, completely crippling the ports, roads and railway lines. But even victory against Rhodesia wouldn't mean the end of Machel's problems. After that, there was the growing conviction that the Soviets would merely use his country as a forward base for the war against South Africa. And as the South African army had the capability to blast its way to Cairo unopposed, it would take South Africa less than a day to control Mozambique. Only the certainty of an international outcry seemed to be holding them back.

In Africa since 1960 – the beginning of decolonisation, there had been over 120 military coups and of these 50 had been successful. The resulting growth in mercenary activity in the area had been enormous.

Rayne leaned back in his seat and closed his eyes. Thinking about Mozambique and her bleak future made him realise that once their mission was accomplished, they must get out of Mozambique – and quickly.

The Boeing 747 winged off lazily from Jan Smuts airport and the Witwatersrand, the economic heart of South Africa, and headed to the east; away from the high altitude and blazing heat of the Transvaal highveld, towards the green rolling hills of Natal, the 'settlers' province on the east coast of South Africa.

The plane took one and a half hours to complete the six-hundred-kilometre journey. It passed over many of the places that had rung to the sounds of battle between the British army and the farmer armies of the Boer republics a hundred years before: Dundee, Elandslaagte, Ladysmith, Isandhlwana. It passed over Pietermaritzburg, a sleepy town on the railway line from Durban to Johannesburg, where in 1893 a young Indian lawyer named Gandhi was told to get off the train because his first-class ticket did not entitle him to ride in coaches reserved exclusively for whites. It crossed the Pietermaritzburg-to-Durban road, the route of the world's greatest long distance road race, the Comrades Marathon, ninety gruelling kilometres. It was from here that Rayne and his men would be launching their operation into the heart of Mozambique.

Just at that moment, however, Rayne was reading the evening edition of the *Johannesburg Star*, unaware of the lands passing beneath him. For the time being he had even forgotten about the mission that had occupied his thoughts almost continuously since his first briefing with John Fry nearly a month before. Instead he was staring at the picture of a woman on the front page; a beauty with long blonde hair who was being heralded as the new Marilyn Monroe.

Penelope O'Keefe. She had always been ambitious. The daughter of Sir George O'Keefe, one of Johannesburg's richest mining magnates, she had been destined for a life of leisure. A year in one of Europe's finest finishing schools had prepared her for a suitable marriage and a comfortable existence. Except that Penelope had been different. She'd returned to South Africa from Europe with a loathing for high society, and greedy for excitement. Her parents had despaired of her, especially when she announced that she wanted to become a model while studying for her BA. But she finally got her way, as she always did.

Rayne had met her in his first year at university. He was sure they hadn't met by chance. He'd noticed her before, watching the rugby trials, enjoying the admiring glances of the young men and parrying their lewd shouts. Then she'd managed to get herself invited into the same English tutorial group as he, and had struck up a casual conversation. Some weeks later he found himself invited to her father's trout lodge in the Eastern Transvaal. He couldn't quite remember when he'd told her that he enjoyed fly fishing, but he accepted with alacrity. Sir George's farm was known to be on one of the best sections of the river.

Fly fishing had not taken up much of that weekend. In fact the only times Rayne's hands had touched the rod were when he took it into the lodge when they arrived, and took it out when they left. The rest of the time had been spent in bed. And for the next year and a half he and Penelope had had a stormy relationship that was the talk of the campus.

He remembered when they'd flown down to the family's house in Port St Johns for Christmas. Port St Johns was a tiny old harbour on the Transkei east coast, just below the province of Natal. They'd narrowly escaped death when Sir George's company plane had crashed just before landing. The pilot had been killed, but miraculously Penelope and Rayne had survived.

Afterwards she'd been a lot keener to leave South Africa. Rayne thought the accident might have been sabotage though that was never confirmed officially.

He and Penelope had graduated in the same year. She scraped through, and he had the highest average of any student in the previous ten years. He had gone on to study further, she'd left for New York, to take up a lucrative modelling contract, and had never looked back.

Rayne looked at the picture in the paper again and smiled ruefully to himself. There certainly weren't going to be any women like that where they were going. He felt an enormous void between his former existence as a law student and what he was now. How would it be if he met Penelope again? Would the same animal magnetism be there? He felt a stab of guilt for his disloyalty to Sam. She was the only woman who had really understood him. And he had let her down.

The noise of the flaps going down, ready for landing, pulled him from such thoughts.

'Well, here we are. It's all stations go.' Michael's voice was confident. Rayne wondered if it would still be confident in a week's time.

Lois was at the airport to meet them. He'd bought a used Land Rover to ferry them all to the base camp. After a brief exchange of greetings they sped off north into the night.

The high humidity of the Natal coastal belt hit them immediately. Rayne's London clothes became uncomfortable in the sticky heat. Lois was ideally dressed in a wide-collared open-neck white shirt, khaki shorts and leather sandals.

'No one's been poking around or asking any questions, Lois?' He had to shout above the noise of the Land Rover engine.

'Nothing at all. As far as the locals are concerned you're a group of businessmen arriving for a sales conference. We're too far away from anywhere to attract much attention.'

Rayne had chosen the location of the camp himself. He'd been there on holiday when he was much younger and had realised even then that it was the perfect hide-out. The only thing he feared was that the local African population might get curious, especially if they heard them testing their weapons. No, they'd probably steer well clear. In South Africa it was always a good policy to stick to one's own business.

'Have you got everything I wanted, Lois?'

'You name it, I've got it. The stuff is all unused. Pistols. Assault rifles. Grenades. Rocket-launchers.'

'And the other piece of equipment I mentioned?'

'Yes. That too.'

Rayne smiled. Lois had proved his worth.

The inside of the Land Rover was dark except for the warm glow of the instruments on the dashboard. Outside, lush vegetation flashed by. For a few moments Rayne imagined that they were travelling through a green tunnel that led on for ever through the darkness.

Lois drove with his foot flat, the white speedometer needle dancing between a hundred and a hundred and twenty kilometres per hour. The men sat in silence, each locked into his own particular thoughts and worries.

The comfortable, tranquil towns of the Natal east coast sped past. It was hard to imagine that much further north along this coastline the atmosphere was so completely different. In Mozambique, as Rayne knew all too well, tranquillity was the last thing they would find.

After two hundred kilometres they passed the turn to Richard's Bay, and the road moved inland to avoid the giant mass of water that was Lake St Lucia. The country grew more isolated. The area to their right was Tongaland, over nine thousand square kilometres of almost uninhabited wilderness. Further along, Lois swung the Land Rover off the main road and onto a single-lane sandy track which deteriorated steadily as they journeyed along it.

Rayne looked round in satisfaction as they arrived at the thatched huts that were to be their home for the next week. The place looked just like a holiday retreat. A few boats were lying around, garden furniture was set out on the freshly mown lawn, a pile of bottles surrounded the waste bins. Lois and the other men had not been idle. Of course he would have to wait till first light to make sure that everything was a hundred per cent all right, but Rayne was sure that from the air no one would be in the least suspicious.

Lois showed them to their huts. Rayne and Michael's hut was neat, if somewhat on the spartan side. The mosquito coil glowed pleasantly in the darkness, its distinctive smell gradually filling the whole room.

'Good God, Rayne, how the hell does anyone live here?' The Colonel's voice echoed against the darkness.

'Not many people do. In fact, because of the mosquito and the tsetse fly, this part of the world used to be virtually uninhabitable. That's why I made you and the others start taking those tablets. There are actually only two species of mosquito that carry malaria, and they aren't particularly prevalent here, but it doesn't do to take risks. If you take your anti-malaria tablets all the time you're here, you're in no danger at all.'

The Colonel smiled grimly in the dark. 'In future,' he said, 'I think I'll be taking my holidays in the South of France.'

Sam

Sam was furious. Every time she thought about it she became angry. He'd hurt her even more deeply than she could have imagined. Now, as she angrily strode through the bush, she tried to blot him out of her mind. A branch of a tree came up without warning and hit her in the face, and she shouted, 'Fuck you! Just fuck off!'

How could he have been such an absolute bastard – after all the promises he'd made! She'd come out here to forget him, but instead she was feeling even worse. She had immersed herself in her work – that was why she was here, on this small farm to the north of Umtali, two hundred kilometres south-east of Salisbury. Today she had gone out from the farmhouse on her own, a highly dangerous thing to do. But she didn't care. She felt reckless after what Rayne had done to her.

The farm's setting was idyllic. Not far to the east were the mountains that marked the border between Rhodesia and Mozambique; the whole Umtali valley was a Garden of Eden, warm and fertile, filled with luxuriant vegetation. Yet in this perfect place life had become a hell for the inhabitants. They were in a no-man's-land, caught between the Rhodesian forces and the ZANLA guerrillas who infiltrated across the Mozambique border only thirty kilometres away. Many of the farmers had fled, opting for the safety of the town of Umtali and letting their crops go to ruin. People drove everywhere in convoy, eyes constantly scanning the dirt roads for land-mines.

For the rural black African population there was no way out of the war. The guerillas demanded that they inform on their white employees, and if the tribesmen didn't cooperate they were tortured or killed. If they did cooperate, they didn't fare much better at the hands of the Rhodesian police. Every farm that was still occupied was linked up to the Agric-Alert system, which enabled isolated farmers to stay in constant touch with their closest police headquarters. A break in contact would automatically lead to an alert, and an immediate police or army investigation.

Sam had long been wanting to do a story on the life of the farmers on Rhodesia's eastern frontier, and now her editor had thought a piece on how hard the Rhodesians were having it might be newsworthy. That was all the prodding she had needed – given the mood she was in – and she had set off looking for the distraction that the story would bring. But it had all been rather depressing. The scenery and the beautiful locations should have compensated her for the despair of the people, but instead it threw their condition into even worse relief for her. Everyone wanted the war over, but everyone knew that it would continue for months, whatever the outcome of the elections.

Sam thought of the beautiful jacaranda and flame trees that lined the streets of Umtali. They made the place look sleepy and secure. Set amid stunning mountain ranges, it was rated one of the most beautiful towns in the whole of Africa. The day before, she had taken the scenic route to the south of Umtali to see the Vumba Mountains, and had marvelled at the spectacular vegetation, especially the blood-red leaves of the musasa trees. She knew that in her native America the place would have been swarming with tourists; instead, in Rhodesia, it was completely deserted.

She had seen the fabulous farm Cloudlands, too, which had been donated to the people of Rhodesia by Lionel Cripps and the Bunga Forest. She had walked through the trees in the late afternoon drizzle, trying to imagine what it must have been like to live in the place when there was no threat of death and only the promise of immense wealth and prosperity. She thought what a timeless quality the forest had, like the sea which you know will keep on crashing against the shoreline in just the same way long after you have departed . . .

Still remembering yesterday's expedition, Sam turned round to start walking back to the farmhouse. It was no wonder the white farmers on the borders were bitter and bewildered, she thought. They were caught up in changes they could not understand. They believed that with the elections, and the new government of Bishop Muzorewa, they would be able to settle back into the life they had once thought would go on for ever. Little did they realise that this was only another, passing phase in the history of their troubled land. The black people, so long dominated by the white races, wanted power for themselves – and not merely power which was handed over to them at secondhand by a white government abroad. Too many of the black leaders now knew that their only option was a bloody one; they had learned this lesson from the successive white governments that had imprisoned and oppressed them for more than twenty years . . .

Noticing the light was beginning to fade, Sam suddenly felt apprehensive. The farmer she'd been interviewing had told her she was crazy to go for a walk on her own. Heart beating hard for no apparent reason, she broke into a half-run. She began to breathe a little easier as she glimpsed the farmhouse through the trees, but the feeling of relief didn't last long.

When she'd left the farmhouse there had been quite a few men working nearby, but now the area round the homestead seemed strangely deserted. For a moment she thought she glimpsed someone in the bush, but then she realised she must have imagined it. Closer to the farmhouse, she was startled by a loud bang that sounded like a shotgun. Another bang came moments later, and then a loud burst of automatic rifle fire.

To her horror Sam realised that the farm must be under attack by a ZANLA unit. To run back to the farmhouse would be suicide. They would have seen her car. What was she going to do?

She ran towards the bush without even thinking, the branches tearing at her clothes while more automatic fire sounded in the distance. Now she was nearing the top of the hill where the ground was more open, and she kept to the edge of the trees, turning back every so often to make sure she was not being followed.

She must get out of the valley and over to the other side of the ridge, then she could make her way back west until she hit the main road from Watsomba to Umtali. There, she calculated, she could hide and wait until a convoy came along. She had heard on the radio that morning that the army was well in control of the operational area Thrasher, where she was now. It could only be a matter of time before the security forces were on the scene.

She could not know that her host, Stuart Gregg, had become worried that she was walking too far away from the farm buildings and had walked after her with his shotgun. Too late he had realised that something was amiss – that all his farmworkers had disappeared, a sure sign there were terrs in the area. He had already started to run back to the farm when he saw the shadowy forms amongst the trees. He kept going, weaving from side to side, hoping to present a bad target. He fired once, cutting one man down. He was within fifty metres of the front door when the first burst of fire from an AK-47 hit him in the legs.

Desperately he had tried to leopard-crawl to the open back door, but he hadn't stood a chance. A second spurt of fire caught him in the back. He reared up and fired his shotgun, killing another terr. Then a bullet struck him in the forehead and he slumped over. Another casualty of the border conflict, his hopes and dreams gone forever, waiting to be collected when his six o'clock alert call did not come in at the police station . . .

The guerillas trooped past the dead body into the farmhouse. They were looking for anything of value they could take with them. They ripped the telephone out of its socket and smashed it to pieces. There was no fear in these men. They had little enough to lose – certainly no home like this to return to. Many of them had left home years before to lead a guerrilla's life in the bush and fight for the cause they believed in.

Soon it was clear to them that the farmer had lived alone. But there was another car parked behind the farmhouse as well as the farmer's Land Rover. The farmer must have had a visitor. The question was, where was he?

Comrade Mnangagwa looked across the green valley, down to where the river glistened in the last sunlight of the day. How many more would it take? How many of these white settlers would have to die before they accepted what was inevitable? Enough of this stupid election and these interfering British politicians! He was sick of their sanctimonious attitude. This country was named after one of their kind, as were most of the cities and towns. The logic of Western politics evaded Comrade

Mnangagwa. They were all so sorry now, these white men from their strange, cold land over the seas.

And these Rhodesians who called him a terrorist. What would killing a few white farmers do to make up for all that he and his people had suffered at their hands? He thought of his own son, buried in an unmarked grave after dying in detention. Yes, he, Mnangagwa, would have liked to own a farm like this; but under white rule it could only ever be a dream. When ZANLA had control, he would become what he had always wanted to be, a city man. A lawyer. He had been lucky enough to get an education before he joined the cause.

He pulled the leaflet out of his pocket, studied the crude drawing and laughed aloud. His fellow comrades also laughed because they feared him, this educated man whose discipline was a legend amongst them. They thought he laughed at the death of the farmer.

The headline on the leaflet Mnangagwa was holding read 'Terror and death is the way of the communist camp instructors in Mozambique.' The picture showed a man beating a new recruit and the story told how all the men in the Mozambique communist training camps lived in fear, expecting torture or death any minute. He knew that only the most illiterate tribesman would believe this story – but such a man would not be able to read it anyway. Mnangagwa wondered how the men in Salisbury who were so good at waging war could be so naive when it came to propaganda. But then the white men were stupid enough to believe that the people would accept the puppet president Gumede and the sell-out Bishop Abel Muzorewa. He knew that those who had fought for so long would never accept such a ridiculous situation.

For Mnangagwa the only acceptable answer would come when the supreme commander of ZANLA, Robert Mugabe, ruled the country. Mugabe was a Mashona like himself, and the Shona peoples were in the majority. Their sworn tribal enemies were the Matabele, and these people made up the ZIPRA forces to the west of Rhodesia under the command of Joshua Nkomo. As far as Mnangagwa was concerned, Joshua Nkomo would always be an also-ran, he could never be president and rule over the Shona peoples. Mugabe was the only choice. After all, he had the support of President Samora Machel of Mozambique, and only Machel could guarantee that the new state would have a route to the sea. That was essential, for it would only be a matter of time before relations between the new state and South Africa soured. After Rhodesia, South Africa was the next goal. But that would be another war, one not even worth contemplating till this one was well finished.

A man was running towards him at great speed. As the man got closer, Mnangagwa saw that it was one of his privates, Comrade Dagger, a quiet and efficient fighter. His skill with the hunting knife he always carried had earned him his name. The man stopped within a metre of him and stood loosely to attention.

'Comrade Commander.'

'I hear you, Comrade Dagger. Speak.'

'Comrade Commander. There is a white woman on this land. She has a camera.'

The man addressed him simply as 'Commander'. Names of commanding officers were rarely used because of the danger of their being found out by the hated Selous Scouts. Comrade Dagger wore the safety-pin identity tag they had all adopted for that week. Only trusted men in the units would be aware of the importance of the little safety-pin; the absence of it would result in questioning, and death if the right answers were not forthcoming.

Mnangagwa listened to the words of Comrade Dagger and felt a tenseness creeping over his body. Perhaps they had been incorrectly informed. Perhaps the farmer did have a wife. But then he had seen no women's clothes in the house. And a farmer's wife would never be stupid enough to walk unarmed, alone, with only a camera, in this area. No, it must be someone else. A friend? A visitor?

'Where is this white woman, Comrade Dagger? Why did you not kill her?' The edge must always be there, he could never allow a moment's weakness. Their role was to terrorise the population, softness got them nowhere.

'She was not armed. She does not know that I saw her.'

'Is the coward's blood of the Matabele dog in your veins?'

'She ran up the ridge. She will not get far. We will capture her and make her sing. It will be dark soon.'

He knew that Comrade Dagger did not want to march through the night, but they must find this woman quickly and silence her. She had seen them and that was bad. Perhaps she had taken pictures. He knew that she would make for the main road between Umtali and Watsomba, then she would wait for one of the patrols.

It would not be difficult to catch her. His men would have to leave all the things they had taken from the farm because the weight would slow them down. He himself never soiled his hands with the white man's things, but his troops would not like leaving what they had taken. That was good. It would teach them a lesson. Especially as they would not be able to return to collect them, because later there would undoubtedly be security forces in the area, checking out the farmer's death.

He yelled at them to regroup. They stood in front of him, laden with booty from the farmhouse. On his command they dropped it to the ground. He could see the veiled anger in their eyes – fifteen of them including himself.

'The white woman. She must be caught. I want her camera, and I want her alive – only kill her if you have to. We will split into three groups of five. I will command one; Dagger, you the other, and Sithole the rest. We will start off now over the north ridge. We will skirt along the edge till we come to the main road, then we will separate and head back. We will find her as she makes for the road. We will meet tomorrow night at the place of the hyena.'

Mnangagwa watched the other two groups disappear quickly into the bush, then he went back to the car behind the farmhouse. He searched through it and in the cubby-hole found a notebook, some pictures and a passport. An American passport.

He opened it and stared at the picture. An attractive white woman. The document was a mass of stamps and he noted that she was a journalist. A rare catch if they got her. He stuffed the papers into the breast-pocket of his shirt.

They left the grounds surrounding the farm house and disappeared into the bush, heading for the ridge, moving fast. In an evening they could cover forty kilometres if the terrain was not too bad. This was their life, moving from place to place, never forming a permanent camp unless they were well inside the Mozambique border. They always obtained food and shelter, whenever they needed it, from the people who worked on the farms. Now in the darkness they moved with practised ease, rarely bumping into a tree or rock and never making any noise.

They had set up so many ambushes themselves that they were careful to avoid those set by the enemy.

Comrade Sithole was bitter. He had taken an excellent transistor radio from the farm, a powerful unit with four shortwave bands. It was something he had always wanted, and now, because of the white woman, he'd had to leave it behind. That was the way it was with the white people. No good ever came from his dealings with them.

Sithole was a tall, thin man with a stoop; he had an ugly face with bulging eyes and a straggly beard. He loped rather than walked, and had the habit of standing a little too close to people when he talked.

As he covered the ground Sithole thought back to the jobs he had held in Salisbury, especially the one where he hadn't been paid after three months. That had been when he was a waiter. At first he had shouted at the white woman who ran the restaurant, but she had laughed at him, her thin lips drawn back in mirth. Then he had threatened her. The police had come the next day. They had taken him to a cell where they beat him. It was after that he had decided he must overthrow the government. But first he had got his revenge. He had grabbed the white woman as she walked to her car behind the restaurant, pulled off her panties and stuffed them in her mouth. Then he had raped her.

That had been two years ago now. And he had nothing to show for his fighting except more bitterness. When it was over, he promised himself that he would have a farm of his own, a pretty wife and big strong sons. Then it would have been worth it. He wasn't interested in politics, but if the Russians gave him a gun then he would listen to their Marxism, whatever it meant. Soon he would be able to walk down the streets of Salisbury again, but this time as a citizen who would be paid for the work he did, someone whom the police would treat with respect.

Before long it would be dawn. Sithole looked proudly down at the watch he had taken from the dead farmer's hand for confirmation. They couldn't be far from the main road now, soon they would break into separate groups. He had been nominated to go furthest north and he knew why. He was a natural tracker, his sight was exceptional, like his other senses. He would always see signs that the other men missed; several times on this mission he had saved them from walking into enemy patrols and land-mines. Soon he would be commanding his own unit, just like Comrade Mnangagwa.

A loud whistle from far in the distance indicated that they were close to the road and should head off north. The order was to be his group, then Dagger's and then Mnangagwa's. They all knew that the woman could never have moved as quickly as they had through the darkness. The only danger to them now were the passing patrols that came along the main road early in the morning – but these patrols would only be concerned with getting to the farm they had just raided as quickly as possible.

The sun rose just after five and Comrade Sithole still had another three kilometres to cover with his men before they turned back east and began to comb the countryside. Their eyes constantly watched the road in the distance.

The noise of an approaching vehicle caused them to dive for cover and lie flat in the bush, each man with his finger curled around the trigger of his AK-47, hoping that he wouldn't be spotted. The sound got progressively louder until the first vehicle came past them, a Land Rover with two armed police reservists. This was followed by a light truck, also with two armed policemen in the cab, and after that came a stream of ordinary vehicles driven by farmers and their wives, all heavily armed.

They could have tried to ambush the convoy but it would have been very dangerous. The Land Rover might radio for help and the next moment the area would be crawling with members of the Rhodesian Light Infantry. So they let the convoy pass by, none the wiser. They got up moments later and moved onto the road – for it was unlikely that a second convoy would come by for some time. Less than an hour later they turned off the road and began to head east towards Mozambique.

Keeping a distance of approximately one hundred metres apart, they were covering an area of around six hundred metres as they walked forwards. They were the last group to start off. The plan was a good one, for if the woman saw the first group and she headed north, sooner or later she would run into a second group. They moved very slowly now, listening for any suspicious noise, knowing it might take them more than a day to find her.

*

Sam felt better as the first rays of sunlight appeared over the horizon, and she began to warm up after the cold night she had spent under a rock overhang. The area on the other side of the ridge had been much flatter than she had expected, though she still found it impossible to keep moving in the darkness.

There were no noises behind her and she suspected that the terrorists had given up the chase. She avoided open patches of ground and kept to where the vegetation was most bushy. Her mouth was dry and she needed a drink of water badly. If she could just make it back to the main road she would be all right.

The bush was getting thicker now and she felt a little more secure. Maybe the army was searching for her. If the farmer had sounded the Agric-Alert she was sure they would be. And if the security forces were active in the area she would have nothing to worry about at all.

For a while she headed north, hoping to catch a dirt track coming from one of the outlying farms that had now been deserted. Eventually she found a track leading off to the west, and followed it in the hope that it would take her back to the main road. Unfortunately it turned out to be a meandering path that only linked the many unpopulated farms. By the middle of the day the sweat was pouring off her and she was feeling giddy.

She decided to rest under a tree for a time until the heat of the day had passed. In the cool of the shade she stretched out and, utterly exhausted, dropped off to sleep. In her dreams she imagined Rayne coming down the track, seeing her, running towards her with a smile on his face. Then bullets started to fly and red marks appeared across the front of his uniform. Now he was crawling towards her, but as much as she tried she could not move towards him. He was dying and she wanted to try and help him . . .

She woke up feeling very cold and scared. It was much later in the afternoon and she realised with horror that she had been sleeping a long time. Something did not feel at all right. She must move away from this place as quickly as possible.

It was then she noticed the man staring at her, not ten metres from where she was lying – a tall, ugly man dressed in a torn jacket and dirty jeans. A back-pack lay next to him on the ground, and an AK-47 rifle rested in his hands as if he had been born carrying it. He was stooping, his big, bulging eyes staring at her. Now she noticed the four others. They were behind him, crouching down in the bush.

She realised they were making sure she wasn't armed. The man gestured for those behind him to come forward and at the same time he rose to his feet, still keeping the barrel of his rifle trained on her. He moved closer till she could smell the stale perspiration on him. He was only a pace or two away from her now, the tip of the rifle barrel almost touching her skin.

She rose instinctively and backed towards the trunks of the trees. He came forward and hit her hard across the face with the back of his left hand, and she fell to the ground. He leant down and snatched the watch off her hand and stuffed it into his jacket pocket. Then he tried to pull the diamond ring that her grandmother had given her off her left hand. She had never taken it off; no one was ever going to take it from her.

'Give me the ring.'

He had hurt her hand badly and she was angry. She curled her fingers and smashed her right hand into his face. Then she raked him with the fingernails of her left hand, the ring he had tried to remove catching his skin and cutting into it. Blood ran from his face. He staggered back, dropped the rifle and put his hands to the wound.

She ran forward and tried to pick up the rifle he had dropped. He moved quickly, slamming his boot against her fingers as they gripped the rifle barrel. She screamed with pain, staggering backwards and landing flat on the ground.

She could hear the men behind laughing. Now her attacker was furious and he grabbed her blonde hair and twisted it savagely, dragging her to her feet.

'Give me the ring!'

She pulled the ring off her finger and flung it into the bush where they could never find it. Then she spat in his face.

She instantly regretted it. He wrenched her hair again, yanking her back onto his chest and then clamping the rifle barrel across her throat so she could hardly breathe. Now she was hanging from his chest, held up from the neck by the rifle barrel and swinging like a puppet. His left hand came up and fastened round her throat and he dropped the rifle. Then his right hand tore her bush pants down, along with her panties.

The other men came up now and, terrified, she saw the excitement on their faces. He ripped her shirt and bra off and dropped her naked to the ground. With the pants round her ankles, she awkwardly tried to run, but he kicked her legs from under her so that she fell heavily.

Then they were on her. Two of the men grabbed her arms and she was dragged onto the dirt, face up. They pulled her arms in opposite directions, each man pushing a boot in below her armpit to brace himself. Her legs still thrashed wildly as the one who had hit her unfastened his jeans. Then he pulled her legs savagely apart and knelt on them so that she was completely pinioned. His hands worked their way over her breasts and she screamed again and tried to bite him. A leather belt was fastened around her mouth, forcing it wide open and splitting her lips. Mustering all her courage, Sam stared at the man in front of her defiantly.

Comrade Sithole thought that he would die. The pain shot through him so hard that he could hardly breathe. He had felt the tip of the boot as it connected with the bone area of his groin and caught his balls in its path.

He was knocked to the ground again as a rifle butt impacted into his skull. 'You scum, Comrade Sithole. You disgrace your mother. Get up and face me.'

Mnangagwa was mad. They had defied him, disobeyed his orders. They had become a rabble. This was what he had to fight most against; there had to be discipline; without it they were nothing. Sithole was staring at him, defiant – and he could sense that the other men were behind Sithole. He would change that, quickly.

Sithole staggered to his feet and looked angrily at Mnangagwa. 'I want the white whore, Comrade. She is mine. She deserves this. Her men have raped our women and taken our children to work on their farms. It is time for revenge.'

Mnangagwa realised he would have to set an example. Sithole was talking as if he commanded the men. He gestured for Comrade Dagger to come forward. Dagger was at his side immediately. Then Mnangagwa dragged Sithole to the tree where the naked white woman lay writhing on the ground, the leather belt still tight across her mouth. She tried to cover her naked breasts with her hands.

Sithole became erect again. Mnangagwa was pleased; this would teach the others a good lesson. He ordered Comrade

Dagger to tie Sithole's hands behind his back, turning him to face the other men, naked from the waist down, his proud erection visible to them all. The white woman was lying at his feet.

Mnangagwa pulled out his Makarov pistol. He spoke quietly to the men. 'Disobey me again, any one of you, and you will die. Comrade Sithole will live, but only to serve as an example to you. As members of ZANLA we obey the rules – the rules of behaviour. Number eight states that we should not take liberty with women, number nine that we should not ill-treat captives.'

He swung round to face Sithole and neatly shot off both his testicles.

The security forces had come to the farm that morning and discovered the dead body of the farmer. They were surprised that all the booty from the farmhouse had been unceremoniously dropped outside the back door, and came to the conclusion that the terrorists must have been surprised by something.

They found Samantha Elliot's car and started to search for her body, moving out from the farmhouse in wider and wider circles. By dusk they had still found no trace of her. They knew how easy it was for the terrs to vanish into thin air after an attack of this nature. Either Miss Elliot was lying dead further out in the bush or she had been taken hostage.

They felt none too comfortable in this outlying homestead with the body of the dead farmer as their only company. Darkness came quickly, and having gathered together everything of value from the house, they returned to headquarters in Umtali where they laconically reported the death of yet another farmer in the Thrasher operational area.

The commander of the police station rubbed his eyes as he completed the report, and consigned it to the growing pile at the corner of his desk. Then he took it off the pile and stared at the section on Miss Elliot.

At over sixty he had been through the Second World War and had had quite enough of death for one lifetime. He often wondered what quirk of fate had caused him finally to settle in this place, where he had thought he was retiring to a peaceful life. He had met the dead farmer a few times and had found him a pleasant, quiet fellow, not the sort to mistreat his black workers. At least it was fortunate he hadn't a wife and children left behind to face the world alone.

Miss Elliot was a problem. An embarrassment.

As he tidied up his desk and positioned the in-tray in readiness for the next morning's reports, he noticed a telegram that had been dropped on his desk some fifteen minutes before. It was from an American magazine editor, wanting to contact Miss Elliot urgently.

The commander started sweating. If Miss Elliot had been kidnapped it could cause him no end of problems. Reluctantly he picked up the phone and rang high command in Salisbury. There was a long silence after he had told them the story. He was ordered to keep quiet and wait for instructions. He put the phone down ruefully.

The commander locked the door of his office behind him and, as he walked down the corridor, he congratulated himself on selling off his farm years before, just when the going was beginning to get rough. At least he had some money in the bank, as well as some inherited money in England. He could always consider emigrating to South Africa if things got really bad, unlike that poor bastard out there who would soon be put to rest in the church graveyard.

Nice place, that farm. You could probably pick it up for next to nothing now, but no one would want it. Things were just too uncertain.

'Welcome to Camp Siberia. It's not a pleasant place but at least the Rhodesians and their bombers can't find it. I have little time for dealing with prisoners, so please tell me the story of your capture, and something of your background. Then I will decide on your future.'

Mnangagwa had brought her to this place, to see this man, one of the high commanders of ZANLA. His tone irritated her. Sam was not the sort of person who liked to be told what to do.

'Does it really matter to you? What's the choice? Death, rape, or long-term imprisonment? It's not my fault I was brought here. If I'd resisted I'd have been killed. I don't know anything of use to you so there's little point in your questioning me.'

He smiled as she spoke, a wry smile. He was an enormous man, not just physically big, but with a magnetic personality. His dark eyes were hypnotic. He had a chiselled jaw, perfectly square, and above it, sensitive lips that often smiled to reveal the neat line of his teeth. Most of the terrorists she had seen over the past two days looked scruffy in their dark jeans and green denim shirts, but this man looked as if the uniform had been tailor-made for him. Over the shirt he wore a light camouflage jacket and on his head a peaked cap.

'You are an American. An American journalist in Rhodesia. This is very unusual. I find it strange that your capture has not been reported on the Rhodesian radio service. It crosses my mind that you might be a spy.' His voice was very deep, and his speech precise. No word was wasted.

'Tell me your name, American woman.'

'Samantha Elliot. I am a reporter for a leading American magazine. I've been covering this war for the last three years. I was doing an article on the farmers of the eastern frontier when your men captured me.' She was worried that her disappearance had not been reported. What had happened to the farmer? She wanted to be alone, to rest and think.

The man laughed long and loud. 'You are very lucky, Miss Elliot. You have told me the truth. Now you will be able to see the war from the point of view of the other side. You will be able to see what pleasant people your Rhodesian friends really are.'

'You misunderstand me. The people who read *Time* revel in my reports on the destruction of Rhodesia. They like to see the Smith regime suffer. They wait like vultures for the kill. The whole war has become an important American issue.'

She found she was getting irritated. Why was she having to defend herself and her work?

'You are cynical, Miss Elliot.'

'This is not my first war. I was in Vietnam, where I worked as a correspondent. I had to take risks – you only got noticed if you went where the killing was. It's the risk of death that carries the interest in war, just as it is in motor-racing or boxing. Except that as a war reporter the price of a good shot is a lot higher.'

'You love violence?'

She was shocked. He was very perceptive, this ZANLA commander. She had not imagined men like this directing the terrorist war. He was looking at her threateningly, his eyes running up and down her body. She was still standing in front of him, he had not asked her to sit. She decided she didn't care any longer. She opened the front of her shirt and swung her naked breasts in front of his eyes.

'See. This is what you want, isn't it? The first thing your "freedom fighters" tried to do when they caught me was rape me. I suppose if I hadn't been lucky they would have shot me after that. Fair enough. Life's cheap around here. If you want a fuck, take it, buster.'

She saw the anger cross his face like a ripple across a pool. 'Cover yourself! You will see what sort of men we are. You will see what this war has done to us. We have suffered and continue to suffer.'

'Enough of the self-pity, you think the white people don't suffer? They are also paying the price.' She was tired of the conversation, she wanted an end to it. 'What's your name?' she said.

'It is Tongogara.'

She shuddered. Tongogara, the deputy-commander of ZANLA.

He smiled. 'And now you are afraid, Miss Elliot. You have heard stories, no doubt?'

'I have only heard that you are a very able commander, Mr Tongogara.'

'Comrade, if you please. Now I must decide your fate.'

'I want to be returned to the place I was taken from. You have my word that this camp will remain a secret. I won't mention anything to anyone.' She didn't hold much hope that he'd let her go, but it was worth a try anyway.

Tongogara frowned. 'No. You are my prisoner. I'm not going to let you go. FRELIMO has heard that you are here. Besides, we don't get any journalists from the West who want to cover our side of the war. But it is true, what you say. The journalists only want to see blood.'

He stood up and started to pace up and down the narrow room.

'I will show you, Miss Elliot, how we live and how we fight. You can write our story. People must hear our story, the story of the victors.'

'Maybe you won't like what I write about you. Perhaps it won't reflect well upon you.'

He turned and stood towering above her. 'Sit down. You have courage, white woman.'

She sat down on one of the storage cases and he returned to his seat behind a makeshift desk.

'I will show you the war as it is from the point of view of ZANLA. Then you can write what you want. All I ask is that you make the effort to see. Most white people are very blind. They cannot even recognise their servants, let alone remember their full names.'

He was silent for a while, as if reflecting on something.

'There was one who was different. He fought with the Selous Scouts. He thinks like a black man, yet he fights us. We tried to kill him many times. This man is like an animal but he has my respect, he is not like the others of his kind. You know what most of them do. They come amongst our people disguised as us, ZANLA troops. Then they find the headman of the village and execute him for cooperating with the Rhodesians. After that the village people will not talk to us. The man of whom I speak has never done this. My brothers tell me that his own men tried to kill him by accident and he killed them all. I hear he was in the hospital in Salisbury and then he disappeared . . . You are very quiet, Miss Elliot. Do you know him?'

'No. Look, I'm tired. I need to rest. I haven't slept properly since I was captured.'

'You speak of sleep as though it were a right. I suppose that is the privilege of your upbringing. You know, I worked on the South African gold mines. I did not think much of sleep then. You may sleep in this room, it is safe. I will be next door, we will talk again when it is light.'

He got up and handed her a blanket. Then he left the room and pulled an old mattress up next to the open door. He waited till she had bedded down and then turned off the paraffin light.

Sam wanted to cry. Mnangagwa had been kind to her, but she'd had to march at a killing pace for the past two days. She was dirty, her clothes stank. The bruises from where the men had handled her hurt all the time. She felt disgusting. If only she could wash, use a toilet that flushed . . .

Her mind was restless in the darkness. She wondered how she would have been feeling now if Mnangagwa had not arrived when he did. She was lucky to be alive, yet she was tormented, for even in this most isolated of places she had not been able to escape thoughts of Rayne.

Occasionally there were scuffling noises underneath the planks of the hut and she guessed there were rats. Sam tried not to think about what was happening to her, but concentrated instead on trying to make herself comfortable on the thin mattress. Eventually she began to doze off, blessedly forgetting for a time where she was and what she had been through.

It seemed as though she had been asleep for only a few minutes when she opened her eyes again and looked out through the door into the dimly lit area beyond. She was sure something was moving around outside the door, though she was uncertain whether it was man or animal. She got up quietly and moved towards the doorway. Outside she could see Tongogara sleeping next to some packing cases. A giant claw-hammer was lying on the table next to the door and she picked it up silently.

A sound to her right almost made her scream out loud but somehow she managed to restrain herself. An eerie shadow passed over her in the half-light.

The man who had made the shadow strode stealthily into view and peered through the door. For a terrified moment Sam thought he had seen her, but he moved softly away from the door towards the sleeping form of Tongogara. As he did so he drew an enormous dagger from his waistband and raised it into the air, ready to strike.

Sam acted instinctively, moving towards the man, swinging her right hand back with the hammer held firmly in its grip. She forced the hammer down against the man's skull. He dropped the knife he was holding and fell across the man he had been about to kill.

Tongogara woke instantly, reared up and grabbed the knife. He pushed his assailant to the ground and brought the knife up against his chin. 'Tell me your name, you traitorous jackal or I'll slit your throat!' But the man's eyes were closed for ever, his lips permanently sealed. Sam had hit the upper part of his spinal column, destroying its vital link to the brain above.

Sam dropped the hammer to the ground, still unable to speak. Tongogara looked across at her.

'You took a terrible risk. If he had seen you he would have killed you. There are people who would like to see me disappear now that the war is almost over; people who worry about who will come to power. I am third in line. It is a dangerous position.'

'I thought I was the one in danger!'

'I owe you my life, Miss Elliot. I will make it known that any man who lays a finger on you will have to reckon with me from now on.'

'You and Mnangagwa.'

'Mnangagwa. He is my half-brother. We have fought many battles together. He told me what happened to you. It will not happen again.'

He stooped down to lift the dead man's body across his massive shoulders. Then he carried the corpse off into the darkness.

It was early in the morning. Tongogara had woken her an hour before and given her breakfast. He gave her camera back to her, though without any film in it, but he had kept her passport. Now they were marching away from the camp – Sam, Tongogara and two other ZANLA guerillas. The pace was quick and she was already sweating with the exertion. Her clothes were badly torn and she ached all over. She was also ridden with guilt about the man she had killed. She couldn't have felt much worse.

Tongogara moved closer to her and spoke softly.

'Don't worry, we do not have far to go. We must get away from the camp, it is dangerous for me. I have hidden the body of my assassin, but there are others. It will not be long before they find it.' Before she could reply, he had pulled away from her, maintaining the rear guard.

Now she could see that they were moving downwards. Suddenly the men in front of her turned and moved into a thicket. They began throwing aside loose branches, and in a matter of minutes had uncovered an open safari Land Rover that had been hidden beneath the brush. Next to it were several jerry-cans, and they unscrewed the fuel cap and filled up the tank. Again Tongogara spoke to Sam.

'We have to be careful. The Rhodesians are always setting light to the bush, so we cannot leave the vehicle with petrol in the tank. Another danger is that the Rhodesians may see the tyre tracks from the air and strafe the bushes. That's their biggest advantage over us, air support. Of course they haven't been in such a good position since the South Africans took their helicopters back in the mid-seventies. But they still have the edge.'

Now they all got into the Land Rover. The engine fired first time and they pulled off down the dirt track at a brisk rate. The driver slowed down over a particularly rough section and Tongogara yelled at him to keep moving quickly. The man accelerated, and Sam had to hold on to the grab-rail behind the driver's seat so that she wouldn't be thrown out.

The countryside they travelled through revealed scenes of desolation Sam had not seen since the napalm bombings in Vietnam. The bush was burnt in many places, and most of the buildings she saw were charred and wrecked. Occasionally they would pass the skeleton of a burnt-out military vehicle lying by the side of the track. Nowhere did they see any sign of human existence. Against the roar of the wind-noise Tongogara shouted into her left ear.

'We were fools when we started fighting. We were up against the Portuguese and the Rhodesians. That lasted until 1974. Then FRELIMO gained power in Mozambique. Up to that time the Rhodesians operated in this area quite freely. Here, we're still less than a hundred kilometres inside the Mozambique border. You can see the devastation.

'Machel and his FRELIMO troops now support us – so the Rhodesians have started attacking FRELIMO bases as well. They've conducted many full-scale raids, especially against our training camps.'

She saw his face tense as he said this. Clearly the Rhodesian operations had been successful.

'Did they hit you badly in these attacks?' she asked. She wanted to know the truth behind the figures the Rhodesians had released on the number of terrorists killed on some of their raids. The vehicle was travelling more smoothly now as the track improved, and it was easier for her to listen to Tongogara.

'In 1976 a group of Selous Scouts disguised as FRELIMO soldiers crossed the Mozambique border, heading towards the town of Vila de Manica in an armed column of thirteen vehicles. On Monday the ninth of August they entered our training camp at Nyadzonya Pungwe.

'Our men were expecting a FRELIMO supply column, so when these vehicles drew up on the parade ground they didn't suspect a thing. The entire camp was on morning parade. I don't know what the Selous Scouts' original plan was, but one of my men recognised a heavily bearded white man behind the guns of one of the vehicles. He screamed out a warning to the others.

'The Selous Scouts opened fire at point-blank range, a wave

73

of bullets that only stopped when every man on the parade ground was dead. Then they moved through the base, destroying everything. Even the hospital went up in flames, the wounded dying inside. By the time the Selous Scouts had finished the entire base had been razed. Then they pulled out and blew up the bridges on the road as they left. Not one of them was captured and only a few were wounded.'

He was silent then, and she waited a few minutes before she spoke.

'How many of your people died?'

'Our official report to the United Nations didn't tell the full story. To be honest, there were over five thousand people at the base at that time and nearly all of them died. We were fools to have established such a large training camp. They caught us unawares. It was a day none of us who were there will forget for as long as we live.'

He leaned forwards and hurled another command at the driver in Shona. Then he continued his story.

'That raid taught us a lesson. In a way, it's helping us to win the war. Now our training centres are smaller, and spread out over a vast area. There are no high concentrations of men any longer.

'Another raid, which we never reported, took place that same day at Vila Machado, on the Beira–Umtali railway line. The casualties there numbered over a thousand. We kept quiet about it, so as not to dispirit our people. But the fact that we can carry on, despite such high casualties, must show the Rhodesians they can never win this bush war.'

They were now on a proper sand road and were able to move much faster. There were no signs along the road – this, said Tongogara, was to confuse Rhodesians operating over the border.

After an hour Sam was aware of a railway line to her left and realised that this must be the main line from Umtali to Beira. She noticed that large sections of it had been torn up. From the rust on the upper part of the rails it was clear that the line had not been used for a considerable time. A little later the road started to descend, and she realised that they were leaving the inland plateau and moving towards the lower ground of the coastal plain. The road curved round to meet the railway line again, and crossed it amidst a scene of total devastation. Both the road and the railway line had been blown up, and torn pieces of metal covered the entire area. The road had to weave its way between mounds of earth and only straightened out again a hundred metres further on.

After another half hour's fast driving they pulled up beside a colonial-looking building which Tongogara informed her was the local police station. He leapt out of the Land Rover and went towards the main entrance. It was a huge, crumbling structure with a pillared portico topped by a sculpture of a giant eagle. The enormous wooden doors were stuck permanently ajar and Tongogara disappeared inside. Sam, remaining in the Land Rover with the two men, ran her eyes over the flaking plaster and peeling paintwork. The whole place had the atmosphere of a sleepy ruin. Then Tongogara came outside again and beckoned her in.

She walked into a large, musty-smelling room. At one end, behind a giant desk, sat a darkly tanned man. He was about thirty years old, wearing a white officer's cap and a crumpled khaki uniform that was loose at the collar. She judged him to be a half-caste. He was fat, and beads of perspiration covered his forehead. She could smell him – a combination of sweat, garlic and whisky. There was a pistol lying on the desk in front of him. He indicated that she should sit. Tongogara remained standing.

The man addressed her in a language she guessed was Portuguese. Tongogara spoke to him quickly, and the man smiled and spoke again, this time in English with a thick Portuguese accent.

'You are Samantha Elliot, the prisoner of Comrade Tongogara?'

He picked up her passport which was lying in front of him and flicked through it idly. His eyes met hers again. 'Mmmmm. What were you doing in Rhodesia?'

Samantha was going to reply when she heard Tongogara speak. 'She's a reporter, Captain Georgio.'

'All right, Tongogara, what do you want me to do with her?'

'Keep her here for three days.'

'Let me remind you, Comrade. Prisoners are the business of FRELIMO. They must be handed over to us for interrogation, then sent for correctional training. This was agreed upon by Mugabe and President Machel.'

Tongogara smiled evilly. 'Suppose, Captain, I was to let high command know about some of your other activities . . .'

Georgio sat up quickly. 'You wouldn't dare.'

'Of course not. All I'm asking for is a favour.'

Georgio could hardly speak and his face was turning white. 'Tongogara . . . you go too far . . . you are not liked in high command. This will be reported . . . You know that.'

Captain Georgio's speech didn't seem to scare Tongogara. He gestured for Sam to get up. 'Say goodbye to your career, Georgio.'

Georgio immediately rose and ran in front of them, blocking the door and smiling obsequiously. 'Forgive me, Tongogara. I apologise. Of course I'll look after her.'

Tongogara walked up close to Georgio and stared down into his eyes. 'You touch her or harm her and I'll blow your brains out. And if I'm not around to do it, one of my men will do it with pleasure.'

The Captain walked back behind his desk and sat down. He took out a bottle of whisky and two glasses from his desk. Tongogara declined the offer of a drink but he did take a seat next to Sam. She gazed up at the big fan on the ceiling above her, turning lazily in the mid-day heat. She was terrified. How could Tongogara leave her with this man?

The two men discussed routine matters in Portuguese, including the fate of some prisoners currently being held in the cells of the police station. Then they came back to the subject of Sam. Georgio was most conciliatory.

'There is a small flat behind the station. It is quite comfortable, she can stay there. But I warn you, if she escapes you will be in more danger than you realise.'

'That's my problem, Georgio. I must leave now. I'll talk to her for a few minutes privately, then she will be your responsibility.'

Sam followed Tongogara out of the office, and he led her into another room and closed the door. Never in her life had she felt so desperate, so little in control of events. He held her shoulders in his massive hands.

'Trust me, Samantha Elliot. If you stay with me you will be in grave danger – high command will insist I hand you over. I owe you my life, and I will come back in three days' time to get you. At least here you can clean yourself and rest.'

'I don't trust him!'

'He will do nothing. I have too much on him.'

The room was quiet except for the sound of flies buzzing in the hot afternoon air. Far in the distance she heard a dog barking; for the first time in her life she understood the real meaning of the word 'freedom'. Yet she trusted a man whom she had only known for two days, and something told her that he would not let her down.

In Salisbury the evening before, Sam's disappearance had created a few problems for the interim government. The death of a farmer on the Mozambican border was one thing, the suspected abduction of an American reporter quite another. With the tense situation that now existed in the country, the last thing Bishop Abel Muzorewa's government needed was an incident that focused the world's attention on the bush war. At all costs, the impression must continue to be given that things were well under control.

The chief difficulty was that the editor of *Time* had threatened to fly out to find the true facts behind the disappearance of one of his top war reporters. After all, he had reasoned, if she could cope with Vietnam, she could cope with anything. He had said he was going to release the story to the world media.

Government officials, anxious to avert a crisis, argued that this might well endanger Miss Elliot's chances of survival, if she were still alive. They asked him for a few days' grace so that the army could comb the Umtali area in one last attempt to find Miss Elliot.

The moment Tongogara left the police station and Samantha had been safely removed to the bungalow behind it, Captain Georgio darted back into his office and dialled a number on the phone. Speaking in English, he asked for General Vorotnikov and was immediately connected.

'General Vorotnikov. Speak.'

As usual the voice made Captain Georgio freeze with fear. He tried desperately to maintain his composure.

'Comrade General, you told me to report anything to you that might be of assistance to the Soviet Union. I am in the Manica E Sofala area. I have captured an American reporter who was operating on the eastern border of Rhodesia.'

'Have him shot. He is most likely a capitalist mercenary.'

'No, Comrade . . .'

77

'You know the punishment for not obeying an order.'

Captain Georgio began to wonder about the wisdom of calling the General. But he was sick of the police station. He wanted a promotion and this was an opportunity to get noticed.

'General Vorotnikov, she is a woman. I have seen her name in the capitalist propaganda magazine *Time*. She is famous.'

'You read such imperialist rubbish? It is punishable, do you understand? Where is this American woman?'

'Here, Comrade. You want me to kill her?'

'Do not make fun of me, Captain Georgio. Men who make fun of their commanders live short lives. Do not wreck your chances.'

'I apologise, Comrade. What are your orders?'

'Keep her . . . Now tell me, who really captured her?'

'Comrade Tongogara.'

There was a lengthy silence on the other end of the phone. Captain Georgio knew why: Comrade Tongogara was not popular with the Soviet military. He had threatened them, told them they should not expect the new state of Zimbabwe to be a communist puppet.

'Interesting. Is Comrade Tongogara involved with this woman?'

'I am not sure, but I think they are lovers. He threatened to kill me if anything happened to her. I told him I would look after her. But I know of the debt that ZANLA owes to FRELIMO and to the Soviet Union. That is why I called you.'

'You did well, Captain Georgio. Keep the woman. I will contact you again in the morning. If anything happens to her, you will be disciplined.'

'But . . .'

The phone was dead before Captain Georgio could continue. The sweat poured off his forehead. If Tongogara came back for her, then he would accompany them. She was *his* prisoner. He would make sure that Tongogara was arrested as a traitor; he would like to see them kill him very slowly . . . These ZANLA soldiers thought they were a cut above the rest. Well, he would show them who was in charge. ZANLA were nothing without the Soviet support that kept them going. The new Rhodesia would be a Marxist state, of that there could be no doubt.

He, Georgio, had been one of the few citizens of Mozambique who had been selected to go to Moscow for training. He had expected promotion and respect on his return, but instead he had been sitting in this derelict police station for nearly a year. It was not his fault that he did not have the gift of intelligence or the ability to fire a rifle accurately. Well, now he would earn a position where men would accord him the respect he deserved. Tonight, he would have some enjoyment with this white bitch.

He pulled out the bottle of whisky that he kept in the bottom drawer of his desk, and took a hefty slug. The smooth brown liquid felt good as it trickled down his throat and put fire into his stomach.

Sam was feeling much better. She'd had a hot bath and changed into some of Georgio's clothes. Perhaps she had been over-reacting when Tongogara left her.

She was surprised when Georgio came into her room. He set two glasses down on the table and tried to pour whisky into both of them. At the first attempt he missed, but he didn't seem to care much. He handed Sam a full glass which she reluctantly took from him.

'To your future, Miss Elliot.'

She put the glass to her mouth but did not drink.

'Good whisky?'

'I prefer bourbon.'

She decided that she'd have to get rid of him as politely as possible. She was tired, and had no intention of putting up with a drunk.

'You Americans. You like to be different. I've never met an American woman before. Perhaps the American consul might have some bourbon. If you're nice to me I might let you talk to him.'

Sam's heart skipped a beat. Perhaps she could persuade this fool to take her to the consul.

Georgio got up and staggered outside. She saw him through the window as, whistling, he fumbled with his pants, then let them slide to the ground and urinated noisily in the sand. He lumbered back into the room again and picked up the whisky. 'Like another drink?'

She passed over her nearly full glass and he slopped some more whisky into it. He pulled a cigar out of his top pocket, lit it, and inhaled deeply. He sat looking at her.

'Come here.'

This was what she had expected. She had no intention of putting up with this pig. 'I'm quite comfortable here, thank you, Captain.'

'I told you. Come here.'

She got up and walked over to him, pretending to look seductive to get him off guard. Suddenly, she threw the whisky in his face. Then she whipped up her right knee, hard into his groin. She had known how much stronger he would be than she was, and had waited for this opportunity. Now he rolled on the floor at her feet – and the image came back to her of Sithole lying on the ground after Mnangagwa had shot his balls off.

'Bitch. Fucking white bitch.'

She picked up his gun and pointed it at his head.

'Comrades!'

She heard the shouts outside the bungalow and two men rushed into the room. She found herself shaking with fear, unable to pull the trigger.

Georgio screamed at the man closest to him. 'You baboon's arse! Help me up.' The other grabbed Sam and savagely twisted her right arm. She cried out in pain and dropped the gun.

'Take the bitch to the cells!' yelled Georgio. 'Give her the water!'

The two men dragged Sam roughly back towards the police station. She started to scream, but received a hefty blow across the side of her face. They pulled her down a flight of stone stairs into the basement. A nauseating smell of vomit and urine filled her nostrils. It was almost pitch dark here, except for the light thrown by a few candles on the walls. She was thrust into a square cell with a chair at its centre. They frog-marched her over to the chair and forced her to sit on it; then they forced her arms through the struts that ran down the back and fastened her hands behind her with an old-fashioned set of screw handcuffs that bit through her wrists. She cried out again but was ignored. They lashed her legs to the base of the chair and then left the cell, not bothering to lock the door. Clearly they were going to leave her here for the night as punishment for what she had done. In front of her was what looked like a horse's drinking trough, filled with foul-smelling water.

Sam could hear noises coming from the other cells, the sounds of people sleeping uneasily. She tried to relax, but every time she nodded off to sleep she sank forwards and the pain in her wrists woke her up.

It was much, much later when she heard the sounds of men coming down the stairs towards her cell. The light in the cell got brighter and she saw that they were carrying a gas lantern.

Georgio and his two henchmen came in.

'Hallo, Samantha. Did we wake you?'

Georgio's laughter echoed hideously round the cell. He had another bottle of whisky with him, and he was having difficulty in walking. He pulled up a stool and sat down next to her. Then he pulled a cigar from his pocket and lit it. He inhaled slowly, watching the end of the cigar as it became brighter. He let out a puff of tobacco smoke – and then he nodded at the two men.

Before Sam realised what they were doing, they had picked her up and carried her and the chair to the water trough. They tipped her forwards until her nose was just touching the water. She started to retch because of the smell.

'Not pleasant, is it, bitch? But then you obviously don't think I'm pleasant either. You wouldn't drink with me – we'll see if you prefer this kind of drink.'

The guards pulled the chair back and wrenched her mouth open. Georgio took the whisky bottle and upended it in her mouth. He clamped his fingers over her nose and as she tried to breathe, whisky poured down her throat.

Just as she thought she was going to black out, he pulled the bottle away – and the moment she started to breathe in, they up-ended the chair in the trough, forcing her head beneath the water.

For a while she managed to hold her breath, but the whisky affected her resolve and she started to take in deep mouthfuls of water. She had heard that drowning was a pleasant death, but this was like suffocating.

They pulled her out of the water at last. She vomited into it. All she was aware of was the noise of laughter echoing round the cell.

She must have lost consciousness. She came round as they slapped her face. They looked worried now. They untied her, and pushed her onto the floor. One of the men pushed her stomach and she threw up a foul-smelling vomit. The man felt her pulse. 'She'll live.'

They left her on the concrete floor and locked the cell door behind them. Their footsteps echoed up the stairs.

She lay in the darkness on the cold floor. At least she was alive. A strong feeling filled her body, the desire to kill. She had killed Tongogara's assassin by accident, but this man, Georgio, she genuinely wanted to murder. What she felt for him was not the impersonal hostility of war but a deep, personal hatred. He had destroyed her pride. She would destroy him.

Captain Georgio felt the throbbing in his head. He opened his eyes, to see the roof of the bungalow revolving in front of him. He felt the pain between his legs and remembered the night before.

There were noises in the distance, and that was strange because it was Sunday, and generally nothing at all happened on Sunday. It occurred to him that the throbbing sound might not just be in his head, but coming from outside the bungalow.

He staggered to his feet and knocked over the bottle standing next to the bed. The smell of whisky nearly caused him to pass out. He peered out of the window and saw a Soviet helicopter gunship coming in to land in a storm of dust. What was it doing here, today of all days? He remembered quickly and tore out of the room, but it was too late. General Vorotnikov appeared out of the dust storm, tall and forbidding, followed by six of his bodyguard. He saluted Georgio, who responded with difficulty.

'Captain Georgio. Where is the prisoner?'

'Prisoner, Comrade General?'

'Yes, you fool. The American woman we spoke of yesterday.'

'She is not here.'

'Captain Georgio, if this is some elaborate joke you will pay for it dearly.'

Vorotnikov's voice was like a whip. He was a tall, lean man in his mid-fifties, his black hair streaked with grey, but his body was that of a younger man and there was a spring in his step. He was immaculately kitted out in a camouflage uniform bearing no insignia of rank. He didn't need insignia – he exuded power.

Vorotnikov's face had a Germanic look to it, enhanced by the thin, stainless steel spectacles that were perched on his nose. The strong jaw-line, the elegant cheek bones and the cool grey eyes, all these spoke of an aristocratic background. To Georgio this man was a typical Russian; no understanding, no time to wait.

'Where is she, Captain Georgio?'

'Not far from here, Comrade General. It was dangerous to keep her here. The Selous Scouts operate in this area.'

Captain Georgio noted with relief that the hardness of General Vorotnikov's jaw had softened. He had won some time.

'Of course. However, I am not a Selous Scout, I am a Russian general. Fetch her, please. We will wait.'

Georgio staggered off to the dormitory that was housed within the police station. The room was filled with snores and he laid about him with the riding crop he usually carried. He must get these fools up, and then get the woman out of the cell.

'Get up, you idiots. The General Vorotnikov is here. If he finds the woman in the cell he will kill us all. You, Gomez, drive the truck away, make as if we are fetching the woman from the bush. Grab one of the women from the village, bring her back with a sack over her head and take her into my office. We will fool the General yet.'

'What if the American woman is dead, Captain?'

'Then we are too, Gomez.'

General Vorotnikov leaned against the side of the gunship smoking a Turkish-blend cigarette. He reckoned Captain Georgio had earned his promotion. The capture of this journalist could really embarrass the Americans, especially as their Dr Kissinger had been trying to interfere in the Rhodesia peace settlement. Some marvellous publicity could be made out of this.

He saw the truck drive away from the police station and smiled, for he knew the woman would soon be in his hands. Well, there was no reason for him to waste his time. He might as well take a look around the police station, an interesting imperialist structure. It was always a good thing to look, observe, be aware. His years in command had taught him the value of constant vigilance.

He looked inside the bungalow Georgio had come from. It stank of whisky. But two glasses. Who would he have been drinking with? A woman – two men would drink from the bottle. A policeman in an area like this could have any woman he liked, all he had to do was arrest her. So why bother to entertain? Yes, it would be the American woman. Who could blame him, especially if she was attractive. An attractive woman would make much better publicity.

Vorotnikov left the bungalow and walked over to the police station. What a mess. Captain Georgio could at least have tried to maintain some order. He passed down a passage and into a courtyard. The Portuguese had been efficient colonisers, pity that such a good building had gone to rack and ruin. He entered the other side of the building through a large door and guessed correctly that he was in Captain Georgio's office.

Chaos. Even clothes lying on the floor. The man obviously had no pride. General Vorotnikov rummaged through the papers on the desk top and found nothing of interest. Next he went through the drawers and found a half-empty bottle of whisky. The man was boring and weak, a useful person to have under his control.

He got up from the chair behind the desk and strolled back into the passage. Most of the other offices were empty and full of cobwebs. He walked into one and watched the crew of the helicopter gunship checking the engines and waiting for take-off. Good men, disciplined men. He noted that his own men were to one side, sitting down in the shade. Every one of them was hand-picked. They would never be used like the blacks, as cannon fodder for the Rhodesians.

He was sick of this war. The bloody British settlers would never give up. Stupid bastards getting blown to pieces for a stupid war ethic. They probably thought they were fighting the Second World War all over again. Fine troops, excellent discipline, but all thrown away on a war they couldn't win. It would all be over for them soon. Then he would concentrate on the jewel. South Africa.

Yes, that was a jewel. Complete control of the Cape sea-route. Control of the world gold market, the diamond market, the strategic minerals – radioactive and otherwise. Control of a whole continent. He, Alexei Vorotnikov, would achieve all of this, and soon.

He proceeded down the passage. A narrow stairway led downwards – to the cells, he guessed. He did not feel like looking around that foul-smelling area, his breakfast was still in his stomach. He was about to walk on when he heard a scream that stopped him in his tracks.

It was definitely a woman's scream. He changed his mind and walked down the steps. God, the place stank.

Another scream and he upped his pace. The door at the end of the row of cells was open. Inside he saw a woman, half-naked, lying on the floor. Her face was deathly white.

The instinct that had earned him the reputation of being one of the best combat soldiers in his regiment saved his life. He ducked as the piece of concrete brushed against the grey hairs on his skull, then turned to see Captain Georgio facing him, pointing a pistol directly at him. Vorotnikov kicked the pistol out of Georgio's hand and it clattered noisily to the floor. Georgio stood shivering, unarmed, in the corner. There was no sign of his men.

'What have you done to her, you dog?'

'She refused to cooperate.'

'Don't lie to me.'

They heard a cough and both turned to look down at the woman lying on the floor of the cell. Long blonde hair, a beautiful face and green eyes that flashed. She was covered in slime and her blouse was torn open, exposing her breasts. She spoke very softly.

'He tried to rape me. Then they tried to drown me in the trough.'

Vorotnikov untied her carefully. Then he gestured for Georgio to sit down on the chair.

'Do as I command, Captain, or you're a dead man.'

When he had securely bound Georgio he helped Samantha out of the cell and into Georgio's office. She looked close to death.

'What would you have me do with him?' he asked.

'Kill him.' Her voice was cold.

He went out into the sun and called his men into the building.

'Take her to the gunship and make sure she is well cared for.'

Then he walked back down to the cell and looked at the Captain who was now shaking with fear. He picked up a piece of wood from the floor and tested the depth of the water in the trough with it. It protruded by about ten centimetres.

'Let's see how long you can live.'

He picked up the chair with Georgio on it and balanced the full length of it over the trough, its legs resting along the trough's edges, so that the man was lying lengthways, looking down into the water.

'Open your mouth.'

He moved his grip from Georgio's collar to his hair, and the man screamed out as his hair took his whole bodyweight. The General rammed the piece of wood between Georgio's teeth.

'Bite it.'

He let Georgio down so that his body was only prevented from falling forwards into the water by the piece of wood he was biting against. The General closed the door of the cell.

After five minutes Georgio's jaw gave in. The wood shot up hard into his throat; for an instant he was suspended less than a centimetre above the water – then he sank beneath the surface, never to breathe again.

The group of doctors stood round the hospital bed, all staring at the patient. Even though she was pale and thin, you could see that she was a very beautiful woman. There was a noise outside the door of the room and they turned to see a massive black man in combat uniform easily pushing aside the medical orderlies who sought to block his path. His voice was deep and powerful.

'I don't care what you say. I have come to see the American woman, Comrade Elliot, and you are not going to stop me.'

He slammed the door of the room shut behind him as he entered. The doctors examined him as they might a specimen on the dissecting table.

'How is she?'

The question boomed across the floor. Dr Dmitri Suvorov smoothed the jet-black hair across his enormous head and peered into the man's eyes. A physician of some note, he did not appreciate his present position as consultant in the tiny hospital in Beira. However, he was a Party man, and the Party had ordered him here. He was not intimidated by this black man.

'General Vorotnikov himself ordered that no one should see this woman. You realise the penalty for disobeying such a command?'

The black man moved closer and towered imposingly over the brilliant young doctor from Leningrad.

'Enough of your General, Comrade Doctor. I am a comrade

and you are a comrade. This country belongs to me and my people, not you Russians. Now tell, how is the woman?'

Dmitri Suvorov trembled with rage. He was not used to being talked to like this; men feared him for his power within the Party. He would see that this black man suffered for his impertinence.

'She has been very ill, Comrade. She swallowed a large quantity of infected water and has been delirious for the past seven days. But she has a strong body. She has survived, and she has responded well to the drugs I have administered. It is only a matter of time before she will be completely recovered.'

'Then why are you all so concerned about her condition, Comrade Doctor?'

'It is General Vorotnikov who is particularly concerned. He warned that should she not recover he would regard me and my assistants as personally responsible.'

'I am glad the General is concerned.'

Suvorov watched the black giant move towards the bed and examine the American woman closely. He heard the words the man was speaking to himself: 'I should never have left her with Georgio.'

Dr Suvorov felt a little more sympathetic, some words of comfort were in order. 'A fine genetic specimen, Comrade, she will live to a good age. The only effect of the torture she endured will be slight psychological damage. That is not my area of expertise, however, and I cannot comment on it.'

'Just make sure that she gets better, doctor.'

'Who shall I say called, if the General should ask me?'

'Comrade Tongogara. Go tell that to your General.'

'Do not fear, comrade, I most certainly will.'

'And here is this evening's news. Five days ago, top American reporter Samantha Elliot disappeared in the Umtali area while visiting an outlying farm. The farmer was shot dead by ZANLA terrorists. The body of Miss Elliot, however, has not been found, and it is believed that she may have been abducted by ZANLA. Miss Elliot is well known for her controversial reporting on this country. Anyone who might be able to assist in tracing her should contact their closest police station as soon as possible.'

Major Martin Long turned off the radio and paced up and down his office. Rayne would never forgive him. How could she have been so stupid? They'd both told her a thousand times not to move in the operational area without members of the security forces. She was probably lying in a ditch somewhere, after being raped and then beaten to death.

He was furious when he heard that they had tried to keep her disappearance quiet. He had demanded that it be broadcast immediately, but already it was probably too late. The only chance was that she might be in a Mozambican jail, alive – more or less.

As a man of action in this situation he felt totally frustrated. He was stricken with guilt; he had sent Rayne on a crazy mission and now Sam was as good as dead. It was all his fault. God, he owed it to Rayne to try and find her. At least that was something he could do.

With the coming of the Rhodesian elections, the worst part of the conflict would be over, but the Major's job was a continuing nightmare. He had to keep ZIPRA and ZANLA apart, because if the Mashona and the Matabele clashed, the country would descend into a bloody civil war. The trouble was that neither faction was prepared to hand over its weapons – especially as each believed its own candidate would soon be president. Then the Major had his own men to worry about. Most of them just wanted to keep on infiltrating the enemy bases across the border, to prove they could still win the war; he had to keep them in order too. He was particularly anxious for his black troops after Independence. Would they be singled out and persecuted? It was so much easier for whites; they could always move over the border to South Africa or back to Britain where most of them still had connections.

He worried, too, about the future of the country in general. The new government would have to take a stance on the South African problem, and in the end that could only lead to war. Rhodesia – or, as she was now to be called, Zimbabwe – was still a great country, but she could not cope with such a war. The worldwide sanctions of the last few years had cut her off from lucrative international markets; she needed to build up her economy; she needed a period of stability so that she could get going from within.

Martin Long sat down at his desk and stared at the map of the war zones into which Rhodesia had been divided. Why had he sent Rayne on that assignment? John Fry was a bastard. The trouble was, nobody cared any more about sending men to their death. This war had gone on too long. Death had become a habit.

He thought again about the Selous Scouts. The 'pseudo' concept had overreached itself. Turned terrorists who had agreed to become pseudo terrorists had turned again, and reverted to being real terrorists. And though the pseudo concept had allowed the Scouts to kill off large numbers of terrs – in fact over sixty-eight per cent of all terrorist casualties in the Rhodesian war were a direct result of the activities of the Selous Scouts – still these figures did not add up to any real gain because they had failed to regain control of the rural areas. It was this lack of real victory that sapped the morale of the civilian population more than anything else.

Major Long sighed. There was bugger all he could do now for Rhodesia, but he could do something for Rayne. He could try and find Sam.

Smiling broadly, General Vorotnikov switched off his radio. This was much better than he had expected – the Rhodesians were obviously very worried about the disappearance of the American woman. They had taken a long time to make the announcement, a sure sign of behind-the-scenes anxiety. Yes, he had no doubt now that the woman could be used to make some very positive public statements about ZANLA and the way the Soviet Union was helping the peoples of Mozambique and Rhodesia. The more pressure they could put on Mugabe now, the better. Vorotnikov wanted no agreements between the new state of Zimbabwe and South Africa; rather, he wanted a stepping up of the hostilities between the two countries. He wanted to see Zimbabwe firmly clasped in the Marxist embrace.

The first important step would be the opening up of the Beira to Umtali railway line and the restructuring of Beira as a major port and Soviet military centre. This would give the new state of Zimbabwe access to the sea, and independence from South Africa. Then the border with South Africa at Beit Bridge must be closed as soon as possible, and all air links between South Africa and Zimbabwe severed. The way to achieve that, he knew, would be to convince the rulers of the new state that there was no advantage to such links – that they were much better off with neighbouring Marxist states as their allies.

But already there had been irritating developments that threatened Vorotnikov's grand plan. The South Africans and Rhodesians had together been aiding a right-wing guerilla group in the northern part of Mozambique. This group, RENAMO, was turning out to be a more potent force than Vorotnikov had guessed. They were harassing FRELIMO and making things very hard for Machel's Marxist government. Then there was the problem of Malawi. The state of Malawi still refused to bend to Soviet imperialism and Dr Hastings Banda, Malawi's ruler, remained as intractable as ever. Worse, Banda enjoyed good relations with the South African government. In Angola, too, there were problems. The rebel group UNITA, with South African backing, was trying to overthrow the Marxist government in Luanda. Unfortunately this had necessitated the bringing in of Cuban troops to strengthen the position of the ruling party.

Vorotnikov knew what he wanted in Africa: strong black dictatorships that would impose the doctrine of Marxism on the new generation. The trouble was that many black leaders were now becoming wary of the Soviet Union. This American woman, Samantha Elliot, could speak to the world. She could prove that the Soviet Union was only in Africa to free the peoples from oppressive white rule, and that the only problems in the region were being caused by the Afrikaner government in South Africa. And speed was all-important, for the South African military machine was gaining in strength daily as the black states desperately wrestled to get their weak economies into shape.

Vorotnikov gazed reflectively out of his office window at the Beira coastline and the sea beyond. This penthouse suite had once belonged to a wealthy South African businessman, now it was the centre of Soviet command and intelligence for the region.

When the woman had recovered he would have her moved to a secret location – though, of course, he would inform his associates that she was still in Beira: the last thing he needed was a bunch of hot-blooded Rhodesians racing in in helicopters and plucking her from his grasp. She must be kept well out of sight of the operation that was currently in progress. In fact, if she was shown round some of their disused facilities, she might actually believe the Soviet forces were *dismantling* their military installations, which would be an excellent message to send to Rhodesia and the outside world . . .

Vorotnikov allowed himself to contemplate the final victory; the immense satisfaction of seeing the Rhodesian commander, General Walls, publicly executed, and along with him, Mr Ian Smith. And a bloody end to white rule in Rhodesia – the wholesale slaughter he planned – would create just the right atmosphere in South Africa, the dramatic swing to the right that would prepare the ground for the greatest coup of all.

He smiled grimly, thinking of his most important asset; of Bernard Aschaar, the man who was the head of one of Africa's largest mining consortia. This man had already promised Vorotnikov that he would secure for him the complete take-over of the mining industries in both South Africa and Rhodesia after the Revolution. That meant total power for Vorotnikov over all southern Africa. An excellent foundation to push him right to the top of the Kremlin.

It was night, and she was alone. Sam tiptoed across the linoleum floor of her hospital room to the door, and slowly turned the knob. She pulled at the door but it refused to open. Locked, as she had guessed it would be. She moved to the window and looked down across the car park, which was bathed in electric light and almost empty. She could see that her chances were slim, but she was going to try. With her experiences in the cell at the hands of Captain Georgio so fresh in her memory she had only one intention – to escape. The Russian physician, Dr Suvorov, frightened her; he seemed to regard her more as an interesting breed of animal than a person . . . If she could escape from the hospital she figured she might be able to make it to the American consul and seek asylum.

Sam eased herself over the windowsill and gauged the distance to the ground. Probably not more than three metres – she was only on the first floor. There didn't seem to be any guards in sight, so she worked her way right out of the window and lowered herself from the outer sill. Now she was hanging from her hands, her toes still two metres from the tarmac below.

She let go, falling silently through the cool evening air. The ground came up hard. She landed noisily and was temporarily stunned by the impact, but after a few moments she tentatively stretched out her legs to see if she was still in one piece. No bones broken, to her relief. She looked around her. What she hadn't seen from the window of her room was that the brightly lit hospital reception area to her left commanded a first-class view of the whole car park, making it virtually impossible for her to move across it without detection. For a time she could edge her way along the car park wall, but in the end she would have no choice but to move out across the tarmac and just hope no one noticed her. The white hospital gown she was wearing wouldn't make that any easier.

Slowly Sam crawled along beside the wall of the car park. She had almost reached the far corner of it when she heard the noise of a car engine in the street outside and then the squeal of tyres as the vehicle turned in to the hospital. The bright headlights lit up the entire side wall of the car park. As the car pulled up close to the reception area, Sam made a mad rush for some rubbish bins and dived behind them for cover. Heart beating hard, she saw a tall, dignified-looking man get out of the driver's seat and walk into reception. It was only when he was in the light that she realised it was General Vorotnikov. He must be coming to see her.

There was no time to lose now. Sam sprinted to the front entrance. Just beside the gate she saw a large bush and moved behind it. There were two men in the guard post beside the gate, smoking cigarettes and talking. Now she was effectively trapped: if she moved out from the bush and tried to make it to the road, the guards would see her, but to go back to the car park also meant immediate detection. As if to confirm her thoughts, a siren suddenly screamed out from inside the hospital, and the whole area was flooded with light. Sam now crawled right into the bush; she was able to sit up quite comfortably in the middle of it, perfectly shielded from the outside world by the foliage.

People were pouring out into the car park now, obviously trying to find her. She recognised Vorotnikov's voice as he shouted out a command. 'On no account must she be hurt. On no account!'

A sound below her – a sort of scratching noise – almost caused her to scream out with fright. Puzzled, she parted the leaves to see that a mongrel had discovered her scent. She quickly scooped up a handful of sand and, hardening her heart, threw it in the dog's face. It hurried off into the blackness and she started to breathe a little more easily.

The commotion in the car park was moving closer and closer to her hiding-place. The two guards at the gate stepped out of their hut to meet an approaching officer. Sam heard his voice punctuate the darkness.

'You two fools. Did you see the woman?'

The men looked dumbly at the Russian officer. Now he was standing just next to the bush in which Sam was hiding.

'I saw you as I came out. Sitting around and not paying any attention! One day someone's going to come up and kill you – if I don't do it myself in the next five minutes. Find her!'

The two men darted into the guard post and then reappeared, armed with powerful torches which they shone out desperately into the darkness.

'Idiots! Search along the wall! Split up! Shoot her, and I will have you tortured, very slowly.'

Moments later, General Vorotnikov appeared at the gateway. Studying him, Sam thought he looked like a German conductor she had once seen at a symphony concert in London. His face reflected an intense concentration. He pulled out a cigarette and lit it, staring out into the darkness – she smelt the strong aroma of Turkish tobacco. He lifted his left hand and rubbed at an area round his neck that was evidently causing him some pain. Then the little mongrel came back up to the bush again, and Sam almost felt her heart would stop. When the dog started to lick the General's boots, he did not kick it away as she had expected him to, but studied the animal with a curious kind of detachment. It was almost as if he grudgingly welcomed the animal's company, when he was otherwise surrounded by such fools.

'General Vorotnikov, sir. She must have escaped into the bush. There's no way we will find her until the morning.' It was one of the troops returning from his search along the wall.

'You blockhead. Don't tell me what to do. Now shut up and search the other side of the road.'

A car came flying down the road and skidded to a halt outside the guard post. Dr Suvorov stepped out, his mop of black hair soaking with sweat.

'General. The American woman, she has escaped?'

'You fool, Suvorov, why do you always insist on such low security at the hospital?'

'The intention is to cure, not to kill, General Vorotnikov. The woman is strong, she has an incredible desire to live. Now that she has recovered she has manifested this desire by escaping.'

'You analyse too much. If I didn't know you better I might think that you admired the capitalist system. How far do you think she might be able to walk?'

'As far as she wants. She's made an astonishing recovery.'

'You should have realised she might try to escape.'

'The door of the room was locked, General. The window was nearly three metres above ground-level, only a madman would jump from such a height onto hard tarmac.'

'Not everyone shares your fear of heights, Comrade Doctor. I must find her because alone in this country she will end up dead rather than free.'

'I see you have acquired a canine friend, General.'

The doctor leaned down and scratched the dog behind the ears, a gesture which the scrawny animal much appreciated.

'Incredible, is it not, General? The animal is covered with ticks. How it does not die is a miracle. Yet it will probably live till the day it can no longer find any food. He likes you, you should keep him for good luck.'

'You never cease to amaze me, Doctor. That is why I cannot dislike you.' He pushed the animal away – and in terror Sam watched as it trotted back to the bush where she was hiding. It started to sniff noisily as it got closer to her. It lifted its rear leg up and made its mark on its new-found territory. A voice sounded again, closer to the bush.

'The dog senses your attitude, General. He is now searching for a new friend.'

The dog was looking straight at Sam, flicking up the earth with its back paws and whining noisily.

'You are right. Animals cannot lie. They are doomed to complete honesty of feeling.' The General walked up to the bush. 'You can come out now, Miss Elliot, the game is up.'

Frantically Sam tried to push her way out, but he was too quick for her and tripped her up. She felt his vice-like grip on her arm as he helped her up. She refused to give him the satisfaction of seeing her cry

'Please don't aggravate the situation, my dear. You've been caught. There's nowhere for you to run to, so don't bother.' He handed her carefully to Suvorov. 'Take her back to the hospital, Doctor. This time put her somewhere she cannot escape from.

Put a permanent guard on the door and tell him he will die should she get away.'

'Yes, Comrade General.'

Vorotnikov bent down and picked up the little mongrel. 'I shall keep the dog, Doctor. Make of that what you will.'

The General stood outside the gates of the hospital, scratching the dog's ears. The dog now accepted his new owner with the conviction that made his species man's most enduring and popular companion.

The General was smiling to himself. The luck that had played such an important role in his career so far had not deserted him. The woman was strong, she had courage and determination. These were qualities he could exploit to the advantage of the Soviet Union.

He must think of a name for this dog, a creature of no pedigree and a dubious background at best. The name came to him in a flash of inspiration that satisfied his own mischievous sense of humour. He would call him Rhodes. If his comrades ever asked him what the name meant, he would merely say that the dog had already been named when it was given to him.

He laughed aloud in the darkness, for he knew that before long his dog would be the only thing left in Africa that bore the name of the great British imperialist.

The Land Rover headed north towards the outskirts of Beira. In the darkness a constant procession of vehicles travelled along the road, moving to and from the Russian barracks that lay between the main road and the sea far to the right.

The sea air imparted a freshness to the air that Tongogara always found invigorating, especially after being inland for such a long time. But he wished he hadn't involved Mnangagwa in this crazy scheme of his. It had seemed so simple at the outset, but now he was less sure. He had gone to see Sam at the hospital the day before; when he found that she'd been taken away, he'd made a few enquiries and learned that she had tried to escape and that the General had had her moved to the barracks. Now he and Mnangagwa were going there.

'Next turn to the right.' Mnangagwa obeyed Tongogara's instruction and turned towards the blaze of floodlights that illuminated the Russian barracks. Tongogara felt his heart beat faster. He scrutinized Mnangagwa's neatly starched dress-uniform and beret, then his own. They certainly looked the part – now it was a question of some good acting.

They pulled up in front of the boom with sentry-boxes on either side. This was the first test of their nerve, thought Tongogara. A Russian officer strode up to the Land Rover and looked cursorily inside.

'What do you want?'

'I have come to take away the new prisoner. Direct orders from General Vorotñikov,' Tongogara lied.

'I have heard of no such orders.' The officer peered into the cab, and saw Tongogara's insignia glinting in the darkness.

'Call the General if you want to,' Tongogara said nonchalantly. 'I'm sure he'll welcome being disturbed at this late hour.'

The officer pulled away from the cab and gestured angrily at the guard to lift the boom. 'Let them through!'

Mnangagwa smiled grimly as he drew up in front of the main building. The guards outside jumped stiffly to attention as Tongogara leapt out. 'At ease. Take me to the new prisoner immediately,' he barked, then looked back at Mnangagwa. They had agreed that Mnangagwa would stay in the Land Rover while he fetched Sam. If anything went wrong it would give him more chance of making a getaway – though the chances of escape, if anyone really suspected what they were up to, were virtually non-existent.

Tongogara followed one of the Russian soldiers up two flights of stairs. The soldier stopped outside a door, which he unlocked. 'She's inside with the doctor, sir. I'll wait for you out here.'

Tongogara's heart skipped a beat. He had not reckoned on the doctor's being with Sam. Suvorov would immediately know that the General would never have ordered Sam's removal.

Tongogara looked the Russian soldier directly in the eye. 'I'll be a few minutes. We are not to be disturbed.'

'Yes, sir.' The man stood to attention, and Tongogara opened the door.

He found himself facing the barrel of an automatic pistol.

'Comrade Tongogara, how nice to see you. Please sit down.' Dr Suvorov gestured towards an upright chair in the middle of the room. 'Yes, you thought I was a fool, you and your half-brother Mnangagwa. The General told me you were at the hospital looking for Miss Elliot this morning. I've been expecting you.'

Sam looked on desperately from her bed. She realised the risks Tongogara must have taken to get into the barracks; he had jeopardised his career and position for her. And now he was cornered. She stared at Dr Suvorov, sitting at the end of her bed. He had his back to her . . . In an instant she realised she had to act. She leapt forward and dug her nails into the doctor's eyes.

'Ahhhh!'

Suvorov screamed out in agony and dropped the gun. Tongogara snatched it up, then clipped the doctor across the ear as he fought back against Sam. The doctor staggered back, blood dripping from his face. 'You bitch!'

Tongogara kicked the doctor's legs from under him and Suvorov toppled to the floor. He looked up at the gun in Tongogara's hand. 'You'll never get away with this. You're finished. You're a traitor.'

'Shut up. Where are Miss Elliot's clothes?'

Suvorov gestured to a cabinet in the corner. 'Fetch them here, Doctor, and don't try anything stupid.'

Sam dressed quickly while Tongogara spoke to Suvorov. 'You're coming with us. One whimper from you as we walk out of here, and I'll shoot you in the back of the spine.'

'You wouldn't dare. You'd be killed.'

'And so would you.'

Four minutes later the guard in the passage jumped to attention as Tongogara filed out of the room with Dr Suvorov and his patient. He watched the three of them walk down the stairs and wondered how the doctor could have scratched his face so badly.

Once they were outside the main building, Tongogara hustled Dr Suvorov into the front seat of the Land Rover, then helped Sam into the back. 'Now let's drive away slowly,' he whispered to Mnangagwa as he pressed the barrel of his pistol into Dr Suvorov's neck.

They passed the main guard post and Mnangagwa let out a sigh of relief. Dr Suvorov stared at him menacingly.

'Neither of you will get away with this. General Vorotnikov is not a fool. He knows you're both anti-Russian – there will be no place for either of you in the new government.'

Tongogara said nothing, but Suvorov's words served to reinforce suspicions that had been growing in him for some time. The Russians were not genuinely interested in helping the black resistance to overthrow the white government in Zimbabwe; Vorotnikov intended to use the new black leaders as his puppets; he and the Russians intended to control Zimbabwe themselves.

Mnangagwa stopped some ten kilometres north of the barracks. The noise of the engine died, and was followed by a cold, disconcerting silence which no one wanted to break. The sound of the insects became louder outside, as if challenging them to take action. Tongogara lit a cigarette, then got down from the vehicle and walked round to the passenger door. He gestured for Dr Suvorov to get out.

In the darkness he led the doctor to a tree, and took a rope out of his pocket.

'Thank you, Doctor Suvorov. Now I think it is time for us to leave you.'

'You won't get away with this, Tongogara.'

'I already have, Doctor Suvorov, I already have. Now enjoy your evening. Someone will pass by in the morning and untie you. This is a busy road.'

Tongogara walked back to the Land Rover and got into the back seat next to Sam. He thought she looked even more beautiful in the moonlight. She smiled up at him as he came closer.

'You know you're mad, Tongogara. You can't get away with this – Suvorov and the guard both saw you. Still, I'm very grateful. I don't know what they intended to do with me.'

'I did what I believed to be necessary. It won't take them long to figure out I was involved, so there was no point in killing Suvorov.'

'They'll kill you, Tongogara.'

'I have achieved my objective, you are free. From here on it is a question of survival.'

The lioness moved silently through the undergrowth, her eyes focused on the man next to the tree. She wondered why he did not move at all. Hunger raged in her stomach; hunting had been difficult for her over the past few months because of all the

98

military activity in the area. There was no small game, and the smell of man had become an increasing fascination for her.

Usually the men were dangerous. The strange sticks they carried made loud noises, and once there had been a searing pain in her left paw, and sometimes it still hurt her so that she limped. She had stayed away from men for a time after that, but now the temptation had returned. This man carried no stick. She moved in closer, so that his smell made her salivate.

Dr Suvorov could have sworn he had heard a noise. It was like a faint breathing sound, not far from where he was sitting. He had been dozing, but now he was wide awake, his eyes peering into the darkness.

Then the lioness came out of the trees and stood at a distance, coolly sizing him up. Suvorov wanted to scream out, but he thought that might make her attack. The beast moved closer, a deep growl rising from the depths of her stomach – a growl that almost caused his heart to stop beating.

Frantically Suvorov tried to think of some way to scare her off. He managed to draw his knees up to his chest and then raise himself to a standing position – and the animal backed away. He realised that the rope that bound his wrists was not tied very tightly, and he pulled against the knot with the desperate strength of a man trying to escape as he is dragged towards the gallows. Gradually he felt the knot coming looser.

The lioness took another step towards him, and he swore at her. Again she retreated, but she continued to stare at him. Now his hands were almost free, and he felt the tension mounting, for now at least he had a chance. He had to climb high in the tree where she wouldn't be able to get at him. He began to edge his way round the tree trunk, never taking his eyes off his adversary and shouting at her again. She watched him, growling softly and revealing her enormous teeth.

The tree trunk was almost featureless except for a branch growing out just above his head. If he could pull up on this . . . His hands now completely free, he leapt for the branch above him. He caught it first time and pulled himself up. He began to breathe more easily. She would never be able to get him in the tree.

He was almost on top of the branch when the lioness roared.

Then she bounded forward, her whole body a mass of rippling muscle.

A giant paw latched onto his leg, almost tearing it off as he clung desperately to the branch. Now he was screaming uncontrollably. His hands gripped the branch, but he was powerless against her strength. He could smell her fetid breath, the stench of death, as he was torn from the tree, still conscious, the blood pouring from the torn artery in his leg.

When Sam woke she had no idea of where she was, and was amazed to see the folds of the dark green tent flapping above her in the wind. She felt hot and uncomfortable. She pulled herself out of the sticky nylon sleeping-bag and edged towards the closed door-flaps on her hands and knees. Undoing one of the knots, she slid out into the open and immediately began to feel much better.

The sun had not yet risen, but she could see clearly in the reddish light of the early dawn. Behind her was a giant range of cliffs, towering up into the clouds. Below the cliffs a long scree slope ended in thick bush, which then petered out some distance behind her tent. To her right a guard sat hunched over the dying embers of a fire. He was snoring noisily, oblivious to the outside world and anyone who might attack the little bush camp. In the distance she could see other tents, but most of the people in the camp seemed to be sleeping outside on ground-sheets.

Just as she was thinking she could walk away undetected, she noticed that the guard at the fire had woken up and was watching her warily. The gun cradled in his arms took on a forbidding aspect. She pulled over an empty billy-can that was lying nearby and filled it with water from the bottle next to the tent. Then she put the billy on the fire and watched for the tiny bubbles that would rise to the top as it began to boil.

'You know, Miss Elliot, you are a very beautiful woman.'

She jumped with fright as she heard the deep voice behind her. She wheeled round to see Tongogara staring at her from his sleeping place, his body propped up on his right elbow. He was naked from the waist up, and his ebony skin was latticed with cords of muscle. The strong face was lit with a radiant smile.

'Thank you, Tongogara. This is a very beautiful place. But I don't understand why there are so many Russians here. I thought your backing came from the Chinese?'

Tongogara laughed. 'This is the thinking of the Smith regime. The two-pronged attack, Chinese to the right, Russians to the left. Unfortunately the reality is a little different – we take our support wherever we can find it. Our aim is simple: to overthrow the Smith regime, not to accept some phoney government imposed on us by British and American politicians. Our people long for freedom.'

Sam stared across at him, deadly serious. 'And the poverty, the hunger and the death? These are real enough. Will they go away with "freedom"?'

His face hardened. Now he looked much older. 'We have to accept suffering. We have lived with it since the white man and his strange god came to our shores. We are the ones who cannot afford to forget. We will never be repaid for our suffering. Thousands of us have had to die in order that we may win this struggle. We could win by sheer numbers alone, there are enough of us for that.'

She eased the billy of now boiling water off the fire and looked up into Tongogara's eyes. 'Your generation will not gain much from that victory, Tongogara.'

He picked up some sand from the ground next to the fire and crumbled it between his fingers. 'Our children will grow up in a land that is their own, a society in which black consciousness has a pride in itself. Already the younger cadres argue that men such as myself are too moderate, that our energy has been sapped by the West. I cannot argue with them, they are my own flesh and blood.'

Sam watched as the cliffs behind them became a deep red in the first morning sunlight. Red, the colour of Africa. Tongogara held her spellbound.

'Who gives a damn whether it's the Russians or the Chinese who are behind us? That disguises the real issue. I have faith in your intelligence, Miss Elliot, which is why I am going to make sure you get out of Mozambique alive. Perhaps you can tell the world of the real issue here in Africa. We have almost won the battle for Zimbabwe, but the wider struggle has only just begun. The country to the south, the country of the Afrikaner tribe, is our biggest enemy. Those people will take a very long time to defeat.'

The sunlight fell across Tongogara's face, throwing his profile into dramatic relief. She knew what he said was true, especially about the suffering of his people. With his intelligence and integrity he would make a good ruler.

'Do you have any children, Tongogara?'

His face lit up at the question. 'I have five sons, a tribute to my wife. They are all strong men who will become leaders.'

'And your wife?'

A cloud passed across his face, robbing it of its life and passion. 'Do not talk of my wife, Miss Elliot.'

But Sam wanted to know, her reporter's instinct demanded that she know. 'No. You want me to tell the story of your people? Then you must explain it to me through your own history.'

He sat down cross-legged in front of the fire and gestured for her to do the same. For some time he stared at the burning embers, as if trying to find some essential message in the slow destruction that was the heart of the fire. She handed him a cup of black coffee and he sipped at it meditatively.

'My children are men now. My wife had the first when she was seventeen and the last when she was twenty-six. They all live in Soweto, the scar on the earth that lies south-west of Johannesburg. Egoli, the city of gold. I went there when I was young, I left Umtali and poverty to seek my fortune in the gold mines. I made money, I found a wife and I learned to hate the white man. Now my children live for the Revolution. I would like them to leave Soweto and join me in the new Zimbabwe, but they will not.'

'Surely they don't all want to fight? There's always one child different from the rest.'

He sprang to his feet like a giant cat and stared into the rising sun. His face reflected only bitterness.

'Yes, I was given five sons, but they were taken away from me. I was forced to leave South Africa and I will be imprisoned if I return there; I tried to start a union at the mine – a dreadful crime! I am the one who should be bitter, but my sons took my bitterness for their own. It is a long time since my wife died, but the memory of her death is still fresh to me, as it is to them.'

'How did she die?' Sam asked softly, almost afraid of the answer he might give.

'She was murdered. She went to Maputo for the cause and worked with the white woman called Ruth First – I think you may have heard of her. Ruth had to go to Lesotho with my wife for a secret meeting, but Ruth became sick so my wife went alone. Neither of them knew it was a trap. She was killed by a bomb that went off in her hotel in Maseru.'

'Oh, Tongogara – '

'A right-wing Lesotho political group was blamed for the explosion, but I did not believe this. For me it was a terrible blow, but for my sons it was the last straw. I had hoped that some of them might make it to university, but now they only live to fight. The South Africans must learn, violence begets violence. I refuse to degenerate to the level of the men who killed my wife.

'Perhaps I am stupid, but I do not want to see our new state of Zimbabwe begun in a bloody purge. Our children need education so that they can rule with intelligence and understanding, so that our civilisation can stand proud amongst the others of the world. I am over forty, and my chief skill is the effectiveness with which I command my men and wield my gun. That is no way to live.'

Sam stared up at him, almost in tears.

'I will tell the world your story, Tongogara. I will not try to escape from here, though I believe General Vorotnikov will try to kill you for rescuing me.'

'Generals are good politicians. Vorotnikov is no different. He will see reason.'

The sun was now well above the horizon and already Sam could feel the intense heat of the coming day. Tongogara walked over to the sentry and talked to him for a few minutes, then he turned away towards the main camp.

Sam went back to her tent. In the distance the cliffs glistened. She understood Tongogara's yearning. How terrible it must be to live, and yet not to have a country one could call one's own.

Deon

It had been a typical Saturday night. The usual procession of people who had had too much to drink had been brought in and put to sleep in the cells.

Four reports of break-ins had been passed on to the Flying Squad – one of the calls had turned out to be a hoax and another had resulted in an arrest. Then there had been a shoot-out; no one had been hurt but the robbers had got away. Deon remembered having read somewhere that white South Africans were the most heavily armed people in the world. Well, he could believe it.

It was two o'clock in the morning, and he was sitting with Captain Pinkus Smit of the Flying Squad over a cup of putrid canteen coffee. They were just getting down to a good heart-to-heart on who would win the next Curry Cup rugby final, when one of his men came in with a report of a break-in taking place at an expensive home on Westcliff Ridge. It was all the excuse he and Smit needed. They'd both had enough of sitting around John Vorster Square – the Johannesburg police headquarters – at that time of the morning.

Moments later they were flying down the motorway, sirens screaming. A second car followed. If there were still robbers in the house, they weren't going to take any chances.

Captain Smit was a fast driver and the car was one of the new BMWs they'd just bought for the force. They were outside the house in five minutes. The story was typical, the owners had gone to Cape Town for the weekend, a neighbour had heard glass breaking . . . Deon had told his men to switch off the sirens as they came into Westcliff. If the robbers were still in the house, they wouldn't know that the Flying Squad was now outside.

While Deon took a statement from the neighbour, carefully listing all the details, Captain Smit and a junior officer began investigating.

Captain Smit had located the window where the burglars had entered the house: typical point of entry, the kitchen side-window. A professional job – they'd bypassed the burglar alarm system easily. Sergeant Venter went in first and Captain Smit followed. Before Smit could say anything, Venter was through the hall and heading up the stairs.

Smit saw the muzzle flashes as Sergeant Venter was thrown down the stairs. He landed on a glass table at the bottom which exploded into pieces. Immediately Smit swung the riot-pump shotgun up at the stairwell and ripped off two shots. His ears sang with the noise of the explosion, but he still heard the sound of breaking glass at the top of the stairwell.

He ran up the steps and jumped over the blood-soaked body of the man he must have hit. He looked out of the broken window and saw a figure running across the back garden towards the bushes. Dropping to a crouch, he aimed carefully along the barrel of the shotgun and squeezed the trigger.

There was a muffled scream and the man toppled over. Another man came into view, and Smit was about to fire again when he realised it was Major Deon de Wet. Smit shivered involuntarily and relaxed his finger on the trigger. God, that was close!

Lights came on in the surrounding houses. Smit wasn't surprised, the riot-pump made one hell of a racket. He searched for the light switch and found it, bathing the hall in light. He'd hit the man on the stairs in the face, killing him instantly.

Sergeant Venter was lying still in a mass of glass shards at the bottom of the stairs. Smit walked down and felt Venter's pulse. Two shots in the stomach, the poor kid hadn't had a chance. He walked over and opened the front door to find the drive was filled with people.

Before he could stop her, a woman ran into the hall, and the next minute she was screaming her head off. Then Major de Wet appeared in the doorway and carried her out. Captain Smit watched as he addressed the gathering of worried neighbours.

'I'm Major de Wet from the Murder and Robbery Squad. Everything is under control now, so I am asking you to please return to your homes. People have been killed here, it isn't very pleasant. If you saw anything earlier that could help us with our enquiries and would like to make a statement, please contact me at John Vorster Square in the morning.'

Captain Smit admired the command with which Major de Wet always handled people. De Wet was a big man – he guessed he must weigh at least two hundred pounds. He admired De Wet's dedication, his obvious belief that he had a mission to enforce the law. In the faint light cast by the lamps in the drive, he studied the face of his superior officer – a dark-skinned face, topped by a mop of brown hair. Individually the features might have been described as heavy: the hard jaw-line with the long, full lips above it; the prominent nose, the dark, hypnotic eyes recessed under huge bushy eyebrows, and the high, heavily lined forehead. On some occasions Captain Smit felt that de Wet looked more like a farmer than a police major. He certainly looked all his thirty-nine years.

Captain Smit watched the last of the people disappear into the darkness. Major de Wet turned to him.

'Good shot, Captain Smit. Perhaps too good. The man in the back garden won't be telling us anything.'

'Unfortunately, Major de Wet, neither will the other man who shot at me in the house.'

'And Sergeant Venter?' Captain Smit nodded his head. 'Damn.'

'Major, you know what it's like. He went inside ahead of me and charged up the stairs like an Afrikaner bull.'

'You tell that to his parents, Captain.'

The ambulance arrived five minutes later to take the bodies away. Why an ambulance, which was, after all, for the living? Deon could never understand that. He left the reliable Captain Smit to help the ambulance men, and began his search of the house.

It was a big place, immaculately furnished and with no bric-a-brac lying around. He felt curiously uncomfortable in it, an unusual feeling which he stored in his mind for future reference. Often such feelings came to have a direct bearing on a case.

The first thing that struck him as odd was the absence of servants. Usually in Johannesburg, a house of this size would have at least three servants resident on the property. He opened the kitchen door and walked over to the servants' quarters.

The rooms were locked but it was obvious that the servants must have been on the property the previous day. There were clothes on the washing-line, and in the rubbish bins were remnants of recently eaten food. It would be natural for one or two of the servants to be out on a Saturday night, but not for all of them to have gone away.

The owner was probably a wealthy, single man. The furnishings were dark – a lot of black leather and stainless steel. There were a few vases, no flowers but plenty of indoor plants. Definitely the taste of a man, not a woman.

The paintings on the walls were originals. Major de Wet did not know much about art but he had an instinctive eye for the value of things. Just one of these paintings would certainly fetch more than the modest house in Parktown he had worked hard for ten years to put down the deposit on. The fact did not make him jealous, it rather appealed to his own Calvinistic view of the role of the policeman in society.

One of the black lacquer cabinets bordering the sitting room was hanging open. Inside was a case containing a magnificent Georgian silver tea service. He'd dealt with a case of forgery recently and had become something of an expert on antique silver. He took the service in its case out into the light and examined a few of the pieces carefully. All the hallmarks matched, all the pieces were of the same set, it was perfect. He took a long, deep breath. He knew what this collection might fetch at an auction at Christie's in London. Had this been an attempt at a theft to gain insurance money? There were no burglar bars on the windows of this room, and only an idiot would leave articles of such value unprotected.

Deon's eyes combed the walls of the room, finally spotting an electronic movement-detector mounted close to the ceiling. It had been disarmed. So, whoever they were, they were professionals.

He moved carefully up the blood-soaked staircase, past the chalk-marked areas that marked where the bodies had fallen. The smell of death was strong. He wondered cynically if the owner would demand compensation from the South African Police for the glass table Sergeant Venter had broken.

He walked towards the open door at the end of the spacious

passageway, his feet sinking into the deep-cut pile. This must be the master bedroom. It was stark, with a square white bed in the centre. All along one wall were fitted cupboards, along the opposite wall a full-length mirror. He stared at his reflection, then turned away; he did not particularly like the look of the cold, hard man in the mirror.

A third wall was all window, from ceiling to floor. He had never seen anything like it – it must have cost a small fortune to install. The en suite bathroom contained its own jacuzzi and sauna. Like the rest of the house, it was fitted with every possible luxury.

He came out of the bathroom and looked again in the mirror. Something about it was odd. It was as if the mirror had come apart from the wall at one side. He walked up close to it, touched it lightly – and the mirror shifted effortlessly to one side, into a recess in the far wall. He wondered if the runners were mercury-filled, it shifted so silently.

Behind the mirror was a narrow passage that ended in a sophisticated vault door. Deon thought the door was locked, but when he tried the handle it swung open easily. Beyond was a small square room. It was lined with shelves filled with files, safety-deposit boxes, computer discs and reels of film.

De Wet slipped on the thin cotton gloves he always carried. He would be examining articles that might need to be finger-printed later. He prised open one of the cylindrical cases that held a 16mm film spool, unwound the shiny black film inside and held it up to the light.

Porn, he thought to himself. A skeleton in a rich man's closet. He closed the metal canister and slipped the reel of film into his pocket. He pulled down one of the files and found himself looking at what resembled a series of personal dossiers. He noted that the numbers on the files corresponded to numbers on the film canisters. He put the file back, and took out the one with the same number as the film spool he had just confiscated.

Photographs. Pages of descriptions. Perhaps this was the way top businessmen analysed their staff? But then there were pictures of a woman. Could it be the woman he had just looked at on the film?

There was a noise on the stairs. Quickly Deon tore from the file the section of photographs that seemed to match the film, and stuffed it inside his jacket. Then he walked out, closed the door and swung the mirror back, hiding the safe.

He walked back into the bedroom just as someone entered through the door. He found himself face to face with General Muller.

'Major de Wet, what the hell's going on!'

It sounded more like a threat than a question. And those eyes, always those bloody eyes. They gave him the creeps, never staying in one place, always shifting, pale yellow orbs recessed in Muller's toad-like visage. The man was short and round, his uniform bulging at the seams. There was a pistol in one fat hand and De Wet wondered for a few seconds if General Muller would shoot him. This was the man who could make or break his career in the police force.

'Major de Wet, what are you doing in this room?'

De Wet was usually scrupulously honest, but this time, for some reason, he decided to lie.

'Looking for clues. We obviously surprised them, sir.'

'Major de Wet, this is not the home of some middle-class businessman. You have no right to be in this room. You are trespassing.'

'Three men dead, one of them a policeman. I suppose that's incidental.'

He waited for General Muller to explode at his impertinence, but the General's mind was clearly occupied with another matter.

'You've made your point, de Wet,' he said mildly, and walked past him towards the mirror.

De Wet felt the hair rising on the back of his neck. He was scared and he wasn't shy of admitting it. It was as if Muller knew there was a safe behind the mirror . . .

'Well, de Wet, I'm sure you're not going to find much up here. I suggest you concentrate your efforts on the staircase. Obviously a couple of professional house-breakers – some of the silver service is missing from downstairs.'

'But General, the silver . . .' De Wet had said it before he could stop himself.

'What, Major? Didn't you notice the empty case?'

'No, sir.'

'I'm surprised at you. A simple case of house-breaking and

you haven't checked what's missing? Get out of this room, man. You may have a good record, but sloppy work is unforgivable.'

'There may be more to this case, General Muller.'

'That's quite enough, de Wet. You should never have left the station, you're supposed to be in command. Get back to your office. I want a full report on my desk by six o'clock this morning. Do I make myself clear?'

'Yes, sir.'

The light of dawn was breaking as Major Deon de Wet drove past the buildings of the University of the Witwatersrand. It was the best university in Johannesburg, if not in the country, with a reputation for liberal thinking. He was slightly in awe of it, of what it represented, and yet he wondered now, as he drove past, whether its liberal academics really had any idea what it was like to be a policeman in South Africa today – or whether they even cared.

He took the Braamfontein off-ramp and swung down into Smit Street, travelling parallel to the Braamfontein Cemetery. As he entered the suburb of Pageview he turned left down Mint Road. After driving for another kilometre he pulled over and switched the engine off. He went round to the boot, pulled off his blue uniform jacket and donned a dark green windcheater that he kept in a holdall with some other clothes. There was no one about.

He walked towards the west, without any fixed destination in mind. Gradually, the thoughts that had filled his head drained away into his subconscious and he began to relax a little. The argument with Muller had set him on edge.

The streets became familiar, evoking memories from his youth, many of them unhappy. There wasn't much to be happy about in Fordsburg in those days, even less now. Almost without realising it, he arrived at the pokey little house.

It was a terrible mess, and the front yard was filled with rubbish – cans and old motor-car parts. He walked quickly past, afraid that, even at this early hour, someone might see him and recognise him. Then he looked back at it, and remembered . . .

As the first born, from the moment he was able to walk Deon had been given every attention. His father, Carel de Wet, was a brilliant attorney, a man who lived life to the full, enjoying alcohol, women – even other men's wives – a giant of a man with saturnine features and eyes that seemed to see right into your soul. Sometimes Deon wished he could have loved his father when he had been alive instead of when he was dead.

They hadn't lived in the house in Fordsburg then, they'd lived in Kensington, the best suburb of Johannesburg. But he had been too young to remember it well. There were parties that were the talk of Johannesburg's high society. In those days, his mother had told him, Carel de Wet could do no wrong. His law company was growing at an incredible pace attracting clients from the major mining houses. His courtroom successes were legendary. He could always find a flaw in his opponent's case and then exploit that weakness to the full. He had the kind of iron constitution that enabled him to wine and dine till the early hours of the morning and still appear in court next day as fresh as a daisy. Nothing, it seemed, could stop his meteoric rise.

Then he took on a case for Max Golden, the owner of one of South Africa's biggest mining companies. The two were often seen at each other's houses, their wives became intimate. Suddenly the relationship soured. For some reason that no one could really understand, Carel de Wet refused to represent Max Golden. There was a vague rumour that he had found Golden's business dealings unethical, and had said so.

The crash came out of the blue. It began with a report in a Sunday paper of corruption in the leading law firm of De Wet and Partners. At first it was dismissed as the work of an over-zealous young reporter, anxious to make a name for himself, but then the evidence had begun to mount up, and though Carel de Wet insisted on his innocence, people began to ask themselves if he was in fact a man who could be trusted. The rumours accelerated. The Bar Council demanded a thorough investigation.

In the weeks that followed Carel de Wet's name was linked to scandal after scandal: affairs with prostitutes; indiscretions with clients' trusted information; the bribing of key trial witnesses and the misappropriation of a large sum of money belonging to a leading businessman. Still Carel de Wet declared his innocence, but in a matter of months men who had been proud to say they were his friends were openly stating that they had never had much time for him. The big house in Kensington became a morgue and the bank foreclosed.

Carel de Wet was a broken man. After the crash he lost himself in a self-created hell of low-class women and alcohol. He made a small amount of money by giving legal advice to people and also by playing the piano – a talent he'd never before considered to be of economic value.

Deon, who had never consciously known the wealth of the previous household, accepted their poverty as his natural condition. When he wasn't running errands for his father or helping his mother in the house, he would play with the other children out in the street. He was respected because of his size, and the other children gravitated towards him because of his natural authority. He had a silent disposition and soon learned that on the street his fists offered the best means of communication.

When he was a bit older, Deon started to earn money by playing as lead guitarist with a local band, The Flyers. He enjoyed the success with girls that playing in the band gave him, and also the night life, but his friends often wondered at his strange, almost religious obsession with doing what was right. Deon never took drugs or drank any alcohol. If he did sleep with a girl, he always took precautions. It was just the way he was. The band would often steal ashtrays and beer mugs from a gig, but Deon would always return them. Once they had been playing at a private function and some men had tried to gang-rape a girl. Deon had laid every one of them out on the floor. No one in the band spoke to Deon on the way back to Fordsburg that evening, but they all silently respected him. . .

Major Deon de Wet continued walking the early morning streets – walking and thinking. Most children in this area would have little chance of ever getting anywhere. At best they'd probably end up like his younger brother Pieter – a gang man, a gutter fighter with no goal in life except survival. What could anyone really do to change this? He was stupid even asking himself such questions, he knew. Yet the teachers in the schools really tried, and so did many of the parents. It was just that the place was against them. He'd once taken a holiday in England and spent a day in the industrial town of Birmingham. The same sort of place, the same sort of problems.

Deon kicked a can in front of him and thought proudly of his own children. They'd pleased him more than he'd ever dreamed possible. To have enabled his kids to avoid this poverty, this hopelessness, was an achievement in itself.

Yet he did realise that many of his own childhood friends who were now hardened criminals still had their own code of ethics. There were certain things they would never do, and he could never regard them as being essentially bad. But just tonight, in the house of an incredibly wealthy businessman, the sort of house he could never dream of owning, he had found evidence of the lowest form of criminal activity. It was only luck that had produced that evidence; if it had not been for the robbery, he would never have found it.

Deon thought back to the things he had found in the secret safe of the luxurious Westcliff home – things that betrayed a depth of evil that he both despised and was fascinated by. He had come upon this evil in the residence of a certain Mr Bernard Aschaar, head of the Goldcorp Group, South Africa's largest mining company.

He wondered what the robbers had really been after. He wished he had had more time to search the safe, to discover what it was that had been worth dying for. And what was General Muller's involvement? Why had he been so anxious to get Deon out of that bedroom? Had he deliberately removed some of the silver to make it look more like real burglary?

Deon kicked an empty can along the gutter and for no reason he could exactly understand, began to cry. Memories of his father's death, long suppressed, came flooding back to him. He remembered that appallingly hot midsummer's day a few weeks before the Christmas of 1956 – the day the fateful letter had come, the letter that had decided him on his present career . . .

With his very excellent academic record, Deon was surprised at first that he should have been turned down for a legal scholarship. He had accepted that it was probably because of his poor background and the school he had been to – but then his father had picked up the letter. Carel de Wet had been quiet for a while. Then he had laughed. It was a sarcastic, bitter laugh. He looked his son straight in the eye.

'Think of this as a favour, my boy. Now you know your place in life.'

Then he had disappeared into the little room that he called his study.

Deon could remember standing there, quite still, with the

letter in his hand. He could remember deciding that there was not another person on earth whom he despised as much as his father – a man who had been exposed as a cheat and a liar. He could remember vowing that those things would never be said about himself. Then he had walked out of the house to visit one of the members of his band, and they'd spent the rest of the afternoon rehearsing a new song.

He had returned home in the late afternoon. He'd been surprised to see a policeman waiting for him with his brother. Their father had shot himself just after lunch. Very professionally done, he'd put the barrel in his mouth and pulled the trigger. On discovering the body, Mrs de Wet had had a stroke. One burial, two coffins.

As a result of his father's suicide, Deon had made the decision to join the police force. If he couldn't read law, then he'd enforce it. The little money he got from the sale of the house, he used to send Pieter to boarding school . . .

Now, when he walked down this street, the memories were as vivid as ever. The police force had saved him, and for that he was very grateful. He had taken a challenging post on the Angolan border with the South African Police, and the fighting and the action had helped him forget the cruel events in Fordsburg. Since then, everything had gone well for him. His promotion within the force had been rapid, he had an attractive wife and two very healthy children.

For Pieter things had gone less well. He had refused to knuckle down and work, and in the end had run away from boarding school. Deon knew that it was useless to try and keep his brother on the straight and narrow, so he gave up any further attempts to impose an education on him, and had to watch him go his own way.

Now, as he walked the dismal streets, the first sunlight began to appear in the sky. This place was his security. Most of the time he liked to kid himself that Fordsburg was a thing of the past. And then, in moments such as this, he needed to come back. He knew he could be thrown back into it and survive. That was his strength against people with money and influence, people like General Muller and Mr Bernard Aschaar. What bothered Major Deon de Wet was his reponsibility to his own family. Would they stand by him, if things got difficult? At least

114

they would never be able to look on him the way he had looked on his own father.

He got back to his car and slipped behind the steering wheel, catching sight of his face, torn and disturbed, in the rear-view mirror. The car started easily and he pulled away from the kerb. His mind began carefully to put together the report of a simple case of house-breaking that had resulted in three deaths, and the mysterious disappearance of silver *after* the robbery. A report that somehow included his almost certain knowledge that General Muller had deliberately steered attention away from the real motives for the break-in.

He knew he was beginning his own silent battle against the real culprits.

Major Deon de Wet's full file on the robbery of Mr Bernard Aschaar's house in Westcliff was not to be found at police headquarters, nor was it in his desk at home. If his wife had been asked if she knew of the existence of such a file, she would have reliably reported that she didn't. It was hidden in a metal box buried at the bottom of the de Wet garden. In the box lay also the documents and the film Deon had found in the safe.

Deon knew that he had latched onto something very important. Muller's behaviour in the house still bothered him. He had always had a basic mistrust of Muller, and now this case had reinforced his suspicions. Bernard Aschaar was a wealthy and powerful businessman – it was not unthinkable that he was paying Muller off.

Deep down, though Deon would have refused to admit it, there was another reason for his interest in the contents of the safe. The mining company Aschaar ran, Goldcorp, was still owned by Max Golden, who had had something to do with his father's fall from grace. Deon remembered his father's insistence that Golden was corrupt; his policeman's mind had filed the information away, keeping it permanently on hold.

Unfortunately, because he worked in the murder and robbery section of the force, Deon did not automatically have access to the information he needed to pursue his enquiries – and to ask his colleagues too many questions would be to give the game away. So Deon began by investigating the supposed theft of the Georgian silver he had seen at the house. He knew it hadn't been stolen, but the thieves were dead and no one would believe his story. If Muller said the silver had gone, then it had gone. Where to, was another question.

He got in touch with a useful contact, an expert in antique silver. The man was not only able to tell him where the service had been bought, but he also knew about the unusual hallmarks Deon had seen on it. He had then made a call to a friend of his who sold antiques to Aschaar. This man relayed the information that a toad-like individual in a badly fitting suit had delivered a metal case to him for safe-keeping for Mr Aschaar that same day. Deon had no doubt that the silver was locked inside it.

The office was enormous, and spartan. Through the two high windows the last rays of sunshine poured in like spotlights on a stage. Deon de Wet could see dust swirling in the pools of sunlight, and beyond, a figure seated at an ancient desk.

The man was writing, and did not bother to look up as he came into the room. Deon walked up to the table and saluted. Still the Minister continued to write, and Deon wondered if he was actually aware that there was anyone else in the room.

'You may sit down, Major de Wet.'

Still he carried on writing, a precise script that never faltered, the head bent over the clean white paper, the thin blond-grey hair barely covering the pale, freckled scalp. This man had fought his way up to one of the most powerful positions of government and demanded respect from everyone who worked for him. Major de Wet had felt courageous at many times of his life, but at this precise moment he was feeling distinctly uneasy.

The Minister put his pen down, leaned back and placed his hands behind his head. The cold, grey eyes stared.

'Major de Wet. I don't think that there is another man in South Africa's police force with a record comparable to your own. As you no doubt realise, we struggle to get recruits of high calibre. You are a very intelligent young man and, without doubt, remarkably good at your job.

'Your family past is of no interest to this force as long as it does not interfere with your work. One cannot be held responsible for the actions of one's parents or one's brother. You married an Afrikaner, your children go to a good Afrikaans school. All these things bode well for your future, Major de Wet.'

Deon trembled as he waited for the crunch line.

'I am pleased to announce your appointment as major-general with effect from today.'

Deon felt himself swaying on his feet. This was the last thing he had expected; he had not believed he would get another big promotion for at least five years. But he refused to admit a smile; he could tell there was something more the Minister had to say, and that it would refer to his own sphere of influence within the police force.

'Please sit down, Major-General de Wet.'

Deon took a chair. Obviously his new rank allowed a little more informality with the Minister.

'Congratulations are also in order for your handling of the burglary at Mr Bernard Aschaar's house last Saturday. General Muller tells me you caught the robbers red-handed.' The Minister paused, and stared directly at De Wet. 'The robbery, it turns out, is of interest to the Bureau of State Security and it has been handed over for their investigation. I would appreciate it if you would assist them with the details of the affair. Naturally, your own investigations on this matter will cease forthwith.'

The smile was icy. The word 'forthwith' had been enunciated with particular emphasis. Deon had the distinct impression that he was being bought. This appointment could only have been as a result of General Muller's direct commendation.

He got to his feet. 'Thank you, sir. I hope I will be able to do justice to the position you have given me.'

The following weekend, Teresa de Wet decided to visit her mother with the children. Deon stayed at home, pleading work. On Saturday afternoon, checking that none of the neighbours was around, he walked nonchalantly down to the bottom of the garden. He looked just like any other middle-class South African husband who had decided on the spur of the moment to do a little weekend gardening.

The spade cut easily through the ground and soon he had unearthed the metal box. It came out smoothly from its resting place, and he carried it to the room at the back of the garage. He locked the door behind him and prised open the lid.

Suddenly there was a rap on the door; then another. Deon froze, unsure of what to do. In an instant he had pulled himself together, leapt up onto the workbench and hidden the box on the wooden rafters that supported the roof. Jumping to the floor, he pushed a set of garden shears into the industrial vice set into the corner of his work bench. Another rap on the door. He opened it quickly.

'God, Deon, what the hell are you up to? Oiling your shears! You police guys take this secrecy business a bit too far. Have you got some petrol? My lawnmower's run out and I can't get any more this weekend because of the bloody restrictions.'

Deon felt the relief soaring through his body. It was his next-door neighbour, John Tillson, a Yorkshireman out in South Africa on contract for his company.

'No problem, John. I've got several jerry-cans in the front of the garage. Guess I've got used to doing things behind closed doors!'

They walked round to the front of the garage, and Deon handed John a jerry-can of petrol.

'Bloody hell, I don't want to fill my car up, Deon. You could get arrested with that lot, you should know, the law states only a ten-litre can of petrol can be kept on the premises.'

'You see, even a policeman can be a crook at times. Actually I've got a licence to keep this lot here. It's in case of emergencies, you can't have the Flying Squad running out of petrol, you know.'

'Well, thanks, Deon, I'll bring the can back full on Monday morning. Otherwise, no doubt, you'll have me up for obstructing a police officer in the course of his duty!'

He waited for John to disappear and then walked back into the garage. It wasn't like him to be so jumpy.

What he wanted to do was quite simple and would not excite any attention. He'd made sure the incinerator was packed with leaves and old grass, and the things he wanted to destroy could easily be placed within this rubbish and would burn to ashes, which he then planned to bury in the garden. No one knew he had the material, so no one would come looking for it.

Deon locked the garage door behind him again and took the box down from the rafters. The lid had jammed, and he had to force it open with a screwdriver. It came loose, at last – so violently that the contents of the file flew across the floor as it fell out. He picked up the pieces of paper first because he knew they would burn the easiest.

A photograph caught his eye. He tried not to look at it but it was no good. The woman was naked, lying face-down on a table, her legs dangling to the floor. Her hands were tied to the far corners of the table. A man stood above her holding a rubber whip – a sjambok – and another looked on smiling. There were heavy weals across her back and buttocks. The next photograph featured the same woman and man, but this time he was assaulting her. Deon knew these were not posed pornographic pictures, rather they were snapshots of an actual event that someone wanted recorded.

He felt something rise up deep within him, something the boys who had been at the dance had seen so many years before: a hatred of evil. He knew he would not be able to leave this thing alone.

In the enlargement that Deon had had made, the woman on the table looked as if she were in her late teens – the lines on her face were only there because she was in a lot of pain. She was extremely attractive; a slim body, from what he could see, perfectly formed. Her hair was dark and short. What was the story behind this photograph? How could this man have performed such a bestial act on such a beautiful creature?

The man next to Deon coughed to break the silence. He was a slight, anaemic-looking man wearing blotchy horn-rimmed spectacles; Major-General Deon de Wet made him feel uneasy, and the claustrophobic atmosphere of the darkroom put him on edge.

'Good picture, don't you think, Marcus?'

'Well, sir, it could be clearer, but then with this sort of enlargement one does lose a little detail. Who is she?'

Deon had prepared a story to ward off probing questions such as this. 'Oh, some prostitute who I think could answer a few interesting questions on the Weppener murder. She may not even be alive, this picture could have been taken twenty years ago.'

He felt the lie sounded very convincing. The Weppener case was genuine, he had just added a few more leads to it that hadn't been there before.

'But the paper is quite new, sir.'

'Are you sure, Marcus?'

'Yes, sir. Ten to eleven years old at the most.'

He would have to watch himself. Marcus was obviously no fool.

'Don't worry, sir. I'll have it checked through every file we've got. I can promise we'll go back fifteen years – further, if we don't come up with anything. Pity you've only got a bit of it. How come it's cut round the edges?'

'Er. I found it in an album. Someone obviously cut it out from a larger shot.'

'Anyway here are the enlarged prints you wanted, sir.'

Major-General de Wet felt uncomfortable. He let himself out of the darkroom. What if they couldn't find out who she was?

Deon met Abe Solomon at the bar of the Carlton Hotel. The place was crowded but they found a quiet corner. Abe was a crime reporter he relied on for the occasional lead; in return he gave him a lot of good stories.

Now he eased the black-and-white photo from his pocket. Anyone who knew this woman would be able to recognise her. The police records department were checking it against their files of convicted prostitutes; she might be a prostitute, but he didn't think so.

'God, the expression on her face is awful. Do you want it in the paper?'

'Definitely not. I'm following up something that could be very interesting, though I'm afraid I can't tell you what it is now.'

Abe drew in closer. He sensed that Deon felt he was onto something big. 'I'll tell you what. I'm not too busy at the moment, crime's having a holiday. I'll show this picture to every person I know who I think might be able to put a name to the face.'

'That's a good idea, Abe. How soon can you start?'

'Right away.'

Sonja Seyton-Waugh turned away, hoping that her friend would not notice how she had reacted.

'Sonja, are you all right? You look as though you're going to faint.'

Hermione du Plessis, journalist-turned-authoress, was one of Sonja's best friends. They'd been at university together, and later Sonja had provided Hermione with the finance to write two books on the people of Soweto. The books had created a stir abroad, and put more pressure on the South African government to improve conditions in the township.

Now Hermione watched her friend with concern. She had always admired Sonja, a woman so wealthy she employed an investment team to manage her interests. Normally Sonja's manner was calm, even cool, but the casual remark Hermione had made about her boyfriend Abe and his search for the woman in a photograph taken some ten years before, had clearly affected Sonja deeply.

Sonja was very tall, with a beautifully slim figure that could have made her a top model. The face was aristocratic, with high cheek-bones, an exquisite small nose and piercing green eyes. Her hair was dark, worn short round her head in a page-boy style. Hermione had often wondered why Sonja had never married. Even now, sitting in the exclusive restaurant in Johannesburg's luxurious Hyde Park shopping centre, she was attracting admiring glances. Her dress was fashionably short, revealing long legs in pale stockings. Hermione couldn't help being envious. An attractive woman herself, she was nothing in comparison to Sonja.

Sonja's main interest in life, apart from running the giant mining company she had inherited from her father, was expanding the consciousness of modern women. She wanted to stimulate more women to work in commerce and industry. She had a doctorate in business administration from Harvard and was known as a brilliant speaker on business matters throughout the world. It had been said by a leading international magazine that Sonja Seyton-Waugh had done more for the women's movement than any of the most ardent feminists in the United States. People gossiped that she might be a lesbian, but most of her friends realised that she was just more interested in business than men.

Hermione called the waiter and asked him to bring a glass of water. 'Sonja, you should see a doctor. I think you've been pushing yourself too hard lately.'

'I'll be fine, really. If you'll excuse me I think I should go now. I haven't been sleeping much lately, that's all it is.' Sonja got up, and Hermione watched her with concern.

'Why don't you wait? Abe will be here in a minute, he'll drive you home.'

'No!'

Hermione looked at Sonja aghast. She'd never shouted at her like that in all the ten years she'd known her . . .

121

Sonja was shaking as she got into her car. She couldn't believe this was happening; they must have released the photograph. They had promised they wouldn't as long as she did what they told her to.

God, the disgrace. How could she possibly live with it?

Deon put the phone down. It was a lead of sorts, nothing really substantial, but worth following up – Abe Solomon's information was always accurate. It was just that Deon had seen several photographs of Sonja Seyton-Waugh – she was always appearing in the press – and from what he could remember she didn't look much like the woman in the photograph. Still, it had been taken at least ten years ago. People changed.

Deon phoned Miss Seyton-Waugh and was greeted by an answering-machine. All right, he thought, I'll go over.

The house was of a very modern design, the front door a polished wooden square with a large yellow handle in the middle. The stone walls that surrounded it soared up into the evening sky. To his left was an open garage and Deon could just glimpse the outlines of a couple of cars that were certainly worth more than everything he owned.

He rapped on the door several times before it was answered by a coloured woman who was obviously a personal secretary. She was well-spoken, and clearly regarded him with suspicion. He had taken the precaution of wearing plain clothes; this was private business.

'I'd like to see Miss Seyton-Waugh, please.'

'She is not at home.'

'She most definitely is.'

He hoped to hell she *was* at home. If not, he wasn't going to leave this house until he knew where he could find her.

'I will call the police if you do not leave.'

'I am the police.'

'You don't have a uniform!'

He pulled out his police identity document. She glanced down at it cursorily and said, 'You do not have a warrant?'

'If you don't let me in I'll break this door down!'

What was he saying? He could be demoted for this sort of behaviour. He pushed the door open, walked past the woman and into what was obviously a reception room. The coloured woman screamed out from behind him, 'Miss Seyton! Miss Seyton!'

A woman walked into the room, and her beauty took his breath away. She showed no fear. 'Who the hell are you?' she said coolly. 'How dare you force your way into my house!'

'Major-General de Wet, Miss Seyton-Waugh. I felt obliged to see you personally.'

'You may leave, Sally.' Then she turned back to Deon. 'Major-General de Wet, you act more like a thug than a policeman. I would appreciate it if you would leave this house immediately.'

Everything about her was perfect. He had never in his life seen a woman so well groomed, so beautiful. 'I think we should talk, Miss Seyton-Waugh.'

He saw her mouth tremble. She was losing control. Instinctively, he knew why.

'Sit, sit down,' she said. He relaxed into the leather suite and tried his best to put her at her ease.

'This is not an official police matter, Miss Seyton-Waugh. I have come to talk to you in a personal capacity. As you have no doubt guessed, it is in connection with what you discussed with Miss du Plessis this morning.'

'I think you must have the wrong end of the stick, Major-General de Wet. I don't know what you're talking about.'

He studied her face closely, the photograph still in his mind's eye. There was definitely a resemblance.

'Why are you looking at me like that?' She stared at him coldly. He took the full picture out of his jacket pocket.

'Do you recognise this?'

He noticed the tremor of her lips, and then she turned on him. 'How dare you show me such a picture. Get out!'

He strode over to her and grabbed her hands. She tried to scream but he picked up one of the cushions and held it over her mouth. He unfastened the back of her dress and ran his left hand down her back.

He felt her skin hot beneath his hands. She struggled to get loose and he firmed his grip. She screamed out with pain. Then he dragged her from the settee towards the mirror in the hall. He lifted the cushion from her mouth.

'Scream, and I'll put it back.'

He turned her head so that she could see the back of her body in the mirror. Slowly he let his fingers work their way down her back to her buttocks.

'Miss Seyton-Waugh, plastic surgery can hide many things, but not perfectly. Your face has been subtly, beautifully changed – but there are still the faint outlines of scars on your back. Only you can tell me who gave you those scars and why.'

She fainted in his arms. He carried her back to the lounge and saw that Sally was watching him from the other doorway, terrified. He turned to her.

'Get me some cold water and some towels. And please don't worry. I had to do this. I don't want to harm her, I want to help her.'

The first words Sonja spoke when she opened her eyes five minutes later were to Sally. 'This man will do me no harm. Don't worry, and please, above all, don't tell a soul about this.' She waited till Sally had left the house and she'd heard the front door close behind her. Then she raised herself up and stared at Deon, tears running down the smooth skin of her face.

'You can't know what it's been like for me. All these years and no one I could talk to. People wonder why I've never married, the men wonder why I won't sleep with them. God, if only they knew. I've worked to forget, I've worked so hard, and still the memory of it, the pain of it, won't go away. I was twenty years old at the time and still a virgin.'

She was crying openly now. He was appalled, he had opened the door into a place which perhaps he should never have entered, but now he knew there was no turning back.

'Miss Seyton-Waugh, I apologise for my behaviour. I hope I didn't hurt you. That photograph I showed you is one of many, along with a film of the same incident. You see, I had to find the woman in it. I am determined that the man who abused you should be brought to justice.'

She looked horrified. 'Photographs? They must have released them. Oh my God.'

'No, I found them in a safe, in a house where I was investigating a robbery.'

'Whose safe?'

'Bernard Aschaar's. Your secret is safe with me, you must trust me. I will bring that man to justice.'

'You know who the man in the photograph is?'

'No.'

'Bernard Aschaar was there, but he must have stayed out of the picture. The man in the photograph is Jay Golden. Yes, *the* Jay Golden. He'd asked me out that particular night. He's good-looking and wealthy, I found him attractive at that time, God alone knows why.

'When he arrived to collect me, he was the epitome of charm, politeness itself. Anyway, we went to a night club. I enjoyed myself and he invited me back to his house for a nightcap. I accepted.

'Aschaar was there when we arrived. He was also pleasant, and we sat and had drinks together. Then Jay Golden came up to me and hit me across the face. He laughed. Bernard Aschaar did nothing. Then Jay hit me again and told me to kneel. I said I wanted to leave. Aschaar locked the door, I screamed but they didn't care. Jay Golden hit me quite a few times after that, across the head, with a telephone directory. I was pretty groggy. They made me take off my clothes.

'Jay asked me to do certain things. He wanted me to kneel down and suck him. When I wouldn't they said I was frigid. I remember pictures being taken. I wasn't feeling too good after Jay hit me.

'They dragged me over to the table and tied me down onto it. Jay explored my body with his hands. I bit him. That was when he got the sjambok – he went berserk. Then he raped me from behind.

'It went on the whole evening. I couldn't stand the pain of being whipped so I did what he asked me to. God, they even filmed the whole thing.

'They took me home much, much later. When I said I'd go to the police they laughed and said that was typical of a whore.

'A friend of my late father's, a plastic surgeon I knew well, operated on my back the next day. I asked him to alter my face. If the photographs ever came to light, I didn't want to be recognised. I told him never ever to mention my back to anyone. He's a good man, he never has. I told everyone else I'd had a car accident.'

'But why are you still so scared?'

'They've been blackmailing me, threatening to release the pictures if I try to interfere with their mining operations. If it hadn't been for that I would have expanded my interests more.

The way they treat their mine workers is appalling, they deserve to be exposed.

Deon got up and touched her shoulder. 'I vow that you will never live in fear again, Miss Seyton-Waugh. I'll get those bastards, whatever the cost.'

Bernard

Helen Jamieson, Bernard Aschaar's new secretary, sat silently at her desk. She had meant to go out for lunch, but now she didn't want to eat, she wanted to wait and see what happened. She'd handed a letter to Mr Aschaar some minutes before – she hadn't opened it herself – and it had made him very angry. He had called Jay Golden across to discuss the contents of the letter.

She thought about the man she worked for, the managing director of the Goldcorp Group and rumoured to be South Africa's highest-paid businessman. Bernard was a big, heavy man, just over six foot tall. She knew most men thought he was bigger than that because he exuded such power and confidence; he had boxed professionally when he left university and had never lost a heavyweight bout. He still trained every morning, and at forty years old his body was a solid pack of muscle. Women found him irresistible.

He always smiled – sometimes coldly, sometimes warmly, and mostly out of habit. People remembered him for his smile – and for his unfashionably long, lustrous, curling black hair. He had the look of a noble savage.

Helen was awakened from her thoughts as Jay Golden bounded into her office. Jay was in his late twenties, with a lightly sun-tanned skin and white-blond hair. It was said he went out with a different woman every day of the year – not surprising, since he was heir to one of the largest fortunes in Africa. Helen liked Jay, and she intended to sleep with him, but on her terms. Jay could give her both money and power. Now his bright blue eyes stared directly into hers.

'Something wrong, Helen?'

127

'He's in a bad mood, Mr Golden.'

'Well, I'm not!' She smelt his expensive aftershave as he breezed past her into Bernard Aschaar's office.

'Hey, Bernard, don't look so heavy. It doesn't suit you. I'd like a Scotch and soda, please. After all, I should have some reward for the effort I've made to come and see you.'

Bernard calmly poured Jay's drink, then a neat Scotch for himself. He watched as Jay studied the photograph on the table and the note that had come with it.

When he finally spoke, Jay had a slight edge to his voice. 'I thought you'd destroyed the stuff with me in it.'

'No, Jay, I kept it. Someone who obviously knew about it took the photographs, the film and the file from my safe. What do you think your father will say when he sees the photographs?'

Jay looked at him in silence, thinking things over. 'He won't see them. We'll do whatever they ask.'

'They haven't asked for anything so far, Jay. They're just threatening, get it? This is revenge.'

'You're in trouble, Bernard. It must have been Sonja Seyton-Waugh who organised the break-in. After what we've been doing to her, she'd be desperate for those photographs.'

Bernard gave Jay one of his famous smiles. 'Firstly, Jay, I'm not the one in trouble; I'm not in the photographs. And I'm not going to inherit the Goldcorp Group. But you are – at least, if your father doesn't see those pictures. Secondly, I have duplicates of all this material. If it's Sonja, she won't move so fast once she knows that.'

'God. What the hell am I going to do?'

'Simple, Jay. Get the photographs back.'

'So we take this one to the police, I suppose?'

Bernard did not laugh. Jay had just come up with a very good idea. 'Yes Jay, that's exactly what we do.'

'Over my dead body!'

'Listen to me. People aren't interested in reality, only in their perception of reality. We got a blackmail note. The only problem with it is that you are in the photograph along with Sonja Seyton-Waugh. The solution is simple: we re-stage the photograph. Your fiancée instead of Sonja Seyton-Waugh, and some other sucker instead of you.'

'But I haven't got a fiancée!'

'You'll get one. In fact I know just the girl.'

'Then we give the new photo and the same blackmail note to the police?'

'Exactly. I'll speak to our friend General Muller. I'll tell him that your fiancée is being blackmailed, that the photograph is of an ugly incident that happened to her many years ago. I'll say I paid the blackmailers for the pictures and put them in my safe, meaning to destroy them. These men then obviously broke into my house, recovered the pictures and demanded more money. I'll tell Muller that we want the photographs found and destroyed, and the blackmailer eliminated.'

'You're a genius, Bernard. But what about making the substitute photo look real? Are you going to use a make-up artist to create the whip-marks on my fiancée's back?'

'Who said anything about faking it? This will be the real thing done to a real lady!' And Bernard roared with laughter as he explained the rest of his plan to Jay.

Helen couldn't quite believe it had happened; it was exactly what she'd been planning. Jay had asked her out for dinner. She could see he was infatuated with her. Well, she would continue to keep him at a distance and control the whole affair very coolly. Her price would be high – marriage, if possible. She had always dreamed of living the way Jay did, driving an exotic sports car and wearing the latest designer clothes.

She got home just after six that evening and phoned her boyfriend, Nigel, to cancel their date. She'd been thinking of ditching him for a long time now, so she felt nothing of standing him up. She actually got a strange kick out of hearing his disappointment at the other end of the line. She slammed the phone down with satisfaction – men like Nigel would soon be a thing of the past. Jay was in a different class altogether; he could offer her everything she wanted. It gave her a thrill to be in the company of a man who had so much power.

Now she had to think about what to wear that evening. She prided herself on her wardrobe – not a lot of clothes, but all of them carefully chosen. She never bought cheap and only chose the sort of things that never went out of fashion. She knew that the way she looked and dressed was an important part of her success. There were many secretaries who wanted to work for the Goldcorp Group, and she'd got the job because of her poise, her looks, and her falsified references. She'd gone to elocution lessons to remove the last traces of her guttural South African accent, and the references made out that she'd attended Johannesburg's top private school for girls. Rhodean.

First she chose some French underwear, a low-cut lace bra and a black suspender-belt with a very brief pair of panties. The satin-smooth black silk stockings enhanced the sensual shape of her legs and she admired herself in the long mirror in her bedroom. Now she would have the time really to arouse Jay. The black evening dress fitted her like a glove, with a daring plunge behind that left her whole back naked. Her breasts pressed invitingly against the thin black material and hinted at the excitement that lay beneath.

The car swung off the M1 South and turned right onto the M2 West, heading towards Krugersdorp. Helen thought for a moment that they were going to the exclusive Crown Mines restaurant but was surprised when the car turned back north towards the industrial suburb of Amalgam.

She was about to say that she knew the area well when she realised that that would conflict with the information on her curriculum vitae. She was supposed to have lived in the exclusive suburb of Houghton . . . The buildings that they were now passing evoked strong memories of her childhood. Perhaps Jay was taking her to see a new factory before going on to a restaurant?

'This is a very exclusive club we're going to, Helen.' He turned the car right and drove in through the open doors of a large warehouse. As they entered, the doors began to close behind them automatically. Inside, it was pitch black. They got out of the car and Jay held her arm, escorting her through the darkness. She heard a door opening and the sound of other voices.

'Friends.'

In the darkness Jay's voice seemed to have an almost threatening tone to it. She had never heard him speak like this before. Suddenly she felt out of her depth and scared. 'Where are we?'

'In the middle of fucking nowhere, lady.'

Another voice, it sounded guttural, low-class and unpleasant. Helen wondered how Jay could allow this man to speak to her in such a way.

The lights came on. They were so bright that she could hardly see anything for a time – large lights, like the sort they used in film studios; steam rose eerily above them. She was standing alone in the middle of the warehouse which smelt of damp and male sweat.

Two men stood behind one of the lamps, and she could see that they both held cans of beer in their hands. She turned round and saw Jay sitting on a chair in the corner. Next to him was Bernard Aschaar. There was a movie camera on a tripod next to them, and several aluminium camera cases on the floor. The only other object in the warehouse was a big wooden table that stood next to her. For reassurance, she began to walk towards Jay and Bernard.

'Stay right where you are.' Jay's voice was cold and commanding. She obeyed it, and shivered, even though the warehouse was quite warm inside.

'Don't worry, dear, we'll soon warm you up.'

All of them laughed, and she laughed nervously too. She heard the sound of a drink being poured. One of the men came forward and handed her a full glass of neat whisky.

'Drink.'

He said the word slowly. She took the glass and poured the contents on the floor. She was tired of their games. She walked bravely towards Jay and Bernard, who looked at her coldly.

The next minute the man had grabbed her hair and twisted it so savagely she screamed out.

'Shut up, bitch. Johnny, fill me another glass.'

He didn't let go of her hair and she thought it would come out at the roots. 'Please. Please. Mr Aschaar, help me.'

She cried out in desperation, she couldn't work out what they wanted. Another glass was handed to her and the man released his grip on her hair.

'Drink.'

She drank the whisky, feeling it burn as it went down her throat. She wanted to be sick. She lowered the glass but the man held it up to her mouth again. Now she almost choked as the whisky continued to pour down her throat. She felt giddy, but at least the pain of her pulled hair wasn't so bad.

'Give her another glass, Johnny.'

'I can't drink any more.'

'Shut up or I'll break your fucking teeth.'

'Easy does it, Sidney.' Jay's voice echoed across the room.

131

Maybe he would help her. But his next words dashed that hope. 'She's got to look good for the pictures. Can't have her mouth bleeding.'

'You're the boss, sir. She'll look real pretty, don't you worry.'

The full glass was thrust up against her mouth, and again he yanked her hair back. She wouldn't drink, so he punched her in the stomach and she sucked the whisky down.

'That's enough, Sidney. We don't want her pissed, do we?'

'All right, bitch, now you can strip.'

She couldn't believe what she was hearing.

'There won't be any music, lady, so you'd better make it good.'

'Just do it next to the table, Helen.' Jay's voice sounded cruel. She was seeing a side of him that she would never have believed existed. Now he was behind the movie camera, focusing it on her.

'I won't. I want to go home, Jay.'

'You don't make it easy on yerself, do yer, lady.'

'You pig.'

'Can we use force again, Mr Aschaar?'

'Yes, but don't mark her too badly, Sidney.'

Before she could move, Sidney and Johnny had grabbed her. They forced her over the table, face-down, with only her feet protruding over the edge. Then they tied her down with baggage straps.

She felt her shoes being pulled off and something strike the soles of her feet very lightly. She heard the sound of more drinks being poured and a cigarette being lighted. She smelt the familiar smell of Bernard's Turkish-blend tobacco.

'No one will hear, Sidney. So as hard as you like, but keep it in the centre of the soles. We want her to be able to stand up when you've finished. Lightly to start with.'

Mr Aschaar sounded as though he were delivering a management paper at a conference. She couldn't believe that they hadn't tried to rape her. There were more soft blows against her soles and she wondered what sort of game they were playing at.

The blows continued regularly so that a pins-and-needles feeling developed in her feet. She thought that if this was all they were going to do, she could handle it. Then suddenly it happened: a vicious blow after the soft ones. She couldn't believe the pain. It shot up her spine and threatened to break her body in two. She screamed so hard that she could feel the blood in her throat. She tried to say that she would do anything they wanted, but she couldn't speak. Another blow, even worse, and she started retching. She managed to scream the words out. 'I'll do anything! Just stop!'

Another blow hit her feet and she thought she was going to die. Then they left her on the table and disappeared out of the giant room. She tried not to think about what was going to happen next.

They came back into the room and the man called Sidney cleaned the vomit off her face with a rag. His face came up close to hers and she began to shake with fear.

'No funny business, remember.'

She felt the straps loosen, and pulled herself up to a sitting position. For a few moments she thought she might pass out, but that avenue of escape evaded her. Instead she became very sober and tried desperately to detach herself from the whole bizarre situation.

She eased herself down from the table and was surprised to find she could walk. She picked up her shoes from the floor and slipped them on. She could feel that they were watching her every movement.

The man called Sidney came forward again with a glass of whisky. 'Drink up.'

'I don't . . .' She was going to object but remembered what they had done to her before, and gulped the drink down quickly.

'That's better, dear. You'll find life here a lot easier if you just do what you're told.'

She hated the sound of Sidney's voice, she could tell he enjoyed her suffering.

'Now you can strip.'

The camera started, and the noise of the motor turning the film broke the silence. Another light was switched on, and for a moment she could not see clearly at all. Then, mechanically, she began to ease her dress off as she stared into space. The camera stopped and there was silence again.

'Now is that what you'd do for your boyfriend? I don't think so. Look as though you're enjoying it or I'll enjoy beating you up.'

Helen began to shiver again but managed to get herself under control. This time when the camera started up she looked at it seductively. She pulled her dress up slightly to reveal more of her legs; she raised it over her head.

'Bend over the table and look as though you're enjoying yourself.'

She did as she was told, and Sidney came over to her, holding a sjambok. The blows came fast and furious. She started to cry. Then he stopped and stepped back. The man called Johnny came up behind her and ripped off her panties. Then he mounted her savagely.

She cried, she couldn't help it, the pain was excruciating. She felt totally humiliated. She prayed that he would stop.

Eventually he pulled away and she felt the pain subside. She wanted to crawl away and hide.

'That's fine. We've got what we want. How about you, Jay?'

She heard a laugh. Jay came towards her and unzipped his pants.

'Now Helen, get off the table and show me how much you love me.'

Bernard stared at Helen who sat in the car seat, bloody and shivering. Perhaps it would be better just to have her eliminated. Jay had lost control of himself as usual.

Still, they had the photographs. He would hand them to Muller in the morning, along with the blackmail note. Helen would effectively drop out of circulation. Muller would never find her, but he might find the blackmailer and the original photographs, which was what they really wanted. Bernard was pleased, in a way; he'd taken some shots of Jay abusing Helen – further material that he could use against Jay in the future.

He pulled a blanket from under the front seat and handed it to Helen. She wrapped it round herself quickly, more as an act of self-concealment than anything else, he thought. She would have to see a doctor as soon as possible. Everything Jay got involved with turned into a mess.

Helen could cause problems. Still, there was an easy way round that; he'd speak to the doctor and they could pump her full of drugs and then keep her out of the way for a while. She might still have her uses, especially for entertaining Jay and the rest of the men.

*

Two days later Major-General Deon de Wet walked into General Muller's office. He had been told to come up for a special confidential briefing.

'Come in, de Wet. Good to see you.'

Well, he thought, this is a change. The General had never before greeted him so effusively.

'General Muller, what can I do to help you?'

'It's a confidential matter. It involves one of the most important members of Johannesburg society, Jay Golden. Here, look at this.'

Deon sucked in his breath. He'd been out-manoeuvred. It was the blackmail note he'd sent to Aschaar, but the photograph was different.

'Disgusting, General Muller.'

'Yes indeed. The woman is his fiancée; you can imagine how upset he is. Now the reason I've decided to put you on to this case is that he doesn't want her involved. It's not in the normal line of police work, but I want you to find the person who sent that note. Evidently that person holds other photographs, even film of this bestial performance. We are to get that material back and sort out the blackmailer.'

'"Sort out", General Muller?'

'Just find the bastard, de Wet. I'll organise the sorting out. You'll get whatever support you need on this one. Naturally I don't think you're going to come up with anything in a hurry.'

'Any suspects, sir?'

'None so far.'

'I'll have to speak to Jay Golden.'

'Just tell me what questions you have and I'll get them answered.'

'I'll do my best, sir, but this really isn't much to go on.'

Deon left the office quickly and caught the lift down to his own floor. By sending the photograph and the blackmail note, he'd wanted to let Jay know that Sonja couldn't be threatened with impunity, but his shot had turned out to be a bit of a curved ball. He would have to play the whole thing very, very carefully.

Deon would have tried to get into the flat by the front door, but there was a guard outside. He'd had to climb up to the back balcony, and now he was crouched there in the dark, watching her through the window.

She was more attractive than he'd expected. There was no one in the room with her. She walked over to the drinks cabinet and poured herself a large Scotch. For a moment she seemed to look straight at him, then she turned and walked over to the mirror on the wall. She stared at her reflection for some time, pulling suggestive faces, then moved to a large earthenware jar in the corner of the room and tipped it over. Whatever she was looking for wasn't there.

'Fuckers.'

She said the word with a smile on her face. He could tell that she wasn't well, though he couldn't be sure exactly what they'd done to her. He'd found her relatively easily. He'd had a blow-up of her face made, as he had done with the original photograph, then he'd given it to his journalist friend Abe Solomon and told him to go snooping round the Goldcorp Group headquarters.

No one, it appeared, had ever seen this woman before, but Abe wasn't one to give up easily. He'd gone to the main bar of the President Hotel – the favourite watering-hole for Goldcorp employees. Abe had waited till late in the evening when a few of the employees were well oiled. He showed the photograph round casually. They recognised the face, but backed off. Clearly they'd been warned. A few more drinks and he got her name out of them.

Of course, Deon had found Helen's flat deserted. But a little more investigative work on Abe's part had revealed a number of properties registered in the name of Jay Golden. He had given the list to Deon and Deon had struck it lucky with the third address on the list, a small flat in the garden suburb of Rosebank.

Now Helen went over to the record player, lifted the turntable from its mounting and pulled out a plastic bag full of dagga. Then she took out some cigarette papers and rolled herself a joint. She lit up and inhaled deeply – he could smell the distinctive aroma. Immediately she became more relaxed. She lay on the settee and stared up at the ceiling.

When she had finished the dagga she got up and poured herself another Scotch. He just hoped she wasn't going to do something irrational like trying to commit suicide, because then he would have to intervene and blow his cover. She put on a record now, and began to dance by herself round the room. The effects of the dagga and the alcohol had loosened her up considerably. She seemed to be enjoying herself.

She sat down on the couch with her legs drawn up against her breasts and stared at the opposite wall. He wondered if they had deliberately taken most of her clothes away, for she was dressed only in underwear. After about fifteen minutes she got up, poured herself yet another Scotch and started to dance round the room more and more erotically. Then she began to take off her underclothes as if she was stripping before an audience, thrusting her pelvis forward aggressively. Her face was covered in a cold sweat.

She pulled her handbag from the side-table and rummaged inside it. Finding what she wanted, she flung the bag into a corner of the room, apparently deaf to the sound of breaking glass as it knocked a vase over. In her hand was a vibrator which she stabbed inside herself repeatedly with a look of savage pleasure on her face. He was sure she must be hurting herself, and now he could hear the words she was screaming.

'Fuck me. Come fuck me. I don't give a fuck. Johnny, fuck me. Come on, Sidney, and how about you, Jay? I like it, give it to me.'

Then she collapsed on the floor, crying with despair. She flung the vibrator away from her and clutched at her sides, her face a hideous mask.

Then she rose and staggered towards the bathroom door – and as she turned he caught his breath, because now he could see her back was a mass of terrible red scars.

Deon let himself down from the balcony and onto the lower roof of the block of flats. He waited for his breathing to return to normal. What was he going to do? What he really wanted to do was to get his riot shotgun from his car and exact his revenge on the man guarding the doorway then and there.

There was a noise beneath him and he froze. Someone was banging on the door of the flat. He pulled himself to the edge of the roof and looked over. Frustratingly, he could see the top of the door but not the person banging on it.

The door was opened, obviously by Helen, and her visitor went inside. Deon edged across to the square opening that looked down to the windows of the bathroom, toilets and kitchen of each flat. The voices from inside Helen's flat echoed up to him.

'Can't you leave me alone, Johnny?'

'You can't have enough of it, can you, you bitch.'

'No, Johnny . . .'

Deon could hear her struggling, and then quite clearly the sound of a whip.

'Johnny, please . . .'

Then there was silence and he wondered if the bastard had killed her. Eventually he heard Johnny's voice again.

'You'd better bloody learn quick, Helen. The boss has been good to you. With what you know, you're lucky to be alive. You listen good. You behave yourself and you'll get better. Cooperate, and we'll make sure you're well looked after.'

'I'm sorry, Johnny.'

'Yeah, Helen, I think we're going to have a lot of good times, you and I.'

Johnny's laugh echoed up and down the hollow ventilation shaft. In the dark the whites of Deon's knuckles stood out like small moons against the black surface of the roof.

Johnny moved casually down the street in the darkness. He'd parked some four blocks away, just to make sure that no one followed him to and from the flat. That was what Mr Aschaar had said he must do. Sidney had come to relieve him at nine o'clock. He actually wished he could have spent the night with Helen, but orders were orders. He knew better than to disobey Mr Aschaar's commands.

God, but she had an amazing body. He could feel himself getting hard just thinking about it. Perhaps he shouldn't have been so rough with her, but she made him lose control.

He knew that Mr Aschaar wouldn't be seeing much of her now; he might even sell her to some Arab. Hell, she was pumped so full of drugs it was a wonder she could string a sentence together.

Now he was getting jumpy – he must be imagining things. Who would be following him down the road in Rosebank? It wasn't the sort of area where people followed you, far too posh.

He dropped back into a hedgerow instinctively and slid the knuckle-duster onto his left hand. Have to teach this jerk a lesson, he thought to himself. The man's shadow fell across the hedge and Johnny braced himself to deliver the first blow.

His fist sailed upwards, but was expertly deflected, and he felt himself being lifted upwards.

'Sorry mate, didn't see you.' He blurted out the words, trying to assess the stature of his attacker. He didn't have a chance: he was forced bodily through the hedge and into an area on the other side filled with garbage bins. A leather-gloved hand gripped his left wrist and then the other one came up under his left elbow. The joint cracked and he screamed.

Johnny's face was forced into a garbage can and he felt his mouth fill up with a foul-smelling liquid as he gasped for air. For a moment he thought his attacker had finished with him. Then he received a blow to his groin that travelled up as far as his stomach.

He staggered backwards. Another blow hit him on the side, breaking some of his ribs. Then his jacket was torn upwards and he was thrown face-first into the dirt.

'Please, I don't deserve this . . .'

He could see the long hair of the woman in his bedroom through the open door of his study . . . He would sort out this person who was playing games on his private line. Again there was a clicking sound in the receiver when he answered the phone. Then there was another click and the line became clear. He could hear a man breathing deeply on the other end of the line.

'Who's that?'

'Johnny.'

'God, you're going to be sorry you phoned me here.'

'Mr Aschaar, I'm gonna die. Someone followed me from Helen's flat. I've got to see a fucking doctor, for God's sake help me.'

'Where are you?'

'In a phone booth, on the corner next to the Rosebank library.'

'OK. Hide yourself nearby. A car will pick you up.'

He slammed the phone down. The man was supposed to be a pro and he'd got himself hurt. Bernard had no respect for incompetence. He picked up the phone and quickly dialled another number.

'Goliath Collections.'

'Jake, this is your uncle. Corner next to Rosebank library, a phone booth. The victim – Johnny – should be nearby. Find out his story, then phone me back.'

'Is the victim to be preserved?'

'No.'

'Understood, sir.'

Bernard put the phone down and walked back into the bedroom.

'Business, Bernard darling?'

'Just a minor irritation.'

'Oh Bernard, forget about that and come over here. Mmm, you've got such strong hands. I hope your little irritation hasn't upset you?'

'No, not at all. I've just decided to scratch it. Always makes me feel better.'

Bernard Aschaar had one ambition: to gain control of the Goldcorp Group. There was only one problem – he was not Max Golden's son. Consequently, one of Bernard's main occupations was boosting Jay Golden's ego, while quietly building up enough evidence to destroy the young Golden completely when the time was ripe.

The next stage in Bernard's master plan to control Goldcorp centred around the forthcoming meeting of the Central Merchandising Consortium. Max Golden had promised Jay that he would hand over the company once Jay became president of the CMC. Bernard knew the incumbent president, Tony Rudd, was about to stand down. In fact, Bernard had arranged to buy Rudd's entire mining group for Goldcorp and thus further strengthen the company's domination of the South African mining industry.

There were three characteristics that chiefly distinguished the Central Merchandising Consortium: exclusivity, secrecy, and influence. Though its members were not permitted to enter certain countries with strong anti-monopoly legislation, such as the United States, sooner or later every government that counted dealt with them – openly or otherwise. Admission to the London headquarters of the CMC was a complicated affair, especially for non-members. They would generally be referred to another building further down the road, their photograph having been taken without their knowledge. A man could truly be said to have made it in the mining industry when he could walk up the steps of the CMC and pass through the doors without being stopped by one of the discreet but firm security guards. And he only retained his membership as long as he held strictly to the Consortium's unwritten rules. Discretion and secrecy were paramount. Many of the members were sworn enemies, but the Central Mining Consortium, with its incredible powers, held them together.

It was known that all the members met twice every year, once in London and once in Kimberley. These meetings were rumoured to dictate the price of gold and world interest rates. To these men, the situation in South Africa was of more than passing importance; a revolution at the right time could create incredible fortunes; at the wrong time it would result in terrifying losses. Several members of the CMC were said to have more power than the South African Prime Minister . . .

The big doors with the gold metal surrounds swung open as Bernard Aschaar walked up the steps toward the entrance of the CMC. Slightly behind him followed Jay Golden, heir to one of the world's greatest fortunes and a gold mining empire. Jay had been admitted to the CMC two years before and had already proved that he had inherited the family flair for business. Only a handful of members realised that it was not Jay but Bernard Aschaar, Max Golden's trusted friend, who was the new genius at Goldcorp.

What everyone did know, however, was that over the past few years the influence of the Goldcorp empire in the CMC had been increasing, and that by buying out more and more of the smaller, privately-owned gold mines across the world, they had strengthened their position. If the Goldcorp Group continued its dynamic growth over the next few years, there was no doubt in the minds of many that Jay Golden would become the first man ever to have total control over the CMC.

The meeting that would take place today would show just how close Goldcorp was to assuming that control. It would also show whether Jay Golden had sufficient capital to buy out the other mining companies he needed to gain over fifty per cent voting control of the CMC.

However, unbeknown to both Jay and Bernard, a special meeting had been urgently called a day before. Several members of the CMC were terrified of what might happen if Goldcorp did gain control. Moves had been made to prevent Goldcorp buying up stock in any more mining houses, but the issue was complicated by the divisions that existed between the other members. Tony Rudd, who owned one of the older mining companies, was intent on getting out of the business and wanted to sell. Unfortunately none of the other members at the meeting had sufficient funds to buy him out – but they all knew that Goldcorp did.

After an hour of wrangling, Sonja Seyton-Waugh, head of the Waugh Mining Company, took the floor. She was the only woman in the room and ten years younger than any of the men – but not one of them was in any doubt about her formidable business skills, especially when it came to the mining industry. She addressed Tony Rudd, a squat bulldog of a man, over sixty years old.

'I don't know why you're doing this, Tony. Your grandfather, Jason Rudd, arrived on the goldfields without a cent in his pocket. He wheeled and dealed like the rest of us – he went bankrupt three times. Jason Rudd believed in free enterprise. He was a founder member of the CMC and he foresaw what is happening today. You sell out to Goldcorp, Tony, and you betray everything your grandfather stood for.'

Sonja saw that Tony was going red in the face and decided that she had said enough. At last she had had the courage to do what she had wanted to do for year. Deon had given her the confidence to fly in the face of Aschaar's blackmail tactics.

Tony stood up to address the table.

'Goddamit, Sonja, you with your fancy words, you make me sound like a hardened criminal. You know my problems; my one son was killed in a university rugby match, the other's a bloody drug addict. There's no one to take over my mines when I go, and I want some peace in my old age. I'm not handing over control, I'm selling. Goldcorp has offered me fifty per cent above the market value of my mines.'

Sonja Seyton-Waugh turned pale. She knew that they'd stepped up their offer, but by fifty per cent, that was crazy! Their capital reserves must be terrifying. She turned and looked up at the oil painting of Jason Rudd that hung on the wall – a handsome man, bearing hardly any resemblance to his mean-looking grandson.

'You've had a very good life, Tony. We're all very sorry about what happened to Tom, but it was a long time ago. As for

Robard, he could still come right. Everyone knows he's a renegade. Self-pity doesn't sit easily on you, Tony; feel lucky your son didn't turn out to be like Jay Golden.'

Everyone was staring at her now. Her hatred of Jay Golden was legendary. Rumour had it that they'd been lovers and he'd dropped her like a lead balloon.

'Jay Golden, like Bernard Aschaar, is amoral and ruthless. He doesn't give a damn. He'll bring down the South African government and finance a bloody revolution, then he'll flood the market with gold, depress the prices and destroy the rest of us. After that he'll create a scarcity and send the gold price through the roof. He'll become one of the most powerful men of this century, along with Bernard Aschaar. Do you want to die knowing you made all that possible, Tony? For heaven's sake, if you sell your mines to Goldcorp they'll have seventy-five per cent control of the Far East Rand goldfields – and then there are their other goldmines, their Russian interests, Australia . . . Give me two years, Tony. Then I'll make you a decent offer for your mines, and so will many of the people in this room.'

Tony got up and stormed out of the room. For a moment no one said a word, then they all began to rise. Sonja held up her hand.

'Wait. I know Tony Rudd. He'll come back in here with an answer. He always does, he's a gentleman at heart.'

The way she said the word 'gentleman' seemed to imply that if any one of them left the room he certainly wasn't worthy of that title. They all sat watching the wall clock, knowing that if Tony Rudd sold out they would be finished – and not just financially. They were all men who made their living out of gold, it was a way of life to them. Take it away, and they would be nothing.

The door swung open and they all turned as Tony Rudd walked back into the room, still as angry as when he had left.

'You win, damn you. I won't sell for two years, that I promise. But when those two years are up, on that day I sell to the highest bidder.'

There was muffled applause from the table, but it stopped when Tony Rudd held up his hand.

'Don't thank me, thank Sonja Seyton-Waugh. I'm doing this for her, not for any of you. And I'm not doing it for the memory of my grandfather, either. This business is people and Sonja's one of the best. Just make sure you keep her ahead of Jay Golden for chairmanship of the committee. As I'm sure you all know, this is my last year.'

Tony Rudd smiled at Sonja and she beamed with satisfaction, then stood up to rousing applause.

'Gentlemen, Mr Rudd has given us a chance, and we must capitalise on it. This meeting is over. Let us make sure that no one outside this room ever knows it took place . . .'

At precisely 11 a.m. the following day, the official meeting of the members of the CMC took place. The doors of the main boardroom were closed and two armed guards stood outside. As it happened, the meeting turned out to be a relatively short one and ended just after two. The guards had noticed nothing particularly unusual happening inside the boardroom, just the usual bouts of shouting and table-banging.

Two members of the CMC left the meeting looking more irritated than usual – in fact they appeared to be purple with rage. They charged through the doors, down the steps and into a waiting Rolls-Royce without bothering to say goodbye to anyone.

'The first meeting we go to without the old man and it's a complete fuck-up. They were ready for us.' Jay was shaking with rage, he had wanted to attack Sonja Seyton-Waugh physically. 'I can tell you, Bernard, when we have control they'll suffer for this. Especially that bitch.'

'She hates you with good cause. Don't ever forget that.' Older and more experienced, Bernard had suppressed his anger in the meeting, and Jay's hot-headed behaviour had annoyed him; it reflected badly on the Goldcorp Group. In his pocket was an envelope that had been pushed into his hand by Tony Rudd as he left the meeting. He was confident about its contents and this considerably helped him to relax. The price had been high, but worth it.

'In six months' time, at the Kimberley meeting, we'll have them eating out of the palms of our hands, Jay. We'll have more power than all of them put together. We'll contest Sonja Seyton-Waugh's presidency and you'll be elected in her place. I'll make sure that your father is present at that meeting. It'll be your crowning glory.'

Short-lived glory, thought Bernard with a private sneer. He

reached into his pocket and took out Rudd's envelope. He opened it slowly, relishing the satisfaction its contents gave him.

'Do you want to hear the best piece of news in the history of the Goldcorp Group, Jay?' Bernard held up the letter, embossed with the Rudd group crest.

'Is that the agreement from Rudd to sell?'

'Yes. Rudd told me he would give us his acceptance after today's meeting. We offered him more than fifty per cent of what he's worth, no one else could have done that, and he knows it.'

'Let me read it.'

Jay read slowly. Bernard noticed his breathing change. 'Jesus. Do you think the fucker's finally found out that we've been pumping his son full of drugs for the past five years!'

Bernard tore the letter out of Jay's trembling hands. He read it for himself: an outright refusal to sell. No, Tony Rudd couldn't have known that they'd been supplying his son Robard with drugs; the connections they'd used had been the very best, and only a genius could have traced the payments back to Goldcorp. Bernard knew how desperate Rudd had been to sell. What in hell could have changed his mind?

The letter explained that Rudd would sell in two years' time to the highest bidder. That was bad news. By that time the gold price could have rocketed, and Rudd Exploration Company shares along with it. Bernard knew the Rudd Company owned important mining rights that they had not exploited on the Far East Rand; Tony Rudd didn't fully appreciate the value of these options, and he didn't have enormous research facilities at his disposal, like Goldcorp. If he had, he would have known that those options were worth more than all his existing mines put together . . . But in two years' time Tony Rudd probably *would* know. Then he would never sell for the price they were offering now.

Bernard felt the bitterness in his stomach. He had put years of work into this deal – years ensuring that Tony Rudd did not have an heir.

They had moved in on Robard Rudd stealthily. He had been a typical spoilt young man, with too much money and not enough wisdom. They discovered that he lived in a luxurious Paris apartment with a girlfriend, and the girlfriend had proved cooperative. It hadn't taken long. In fact after a short time the operation had actually become self-financing, for the moment Robard became a heroin addict he started to pay enormous amounts of money for the drug he craved. Fortunately he went overboard faster than they anticipated, and even the expensive clinics Tony had sent him to had not been able to cure him. If they wanted to, they could kill him now, in less than a week. Bernard knew he must resist the temptation to kill Robard off as revenge for Tony's having held up the deal. It would be a dangerous coincidence – and it could get both Bernard and Jay into big trouble with Max Golden.

Right now, Bernard had other problems to solve, and one was sitting right next to him.

'Jay, you know what happens if you don't become chairman of the CMC in the next two years?'

'Only too well. My father won't pass the Goldcorp Group into my hands because I'll have failed the test he set me. My step-brother Ludwig will get control.'

This scenario was familiar to Bernard. Ludwig Golden was the product of Max Golden's second marriage to Laura. As his first wife, Jay's mother, lay dying, he had promised that the company would go to her son – but Max Golden was no fool, and he had added a proviso that her son should prove worthy of the task. Ludwig Golden, the son of his second marriage, was a self-made multi-millionaire at the age of twenty-eight. Bernard knew that if Ludwig took over the Goldcorp Group, he, Bernard Aschaar, was finished.

'As I see it, we have only one option remaining to us.'

'To acquire Sonja Seyton-Waugh's Waugh Mining?'

'Exactly. To force that bitch to sell out to us. We could do it. The only problem is that she seems to be resisting our blackmail campaign. If she's the one who's got her hands on those photographs, she might be tempted to nail you – she could put you away with that evidence. Provided she had the guts to use it, of course. She'd never admit to the public what you did to her. We know she's never told anyone about it. I think we can deal our ace.'

'Our ace?'

'The other photographs we took that night, Jay. The ones where you forced her to pose on her own.'

'I'd forgotten about them!'

'They weren't stolen from the safe, they were in another file.

146

We could suggest she sell, or that we'll send a couple of glossy prints to *Lord*.'

Jay laughed, and Bernard began to relax again. The plan could work. *Lord* was a man's magazine that revelled in getting wealthy and famous women to take their clothes off.

'Bernard, you're a genius. But first we have to get the other film and photos back. We can't go ahead till we've got those.'

'We proceed as follows. Through our other companies we buy aggressively into the stock of all the companies and mines belonging to Waugh Mining. Finance won't be a problem, we can use the funds we had earmarked for the Rudd acquisition.

'When we get the film and pictures back, we use a third party to blackmail Sonja Seyton-Waugh, and she hands over ten per cent of her fifty-one per cent controlling stock. She won't know it's us, and she won't know that we've bought up all her other stock. Then we move in and fire her as chairwoman, and install you in her place.'

'Bernard, you're a genius.'

The atmosphere was electric. The intimidating power emanated from a single source, the silver-haired man whose head rested on the white desk top, as if he had suddenly fallen asleep.

Bernard and Jay sat facing the desk, a discreet distance away. Looking down through the window they could see the mine dumps, and queues of cars heading through the early morning sunshine, towards the centre of Johannesburg. Neither of them spoke, for that was the unwritten rule.

An immaculately dressed butler came into the room and served them all coffee. He didn't have to ask who wanted what because he had known each of the men for so long. That was why he was paid more than many company directors – his life had been dedicated to the service of the man whose head lay on the desk, in the enormous top-floor office suite of the Goldcorp Group.

Having put down the paper-thin white porcelain cups, the butler left the room as quietly as he had entered. Just as he was about to disappear through the door he heard the familiar voice of his employer.

'Thank you, Raleigh. We are not to be interrupted on any account.'

'Very good, sir.'

147

The butler closed the door behind him and wondered, not for the first time, if his employer was psychic. It had become a sort of game between them both: Raleigh would often come into the office to adjust a piece of furniture, tidy up or deliver some correspondence, while his master was asleep – but he had never yet been able to leave the room undetected, and he could swear that he had never seen the man open his eyes.

The silver grey locks rose up from the desk and for a brief moment Jay and Bernard glimpsed the face beneath them before Max Golden got up and walked over to the giant plate-glass window. Sunlight caught the side of his heavily lined face. People said that Max Golden was Jewish, but that was only part of the truth. His ancestors had been Cossacks and had ridden in the Czar's cavalry; he himself still rode every day – his only relaxation. The two men seated behind him admired the straightness of his back, the ease with which he moved, even though he was over seventy.

Without warning he turned to face them. His brilliant blue eyes surveyed them cursorily, reading their feelings exactly.

'My decision is not negotiable. It was reached because of your singular incompetence, Jay, and nothing that has happened since – least of all the events of the last couple of days – has persuaded me that my original assessment of you was inaccurate.'

He walked back to the table, sat on its edge and stared down stonily at his son.

'You have failed me. That meeting was your chance. Mistakenly, I thought you could handle it – I will not ask you why you neglected to tie up all the details. Obviously there was a secret meeting of the other members beforehand, and your move was blocked. Why were you not aware of this meeting? It was an obvious blocking move – you should have suspected it, taken precautions against it. There was nothing in your mother that indicated failure, she never compromised, not even in death. I cannot believe that you are my son.

'So now you have just two years left before Ludwig takes control of the group – and twenty-four months from this day to undo what you have done so far. Bernard has outlined the details of your strategy. A good plan, but one that will take nerve and intelligence to carry out.'

There was a moment of silence while Jay summoned up enough courage to address his father.

'What will happen to me if Ludwig takes over, sir?'

'If I were Ludwig I would have you fired immediately. You will receive no support from me after that. You must find your own way.'

Jay went red in the face. He could not understand his father sometimes. The man had the ability to cut himself off from any emotion, to fill his heart with ice.

'And if I were you, Bernard, I would begin separating yourself from Jay and consider offering your services to Ludwig. That's if you're thinking of survival.'

Max Golden moved easily back to his desk. He sat down behind it and stared at Jay coldly.

'A word of warning to you. Ruthlessness is the only way to succeed – but you must remember that to enjoy ruthlessness is death. You must aim only for success. You see, when you enjoy doing something, you get careless. You make mistakes.'

He got up again and stared out of the window. The two were unsure if the meeting was now over.

'Father, how was I to know they would fix the meeting?'

'Shut up and get out. And don't call me father, it's an insult. Get out, Jay, before I throw you out.'

Max Golden did not turn round till both Jay and Bernard had left the room. Then he sat down again at his desk and pulled out a large file. He smiled. Jay and Bernard – nothing like playing both ends against the middle! It was fun to watch the manoeuvering as each tried to score over the other, fun to twitch the threads and watch them dance. Jay would put up a good fight, but he'd bet on Bernard Aschaar any day of the week – the man was as clever as a cartload of monkeys. How could they ever believe he would hand the company over to Ludwig!

The forest was very beautiful. She could not remember ever having been in a forest of trees that were so full and green – but then she had never been to England before. She walked barefoot in the cool, early morning dew and felt as if an immense burden had been lifted from her shoulders. The people at the clinic only wanted her to be happy, to recover.

For the first few days she had been suicidal. She'd tried to slash her wrists because they wouldn't give her the drug she craved, and they'd had to bind her down. That period had passed as dramatically as it had come, and now she was a child again – except for some memories that she tried to tuck into a far corner of her mind. She did not think of men at all. That would come later, but she was in no hurry for she knew that with the first physical contact there would come fear.

She would have a visitor, they had said, a beautiful woman like herself. Someone very understanding, a good friend.

She knew her relaxed state was because of the pills. The doctor had gone to great pains to explain to her the withdrawal symptoms and the need to recover as quickly as possible. She often asked them about the man who had rescued her from the flat, the man who had held Sidney against the wall and slowly broken his ribs while she screamed. They always looked at her blankly and said they didn't know about that, but she knew that she should thank this man who had rescued her, and that he wasn't a figment of her imagination.

She dreamed very often, more than she had ever done before. A long dark river appeared again and again in her dreams; she would be lying by the bank and a tall man with dark blond hair in a brilliant white suit would come along in a boat. She would get into it with him and they would smile at each other. With him there was always great peace, and his strong arms would move the oars effortlessly through the deep green waters.

Last night in the dream, the boat had turned over when they saw a friend, and he jumped into the river when they fell in the water. This man swam out to her and took her gently to the river bank. Then he went to find the man in the white suit but he had been swept away. This man then returned to the bank and wept on her shoulder. She felt removed from him, she wanted the man in the white suit to return, for she couldn't believe that he had disappeared beneath the dark green waters . . .

The woman she was waiting for appeared by one of the oak trees and waved to her. She ran over, and was surprised by the woman's incredible beauty. The woman kissed her gently on the cheek and took her hand. Though she was very beautiful, she talked in a voice that hinted at great power and authority.

'Helen. I've wanted to meet you for so long. I know what you've been through.'

Helen drew back. She did not want the memories to be unlocked from the corner of her mind where she was keeping them.

'I'm sorry, I didn't mean to scare you, Helen. My name is Sonja. You can stay here for as long as you like. I want you to get fit and strong again.'

Sonja was torn by a terrible dilemma. Helen must have information that could be used as evidence against Jay and Bernard, but Sonja knew that Jay had almost destroyed Helen, and that any questions at this stage would push Helen back towards the abyss of madness. She would have to be patient; the doctor had told her of the risks and warned her against proceeding too quickly. First Sonja would have to establish a bond between herself and Helen. The doctor said that once that feeling of trust had been established, it would actually be good for Helen to talk about her experience; if she didn't talk about it, he warned, she might retreat inside herself for ever. There was hope, but she was hanging onto sanity by a slender thread. One wrong move and the umbilical cord with reality would be severed for ever.

The discussion with the doctor had fuelled Sonja's hatred for the Goldcorp Group. How many lives had these ruthless men ruined? How many countries would they destroy in their maniacal quest for absolute power? Money they had aplenty, but it was nothing to them. They had to have power. She was determined to smash that power, to humiliate them as they had humiliated her and Helen and countless others.

She continually thought about Deon de Wet, the policeman who had come into her life so unexpectedly and given her renewed courage. There was something about him that stirred her soul. Beneath this man's rugged exterior she was aware of a sensitivity, a basic goodness that she had rarely encountered in any man. There was something deeply reassuring about him. She wanted to see him again, soon.

Deon and Bernard

Dr Jerry Odendal got the call just as he returned home from an evening out with his wife. He had had the usual two bottles of wine to drink and was feeling very pleased with life. At fifty years of age he really had nothing to complain about; since his appointment as district surgeon some twenty years earlier he had made a steady, easy living, and apart from the examination of rape victims, his job was pleasant and undemanding.

When the phone rang, he decided to ignore it – if they wanted a doctor to do a blood test on a drunken driver at this time of night, they could find someone else. But the phone did not give up ringing and his wife insisted that he answer the call. He felt thoroughly irritated. All he wanted to do was sleep.

'Jerry, it's General Piet Muller here. I need you down at the station urgently.'

'Bloody hell, Piet, it's after one. Can't it wait till the morning?'

'Someone's died in detention.'

'So, get Travis, he's really keen.'

'Jerry, this is a difficult situation. I don't need Travis around, he's another of those bloody liberals. I want you on this.'

'All right, I'll be over in about fifteen minutes.'

He slammed the phone down, glared at his wife and walked out of the house to his car. He was in General Muller's debt and now the payment was due.

The main police station was a blaze of lights when he got there, and he wondered how much of the taxpayers' money went on the electricity used in government buildings. The young man at the charge desk gave him a surly look and carried on paging through a magazine full of photographs of scantily clad women.

152

Dr Odendal coughed loudly to get some attention and was again ignored.

'Get me General Muller or I'll make sure he gets to hear about your attitude.'

The young man was on his feet in seconds and staring earnestly into his face with dumb grey-blue eyes. 'Sorry, sir, who shall I say it is?'

'Dr Odendal.'

The young man dialled a number on the telephone and there followed a very terse conversation.

'Sir, if you could make your way to the lifts, General Muller will be waiting for you on the sixth floor.'

The lift arrived on the sixth floor without stopping and Dr Odendal looked straight into General Muller's eyes as the doors opened. Something was seriously wrong – he looked haggard, and the usual aura of confidence was missing.

'I think it would be best if we went to my office. I hope you've brought whatever you need for an examination with you?'

'Of course. Are you all right?'

'I'll be fine once we've got this mess sorted out.'

General Muller's office was spartan, and dominated by the South African flag which hung from a pole in one corner. The doctor did not like flags indoors, he felt they signified bad luck, like an open umbrella. He seated himself on one of the uncomfortable chairs next to the desk. The General sat down too, and pulled out a bottle of whisky from one of the desk drawers. Dr Odendal declined the offer of a drink since he was already concerned about how much alcohol he had consumed that evening, but the General poured himself a very generous glassful. After taking a hefty slug he put his arms behind his head and stared at the doctor.

'We live in troubled times, Jerry. The pressure on this country gets greater every day, and we fight a hard war trying to keep communist elements out of our fair land. A day ago we brought in a suspected communist sympathiser for questioning, a routine inquiry. Now, unfortunately, I have a problem on my hands. The man has died in his cell, the fool fell over and the fall killed him. You can imagine my difficulty. You remember the lies that were spread around a few years ago about suspects jumping from the windows in this building – malicious lies concocted by our enemies in the press? Well, I have reason to believe that these people will try to get mileage out of this man who's died in detention. So I want you to examine his body and get the facts straight.'

Dr Odendal felt himself shaking. The price Muller was asking was high, perhaps too high. True, the General had helped him get off a negligence charge that could have wrecked his private practice, and he had also got him his present job . . . He understood in an instant what it was the General wanted of him.

'And if I find evidence that the man did not die from the fall? That he might have died from some other cause?'

'You won't find such evidence.'

'And if there's a coroner's enquiry?'

'There will be no coroner's enquiry, I guarantee you. But there is an additional problem. I have an adversary, a man who could jeopardise my future, and he's downstairs now, looking after – I mean, watching over – the body of the man I want you to examine. He will ask you questions and you must give him the correct answers. He'll say things have happened to this man, even though you and I know it isn't true. You must convince him that he is mistaken.'

'What if he doesn't believe me?'

'You owe me, Jerry. He will believe you, I've seen you in action. If any man can do it, you can. Just don't mention to him that you know me. But I want you to note whatever he says about me. I want to know.'

'Piet, I just don't know about this.'

'Those charges against you, I had them dropped. They can be brought up again, you could lose your job, your pension. Your son could be found in possession of Mandrax tablets, your daughter could be found to have communist literature. You've got no choice, Jerry. Ask for basement three, cell number sixteen. And if you mess up, forget you had a future.'

Dr Odendal made his way to the lift, thinking hard. Even though it might not be necessary, he would conduct an immediate autopsy. That way, he could destroy any incriminating evidence and no one would be able to figure out what had happened. If what Piet had said was right, he had nothing to lose.

The lift arrived at ground-floor level and he crossed the foyer to the lift that would take him down to the cells. As usual he was confronted by an armed police guard and he flashed his district surgeon's pass at him peremptorily.

The moment he got into the lift he started to breathe deeply in order to relax himself for the coming ordeal. The lift arrived at the corridor leading onto the cells, and he found the stillness faintly disturbing. It was as if everyone had vanished. He wanted to be away from this place and back in the warm comfort of his bed, snuggling up close to his wife. As he walked towards the cell he felt like a man moving towards his own execution. He was about to walk into basement three when an enormous man stepped out, towering over him.

'Are you the doctor?'

'Yes. You are Major-General de Wet?'

The man appeared to miss his question. 'About bloody time too. It's been half an hour since I called for you. Have you seen anyone here?'

'No. I came straight to the cells.'

'How did you know which cell to go to?'

'I asked the officer on guard.'

'Fine. Let's get on with it, then.'

De Wet smiled grimly to himself. So, the bastard was lying. The officer on guard duty had no idea who was in which cell, the doctor must have spoken to General Muller. Perhaps he was one of Muller's cronies – he would see soon enough. De Wet had carefully studied the techniques of medical examination many times – he never felt he could take anyone for granted, there were always slip-ups that cost lives and convictions. This evening, his diligence was to be rewarded.

'I'll have to conduct an autopsy.'

De Wet did not reply. He watched the doctor studying the dead man's skull. He could see that the doctor knew exactly what had happened to this prisoner.

The dead man was black, about five foot ten tall, well-built, with close-cropped black hair and a pencil-line moustache. Dr Odendal winced as he saw the line of cigarette burns down the man's left arm; both wrists were bloody from where the manacles had been tightened. But the worst thing was the side of the man's head which had been smashed in. Dr Odendal guessed that they had beaten the man up with a pickaxe handle, a

155

favourite method of interrogation. Reluctantly he turned up to face the Major-General.

'Major-General de Wet, we'll have to get a stretcher and take him to the state mortuary. Could you arrange that for me, please?'

Deon stood looking at the doctor, who clearly had no idea that his story hadn't worked. Deon had already decided he was going to see this thing through to the end. One of his junior officers had told him he'd heard screams coming from the cells – Muller had been careless, leaving the door open while he and his cronies worked the prisoner over. When Deon arrived, the cell door had been locked and he'd had to get the key. Inside he'd found the dead body. And Muller had told him there had been an accident.

Deon listened sceptically as Dr Odendal pressed his point. 'I'm sorry, Major-General de Wet, but he must be taken there very quickly. A body decomposes rapidly after death.'

De Wet sat down on the floor in the corner of the cell, his knees almost obscuring his face. He saw the puzzled reaction on the doctor's face and waited.

'Are you all right, Major-General?'

'I'm perfectly well, doctor. Would you mind sitting down, I think we should talk.'

'This is no time for flippancy. I insist that the body is moved to the mortuary. I will talk with you later.'

'Doctor, which university did you study at for your doctor's degree?'

'I cannot see that this is an appropriate time to question my ability. Pretoria, if you must know.'

'Yes. That is a fine university. I'm not questioning your ability, doctor, rather your judgement.'

'How dare you!'

'You must have taken the Hippocratic Oath. It is a very solemn oath, I wish we had something of similar standing in the police force. I ask you, is it the correct procedure to conduct an autopsy on this body?'

'Yes.'

'And you say there's no evidence that this man has been physically assaulted?'

'No, he has not. I would imagine that there may be a tumour on his brain which may well have contributed to his death. That

156

is the reason why I must conduct the autopsy. Now, if you please, Major-General de Wet . . .'

Deon noted that the doctor was still steady though there were beads of perspiration running down his forehead. He started when he heard the footsteps coming down the corridor, then Deon could see his shoulders relaxing; it was as if he were trying not to appear scared. The footsteps approached the door of the cell.

'Good evening, Dr Travis. It seems I called you out unnecessarily, Dr Odendal has beaten you to it.'

Dr Odendal was now crouched over the prisoner's body and visibly shaking.

'Good evening, Dr Odendal. I'll be on my way, then.'

Deon could see Dr Odendal was looking relieved as Dr Travis said this. 'Well, Dr Travis,' he said casually, 'you might as well give us a second opinion, just for the record.'

'No, Major-General de Wet, professionally it's not necessary for a case like this. Dr Odendal is far better qualified than I am.'

De Wet admired the young doctor's tact, he wished he could have instilled a little more of it into his own junior officers. He said, 'So you would agree with having an autopsy?'

'But it's obvious what's happened! Er, I mean, I'm not sure . . .'

'Well, Dr Travis, I suggest you drop your professional ethics and have a look for yourself.'

De Wet pulled Dr Odendal away from the body and saw the horrified look on Dr Travis's face. He watched his face harden; Travis had only been doing this job for six months, out of interest, before taking up a lecturing post at the university medical school. Bending down over the body, in a few seconds his professionalism took over.

'So, Major-General, you want me to examine your handiwork?'

'Not mine, Dr Travis. Dr Odendal is of the opinion that this man fell off his chair and died.'

'That is ridiculous. You must know that. This man has been beaten to death. I've never seen someone so savagely beaten!'

'Thank you, doctor. You will now make your report, and you will deliver it to me and no one else. You will most probably have to contest Dr Odendal's opinion in court. I have no doubt that you will tell the truth as I can see you are a man of conviction. Should anything happen to me within the next few weeks, I hope you will have the courage to pursue the matter on your own. This man died under interrogation, and I'm going to make sure that the men who killed him are brought to justice. Dr Travis, I want you to take this body to the morgue and make bloody sure no one tampers with it.'

Dr Travis looked at Major-General de Wet. He knew what courage it must take to do what this man was doing, and he would stand by him whatever the consequences. He turned to Dr Odendal who was crying, shaking with emotion. 'He forced me to do it! Muller said he'd destroy me!'

'Dr Odendal. I will make sure you are struck off the roll.'

A few hours later the body was placed in a refrigerated box in the Johannesburg mortuary. It was to stay there for a long time, and the name of the dead man would appear in newspaper headlines across the world, above wildly conflicting reports of what had happened to him. His death would affect the lives of three people immeasurably.

Deon did not go home that evening. After phoning Teresa he wrote his report on the incident, working and reworking his account of how he had found the prisoner and what had happened afterwards. He knew what would happen when he submitted the report: the spotlight would fall upon him and everything would be done to try to discredit his statement. Driving home late the next day, he realized his career was in serious jeopardy.

The moment Deon got home he realised that something was wrong. Everything looked too tidy – the kids usually left things lying all over the place and Teresa only ever cleared up in the morning.

He noticed these things because of a lifetime's career of searching for tiny clues that would lead to larger conclusions. He walked into the lounge and almost stepped backwards when he saw Teresa sitting on the rocking-chair, rocking backwards and forwards, staring at him.

'You lousy, cheating bastard! Is this what I get for being loyal, for having loved you, for caring for you? I'd like you to tell me it's not true, except that there's just too much evidence for you to argue against.'

He walked straight up to her and tried to take her in his arms. She slapped his face viciously and he felt the blood running down his nose.

'Where are the children, Teresa?'

'At my mother's, where they'll be staying while we arrange a divorce. You don't deserve them, you've betrayed them. Thank God, at least I've got a few friends who'll stand by me. Now it all makes sense. When you rang last night and told me what you were doing, I was so proud of you – then General Muller came round and had the decency to explain what you were really up to.'

'Muller?'

'He showed me those disgusting pictures you keep in your office, you pervert. You disgust me. General Muller told me the whole story; how he found out about your taste for whores, and he told you to behave yourself; how he threatened to tell me if you didn't stop beating up black women – and then you tried to blackmail him with that trumped up story of police brutality. God, Deon, how low can you get?'

'That's all a pack of lies, Teresa. How the hell can you believe him?'

'I can believe photographs, Deon. Photographs don't lie. Muller says you're just like your father, he told me all about him. He says he was corrupt too.'

Deon went white. How could she believe him capable of these things? How could she speak like that of his father, a man she had never known?

Teresa picked up a vase from the fireplace and threw it at him. He ducked, and it sailed past his head through the window. Her face was ugly with anger, he knew he could not reach her. Muller had played his ace, and how cleverly he had used it.

'Get out of this house, Deon. Your clothes are all packed – go and sleep with one of your sluts. And don't come back. I don't want to hear any more of your disgusting lies!'

'Teresa, it's not true. I can't believe this is happening to us.'

'Get out, you pig.'

Deon walked out of the room, picked up the two suitcases from their bedroom and took them out to the battered old Mercedes. As he was packing them into the boot Teresa came out of the front door. He turned; she must have seen sense at

159

last, have realised that Muller had been lying. He began to smile.

'And if I've got some foul disease from you, I'll make sure you pay dearly for it. Don't think I'm going to keep quiet about this, either. I'm speaking to the papers tomorrow, you bastard.'

Deon got into the car and drove. He had no idea how long he went on driving but at last he pulled into a small park and got out in the darkness. Then he walked over to some trees and was violently sick. He lay against one of them, crying like a child. Never in his life had he felt closer to suicide. He reached for his pistol, but before his hand even touched it he thought of his father and he left the pistol in its holster. That was just what Muller would have wanted, too. Then he would become the lying cop who took his own life – the perfect scapegoat on whom to hang a string of further lies and falsehoods. Well, Muller was going to learn that he might have won this round but he hadn't won the fight. Deon still couldn't quite believe that the General had done this to him, it was so cold-blooded.

A moment later Deon strode out from the trees and onto the grassy area beyond. Once he had found a comfortable place, he lay down and stared up at the night sky.

He had been unforgivably naive. The story of the dead prisoner was explosive, and naturally Muller would have received full authority from the highest level not to pull his punches. He had moved with the speed of a striking snake. Deon knew that if he hoped to stand any chance of defeating such a powerful adversary, he too would have to move very fast indeed.

He went to see Sonja Seyton-Waugh the very next day. He had spent the night in a hotel, trying to persuade himself that Teresa would come to her senses. He couldn't quite credit the fact that she had believed Muller. Of course, he had been a fool, he should have come home the previous evening, but then she had always trusted him.

He knocked on the door of Sonja's house with some trepidation. He was scared that she might not be in, and even if she was, perhaps she wouldn't want to see him.

She opened the door and greeted him with a warm smile. 'Deon . . . ! Please, come in.'

To his surprise, she touched his hand as he came through the door, and he felt electricity surge through his body. He turned and found himself staring into her eyes, transfixed.

'I read the paper. I know what you must be going through.' She embraced him, feeling the pain that was in his body. She understood.

They drew apart after a few minutes and went through to the lounge. Sonja gestured for Deon to sit down next to her on one of the large leather couches. He looked into her eyes. Her lips were slightly parted and he sensed the need within her, matching his own. It was his loyalty, his love for Teresa, that had never let him fully admit what he was feeling now. But now he felt himself drawn to her by an irresistible force. His lips touched hers, and they kissed.

Her body felt strange and inviting. He'd never known a woman like this. Suddenly the pangs of guilt swept over him. He thought of the vow he'd made, never to let Teresa down. Then he thought of how she'd believed Muller's lies.

The kiss became more and more passionate. He could feel Sonja's heart beating. The smell of her excited his senses, made his body shudder with excitement. His hands were exploring her body, out of control. He tried to fight the surge of passion that took hold of him but was powerless against it.

She led him upstairs and slowly undressed him. He came to her softly, removing her clothes carefully, conscious of the hurt she had suffered so many years before. She was like a young girl; and though her naked skin was like a flame to his passion, he forced himself to be sensitive to her every need, wanting this experience to be as good for her as it was for him. Only when she began to cry out for him did he penetrate her and feel the waves of excitement consume his body.

Inside her he felt a fulfilment that he had never experienced with Teresa. The guilt was gone. This thing between him and Sonja was beyond his control. He held her tightly in his arms and sank into a deep sleep.

He awoke later, immediately conscious of the darkness outside. She was sleeping, curled up under his arm – this woman who controlled giant corporations and made men such as himself tremble.

Sonja's eyes opened and he could see she was watching him carefully, trying to sense his mood. She pulled herself from beneath his arm and knelt on the bed covers.

161

'What's wrong?'

'My life, Sonja.'

'I don't feel guilty. I love you, Deon.'

He turned over and kissed her again, then drew away. 'I was in love with you from the very first time I saw you, but I wouldn't admit it to myself. It was only when Teresa refused to accept that what I had done was correct, that I realised you were the only person in the world who would understand.'

She pulled him close to her. 'Deon, I'm never going to let you go.'

Much later, over breakfast, Sonja told him about the trouble she was having in getting information out of Helen. The good news was that she was making an excellent recovery; because Helen had not been a conscious addict, the job of the Warwickshire clinic had been that much easier, but the mental problems that accompanied the withdrawal were hard to deal with. Sonja wanted to keep Helen in England, beyond the reach of Goldcorp's tentacles. In the long term, her only hope of evading them would be to assume a new identity. Meanwhile, locked in Helen's mind somewhere, was the information Sonja needed on Bernard and Jay.

'I'm going over in a week's time. I'm going to try again. I'm the only person who can do it because I've been through the same experience myself.'

'You could never take her into the courtroom, Sonja, they'd tear her to pieces. I've seen it enough times to know it can be almost as bad as the experience itself.'

'This business will never be sorted out in a court of law – they wouldn't be so stupid as to let it get to that stage. They'll start to close in on us as we begin to find out more, and then we'll have to strike them where it really hurts. I want them to suffer the way they made me suffer.

'They must be worried already about what's happened to Helen. I just have to keep on working at establishing a bond with Helen. She still doesn't trust me, or anyone else for that matter. By the way, do you think you could provide me with a complete file on her – friends, education, the whole thing?'

'Sonja, if I start checking up on Helen, General Muller will get to know about it and he'll put two and two together with Bernard Aschaar.'

'But there has to be a way.'

'There is. There's the man who led me to you, Abe Solomon. He could investigate her background.'

Everything about it attracted his journalist's instincts. All the ingredients were there for a perfect story, the story of a lifetime. He'd never thought Deon would fight back against evil within the police force itself. He realised that as the members of the force closed ranks to protect themselves, Deon's career would be on the rocks.

Abe drove cheerfully along the sunny Johannesburg highways in his battered Alfa convertible. He changed down to third, and the sound of the well-aspirated, two-litre, double-overhead-camshaft engine sounded good to his ears. The shadows of the trees cast dappled reflections on the red paintwork and chrome surrounds of the Alfa as he zipped easily round the bends of the long crawling snake of a road that was Jan Smuts Avenue, and he grinned with satisfaction as he whipped past a big, ponderous saloon and saw the look of anger on the driver's face. That was Johannesburg all over – bursting with the kind of aggression that pushed everyone to succeed. Whether it was driving your car to church or walking to a bus queue, you still had to win. Most of Abe's friends were making a lot more money than he was, but what the hell, he enjoyed what he did.

He pulled into the drive of Sonja Seyton-Waugh's house – 'palace', he called it – and felt the predictable sting of jealousy. Ordinary houses, however big, never had this effect on him, but this one was something special, just what he would have liked himself. And he knew that behind the garage doors were machines he would have given his eye-teeth to own.

The man in uniform who opened the large front door seemed somehow different from his friend of old. He appeared taller than ever, and the lines of concentration scoring his forehead had become deeper, giving him a more powerful appearance. Not for the first time, Abe felt physically intimidated by Deon. But the grip, as they shook hands, was unmistakable, and he relaxed, seeing the familiar smile come to Deon's face. They went through to the lounge together, where Sonja was waiting.

Abe looked at Sonja. She had an overpowering sexual attractiveness enhanced by an air of vulnerability. He'd seen her before at a distance and then she'd never had this effect on him; perhaps she had changed. Now he positively ached when he

163

looked at her. God, how did any red-blooded businessman stand a chance against her in a meeting? One glance, and all the traditional defences would be down. He realised he'd been looking at her a little too long and turned back to Deon.

'Hell, Deon, why don't you take on Goldcorp as well, and throw in the South African army for good measure. Naturally, I'll do everything I can to put your case across. You're already something of a hero in the foreign press, but the reaction here is likely to be a *little* more guarded.'

Deon's reply shocked him. 'Forget it, Abe. Of course I'll give you my exclusive story. I know you'll make the best of it, I wouldn't expect anything less with your reputation. But that's not the reason I called you here.'

'You mean you *have* decided to take on Goldcorp!'

'In a manner of speaking, yes. You know that secretary who disappeared?'

'Yes. But, Deon, to be quite honest I think you'd be better off fighting your own battle now.'

'There's no point. A lot of people outside the force have offered me their support, but it's only a matter of time before I'll be forced to resign. Dr Ken Norton died because of police interrogation, and hopefully my exposé of that will make sure it doesn't happen again. But the fact is, I've got another, far more important thing to sort out.'

As Deon spoke he turned to meet Sonja's eyes. It was a look that threw Abe totally. He knew how devoted Deon was to his wife and family – yet in that look there was a whole world of feeling.

General Muller was a very worried man. The last thing the South African government wanted was an international scandal, and it looked as if he had just presented them with one on a plate. Why, he was asked, had a young doctor with suspect political beliefs been allowed to examine the dead detainee, Ken Norton? Why had Major-General Deon de Wet become involved in the matter, since he had nothing to do with the interrogation of political suspects? Why hadn't Dr Odendal immediately condemned the younger doctor's findings? Surely it was against medical principles for one doctor, especially a junior, to check out another doctor's work?

General Muller knew he would have to get Dr Odendal on

the witness stand, but he wasn't sure if Jerry Odendal could handle the strain. The man should never have broken down in the first place.

Anyway, at least he had made a good start with Deon de Wet. He thought back to the burglary at Aschaar's house. He should have guessed a lot earlier that the safe in the room had been opened. That was how de Wet must have got hold of the photographs.

Well, it wouldn't take him long to put a stop to whatever it was de Wet and Miss Seyton-Waugh were working on against Aschaar. She'd probably lose interest in de Wet when she realised his career in the police force was in jeopardy. He knew from experience that the last thing the powerful and wealthy liked was a lame dog.

At first she thought it was Deon coming back, but then realised he had taken her Mercedes and not his police one. Who was this in her drive now?

A sharp knock indicated that she was not to be kept in doubt for long, and she opened the door to see a toad-like man of average height staring at her from the step. He was in police uniform and had an ugly half-smile on his face. Her reaction was instantaneous – strong dislike. However, like the hardened businesswoman she was, she showed none of this on her face. Instead a pleasant smile rose to her lips.

'Good afternoon, can I help you?'

'Er, Miss Seyton-Waugh? Could I please have a few moments of your time? I am General Muller of the South African Police.'

Sonja felt the hair at the back of her head rising. It took a considerable effort for her to utter the next sentence. She hoped like hell that Deon would not come back now, she knew he would not react with such self-control.

'General Muller, please come in.'

He sat down in the lounge opposite her on one of the big leather couches. She could see that the attractiveness of the interior design was lost on him, though no doubt the cost of it was not.

'This is, er, a personal matter, Miss Seyton-Waugh. It concerns Major-General de Wet. You know him?'

'You must know I do, or you would not be here.' She was

165

trying her best, and not doing very well. This man must not see how much she hated him.

'Well, Major-General de Wet is in very serious trouble. I don't think he'll be with the force for much longer. He's accused of manipulating evidence and of disobeying orders. Also, his wife is about to divorce him. We have recommended psychiatric treatment, though he has refused it. It is hard for me to tell you all this because Major-General de Wet is a close associate of mine, but my visit is prompted by concern for your personal security, and also your reputation.'

'Thank you, General Muller, that is most interesting. I had no idea of any of this, and of course I can understand that it must be deeply disturbing to you – as it certainly is to me.' Sonja put a concerned expression on her face and resisted the temptation to order this odious man out of her house immediately. He leant slightly closer.

'Take my advice. Lay off Mr Aschaar.'

Sonja went cold. She tried to look as if she didn't understand what he was talking about. Muller slipped his hand inside his uniform and pulled out a photograph. It was one of the photographs that Bernard had taken of her that evening. Sonja felt the blood surge up into her face. She tried to grab the photo from Muller's hand but he pulled it away.

'You wouldn't want this coming to light, would you, Miss Seyton-Waugh? So just follow my advice and stay away from Major-General de Wet.' He handed her a piece of paper. 'If you need any help, here's my personal number; if you should have any trouble, or any information for me, you can reach me here, day or night. And I must ask you to try and act normally if you do see Major-General de Wet. He has a violent temper and I don't think he would react well if he knew that I had been here.'

If Sonja had had a gun in her hand at that moment, she would have killed him. Instead she remained icy calm. 'Don't worry, General Muller, he won't know about our meeting. But I think you should leave immediately; I received a phone call some minutes ago from Major-General de Wet, telling me he would be here shortly.'

At the door, General Muller made one last comment. 'Please remember, Miss Seyton-Waugh, that this is a serious matter. No one else must know of our conversation.'

'No one else will, General.'

It was only when she had closed the door behind her that she started shaking. The meeting with Muller confirmed everything Deon had told her about the man – except that he was even worse than Deon had described. But as she looked at the piece of paper in her hand with the General's number on it, she realised she had been given a powerful weapon which could be used to help Deon out . . .

Meanwhile, General Muller felt very pleased with his visit. Miss Seyton-Waugh's reaction had been just what he had expected – he could tell he'd struck home. After all, what woman of standing would want a photograph of herself like that in the popular press? He was quite sure she wouldn't be seeing de Wet again.

As for himself, he would much rather have Miss Seyton-Waugh as a friend than an enemy. After all, she might be a useful source of revenue in the future. Perhaps a nice little profit could be arranged through third parties who would agree to return the photographs of her for a substantial sum? It would be a pity not to get the maximum yield out of all his hard work.

Pieter de Wet stepped out of his sports car and into the pouring rain. Looking at his watch, he saw that it was after four in the morning. He smiled to himself. He'd won a small fortune at poker that evening and was feeling very good.

He was glad he'd been able to do something for Deon. It had been a small thing to fly that Helen woman over to England and make sure that she was booked into the nursing home, but he could tell it had meant a lot to his brother.

Pieter felt that Deon had never really understood him – Deon, who was always so concerned with doing what was right. Unlike Deon, Pieter saw nothing unethical about the way he made his living. So he bought things that a lot of people wouldn't touch . . . Sometimes they were stolen, sometimes they weren't . . . So what. He had an enormous flat in the exclusive suburb of Killarney, he had a seaside cottage, and he enjoyed life. Except that Deon sometimes made him feel slightly guilty about it, because Deon worked like a galley-slave in the police force and earned only a pittance.

As Pieter walked towards the front entrance of his flat, he saw that a large man was obstructing his path. Immediately Pieter was on his guard. He ducked to the side – and received a punch in the head from a man he had not seen in the shadows. Then the big man was on him before he had a chance. Another blow across the head laid him out flat.

Pieter came round twenty minutes later. He was lying in sand, in front of the headlights of a car. He staggered to his feet, unable to see where he was because of the blinding light, but something told him to get away into the darkness as fast as he could. He started to run when he heard the cold metallic click that spelt death.

The noise of the shot resonated through his skull as the bullet struck him in the small of the back. He grabbed a handful of sand and squeezed it desperately, then rolled over and drew one last, painful breath.

The rain was coming down in sheets. Deon's best pair of shoes was full of water, and the rest of his clothes were soaked through. Close by, another man was holding an umbrella, not for his own protection, but for the man in the black cassock who was reading aloud from the Bible. The minister had asked Deon if he would like any special passage to be read out when Pieter was buried, and Deon had chosen the thirteenth chapter of the First Epistle to the Corinthians.

The Dutch Reformed minister read out the scripture in monosyllabic tones that would have killed most of the beautiful passages of the Bible, but even his deadpan delivery could not dampen the intensity of this sublime piece of poetry.

'. . . When I was a child, I talked like a child, I thought like a child. When I became a man, I put my childish ways behind me. Now we see but a poor reflection; then we shall see face to face. Now I know in part; then I shall know fully, even as I am fully known. And now these three remain: faith, hope and love. But the greatest of these is love.'

The minister finished and was silent. The solemnity of the occasion was broken only by the sound of raindrops beating against the black surface of the coffin.

Deon helped the men lower the coffin into the narrow trench at his feet, then threw the first spadeful of muddy soil across the top of the box. He pulled a small tin soldier out of his pocket, a present Pieter had given him for his seventh birthday. He threw it down into the muddy waters of his brother's final resting place. Then for a few moments he stood watching as the men from the funeral parlour began to cover the rectangular black box with earth.

Across the grave stood Deon's children with their mother. Teresa had refused to speak to him, but he had managed to speak to each of the children – though that had only increased the pain. Until now they had always been his to see whenever he wanted to; now they were estranged from him. Later, when they were older, perhaps they would understand. Now the little boy and the little girl looked back at him across the grave with yearning in their eyes. What had their mother told them about him?

With Anna, Pieter's girlfriend, Deon walked amongst the strange white blocks that lay in ordered rows across the greensward, heading towards the Maserati that lay parked under an oak tree near the cemetery gate. Deon was glad it was raining; the harsh heat of the highveld summer would have been out of keeping with the mood of the occasion. At least, he thought, he had children of his own, who would in some way mark a continuation of his family's line.

He opened the passenger door for Anna, then got into the car with her. They sat watching the rain run down the windscreen. It was all over.

Deon knew that Pieter's death was a warning to him, a clear message: Aschaar and Muller were on to him. But his reaction was completely the opposite of what they had no doubt intended; now he swore he would get them, whatever the cost, however long it took. As far as Deon was concerned, playing by the rules was over.

Bernard pulled out the massive file labelled 'Project Zimbabwe' and began to read through it yet again. Yes, the Russians were hard bargainers, he'd found that out negotiating with them over the price of gold and diamonds. Here, the subject under discussion was rather different: nothing less than the complete take-over of a country. He, and the Russians, with the help of the black African freedom fighters, would take over Rhodesia – Zimbabwe.

For the hundredth time, Bernard smiled to himself as he contemplated the folly of the British who were blindly expecting to have things all their own way and quite unaware that black African leaders did not want a Westminster democracy in

169

Zimbabwe, or anything like it. Democracy – the whole concept made Bernard want to sneer. Power for the people. Who were the 'people' anyway? They never did anything to earn power, just followed one leader after another like a pack of lemmings. Security, warmth, and a good meal each day, if those were provided the 'people' demanded little else. In the plan Bernard had formulated the 'people' of Zimbabwe wouldn't even get those basic things, which was one of the reasons why he found it so appealing.

Once he and the Russians had secured the new state of Zimbabwe, the next step would be alliance with Mozambique and the reopening of the Salisbury-to-Beira railway, so that they were no longer dependent on South Africa for exports and imports. Then, with full Soviet support, an all-out war could be waged on the Afrikaaner regime. They would bring South Africa to its knees. The new government would be headed by a protégé of Bernard's, the country's entire mineral wealth under his control. The new government would be able to seize anything it wanted: banks, farms, public utilities . . . whatever took their fancy. With a Marxist system of government in force, rather than a democracy, there wouldn't be any trouble with trade unions, either, or a welfare state taxing businesses to the hilt. And there'd be Soviet arms and ammunition to crush any opposition. The whole scenario promised Bernard almost limitless wealth and power. He would supply the new state of Zimbabwe with the expertise to run its mines and industry, and in return he would gain increasing control. He would also be able to get anything he wanted out of the puppet government they would establish in South Africa.

Of course, some black politicians were certain to cut up rough. The trick would be either to have them removed by an unfortunate series of accidents, or to elevate them to a position of power where, however principled, every man has his price. The white skilled people in the new state of Zimbabwe would have to be protected. Since the indigenous peoples had not reached a high enough level of technical education to run the essential industries successfully, the white middle class would form the backbone of the economy. The last thing Bernard wanted was to have to import skilled white labour from Europe and America because the Rhodesian whites had been scared away. Imported white labour usually demanded payment in American dollars and wanted lengthy, expensive contracts.

Bernard turned the pages of the fat file. Of course, as any fool could see, the first major step in 'Project Zimbabwe' must be the combining of the two countries of Rhodesia and Mozambique into one unified state. This could not happen overnight. First the army of the new Zimbabwe would have to be built up to formidable proportions, then it could invade and take over Mozambique. In this part of the plan, too, Bernard could see opportunities for profit. Mozambique had a desperately poor economy. After a few years of Soviet-style community farming in both Mozambique and Zimbabwe both countries would inevitably experience a shortage of essential foodstuffs and would have to buy food from outside sources. Then Bernard would lend them money for this purpose, and in return they would hand over to him what little control of the economy he did not have already.

By this stage 'the people' would be grateful for the right to stay alive and the ability to feed their children: labour for his mines would be cheap and plentiful. Mozambique had a vast pool of skilled mineworkers who were employed on the Witwatersrand gold mines surrounding Johannesburg. These men would be 'persuaded' to work for the new state. Bernard grinned. He might even introduce something resembling the punishing 'chiblo' system that the Portuguese had employed so successfully in Mozambique . . .

The next stage in the project now was the meeting he had arranged with the Russians in Beira. It was critical for the achievement of his plans. The money would be exchanged, and the final agreement with General Vorotnikov would be signed. Immediately after this, a pre-emptive strike would be launched against Salisbury that would horrify the western world and blow to smithereens any chance of a British-orchestrated settlement.

A hit-list had been drawn up of important people in Salisbury who had to be eliminated. Bernard knew that when most of the ruling elite had been wiped out, the affairs of the country would be in disarray. South Africa wouldn't dare to intervene, for fear of western condemnation. The British wouldn't want to get too heavily involved either – and the Americans would probably stay well clear of the whole thing. So then martial law could be declared, and a military government installed on Soviet lines.

The rights of the white citizens would be protected, but all their assets would be frozen and no one would be allowed to leave the country for a considerable amount of time. There would be no free press, and the military government would be able to do exactly what it wanted to.

Just the thought of this caused Bernard to smile. Power beyond his wildest dreams.

Mozambique

'You set me a very, very difficult task, Captain Gallagher . . .'
Rayne went cold. He was sure he'd been absolutely right to
choose Lois. There was an elemental hardness about him, no
matter what his sexual preferences might be. He didn't want the
big man to let him down now.

'I had to go back to Johannesburg, and then up to Zaire. I've
got everything you wanted, but now I need to know what
happens next.'

'Lois, you're going to be our back-up. In this operation success
is going to be bloody difficult to achieve. If you tell anyone else
what I'm going to let you know now, the whole operation will
be blown. You're a key element.'

He could see that Lois was excited, and that was what he
wanted. He sensed that the man had never really been extended
to the limit of his capabilities, that Lois relished the thought of
being able to prove himself.

'As you know, the people who are backing me are providing
full air support. The trouble is, though I've no doubt they'll get
us in all right, I wonder if they'll get us out so easily. And I like
to be in charge of my own escape route. So that's where you
come in. I want you to fly in after us with the extra equipment I
told you about, and then make contact with me secretly. There
should be a few places outside Beira where you can land the
helicopter and then keep it hidden.'

A frown appeared on Lois's face. 'How will I know if things
go wrong, Captain Gallagher?'

'We'll make a secret rendezvous. If I haven't arrived there by a certain time after the attack has been launched, you must leave.'

'And what if you're killed?'

'I've got Colonel Michael Strong as second-in-command. He'll know all about this arrangement once we're in Mozambique. If something happens to me, he'll meet you at the rendezvous-point.'

'And how are you going to keep my separate departure a secret?'

'That's the hard part for you, Lois. I'm going to give everyone the option to drop out one last time, and you'll have to act the whole thing, say you've decided to throw in the towel. Then you'll leave the camp and I'll stay secretly in touch with you until it's time for take-off.'

The noise of the rain outside emphasized the silence between them now. Lois looked at him directly. 'That's fine with me. I just hope you know what the hell you're doing.'

'Believe me, I've got this whole thing under tight control.'

But as Lois disappeared into the pouring rain, Rayne wondered if the words he had just spoken weren't more to reassure himself than Lois. If John Fry ever found out about this back-up plan, he'd be for the high jump. Too bad – he wasn't about to end his life in a muddy ditch with a couple of rounds of ammunition in the back of his skull.

In the next few hours Rayne interviewed every man on the team. Some inspired him with absolute confidence, others he was less impressed by, but all of them were right. At least, that was what he felt until Larry Preston sauntered through the door.

'Hi. How are things going?'

The tone was surly and the form of address incorrect. Rayne would not tolerate insubordination of any kind, and he stared coldly at the Englishman until Preston began to shift uneasily on his feet. Eventually it was clear that he could stand the silence no longer.

'So what do you want me for, sir?' There was a veiled sarcasm in Preston's voice and Rayne wondered at the change in him.

'This is your last chance to get out, Preston.'

'And what if I should want to leave tomorrow?'

'You're a mercenary. You follow the rules I make. Go today

174

if you don't like it; go tomorrow, and the only place you'll rest is six foot under.'

'I don't take to being threatened, sir.'

'Then pack your bags and get out.'

Rayne didn't want to lose this man but he wouldn't put up with his attitude. Preston was a first-rate soldier, and more than that, no other man on the team could match his knowledge of explosives. Rayne also knew from Michael Strong that Preston desperately needed money – and he was paying far more than the going rate.

'I'm sorry, sir. I'm in on this one. You won't find me lacking, I can guarantee that.'

Preston would have to be on his team, Rayne thought. If he got out of hand, Rayne would sort him out on the spot.

'OK, Preston. But don't forget who's in charge. And I mean that.'

He saw the last of the men by five-thirty, by which time he was thoroughly exhausted. Now he had to go through with the charade of Lois's wanting to leave. It had to be convincing; he didn't know who might be keeping tabs on him for John Fry.

Half an hour later Michael Strong came through the door, his clothes absolutely sodden, but his smile warm. 'So, how did it go?'

Well, thought Rayne, it was now or never. 'Fine. In fact very well, Michael.'

'You sound as if everything isn't entirely right?'

'There's a slight problem. We're going to be one shorter than expected.'

'You decided to jettison someone?'

'No, it's Lois. He's decided not to come.'

Michael looked anxious. They were operating thinly enough as it was. Rayne looked squarely at him. 'I'd rather he was with us, but it's not the end of the world. They're all bloody good men. What matters is that from here on, it's all systems go.'

Rayne swung off the road, taking a hard dirt track that seemed to stretch on through the darkness into infinity. They crossed a range of hills and went over some small concrete bridges. Rayne talked to Lois as he drove along.

'This farm is the only habitation along here. It's fifteen kilometres from the main road, so I don't think you'll be bothered by anyone, but if someone does pitch up, just use the story we've planned and clear them out as quickly as you can. This farm will have to be one of your escape routes. Not the main one, obviously, but if we have to get someone injured out of Mozambique, this will be the first stop-off point.'

Rayne changed the vehicle into third gear as they went up a particularly steep incline.

'Make sure when you take off that you leave no evidence lying around. Pack everything away very neatly and destroy anything you don't need. Leave the place exactly as you find it.'

'Do you think we'll be followed?'

'No. But if the mission succeeds, a lot of questions may be asked, and no one must know anything about us. We'll disappear into thin air after this.'

They came up to a single wire gate and Lois jumped out to undo it. Rayne watched him unwinding the piece of wire that held the gate shut. Around them was blackness, the earth smelling fresh after the earlier heavy rainfall. If Lois failed him, it could all be over for them. But he had great confidence in the man, and he had learned to count on his gut feelings. Five minutes later, and they hit the paved road that led up to the farmhouse.

The building, designed in the Mediterranean style with a tiled porch with plants growing all round it, was enormous. Rayne drove past the front entrance and continued along the side of the building, passing the bedrooms, until he reached the back. He stopped in front of a junction-box and climbed out of the cab. Moments later the whole place was bathed in light from a series of spotlights mounted high in the trees surrounding the house.

They entered through the kitchen and took a quick look round, then they walked away from the main house and over to a couple of large buildings at the side. Rayne unlocked one of the big sliding doors to reveal a small aircraft-hangar.

'The farmer who owns this place is a multi-millionaire. He's away on business for six months and I've rented it for the entire period. There's just about everything you could want installed in the workshop next door – drilling machine, a couple of lathes, a metal saw. I don't know whether you can get the chopper into this hangar, but there's plenty of room outside as you'll see in the morning.'

Rayne extinguished most of the lights and they walked back to the vehicle. He glanced down at his watch and saw that it was after nine-thirty. Any more time spent showing Lois round would be a waste. Now he must take him quickly to Richard's Bay and then get back to the main camp. He didn't want anyone getting suspicious.

The big diesel truck exploded into life with a deafening roar. The vehicle moved effortlessly out of Richard's Bay and onto the main road, and Lois kept his foot flat on the pedal, holding the speed at around one hundred and twenty kilometres per hour. He hadn't got time to spare. Rayne had set him a tough task.

Having dropped the truck off at the farm, he would drive back on one of the motorcycle scramblers that were packed in the back. He'd head down to the airfield at first light, then fly the chopper back to the farm. That would mean he could start work on it in earnest by midday. He didn't need anyone to tell him that he wouldn't be getting much sleep in the next week.

Rayne made it back to the camp at eleven-thirty that evening – an acceptable time for someone to return who had driven to Richard's Bay and back. No one would have any reason to be suspicious. Colonel Strong came out to greet Rayne as he arrived, and they walked inside together.

'Damned bloody shame about that. But it's for the best, no doubt. Do you think we should try and replace him?'

'No, I'm happy with everyone else and we've got enough men for the job. The final briefing is tomorrow. I want everyone up at six so that I can put them through their paces.'

'Will this be your physical evaluation?'

'Yes. On that basis, I'll decide exactly who's doing what.'

'I'm glad we're getting going, I was beginning to get restless. I just hope *I* don't fail the physical!'

Rayne laughed. Michael was probably fitter than he was. 'Let's get some sleep now, or I'm not going to be in any condition to run anyone off their feet, let alone you, Michael.'

Rayne pushed himself hard up the slope, reflecting on what he'd put them through already: a hard jungle course that ended in a mock fire-fight; several mock manoeuvres involving the use of explosives and camouflage gear; then some regular shooting and unarmed combat training. He now knew that every man he had with him was of the highest military calibre. The only thing left was to see if they were physically fit.

He heard the man closest to him start to breathe more deeply as the gradient began to tell, and soon he felt his own legs burn with the effort of the climb. He broke away from the rough path and began to beat his way upwards through the bush. A hundred metres further on, the ground dropped away into a steep ravine, and Rayne started to work his way down the side. One slip here would be fatal – the muddy ledge he was following bordered on a sheer cliff. Occasionally a loose stone would rattle over the edge and explode into pieces as it hit the rocks below.

The moment Rayne had reached the stream in the bottom of the gully, he turned upwards and followed its course. Now the way was blocked by huge boulders that could only be scrambled over with great difficulty. Rayne didn't stop. He pulled himself up, hand over hand, on an enormous creeper that grew up one side of the waterfall. He came to an overhang and his legs swung out into the void as he followed the creeper over the rock.

After that his arms became weaker, and the last twenty-five metres weren't easy going. He pulled himself over the top and breathed deeply. He looked down and watched the rest of the men who were now making their way up the same route.

Guy Hauser handled it with ease, he moved up the creeper like an acrobat. The rest of the men followed, each tackling the vine with the same formidable determination. Then it was Mick O'Rourke's turn. He started off well, full of confidence and moving quickly. However, as he got further up the vine it was clear that the height of the cliff was beginning to faze him.

At the overhang, O'Rourke hesitated. Then he decided to go for it. He was climbing badly and his legs swung away from the vine. Now he was hanging from his arms, not moving, and losing strength rapidly. Rayne knew that if he let go he was dead. No one stirred. It was only a matter of time before his arms gave in.

In an instant Rayne was climbing back down the vine, the enormous drop below him more apparent now as he moved towards the stricken man. O'Rourke was silent, his eyes looking upwards desperately. He stared directly into Rayne's eyes, the animal terror reflected on his face.

'Mick, you have to let go with one hand. Can you do that?'

178

'I can't.'

'You bloody well can, or I'm going with you! Give me your hand!'

'If I let go I'll fall.'

'Give me your fucking hand, man!'

With a last incredible effort O'Rourke shoved his right hand upwards, and even as he did so Rayne saw his left hand begin to loosen its hold. He gripped the hand, and felt O'Rourke's weight start to drag him down. The man swung out below him, almost pulling Rayne off the face of the cliff.

'Mick, for God's sake get a grip on yourself! Catch hold of the vine again.'

Rayne closed his eyes and began to pull the man up. His left arm screamed with pain as he clung to the vine above him, and he knew that if O'Rourke did not respond soon, they would both go hurtling into the void. Finally O'Rourke gripped the vine and Rayne felt the weight come off his arm.

The next minute O'Rourke was climbing past him for the top. They both made it, and lay gasping for breath as the rest of the men watched. Nothing was said. Nothing needed to be said. Rayne had just proved how much he would go through for any one of them.

He kept them going for another hour, moving through dense bush, wading across muddy pans and then sprinting across open stretches of ground. None of them wavered now, all sticking together in a tight formation. A feeling of comradeship began to grow in them. None of them had been members of such a crack team before. By the time they made it to camp they were all soaked with sweat, thoroughly exhausted, but strangely exhilarated.

Rayne was pleased with his team. Now all he had to do was get them into Mozambique, do what had to be done, and get them out again alive.

The two men in the four-wheel-drive came across the camp that morning. It struck them as odd that there was no one about. They rummaged around and found the weapons. They saw the uniforms.

The two men were not stupid. They could see that this wasn't a regular army unit; what it actually was they weren't sure. It

179

seemed dangerous to stay in the place for long in case the people who were using it came back.

They drove out the way they had come, glad to have got away unnoticed and with no desire to return.

Rayne saw the fresh tracks when he stepped out of the shower. He didn't have a clue who it had been, but he wasn't going to take any chances.

He gathered a duty roster together and drove the men to the main road. When they got there they dug up the hard sand next to the tarmac and covered the track that led to their camp. Next they transplanted a considerable amount of vegetation with great care and used it to cover the spot where the track cut into the bush. By the time they had finished Rayne was satisfied that only an expert tracker would notice that there was something odd about the bush at the side of the road. To the casual observer the track seemed to have vanished into thin air.

Next, Rayne walked some one hundred metres down the tarmac road until he came to a sign indicating a curve coming up for traffic from the south. Rayne pulled out the sign and tossed it deep into the bush. Now there was no way that anyone who might have come upon the track earlier in the day could find it again.

That afternoon Rayne split the men into two attack units, one under his own command which would attack the bank, the other – and by far the larger – under Michael Strong, which would be responsible for destroying the airfield and all the planes. Speed was all-important. Rayne remembered John Fry's words. 'Take the bank, destroy it and the contents of the safe-deposit boxes. Destroy the airport runway and the planes. On no account touch the fuel storage tanks just outside Beira.' As Rayne and a smaller group attacked the bank and created a diversion for the enemy forces in the area, Michael Strong's unit would move in on the airport. The moment that had happened, Bunty Mulbarton would blow up the road to the airport and wreak complete havoc.

Rayne pointed out that this would be no tea-party. The longer they took, the greater the chance of failure. However both units would be fully equipped to masquerade as either ZANLA or FRELIMO.

They would land early in the morning in the Beira area by parachute, along with their equipment, then disperse. Rayne and Guy Hauser would then enter Beira by car, disguised as civilians, and would prepare the way for the other two members of their unit to join them. Then, seven days later, all of them would make their attack. They would escape under cover of darkness and meet at a prearranged point where an aeroplane, organised by John Fry, would collect them and fly them to safety.

Rayne had opted for the attack on the bank and on the airport to take place at exactly five o'clock on a Sunday afternoon. They would be airlifted out just before darkness. If anything did go wrong, in the dark it would be very difficult for the enemy to guess the number of men involved, and this would further add to the chances of a safe escape.

So they would then have ten valuable hours in which to make their getaway. Rayne did not tell the men about the formidable build-up of enemy forces Fry had described in the Beira area. Neither did he tell them about Lois, their secret passport to success should Fry's planes not arrive to take them out. But he made sure they knew that they were all equipped with the finest and most up-to-date weaponry money could buy, including ground-to-air heat-seeking missiles that would be used to destroy any aircraft managing to take off while the attack was being made.

An air of excitement swept through everyone in the camp. They were all looking forward to the action. Except for Rayne. He was the only one who knew what Mozambique was really like.

That evening Rayne went into Richard's Bay for the last time, ostensibly to make a few last-minute arrangements about their air transport. He contacted John Fry using the classified phone number.

'Is that the bird?'

Rayne recognised Fry's distinctive accent, a strange amalgam of English and American. He was using the special code-sequence. Rayne replied quickly. 'No. The eggs have not hatched this season.'

There was a lengthy pause after this and Rayne did not speak. He waited for Fry to open.

'Everything has been organised for you. I telexed the hotel in Beira and they know you will be arriving tomorrow. The car will be as arranged. The bank has accepted a deposit in your name, your front will be perfect.'

'We have had visitors.'

'Who?'

'I don't know, we were out at the time.'

'It's good you are leaving tomorrow morning.'

'Yes, the timing's perfect, my men would start to get restless if they were delayed any longer.'

'The plane will be landing tomorrow morning at three hundred hours. Your ETA in Mozambique will be five hundred hours. The car has been organised for you through our contacts in the Mozambique National Resistance Movement – and that's all the help you'll get from them.'

'How do I find the car?'

'Your pilot's name is Max. He'll explain where to find the car in relation to your jump-zone. If you're captured you must say that you stole the car in Maputo, that'll fit with the car's history.'

'And the hotel?'

'You and Guy Hauser have been booked into the Hotel Beira. As agreed, you'll pose as arms dealers. Bruce Brand and Henri Dubois. Anyone who bothers to check on your references will find them impeccable.'

'Anything else?'

'When you get into the bank you *must* remember to destroy the safe-deposit boxes – it will help us to alleviate certain security risks. And remember the story if you're captured.'

Rayne knew what that was. He was to say he had been employed by a wealthy man who had lived in Mozambique before independence, and that this man was paying him to get out a fortune of jewellery left behind in the safe-deposit boxes of the bank.

'Fine, sir. Next time I speak to you this should all be over.'

'Good luck.'

The phone went dead. Rayne looked at his watch and realised that he hadn't much time to fit in his final visit to Lois.

Rayne 2

Rayne pulled out his gun and moved away from the house into the garden. What the hell was going on? After searching the area very carefully for nearly half an hour, he had put the main power-switch on. The truck was still in the driveway. Some of Lois' clothes were still in the house, but the helicopter wasn't in the main workshop.

Rayne began to sweat. Something was wrong. But there was no way he could find out what had happened, he couldn't stay away from the main camp for too long or people would start asking questions. Without Lois they were naked, they would have to rely on other people for their getaway, and in his book that wasn't good enough. He trusted Lois implicitly. There was no way he would have taken the helicopter, he wasn't that kind of man. But where in hell had he got to?

'I don't have to lecture you; you've all seen plenty of action. But what I do need to stress is that we are one, a team. We have to look after each other, and any man who deserts the group will face the death penalty. Things are going to get ugly out there and we'll only handle them if we stick together. I'm first-in-command, if I get killed Michael takes over, and if he gets killed then Bunty is next in line. If he gets killed . . . then God help us!'

The joke raised a faint laugh. Everyone was aware of the risks they would be taking.

'We should be in and out in just over a week. That doesn't seem very long for the sort of money you're getting, but believe me you'll earn it. We're a small group, operating in the thick of enemy territory, and if we're discovered we won't stand much of a chance. The whole essence of the operation is surprise. We keep low till the moment we attack, and then we get the hell out the minute we've completed our tasks. But it isn't a case of every man for himself; you have the best weapons available and your back-up is outstanding.

'Michael and I have planned this operation very carefully, but things always do go wrong however good your planning, so we've made provision for that too. Now, when this is over you're never to mention it again – not to wives, girlfriends, mates, anybody. Part of the reason why you've been chosen is that you're all known for your ability to keep your mouths shut.'

Rayne paused for a moment. He wanted to make sure that the secrecy element sank well and truly home.

'For the rest, good luck and bon voyage. Enjoy your holiday in Beira.'

The drone of the two enormous Hercules transporters was deafening. They landed precisely within the flares that Rayne had set out. It took five minutes to get all the men and equipment on board and then they flew off into the darkness. Soon they were heading towards the Mozambique border. Inside Rayne's plane was the jeep with a recoil-less cannon, as he had requested, plus a giant army truck painted in Soviet livery.

Rayne made his way towards the cockpit, to get the instructions he needed from the pilot. The giant hold felt like a subterranean cavern that shook every time the plane hit turbulence, and after this the cockpit was strangely comforting. Rayne saw the crew-cut head of an enormous man hunched over the controls. He turned as Rayne came closer, and Rayne saw that his hand moved instinctively to the .45 strapped to his side. No one, evidently, was taking any chances on this one.

'Hallo, Max.'

The pilot stared at him dumbly till Rayne realised that he would have to yell to be heard over the noise of the engines.

'Max. I'm Captain Rayne Gallagher.'

The man took his extended hand and squeezed it in his giant paw.

'Hi, Captain. You're fucking crazy. Absolutely fucking crazy.'

Rayne was silent.

'Listen, buddy, and listen good.' The American's tone was

184

friendly. 'I fly into that fucking place twice every goddamn week and I'm still alive. That's not a country beneath us, it's a cesspit of war and goddamn violence. Nobody gives a fuck down there. If you don't like the look on someone's face, you just blow them away. Maputo is half sane and Beira is barely there. Don't ask me how I know, we just have to keep on supplying and this is my job. I get paid for being stupid. Just like you do. Sorry, you get paid for being fucking mad.

'You'll drop in the dark. Don't worry, I checked out the area last week, it's quite clear. Keep your legs together and you'll still have your balls with you when you touch the ground. The drop zone is a long way from habitation and you shouldn't have any trouble. They won't be expecting you. Here . . .'

He handed him a piece of paper. Rayne opened it and saw a very accurately drawn map, showing the precise location of the car he was going to pick up after landing. The map even included precise compass-bearings, so there was no way he could get lost. He was about to thank Max but the man didn't give him the opportunity.

'Don't bother, buddy, save your breath for a prayer. There's half the Soviet airforce outside Beira at the moment, one sniff of trouble and they'll be on you like a pack of angry timber wolves. Don't know what's happened to the world. Ten or fifteen years ago the good ol' USA would have been there, blown the bastards out of the sky. Now they can get away with murder. I'd like to take my M16 into the United Nations, give those fuckers a taste of the real world. They'll get it when the bloody Reds take over the globe, then they won't be able to sit in endless fuckin' meetings all day.'

Rayne was taken aback. He'd had no idea that there was such a large Soviet presence in Beira. After Max had finished his tirade Rayne asked him another question. 'How long have the Russian aircraft been in there?'

Max shot him a quick sideways glance. 'They don't tell you fuck-all. Hey, I've surprised you. Look, they've been coming in for the past two weeks. Maybe it's part of some manoeuvre, I don't know. A lot of equipment is being off-loaded, a lot of planes are on the ground. Reminds me of Vietnam, like they're preparing for an assault. Strange thing is, I can't understand where. I can't see them leaping into Rhodesia now the Brits are in there successfully buggering things up; it would provoke too

185

many people. But who am I to know, I just ferry nutcases like you in and out of this pit.'

Rayne was patient. Max could be a mine of useful information if primed properly – and once they were down on the ground it would be a lot harder to gauge what was going on.

'Are there a lot of Russians in Beira itself?'

'Hard to tell, but I don't think so. The guys are pretty yellow, don't want to catch any nasty diseases from the locals. Also don't want to create a bad impression, I guess. This is all thumb-suck stuff, you understand, I've never been an on-the-ground operative like you. We'll get you out OK, just as long as you make it to the pick-up point.

'It pays to keep your mouth shut in this part of the world. The trick for you lot is to lie low until you're gonna strike. They'll never notice you're around – they won't be expecting you. The Rhodesians would never dare to hit them when they've got all that heavy air support, and who else could they possibly think would come down on them?'

He roared with laughter, but Rayne felt it difficult to share in his amusement. The heavy build-up of Russian personnel meant that his attack would have to be faster and more efficient than he'd originally planned. He must let Michael know the moment they landed. Michael was in the other plane – two of them on the same plane would be inviting disaster.

'Have I got you worried, Captain Gallagher?' Max's voice interrupted his thoughts.

'No, you've just given me some useful information. I'll have to be a lot more careful than I'd thought.'

'You're a cool bastard, Captain. That I'll say for you.'

Rayne went back into the hold and wondered how cool he'd be once they were on the ground.

He paced heavily along the side of the field, and occasionally he nodded his head knowingly – a thickset man with a white freckled skin and wispy red hair. Eventually he came back to the holidaymaker who'd first stumbled across the place.

'Shit, man, this certainly does look like the army. They laid out flares for a plane to come in by. Very professionally laid out, as well. Now let's have a look at the camp.'

The camp was deserted. Spotlessly clean, not a scrap of paper or a broken bottle to be seen, and the huts were in immaculate condition. Even the ground outside had been swept. Major Piet 'Iron Man' Viljoen's face was looking more and more concerned.

'I don't know, man. I really don't know. There's more to this, that's for sure.'

He moved away from the huts and began to search in the surrounding bush. Again he found nothing. Then he walked to the track that led out of the camp and nodded his head.

'Crafty fucking bastards. Another day and no one would have known. You were correct that this was the place, Mr Retief, but these guys don't remind me of the regular South African Army. They'd never go to all this effort to cover up their tracks. Maybe it's an elite unit. Fuck, whoever runs this outfit has got his men well disciplined, I've never seen a place so well cleaned up. There isn't a single bloody clue that they've been here.

'There are no tracks leading out of here, so they came by road but they didn't leave that way. Must have been a bloody Hercules that took them all out. It doesn't make sense unless they didn't want to be seen or known by anyone. If you ask me, something funny's going on. I think you and your friend were very lucky you didn't bump into these men.'

The other man shivered, then walked quickly back to the car, anxious to leave the place.

Major 'Iron Man' Viljoen scratched the stubble on his chin. Whoever these bastards were, he'd sure as hell find out.

Rayne plunged headlong into the blackness, screaming towards the earth. The cold air rushed past his face, pushing his hair back like a powerful hair-dryer. He immediately pushed out his legs and arms so that he was spread-eagled against the air, gaining control over his fall. He could see no one else in the icy blackness and he didn't expect to. All he did now was concentrate.

In a way, this was the worst part – not knowing where one was going, hoping like hell that when the ground came up there was nothing in the way and no one waiting. As a practice he found this sort of jump exhilarating, in reality it was always quite terrifying. If he broke an ankle now, he would be useless to the whole mission. Instead of the regulation jump-boots he was wearing a light pair of running shoes, his personal preference. They would give him the opportunity to get away quickly once he was on the ground, and leave very few tracks.

He was glad to be away from the mad American and his plane.

The man's cynicism had bothered him; it was the sort of cancer that got you killed in action very quickly. He pulled at the rip-cord that lay packed against his stomach and felt the rush of the shute careering up above him.

His body was jerked upwards as the giant expanse of material above him billowed out and slowed his fall. Suspended in the air, this was the last peace he would know till it was all over. His mind ran quickly over everything they had brought, searching for something that might have been forgotten or overlooked. He thought of Sam for a fleeting moment. Then the ground came towards him very fast.

He hit the dirt hard and rolled over to one side, forming his body into a bundle. Immediately, he was up, checking that the safety on his Browning was off and glancing round quickly. He bundled the shute into a ball, the relief of having made a good landing lasting little more than seconds.

For the moment it would be best to sit still and listen to the others coming down. The vehicles and equipment must have landed minutes earlier, they would be lying somewhere in the bush around him. The biggest worry was that they might have landed in a very open area, contrary to their plans. He heard a noise to his right. Another man coming down. By the sound of it he had landed perfectly too. Rayne heard him pulling in his shute, and used the pre-arranged call-sign.

'Hallo, my brother?'

'I am not your brother, I am your son.'

Fine. It was Guy Hauser. At least one member of his team was on the ground in perfect condition.

'Guy, I'm keeping still till the light comes up. I don't want to do anything till I know exactly where we are.'

'Good, sir. I'll stay here with you.'

Rayne liked this quiet, ruthless man. The iron discipline of the Legion had become a part of his soul, and he was the perfect soldier even if he was not the perfect man. In the distance came the sound of another man landing. Soon they would all be down, nineteen men in a hostile country where the gun was law and little else mattered.

General Vorotnikov did not find the major's barrack-room humour in the least bit funny. How such a common man could have risen to such high command was beyond him.

The General had decided to set about a thorough inspection of the military installations and airforce back-up in Beira. He had not been disappointed; the force was well organised, and carefully disguised to escape detection by aerial reconnaissance. His black colleagues were beaming, this sort of fire-power had never been seen in southern Africa before – the fighter-bombers would annihilate the Rhodesian Airforce in a matter of minutes.

He was pleased that there had been no comment from the West so far. The build-up had been achieved in complete secrecy and there was little chance that anyone could have known what it was all about. They had air-lifted in crack combat troops and heavy artillery. Not that the troops would be used unless things got really out of hand, and Vorotnikov doubted that that would happen. With Salisbury a mass of flames, the Parliament building destroyed and most of the key white leaders captured, the people would be a terrified herd, easy to control. The new People's Republic of Zimbabwe would be declared within twenty-four hours while a stunned world looked on. Certain key whites would be quickly executed for crimes against humanity. Western politicians and journalists would be held for a long time, just to rub salt into the wounds of the Americans and the British.

The hands of the Western super-powers would be tied – his underground agents assured him that no Western army would dare to interfere in Mozambique or Rhodesia, with the memories of Vietnam still so fresh in their minds. But meanwhile, left-wing politicians all over the world would urge their governments to acknowledge the new Zimbabwe, and the coup would be heralded as a victory for the oppressed peoples of Africa, an overthrowing of colonialism and the beginning of a new era of equality. Immediately, behind the scenes, the banks, heavy industries and mines would be nationalised. Key figures in commerce would be arrested for exploitation of the people before the Revolution. The men he was speaking to now would take command within the next few days. All wages would be dropped to an equal level, and people would be asked to 'volunteer' their services to the new republic.

The South African border would remain open, but Soviet forces inside Mozambique would annihilate the Rhodesian-backed Mozambique National Resistance Movement and re-open the Beira corridor. That way the new state would not have to rely on its South African neighbours. It would not take many years before the pressure could really be put on the South African government . . . But, he must not dream of the future now, for fear of neglecting the present. He still had lots to do.

Vorotnikov turned away from the impressive spectacle of the helicopters, bombers and fighters that had been set out for him on the runway. He thought about the woman journalist, Samantha Elliot.

It irritated him that she had been spirited away from him, and he looked forward to the pleasure of seeing Tongogara and Mnangagwa in front of a firing-squad. It was all they deserved, they were traitors of the first order – and his black colleagues' lack of enthusiasm for searching for the the two dissidents irked him considerably.

Still, he was sure Miss Elliot couldn't have escaped the country, and it would be very hard for them to keep her presence here a secret. A blonde white woman in a black republic with its efficient bush-telegraph system had little chance of remaining anonymous for long. Her kind would not be tolerated in the new Africa. The media would be in the hands of the state, firmly controlled.

He saw the major coming towards him and wished that his visit to the airport were already over.

The early morning light gradually revealed the land – a densely bushed area that allowed one to see little more than ten metres ahead at ground level. Rayne couldn't have chosen a better landing place.

Already it was getting warm, and the men were beginning to realise that they weren't going to be particularly comfortable for the next week. The truck had landed badly, buckling its front wheel, and two of the men were already busy fitting a spare. All the other equipment had been found and Rayne was busy burying his parachute. They must all be away from here in a matter of hours. By midday he and Guy must have found the car and be heading into Beira.

Bunty Mulbarton came striding quickly towards him. 'Everything in order except for the truck, sir, and that'll be fixed in a few minutes. The jeep is already running and the cannon is in perfect working order. We'll be ready to set off within the hour to look for better cover. Should Larry Preston and Mick O'Rourke stay with us for the next couple of days?'

'Yes. Guy and I will get familiar with what's going on in Beira, then we can bring Larry and Mick in. I want to minimise the risks at all stages. If Guy's and my cover is blown it still means you've got seventeen men to do the job, and you must just drop the bank plan.'

Bunty's face wrinkled against the sun. 'I don't think there's much chance of that, sir. It seems to me you've got a brilliant cover.'

'I'm not taking any chances, Bunty. Anything can happen, and it probably will. If we decide to change plans at all it must be in the next couple of days – we won't be able to, once we've lost contact with one another. You must hold all our weapons for the moment. Guy and I will only collect ours when we've found a safe storage point.'

When they'd finished fitting the new wheel to the truck, they began moving. Bunty, Michael and Rayne took the jeep, the rest of the men and the equipment were aboard the truck. They'd buried some of their things, and these they would come back for if necessary.

Bunty drove very slowly, making as little noise as possible. Working with the compass, they made it to the main dirt road leading from Beira into the interior.

The moment Rayne and Guy leapt out, Bunty pulled away, and the truck followed. There was no time for pleasantries. The two men watched the back of the truck disappearing down the road and then walked back into the bush ten metres from the roadside. Between them they had two pistols plus an Uzi sub-machine-gun each in their back-packs. Without saying a word they began moving east in the direction of Beira.

Now they had to rely on their wits. The slightest noise or movement was enough to send them down on their stomachs. Fortunately there was little traffic on the road and they were not forced to hide often.

After an hour they came to the left turn marked on Rayne's map. They took it, still keeping well out of sight of the dirt road. Eventually this road became little more than a track and they relaxed slightly, knowing that here there was less chance of discovery.

Another half hour passed and Rayne began to get worried –

they should be nearing the car now. What if it wasn't where the map had indicated? He was beginning to sweat when he saw what was obviously the back bumper of a car sticking out of some bushes.

Rayne gestured for Guy to remain hidden. The Frenchman immediately dropped his pack and took his pistol in both hands. Then Rayne broke cover, walking slowly towards the old Peugeot 404. Its white paintwork was covered with dust, though the interior looked more or less clean. His eyes ran over the tyres and the outer bodywork, checking their condition and finding them satisfactory. Gingerly he opened the door and slipped behind the steering wheel.

His hand searched the top of the sun-visor where the keys should have been and found nothing. Then he checked under the mat beneath the steering wheel. No keys. What the fuck had they done with them? He hadn't got time to waste, he would have to hot-wire the car to get it started.

The bonnet release lever pulled back easily and he heard the noise of the catch releasing. He got out of the car, opened the bonnet and peered inside.

The muzzle of the gun felt cold against the stubble on the side of his cheek. Sweat dribbled lazily down the back of his neck, and he felt himself being relieved of the pistol in the waistband of his trousers. He knew better than to do or say anything. He just waited for the first command.

'All right, sucker. Move slowly back from the car. One funny move and you'll get it through the neck.'

The man, who spoke Portuguese, must have been waiting for him. The tone was surly and confident.

'OK. Kneel on the ground and undo your pants.'

No fool. With his pants round his legs there wasn't much Rayne could do.

Another man came into view, a squat, ugly black man of medium build with a bushy beard. His skin was oily and smooth, his movements easy. Obviously this man had spent much time in the bush. Rayne shivered. Fuck, now there were two of them.

'You must be a wealthy and influential man,' the black man sneered. 'The one who brought the car did not talk easily. It took me and Paolo a long time to get him to say anything. I hope you're not the same.'

'Where is he?'

'Where you'll be if you don't shut up.'

Something hit Rayne hard on the head from behind. What the hell was Guy doing? Who were these men and what did they want?

'I like you, my friend. I am sure we can do business. You pay me enough and I will let you go. I have always valued the lives of the wealthy, they understand my principles. I hope you are going to talk easily, there has been enough violence today. Paolo, I think it is time to give our friend a quick working-over.'

The sound was deafening. Rayne fell forward as he heard the first shot. A red patch spread across Paolo's jacket, and the black man screamed as the second shot ripped into him. Rayne heard the sound of someone else moving closer to him.

'What do you want to know from them?'

The voice with its French accent was cold and emotionless. Already Guy had earned his money. Two shots, two men down. Cool and ruthless.

'Where are the keys to the car? And who are they?'

Rayne pulled himself up as Guy dragged Paolo to his feet by the scruff of his neck. Paolo's body was now covered with blood. Guy's shot had hit him just below the right shoulder-blade, a crippling shot but not enough to kill him – Guy had already realised they would need information from these two.

'Where are the keys?'

Even though he was in great pain, Paolo smiled and spat on the ground. Guy dragged him across to where the black man was still lying, similarly wounded. Guy crouched down next to the black man, holding Paolo. He spoke softly, so Rayne could barely hear what he was saying.

'Your friend Paolo won't tell me where the keys are.'

The black man smiled up at him as Paolo had done. 'Go fuck yourself.'

Guy pushed Paolo's face close to the face of the man lying on the ground, then there was another explosion as Guy put a bullet into the black man's skull.

'The car keys?'

'In his left pocket.'

Rayne went over to the dead man and found the car keys in his pocket. He hoped Guy would finish the Paolo man off quickly.

The man started to gabble. 'I run this area. If you kill me my

193

death will be avenged. No man can threaten me, even the Russians respect me.'

'You are not with the army?'

'I take from the army. I am a brigand.'

'Where is the body of the man who brought the keys?'

'Just near to the car. Behind the tree over there.'

Rayne went over to look at the body. As he had expected, it was badly mutilated. This man, who was to have been their contact, had clearly died in great pain. He walked back to Guy.

'Dead. They tortured him.'

Guy looked into Paolo's face. 'I have no respect for you.' He pulled the trigger and the man's body shuddered as the bullet passed through his heart. Guy threw the corpse down and got up.

'Guy, we must conceal the bodies. It won't take much time and at least there'll be a chance that they won't be discovered.'

'All right, sir. But such scum hardly deserve a burial.'

They found a slight hollow in the ground and moved all three bodies into it, covering them with earth and rocks. By the time they had finished, the area looked just like the surrounding bush.

'This country is no different from anywhere else in Africa. I don't know how any man can live in such a place.'

'Just thank God we'll be out of here in a week.'

'I do not think there will be more trouble from the friends of that man.' Guy spat contemptuously on the ground.

The car started easily, and Rayne drove carefully back along the track till they were almost on the main dirt road, then he pulled over and they both got out. They took the clothes that they would wear for most of their time in Mozambique out of their rucksacks. In a few minutes they were both transformed into rather shady-looking characters dressed in crumpled suits. Guy wore a dented Panama hat on his head that added to his seedy appearance.

'You are now Henri Dubois, an arms dealer of considerable reputation.' Rayne handed Guy his papers, then took out his own. 'I am Bruce Brand, a man who has seen most of the wrong side of Africa. I deal in arms and drugs. We are a natural team. Let's get going.'

Guy nodded in agreement and they got back into the car. Soon they were cruising towards Beira at a leisurely pace.

The road-block was a crude affair – no outlying gunners, and badly placed. If Rayne and Guy had wanted to, they could have taken the men out in a matter of minutes. But they were now civilians, innocently going about their gun-running business. They pulled up next to the guard, who was dressed in a combination of uniforms but spoke to them in Portuguese – in which both Rayne and Guy were fluent.

'Get out of the car. I want to see your papers.'

Guy and Rayne clambered out of the car as lazily as possible. For travellers in Mozambique such stops would be a regular, irritating occurrence; they both had to act as if this was the fiftieth time they had been stopped and as if they found the whole business extremely annoying.

The guard did not seem in the least put out by their lethargy. He examined their papers, more for show than anything else.

'Where are you going?' An idiotic question, seeing that the road led only to Beira. However, even idiotic questions must be treated seriously.

'We are going to Beira.' Guy spoke as nonchalantly as possible. Both guards roared with laughter at his reply. The one who had asked the question then stared at him coldly.

'This road only goes to Beira, my friend. What is your business?'

'We have come to see a friend of ours at the bank, we'll be staying at the hotel. We have some business matters to clear up.'

'I do not like businessmen. They take what belongs to the people and use it to make themselves wealthy.'

The guard stared at them for a few moments. Then he handed them back their documents and waved them through.

Rayne pulled away very slowly, anxious to seem as if he wasn't in a hurry. The men Guy had just killed must have passed through this same road-block, and when they were missed, questions would be asked. He was glad now that they had taken the precaution of burying the bodies.

The road ahead was getting wider though not better. Occasionally they would pass the burnt-out wreck of a car or a truck, lying in the bushes at the side of the road. Then, at last, they came over a crest and found themselves looking down at Beira and the Indian Ocean beyond. They could see the town proper, and a much larger shanty town next to it. Near the main harbour was a giant collection of fuel tanks. Immediately to the south, the Pungwe River snaked its way out to the azure-blue expanse that disappeared into the horizon; while to the north lay the airfield, strangely empty. Yet Rayne was sure he could make out the lines of camouflage covers, and underneath them, undoubtedly, lay a formidable array of modern fighters and helicopters.

Guy voiced his thoughts. 'It is smaller than I imagined. We won't be as inconspicuous as I had thought. It will be dangerous.'

'Don't worry, we have an excellent cover. It'll give us the perfect excuse to be seen all over the place. The only trouble we might have is with the Russians, and we'll have to try and avoid bumping into them at all costs. We're their competitors, in a way; we're selling exactly what they're selling – though for a different reward.'

Rayne eased the car forward and soon they lost their panoramic view of the harbour town and were back in the bush again.

They came up to another road-block just as they were heading into the town itself. Rayne could feel how tense he was becoming. The security was stiffer than he'd realised, they'd really have to watch every step they took.

The line of questioning here was much the same as before, except that this time the commander phoned the hotel to find out if they were expected. Rayne and Guy sweated heavily, hoping that nothing was wrong. If they were arrested at this point, they stood little chance of getting away. Eventually the commander put the phone down and walked over to the car.

'My friends, you are most welcome. The hotel has confirmed your booking. I hope you enjoy Beira.'

Rayne drove slowly along the partially tarred main road. It obviously hadn't seen any attention since the Portuguese left. The town was well laid out in a typically colonial style. Many of the houses had seen better days, though it was clear that the place had never been really prosperous. His eyes noted everything of importance. There were few shops, and virtually no one was on the streets. It was almost like a ghost town. The bank looked run-down, as if it were permanently closed.

The hotel was at the end of the street, overlooking the sea. It was a two-storey structure with pretensions to grandeur. They pulled up outside and walked up the steps to the giant wooden entrance doors standing open.

The entrance hall was vast and gloomy, filled with bad

furniture and dominated by a large reception desk that looked more like a bar. On the main wall above the fireplace was a picture of the Mozambican president, Samora Machel. In the far corner of the room two white men were enjoying a drink. Rayne guessed they must be Russian military personnel.

"Allo. Mr Brand and Mr Dubois?'

They turned to the desk to see a short, stocky Portuguese standing behind it. His hair was swept back from his forehead and glistened with oil, his teeth stood out from his mouth like a chipmunk's and he grinned at them idiotically.

'Welcome to the Hotel Beira.'

Rayne didn't say anything. He was watching the Russians out of the corner of his eye – they didn't appear to be in the least bit interested in him or Guy. He leant over the counter and spoke quietly to the hotel proprietor. 'Who are those men?'

'Ah sir, you are worried? There is no need. They are Russian military advisors. I am Fernandes and I am at your service.'

Rayne shook the oily palm pushed out to him and Guy followed suit.

'I will show you to your rooms, the best that the hotel has to offer.'

They followed him up the wide staircase and along a gloomy corridor. In some places the ceiling was sagging, and huge pieces of plaster were hanging off the walls. At the end of the passage Fernandes flung open a door and stood to one side.

'Both rooms are the same, they look out to the sea. You can order anything you want by phoning me directly. Please keep your door locked when you are not in the room and do not leave anything valuable lying around. There is great poverty here and even the most honest men are not above stealing. Lunch will be served at one o'clock and dinner this evening at eight. Drinks are always available from reception, and the bar is open most of the time. Now I must have your deposits, please.'

'Half the bill has been paid already.' Rayne answered coldly. He did not trust this man.

'I will have the other fifty per cent now, please, Mr Brand.'

'You will have the other fifty per cent when I leave, and only if I am completely happy with the service.'

'This is not fair. I am not a wealthy man.'

'I will pay you in American dollars when I leave. As long as the service is good.'

Realising he wasn't going to win this argument, Fernandes left them and they both breathed a sigh of relief. The best that could be said of the two rooms was that they were clean. The pile of newspapers which were obviously meant to serve as toilet paper said everything about the state of the Mozambican economy. Rayne had hoped there would be more people staying at the hotel, but perhaps he had been a little unrealistic about that.

The balcony door of Rayne's room would not open easily. He had to use all his strength to slide back the bolts which had rusted into place. With the doors open, the room immediately felt better. Rayne wondered how long it had been since it was last used. Perhaps not for over a year; maybe not since independence . . . From the balcony he had an excellent view over the harbour and the river mouth. The sound of the sea blanketed his thoughts for a few moments until he heard a knock on his door and Guy walked in.

'I do not trust the Russians, Rayne. We will have to be wary of them. That scum Fernandes cannot be relied on either. He would sell his mother to the devil for ten dollars.'

'Relax, Guy. We couldn't have a better cover. It allows us to come and go as we please – we can go for a drive around town after lunch, maybe play some cards with Fernandes, let him win a little money and encourage him to drink a bit too much. We have to find out how the town works, who runs what, and what sort of security they have organised. There's no way Fernandes can be in league with the Russians, they probably pay him next to bugger-all and demand everything. He thinks we're loaded with money, which means he'll do everything he can to please us – and I guarantee he knows more about this town than anyone else around.'

Ivan rapped his glass down on the table. He wanted another vodka and he couldn't see Fernandes anywhere. Carl was lucky, he never drank much. Also, he liked Beira. He must be slightly crazy, because of all the places he had ever been posted to, Ivan thought this one was the worst. He banged his glass down again and screamed out at the top of his voice, 'Fernandes!'

Carl roared with laughter at Ivan's irritation. He shuffled the pack of cards again and dealt them each another hand. Ivan scowled at him.

'I'll strangle that bloody Portuguese to death before I leave this place. He disgusts me.'

He looked up as he heard a rattling sound coming from the reception desk and saw Fernandes waddling over with a tray filled with drinks. The Portuguese set another glass in front of Ivan and poured him a strong vodka, spilling some of it on the table.

'You call yourself a barman and you can't even pour a drink straight.'

'Sir, I am not a barman. I am the owner of the hotel. There was a time when I employed five men to work behind the bar.'

Ivan stared at the man and decided that he wasn't worth having an argument with. Besides, there was something he wanted to ask him.

'I see you have guests, Fernandes.'

'Yes, guests with money. Gentlemen who pay their bills. Men of substance.'

'Cut the crap. Who are they?'

'Why don't you ask them yourself? I know nothing.'

'When did they make their booking?'

'Two weeks ago. Cash in advance. These men are in business. All that matters to me is that they pay their bills, what they do to pay them is of no interest to me. I am not your spy.'

'Fernandes, if you know what's good for you, you will cooperate with us.'

The Portuguese turned his back on the Russian and headed for the door. He spoke as he walked away. 'I am sure General Vorotnikov would love to know that there are drunks on his staff.'

Ivan did not reply. It didn't matter; in this place there was plenty of time. Still, he *would* find out what the men were up to. It would help to break the boredom.

The two Russians were the only other people having lunch. Almost as soon as Rayne had seated himself, the larger of the two men came over to him.

'Would you like to join us?' he asked in English. 'We do not see many new faces here.'

This was the last thing Rayne wanted, but he could hardly decline the invitation without appearing hostile. He could see that Guy shared his feelings. Reluctantly they joined the Russians.

'A bottle of wine?' Ivan offered.

The Russian smiled, but Rayne and Guy shook their heads. It would be hard enough acting correctly while they were sober without risking the effects of a heavy drinking session.

'Well, I'll have a bottle by myself. Carl's like you, he also dislikes drinking at lunchtime.'

There was no menu, and they had to wait a considerable time for the first course. They introduced each other and began talking about how run-down Beira was. Rayne carefully steered the questions away from himself and Guy, and Guy said very little. When the first course arrived it was cold tomato soup.

Ivan had clearly had far too much to drink. 'Fernandes!' he shouted. He was beginning to slur his words. They carried on eating and hoped that he would calm down, but this only aggravated him and made him shout more loudly. 'Fernandes, you old bastard, come here!'

'Ivan, leave him alone.'

'It's not good enough, Carl. How can he serve us this cat's piss? It is the first time that our two friends have eaten here, they should not be subjected to this. I am embarrassed for them.'

Rayne wasn't in the mood for this. 'I've eaten worse. Let's just relax and enjoy the meal.'

'No! I cannot accept the way in which you have been treated.' He was about to pour himself another drink but Carl snatched the bottle out of his hand.

'That's enough, Ivan. You've had far too much. I think we must leave these two gentlemen alone.'

He pulled Ivan out of his chair by the scruff of his neck. Rayne was surprised that the bigger man did not fight back, but it was apparent that Carl was in control.

'You must excuse us, gentlemen. We'll eat together another time, I am sorry if you have been embarrassed. Ivan can never tell when he's had too much to drink. Now we must go.'

Rayne heaved an immense sigh of relief as the two Russians left the room.

'We'll have trouble from those two, I can sense it.'

'Well, there's not much we can do about it. Just keep out of their way for as long as possible.'

They finished their coffee and returned to their rooms. It was time for them to start working.

Rayne took a pair of binoculars from his suitcase, and with Guy following, made his way up some back stairs and onto the flat roof of the Hotel Beira. Fortunately the roof was not overlooked by any of the other buildings in the area, and the wall surrounding the outer edge was quite high. They were able to make their way to the front of the hotel and squat down behind the parapet without the slightest risk of being detected from the ground.

After a few moments Rayne raised himself cautiously above the height of the wall and looked around carefully. The main street was completely deserted. He gestured for Guy to come up alongside him, and then focused his binoculars on the front entrance of the bank. He couldn't believe that it was unguarded, yet this appeared to be the case. Now was the time for patience. He moved the glasses up and down the length of the building. Nothing moved.

They took it in turns from then on. At ten-minute intervals they alternated looking through the field-glasses. It was only after an hour that Guy picked up a slight movement in the front side-window of the building. Now they concentrated on the window, and the other windows round it, which wasn't easy from their angle. Eventually Rayne also saw a movement within the building. They would have to get closer to see right into the room but for this afternoon they would remain where they were.

By four o'clock a few people had appeared on the main street, obviously taking a Sunday afternoon stroll. No one paid any attention to the bank.

Rayne took the binoculars again. After a few minutes of watching the window where they kept detecting movement, he moved his field of vision to the street in front of the bank.

There was the sound of a heavy truck in the distance and immediately everyone on the street became more watchful. As the noise grew louder Rayne returned his focus to the front of the bank. Now there was a face looking out of the window. He focused the high-powered binoculars on the figure – a Portuguese in his thirties. The Portuguese had also obviously heard the noise of the truck and was waiting to see who it was. Everyone in the town was on edge. Rayne wondered how long things had been like this. Was it because of the Russians, or had it been this way ever since the Portuguese pull-out?

After the earlier silence of the afternoon, the noise of the truck coming into the street was deafening. The face moved away from the window, and one of the blinds was pulled down.

Rayne moved his focus to the truck, a GAZ-53A with an open rear deck filled with an assortment of troops. It was moving quickly, the V8 engine humming smoothly along. Only a few of the men had their rifles in a ready position, all of them black troops. If Rayne had wanted to, he and Guy could have taken out the truck with ease.

He looked at the driver as the truck drew closer to the hotel, and noted that he was also a black soldier. His passenger carried an automatic rifle across his chest in a ready position. Rayne raised the glasses again and took a quick view of the back.

'Lot of troops around in town. More than I expected.'

'So. We have to move fast. Kill or be killed, as you English say.'

The ruthlessness of the professional soldier, the weighing up of alternatives. Guy had survived by thinking this way.

Rayne was watching the bank again now, his mind beginning to operate with cool precision. 'I'll make enquiries at the bank on Monday. Then I'll draw up a floor plan and calculate our attack.'

Rayne made his way carefully back to his room. From what Fry had told him, he had believed the town to be relatively empty of troops. Already, what he had seen had created precisely the reverse impression. Soldiers seemed to be about the only people in Beira.

Larry, Mick and Guy would be able to do most of the fieldwork on the bank, which would allow him the time to plan their attack faultlessly. He had six days to work the whole thing out. If anyone discovered that there were enemy operators in Beira, security would be stepped up and the chances of successfully hitting the airfield would be greatly reduced.

He walked out onto the balcony of his room and watched the sun setting. What if he found it was impossible to hit the bank? What if there was no way that they could hit the airfield and get out? He drove these questions out of his mind. He had to think of the larger issue at stake – the attack on Salisbury and the loss of the Western peace initiative.

He was back on the roof again at nine o'clock. Fortunately there had been no one in the dining room and he had been able to eat in peace. He found Guy exactly where he had left him, crouched over the wall, staring down at the bank.

Bunty Mulbarton was not in the least bit comfortable. The constant buzz of mosquitoes in the night air was driving him up the wall. He, along with Ted Donnell, was going to have to endure this for another six days. At least they had found a good position relatively easily. He was lying in a small cave in a rocky outcrop that rose above the main road running from Beira to the airport.

He heard a noise beneath him and raised his silenced 9mm pistol, ready to fire. Two short whistles told him that it was Ted coming back up from the road. There was nothing to worry about.

'Sod this.'

Ted's Rhodesian accent stood out against the sounds of the African night. Bunty liked him, a good soldier and one of the men who had fought with Captain Gallagher in Rhodesia.

'Everything OK, Ted?'

'Yes. Dead easy. We'll blow up the whole lot without any problems at all. There's a nice drainage ditch running either side of the road. I've burrowed in on one side already, I'll go down in another three hours and do the other. With the explosives we've got I can lay three good sets of ball-breakers. We can just sit back and let them off one after the other. Usually after two the enemy gives up. I would – I've seen that stuff lift a twenty-five-ton truck in the air. Leaves a crater so bloody big you'd think that the earth had opened up. I'm glad it's not a dirt road; we can lay the entire perimeter with heavy mines and anti-personnel mines. It'll teach those Rusky bastards a good lesson.'

Bunty swatted another mosquito that had just landed on his face. 'Nice work, Ted. Pity about our home, but there doesn't seem to be any air-conditioning and the flies are a pain in the ass.'

'You can say that again, sir. Do you want to take a kip? I'll keep watch for another three hours, then I'll go down again.'

Bunty lay down on the ground with relief and Ted took over

watching the road. In the distance he could see the lights of Beira twinkling in the night and he wondered how Rayne and Guy were making out.

'Fernandes has agreed to let me rent the disused shop he owns next to the hotel. I told him I was bringing in a consignment of goods and that I needed a place to store them. It couldn't be better for our purposes; we can get in and out the back way without being seen, and it affords a good view of the front of the bank.

'I want to get Larry and Mick in there by the middle of today. The sooner they can take over watching the bank, the better. I need time to consolidate our position with the bank manager. I'll stay here while you have breakfast and until the bank opens, then we can make our first visit together. And check on our funds.'

'You mean you've actually got money in this bank?'

'Yes, but we're going to take it back at the end of the week. We have to establish our credentials. I'm going to ask the bank to give us a loan, so the deposit is just a sweetener to show them that we're men of substance.'

'Well, it's your money.'

Guy went across the roof and through the door to the stairwell. Rayne waited till he heard the click of the lock before he sat down with the binoculars. It was Monday morning and he was getting restless. The bank was the centre of his interest. He carefully examined the buildings surrounding the shop to make sure that he hadn't missed any viewpoints.

The guarding routine on the bank was simple: the guard was changed every six hours. Obviously they weren't taking major precautions, but then why should they? Anyone who robbed the bank would find great difficulty in getting away, especially with so many army personnel around. The guard's sole duty was obviously to alert the army if the bank was attacked. That was all.

At nine o'clock a chauffeur-driven Mercedes-Benz pulled up in front of the bank. It was an old model, with funereal black paint and masses of gleaming chrome. An Indian, conservatively dressed in a black suit, got out of the back of the car. Rayne guessed that he was the bank manager. His chauffeur followed behind him, carrying his case.

A slow procession of business people filed into the bank over the following hour, probably collecting their cash float for the day's business. Fernandes was amongst them. Rayne knew that Fernandes was in overdraft and wanted to see as little of the manager as he could. He'd established this over a game of cards with Fernandes the previous evening, which was how the subject of the shop had come up. Rayne realised that more than anything else, Fernandes needed money.

At nine-thirty precisely another large car pulled up outside the bank. An armed guard got out of the front passenger seat with a Soviet AK-47 in his hands. He moved round to the rear, right-hand passenger door, opening it carefully. A white-haired, aristocratic head emerged and after a few seconds Rayne recognised the uniform – a Russian general. The general walked to the door of the bank and turned round to the guard, bellowing an order at him. This was no puppet commander, Rayne thought, this was the real article.

He felt something tap on his shoulder and he swung round in surprise, almost dropping the binoculars. He had forgotten where he was in his fascination with the general.

He looked up to see Guy staring down at him.

'Don't worry Rayne, the door to the roof was locked.'

'I thought you were Fernandes.'

'He won't be coming up here in a hurry. I stole his keys.'

'Good thinking. What's up?'

'Fernandes wants to see you.'

'Mr Brand, you must not go to the bank now, it is not safe. The Russians might arrest you.'

'I'm not scared of them, Fernandes.'

'No, no. You still do not understand. This is no ordinary Russian, it is General Vorotnikov. He is a terrifying man. They say he tortures his victims with drugs – that his victims will say anything once he has got hold of them, and then he sends them back to Russia.'

Rayne remained calm. 'Thank you, Fernandes. I wasn't going to the bank, in fact, but I'll be sure to stay away from it until the General has left. Now I must be on my way.'

'Mr Brand, you have not forgotten about the money?'

It was obvious that Fernandes had only been interested in Rayne's safety because he thought he wouldn't get his money if

Rayne was arrested. Well, that was excellent insurance: as long as Rayne owed Fernandes money, he would have the man under his complete control.

'No, I have not forgotten about the money.'

'You are a good man, Mr Brand. Please do not underestimate the Russians. Carl and Ivan whom you saw last night are always in the company of the General, they are dangerous men.' He moved a little closer to Rayne and whispered quietly in his ear. Rayne winced as he smelt the Portuguese's fetid breath.

'I keep hearing rumours. Evidently there is tight security at the airfield, and troop transporters fly in every night. Beira is quiet, but outside the area is crawling with Russians. I do not know what they are planning, but be careful.'

Rayne pulled away, prising himself from Fernandes' grip.

'Be careful, Mr Brand.'

Rayne drove out of Beira very slowly to the rendezvous with Mick and Larry. He approached the road-block he had passed through the day before, and the guard, who recognised him, waved him through without bothering to check the car. He kept on the main road now, moving closer and closer to the agreed pick-up point and keeping an eye on his rear-view mirror to make sure he had not been followed.

After half an hour of driving, he was beginning to get worried. Perhaps Mick and Larry were on the wrong road? He wouldn't have time to search for them. Just as he was beginning to feel uneasy, a man jumped in front of the car, his face blacked and a riot-pump shotgun in his hands. Rayne slammed his foot hard on the brake and, as the car rolled to a standstill, a second man appeared next to the car door, pointing an assault rifle directly at Rayne's head.

The barrel was not dropped until Larry Preston was one hundred per cent sure it was Rayne.

'What if it hadn't been me, Larry?' Rayne got out of the car breathing an immense sigh of relief.

'Then we would have had to dispose of you, sir.'

Rayne drove the car into the yard behind the shop and closed the gates quickly. The security was perfect – no one could see in from the road. He went quickly round to the back of the car, and at his touch the boot lid sprang back to reveal the two bodies. He dragged them out one after the other, and pushed them both into the shower at the back of the shop. Then he turned the cold water on hard.

After a few minutes they both started to come round. Rayne pulled Larry to his feet, giving him a couple of slaps on the face. If he'd taken much longer at the road-block they might both have died.

'My God . . .'

'Are you all right, Larry?'

'The heat was incredible. We couldn't breathe. It took everything I'd got to stop myself banging on the metal for you to let us out. Mick was out long before I was. I hope the poor bastard's OK.'

In reply Mick staggered to his feet and lifted his face into the heavy spray of cold water. Then he turned to Rayne.

'I thought I was dying. Thank God the bastard didn't open the boot – we wouldn't have been able to do a bloody thing except breathe. We should have cut a couple of holes in the bodywork of the boot before we started off.'

'Mick, I had no idea we were going to be held up for so long.'

'Was the guy grilling you?'

'No. He ordered me to stop while the Russian General in charge of Beira came tearing up the road. If I'd tried to push on, the guard would have got aggressive. There was bugger-all I could do.'

Larry and Mick were in reasonable shape after another ten minutes. Rayne had asked for tough men and he'd certainly got them. He led both of them into the main section of the old shop, where the windows had been blanked out with white paint.

'This used to be a supermarket, it's owned by the Portuguese who runs the hotel. It's completely private and you won't be bothered by anyone. As you can see, the front window gives an excellent view of the bank we're going to attack, and very shortly you'll be able to watch us going in to make our first contact with the manager. Later, you'll take over from Guy and me on the hotel roof where we're keeping watch round the clock – but I don't want you up there until you've completely recovered from this morning's ordeal.'

A couple of days cooped up in the shop, Rayne thought to himself, and they'd be thirsting for action.

'I'll get you plenty of food in town, and I'll bring it back this afternoon. I haven't had the electricity turned on in here because I don't want anyone getting suspicious, so I'll get you a paraffin stove to cook on. Make absolutely sure no one gets even a glimpse of you – the whole town is simply crawling with Russians.'

General Vorotnikov stormed out of the storeroom. He had never come across such gross incompetence in his life. Outside, he screamed out a series of commands, and moments later two guards came up, hauling the quartermaster by his arms. The man was white with fear.

'So. You made a mistake?' It was more of a threat than a question.

'General, I ordered the assault rifles myself, they must be here.'

'Well, you fool, they're not.'

Vorotnikov stormed back into the storeroom and emerged some minutes later with a torn piece of paper in his hands. He thrust it in front of the quartermaster.

'What is this, idiot?'

'That is your order for assault rifles, sir.'

'Why didn't you obey it?'

'Sir, in all reasonableness, I don't think I am going to find those weapons for you.'

Vorotnikov walked angrily away from the quartermaster towards the control tower of the airport. He needed those rifles, he had promised them to ZANLA for the assault on Salisbury. Someone would have to get them for him.

In the ground floor room of the control tower, the commander of the airport stood trembling before him.

'Conrad, you were the fool who employed the quartermaster, now you sort this out. If this operation fails I shall see that your name is directly linked to the failure. You realise what that will do to your career?'

'Yes, sir.' Conrad swallowed hard. 'You shall have your rifles.'

General Vorotnikov turned on his heels without saying anything more and strode back to his car.

Inside, the bank was no different from any other – a large hall lined with frosted glass through which, at regular intervals, the tellers' faces leered at prospective customers. The parquet floor shone from years of polishing and the brass rails that guided customers to the counter gleamed aggressively. They were told to wait for the manager. Perhaps, thought Rayne, John Fry had been lying, and no prior contact with the bank had been made at all.

'Mr Brand. Mr Dubois. My sincere apologies!'

The voice boomed across the length of the hall, causing everyone to turn round. The manager was tall and commanding in his dark suit. Though he looked little more than thirty-five, he nevertheless gave an impression of pomposity. They shook hands and he smiled at them.

'Please, gentlemen, let us go to my office. I apologise for the woman at the counter, she did not know who you were. That will not happen again, I promise. My name is Siva Singh. Would you like tea or coffee?'

Rayne and Guy both requested coffee, their eyes watching the interior of the bank very closely through the door of the manager's office. The bank's working area was full of small desks, each a work-station. At the back the massive doors of the vault were wide open, and people were constantly moving in and out. The bank was clearly very busy.

'You are impressed, Mr Brand?'

Rayne decided that the best way to get on with this man was to play up to his ego. 'Er, yes. I had not expected such a massive vault.'

Mr Singh beamed, pulled out a cigar and lit it reflectively. 'The vault was brought here by Mr Rhodes, that most excellent Englishman,' he said, puffing clouds of smoke over his two clients. 'Mr Rhodes had a dream that he would export his gold through Beira, a dream that unfortunately was never realised – but I still have the vault!'

Mr Singh's office was massive, with an enormous oak desk at its centre. At the windows hung blue velvet curtains, and the oak floor was covered with Persian carpets.

'You must run a very profitable bank, Mr Singh?'

'Indeed I do. Even President Machel is jealous, and maybe that is not a bad thing. It has been said that one should always be in awe of one's banker!'

'But there must be bigger banks in Maputo?'

Mr Singh looked at Rayne scornfully. 'I used to live in the

capital, our bank was always based there. But after the Portuguese left, it seemed logical to move somewhere a little more discreet. My clients feel that their possessions are a lot safer in Beira than in Maputo, and a lot less visible.'

'I am glad you believe in secrecy, Mr Singh. Usually I deal with one of the Swiss banks, but I now find myself in need of substantial funds. I also need a place to deposit large amounts of cash the moment I receive them.'

'Your money will be perfectly safe in this bank, Mr Brand. We have the best security – the Russian Airforce!'

Rayne winced visibly at this, but Singh misinterpreted him. 'Mr Brand, I can assure you that the Russians would never take your money. They have much of their own, and it pays them to have a place of safe custody. I mention them only in the context of security.'

'Please elaborate.' Rayne sucked in his breath and waited for the bad news.

'It's quite simple. We always have a guard posted within the bank. In the event of an attempted robbery, he pushes a warning button which alerts our own army, FRELIMO. They then alert the Russians. So anyone who attempts to rob this bank will be taking on an entire army!'

So an alarm from this bank would be relayed direct to the Russian army, no doubt calling quite a number of troops away from the airfield. John Fry had planned well. Rayne said, 'Good. Now, I would like to know the balance of my account with you at present.'

'Ten dollars. But I was informed by your Swiss bank that you are good for millions!'

Rayne tried to stay relaxed. Why had John Fry put so little money into the bank account?

'Did your bank in Zurich deposit less in the account than you'd expected, Mr Brand?'

'No, no, I was thinking about something else. Mr Singh, I will be depositing a large sum soon and that amount of money always makes me feel uneasy when it's not in Zurich. The day I feel secure is the day I die.'

Mr Singh's face took on a reassuring expression. 'The Russians trust me. They have a large account with me.' He leaned over the desk and smiled conspiratorially. 'We have also had another enormous amount of money transferred here, like yours, from a Swiss account. I am waiting for the depositor to contact me.'

Rayne was astonished by Singh's indiscretion, but was very interested. Who else would want to place large funds in the Bank of Beira?

'Mr Brand,' Singh went on, 'I am aware of your line of business. There are no competitors for you here. You have carte blanche.'

'We always pride ourselves on selling the very best. Naturally, if you could provide any leads for us we would be more than grateful. You would of course be the recipient of a commission.'

'Thank you, Mr Brand. We obviously operate along similar principles! You help me, I help you. In this line of business it is the only way to operate. Do you know Johannesburg, Mr Brand?'

'Maybe yes, maybe no.'

'Ah, I understand. It is just that I am expecting an important visitor from that capital tomorrow. Perhaps you know him?'

'Perhaps I do. What is his name?'

'Mr Aschaar.'

Rayne was surprised. He knew that Aschaar was the head of one of the biggest mining groups in South Africa, but why was he here?

'I've heard of him, but then who hasn't? Now, if we could get down to business, I'd like to make a withdrawal.'

'How much do you require?'

'Five thousand dollars.'

Mr Singh lay back in his chair and put his hands behind his neck. 'We do not give overdrafts.'

'Then forget about any commission you might have thought of earning.'

'I will get it for you. Please wait here.'

Mr Singh scurried off, returning in a few minutes with a bundle of notes which he handed over to Rayne. Rayne counted them out carefully, then he got up with Guy to go. They both shook hands with Mr Singh.

'We look forward to doing good business with you.'

'Only the best, Mr Brand. Only the very best.'

Mr Singh closed the door of his office. Alone now, he had time to think. He paced up and down his office, imagining himself ordering the Swiss banks to deliver funds to him. It was nice to be in a position of power.

These men would be good for business, he could sense it. And his other clients would be most interested in what these two men had to offer, and he could make a tidy forty per cent at least on every transaction. He went over to the large mirror on the wall beside his desk and admired his chubby jowls. Once he'd made some money out of Brand and Dubois he could tell Vorotnikov that they were Rhodesian spies. They wouldn't last a day after that. Then he could keep all the money they had made for himself.

He rubbed his hands together. Business, he thought, was far more exciting than sex.

They sat down in the lounge and ordered two beers.

'Bruce, what's wrong?'

Rayne was glad that Guy remembered to use the false name. Fernandes was in earshot.

'I don't trust that bastard. Mr Singh wouldn't have bothered to pass the time of day with us if it wasn't for my Swiss funds. But maybe we can use him to acquire some very useful information.'

They sipped their beers in silence. The bitter brown liquid tasted good after the heat outside, but Rayne's mind was in turmoil. The Russians had invited him and Guy to dine with them. Of course he could try to use the opportunity to find out more about the deployment of Russian forces round Beira – but what were the Russians hoping to get out of them? They sure as hell hadn't invited them to dinner for the pleasure of their company.

Rayne felt like a man trying to defuse a time bomb, with the fuse ticking away in front of him. The stakes were being raised all the time. What the bloody hell was Fry playing at? He'd promised Rayne there'd be a large deposit waiting for him at the bank. Instead there was virtually nothing. It was as if the CIA man was deliberately trying to abort the mission. If Singh hadn't agreed to the overdraft he would have been in trouble already. What other surprises did Fry have for him?

The appearance of Aschaar was another cause for concern. It appeared that there was a bigger picture of which Rayne was unaware. It was like walking through a minefield blindfold.

What had happened to Lois? He really needed him as a back-up now.

Rayne forced himself to concentrate on the matters directly at hand. With Larry and Mick safely installed he had to concentrate on how he could get in and out of the bank quickly. If they took too long, they'd all be dead.

Alexei

The Lear jet took off from Nairobi airport in the blistering heat. Anyone checking its markings would have found that it was registered in Ireland. Further investigation would have traced the ownership to O'Regan and Son, a small but successful engineering company. Beyond that, however, any investigator would have drawn a total blank.

Bernard Aschaar was annoyed. It wasn't that Goldcorp's operations in Kenya weren't going well – on the contrary, they couldn't have been more profitable. The problem was expansion; the Kenyan government wouldn't let him broaden the scope of his interests any further, and he resented this limitation of his control. Bernard smiled to himself. Never mind. Soon he would be able to bargain with them from a position of unprecedented strength . . . All systems were go for the greatest coup of his life. He had the money Vorotnikov wanted, and all the paperwork: the blueprint for the new Zimbabwean industrial state, and the list of names of all the Rhodesians who had to be eliminated.

As the plane levelled off, Aschaar looked down at the country below. The Yatta Plateau stretched out into the distance; soon the land would drop away as they neared the coast and passed over Mombasa. Then they would head south, following the east coast of Africa with the island of Madagascar to their immediate left.

He pulled a sheaf of computer print-outs from his attaché case, a series of feasibility studies conducted on the main Rhodesian mines. This was his favourite kind of reading matter. It would keep him well occupied for the rest of the trip.

*

Vorotnikov smiled as the executive jet came in to land. Mr Alexei Aschaar was as good as his word; he had wondered, just a little, whether the businessman would have the courage to come to Mozambique. Now, once they had tidied up the final details of running Zimbabwe's essential industries, he could move in quickly. After this, no one would doubt the power of the Soviet Union – and no one would question the Soviets' allegiance to the underprivileged nations of the world.

As the plane taxied to a halt he gestured for his chauffeur to drive forward. The side-door of the fuselage opened and a set of steps snaked its way to the ground. Mr Aschaar appeared at the doorway, looked cursorily around him and then walked confidently down. Vorotnikov admired the poise and self-assurance of the man.

'Mr Aschaar, I welcome you to Mozambique.'

'Thank you, General. I am most impressed.' Bernard's gaze had shifted to the massive shapes under the camouflage sheets to the side of the runway. 'You are evidently ready to launch your attack. I have my side of the agreement ready too. Our business will not take long.'

They shook hands, General Vorotnikov showed Aschaar into the car, and the vehicle pulled away the moment the door was closed. Bernard glanced over his shoulder as the car moved off – and the General laughed.

'Mr Aschaar, you have no cause to be concerned!'

Then he smiled smugly to himself. Aschaar had every cause to be concerned, for he was completely in Russian hands.

'You believe that my safety is in your hands?'

Aschaar's question caught the General off balance. It was as if the man had been reading his mind!

'No . . .'

'General, I've got where I am by looking after myself, and I'm certainly not about to change my operating philosophy now. Let me remind you that every single word that has passed between us over the course of the last year has been taped. I already do extensive business with the Soviet Union through my diamond-mining and diamond-selling operations, and my connections are excellent. So, you pull a fast one on me and you'll drop like lead through water.'

Vorotnikov gritted his teeth, his face white with the mixture of anger and fear that welled up within him. He should have

215

known! He had been a fool. In battle he never made the mistake of underestimating his adversaries. Now, in this business, he had done precisely that. He breathed in deeply, knowing he could not afford to lose control at this vital stage of the proceedings.

They were equal now. His advantage was gone, for he had met his match. Bernard Aschaar might be the product of a corrupt Western democracy, but if he had been in the Party, he too would have risen to the top. Until Vorotnikov could find another way to undermine him, he would have to cooperate with Aschaar.

The General's immediate worry now came to the surface. He had the money with which to solve the problem, but he didn't have the contacts or the business acumen to strike the deal.

'Mr Aschaar, there is one small difficulty. One of my men failed in the uncomplicated task of ordering armaments for the main assault. I need four thousand AK-47 assault rifles in a hurry.'

'I am sure, with the right amount of money, General, something can be arranged.'

It irked Bernard to see the degeneration of Beira. In the past there had been a magnificent colonial harbour flanked by a beautifully laid-out town with outstanding tourist facilities. Now everything was run-down.

He calculated the lost revenue in tourism since independence, and heaved a heavy sigh. It would be an excellent challenge, to transform this place in a matter of years to its former beauty and profitability. Naturally, the harbour facilities would have to be expanded first, then work could begin on the rest of the city. All the poor could be moved to outlying areas – the creation of a ghetto was an excellent way of funding cheap labour and establishing a useful class of small-time criminals . . .

They entered the town on the Avenue Massano de Amorim and the General pointed out the bank. Further on, Bernard noted the dilapidated exterior of the Hotel Beira, and saw that most of the shops in the avenue were closed. They entered the Avenue Pedro Alvares Cabral and then turned right into the Avenue Major Serpa, heading for the area where all the consulates had been, at the edge of the harbour.

The sea and the harbour's edge provided a refreshing change after the depressing spectre of the city centre. But the old consulates were filled with squatters now, and only a shadow of their former glory.

'A fine victory for the people.' Bernard could not help the sarcasm. He hated waste more than anything else. The order of things had to be restored.

'Like most Westerners, you make the false assumption that Communism gives wealth to the people. As you will soon learn, it merely concentrates more power in the hands of the State. I do not approve of what has happened here but my country has to be careful.

'Without wishing to offend the people of Mozambique, I have to say that many countries appear to think they can borrow our expertise to achieve revolution, and then dispense with us. With our help, this country has overthrown its Portuguese tyrants, but what has it achieved on its own? There is no proper government and no functioning economy here. These people need us. They have no choice.'

'Precisely.' Bernard stared across at the General as he spoke.

'The Soviet of United African States. My dream, Mr Aschaar. A whole continent for my country, an achievement that might make me even more famous than Lenin.'

'You are ambitious.'

'What other reason is there for being alive?'

Bernard laughed long and loudly as the harbour disappeared out of sight through the back windscreen, and the beautiful beaches of the Indian Ocean coastline came into view.

Mr Siva Singh stayed late at the bank. He had much to do. The stakes were high and Siva wanted to make sure that he was up to them. His reputation was good and his knowledge in these matters excellent; this was his chance to enter the big league – something he wanted very badly. Still, Mr Aschaar was not a man to be dealt with lightly. He had guessed, when General Vorotnikov first arrived in Beira, that something big was about to take place. Now, with the appearance of Aschaar, he was sure of it.

Aschaar scared him. Meeting him at the bank this afternoon, for the first time, Mr Singh had judged him to be quite ruthless; one false move, and Aschaar would undoubtedly have his enemies eliminated. Siva Singh had only taken money from small operators before, he had never swindled the big fish. He had sensed that he had already been appraised from afar, Mr Aschaar's minions had pored over his history, checked his professional record. Now Mr Aschaar had transferred a very large sum of money into the bank, and Mr Singh wanted to make quite certain that everything about the transfer was correct, and that nothing had been unnecessarily charged for.

At last, satisfied, he took the books into the vault and carefully secured the door. He indicated to the guard that he was about to leave and that his chauffeur should be notified. The security system was not wonderful, but with the Russian army to protect him, he had little to worry about. Secure in the knowledge of a rosy future, Mr Singh left the bank at 8.15 p.m.

Larry Preston squinted through the narrow gap in the white paint on the window and noted that the manager was now leaving the bank. At least someone else was working overtime, he thought to himself. He was still not feeling so good after his experience in the boot of the car yesterday morning.

At first the bank had looked as though it would be a pushover. The one guard could easily be overpowered, then in with the explosives and out with whatever they could carry. But the large number of Russian troops he had seen patrolling up and down the street in heavy trucks bothered Larry. He understood now why Captain Gallagher had spent so long preparing this operation.

It wasn't a case of simply beating the hell out of a vastly inferior force. Now Larry realised why the money for this job was so good and the entry requirements had been so steep. Other men would have banged on the boot of the car if they had been suffocating . . . Only men like himself, who really knew what danger was about and had the guts to die quietly, had qualified for this mission. It would be no picnic.

Rayne was on edge. Dinner with the two Russians was proving to be far more exacting than he had anticipated.

They had met Ivan and Carl at the Grande Hotel, some two kilometres away from the Hotel Beira. They were shown into a private dining room, and after they'd agreed on the wine, an uneasy silence had fallen.

'You have been in Beira for long, gentlemen?' Rayne had asked eventually.

Ivan replied eagerly. 'For over a year, in fact. I have not returned to Russia since we arrived. I don't know how I've stuck it for so long.'

'Does anything interesting happen here?'

'General Vorotnikov has arrived. He's in a foul mood. There's talk that he's still smarting about a captured American journalist who gave him the slip. He's offered an all-expenses-paid holiday on the Black Sea and an instant promotion to any man who can find her! Can you believe it? Just to find a bloody woman. He must have a crush on her.'

Rayne's curiosity was aroused. Perhaps the journalist was a friend of Sam's. 'You don't know her name?'

'What was it again? Samantha. Samantha Elliot. Evidently she's an attractive lady!'

Rayne spilt his wine over the tablecloth. Guy looked at him nervously, and Carl immediately homed in on him. 'You know of her, Mr Brand?'

'Yes, the bitch was in Vietnam.'

This appeared to satisfy Carl, but Rayne's pulse was racing. He had to find out more. Luckily Ivan was voluble on the subject.

'Naturally, the whole camp can talk of nothing else. Two ZANLA men abducted her from the prison in the barracks. One was in the top echelons of ZANLA, Tongogara.'

'Where did she come from?'

'Rumour has it that she was captured by a ZANLA unit on the eastern border of Rhodesia. Researching a story, no doubt. Bloody stupid, if you ask me. They dragged her off to one of their bases, then some idiot tried to rape her. He didn't get far because Vorotnikov flew in on a white charger and whisked her off to Beira.'

They all laughed dutifully at this point, then waited for Ivan to continue.

'I wish General Vorotnikov would forget the whole business. I mean, have you seen a blonde white woman walking around here lately? The only white women here are the Portuguese whores who operate out of the old American consulate in the Mouzinho de Albuquerque, and they certainly aren't blonde.'

Rayne stared down at his plate, willing himself to eat the crayfish the waiter had just placed in front of him. He knew what the Russians had done to the prawn beds that lay off the coast of Mozambique – dredged the channel and shipped most of the prawns off to the USSR to use as fertiliser. A staple industry wiped out – and no doubt the same thing would soon happen to the crayfish . . . Sam. Where in hell was she? What would the Russians do with her if they found her?

Carl said, 'So, my friends, you have heard a lot about us, but we have heard little about you. What brings you to this part of the world, Bruce Brand?'

Rayne smiled at the Russian good-naturedly. 'Henri and I are traders. We've come here because we can see some very good business opportunities. You've been open with us, so I'll return the courtesy: we sell weapons. Of course, we've other sidelines, but gun-running is our main occupation.'

'I could have you arrested. Right now.'

Rayne could feel himself breaking out into a sweat. Had he overplayed his hand? 'Our business is dangerous, Carl. We're always taking risks – you can't have a wife and children in our line. I've seen war in Africa for the last fifteen years and I know nothing will change. I can't think of a better continent for business.'

'You think there will be war in Mozambique?'

'There is perpetual war in Mozambique.'

Ivan and Carl laughed. It amused them that Rayne wasn't scared of the truth. Rayne saw the moment was right to strengthen his links with them.

'May I be frank? Henri and I may do business with you yet. Armies, in my experience, have a habit of running short of things, especially when the pressure steps up. You would be surprised if you knew some of the countries in Africa I have sold weapons to. The trick in our game is: always deliver what you promise.'

Carl smiled at Rayne conspiratorially. 'But how do you make sure that you get paid?'

'We have our means.'

'I would hate to think what those are. How long do you intend to stay in Beira?'

'It's all a question of wait-and-see. My gut feelings tell me that we must be here for a month.'

'The Russian army would never buy from you!'

Rayne smiled. 'Officially no, but maybe behind the scenes. I actually prefer that sort of arrangement.'

The arrival of the second course put a fortunate stop to the conversation. Ice-cream and chocolate sauce were of more interest to the two Russians than illegal arms deals. Carefully, Rayne steered the talk back to the topic that was now dominant in his mind.

'If Henri and I were to find the American journalist, what reward would your General Vorotnikov give us?'

'He would most likely kill you!'

'We would organise the deal properly. No money, no journalist. You must understand that.'

Carl frowned. 'Vorotnikov would pay you if he had to. The holiday by the Black Sea is a big incentive for us, but obviously not for you two.'

'Henri and I will definitely spend the next couple of days searching for this woman. I think we will start at the brothel, eh Henri!'

'Yes, it will be a pleasant change from the bullets and shells.'

They all raised their glasses and Carl proposed a toast. 'To the blonde American journalist. May the best man have her!'

Rayne grimaced. He would kill any man who did.

Sam was worried. They had tried to smuggle her out on board a boat, but failed, and she knew she was becoming a burden to them; if they were caught, they would all be put to death by the Russians. She wished there was some way that she could help but all she could do was obey their instructions and sit here in this small thatched hut, out of view of anyone in the small village. There was no light inside the hut, so all she could do was to peer in between the reeds of the wall and watch the life of the village outside. They had brought her here two days earlier.

She saw no reason for hope; time was running out very quickly. The men in the village had heard that they would have to join their comrades for a final assault. What form this attack would take they didn't know, but it was rumoured to be an all-out push for Salisbury. Perhaps she was lucky. From what she had learnt over the past few days, she guessed that no one in Salisbury would be safe once the attack began.

She wondered where Rayne was. Why had he let her down? How could he just have left without saying goodbye? Had he heard yet that she had disappeared? She couldn't know that in the American and British papers there had been extensive coverage of her disappearance and that she was now classified as missing, presumed dead.

The simple diet of sadza and water that she was given agreed with her system. Occasionally a girl from the village brought her fresh fruit. They were all so desperately poor; real freedom, for them, would be freedom from their poverty. Most of the villagers were illiterate, had never seen the inside of a schoolroom in their lives. Many of them had earned a living on the big British sugar plantations before independence. Now those plantations were deserted, overgrown and neglected. Many of the fittest and ablest young men had gone to South Africa to work on the mines. Their wives waited for them, hoping that they would not find some other woman in the giant, sprawling townships they had heard so much about.

Living in the little village had taught Sam much about the way the majority of people still lived in Mozambique. She had befriended one of the women, an aristocratic beauty whose English was excellent.

Many of those men who left to find work did not return, but chose instead to live illegally in the South African townships. They threw away their roots, Sam's friend told her, and drifted through the townships like men without purpose on the sea of life.

Sam was surprised that this woman, like the others from the village, treated her with so much courtesy, when she brought danger into their lives and was a part of the civilisation they supposedly rejected. It took her some time to realise that they bore her no ill feelings, that they were in fact a peace-loving people.

She was pleased when Tongogara came at midnight. She depended on his company and the reassurance his presence gave her. He sat down next to her and she rested her hand on his leg. Over the days that had passed she felt herself more and more attracted to him.

She turned her face to his, and was irresistibly drawn to his lips. They kissed softly for a minute, then he pushed her gently away.

'Sam, this is madness.'

'Everything in this place is madness, Tongogara. There's nothing wrong with the way I feel about you.'

'There is everything wrong, Sam, a world of wrong.'

She watched his face, barely visible in the darkness. She owed this man her life many times over, but that was not why she felt so much for him. Perhaps it was because he was strong, tougher than any of the soldiers he commanded, a man who was prepared to take risks and didn't care for the opinion of others, only for his own.

'Everything in my life that has caused problems has been white. My struggle is against the white man. You . . .' He could not carry on. She looked up into his eyes and took his hand. At least he would allow her to do that.

'Yes, I am white. But I am also a bridge. I take you to a place you do not want to go.'

He put his arms around her, kissing her long and hard. She was thrilled by his passion – and she could feel the fear in him too. 'What's wrong?' she said softly.

'The Russians are hunting for me and Mnangagwa. My comrades in ZANLA cannot be trusted, I know they would betray me.'

'Why?'

'It is because I don't agree with this attack they're planning. The Russians have too much control.'

Sam felt scared. It could be a bloodbath.

'When will it happen?'

'Not yet, because Vorotnikov does not yet have guns for ZANLA.' He paused. 'He is playing a bigger game than we understand, this Russian general. He does not intend to give us real power, I know it. I should have him killed.'

'Another would have to come in his place, maybe even worse.'

'You are too wise, Sam. I have fought long and hard, I want the power to help my people. There are strange things happening, the pressures are building up on us all. It is as if some have been selected by the Russians and some have not; as if they have secret plans for after the takeover.'

'You must get away, Tongogara. General Vorotnikov will have you killed.'

'That's my problem, not yours, Sam. I wish I could help you get away, but I can't take you any further north. The Gorongosa National Park area is dangerous, and Zambezia and Nampula are even worse. If I could skirt left of the park along the borders of the Manica and Sofala provinces, I might be able to get you to Mutarara, which is about a hundred kilometres from the

Malawi border. The danger there is from the MNR. If they found you, they would kill you.'

He sank forwards, holding his head between his hands. 'I can't think of a way to get you out at present. You'll have to stay in this village. If something does happen to me, Mnangagwa will come and help you.'

'But Tongogara, why don't you just make for the border with me? Come back when things are safer.'

'A lifetime of waiting and my wife dead for the cause – I cannot turn back now, I would be betraying myself. I cannot explain to you how it will feel to be able to walk in the land of my birth knowing that I do not have to fear arrest, that I am not a second-class citizen. Independence on our own terms!'

'Independence on Russian terms.'

Now he was angry. 'That is why I must stay! I do not want to see the Russians take control. They will be welcome as advisers, nothing more. I fear for my people who have fought for so long and at such a high cost. It is my responsibility to see that they are not betrayed.'

'I'm scared for you, Tongogara. You're dealing with a great power, I don't think you can win.'

The village was quiet outside, only the ordinary sounds of the African night broke the stillness.

Before he left Tongogara kissed her again – a man caught between his own ideals and the grosser ambitions of power politics. He didn't stand a chance, she knew.

Much later, she stepped outside, the night air cool and refreshing after the closeness of the reed hut. At least she was alive, and would stay that way as long as she remained hidden. Just the fact that Tongogara had come to visit her had lifted her spirits. She had made it this far – she would not give up the hope of getting out of Mozambique.

Sam thought about the powerful nations that had ruled the world through history, how they had all eventually been overrun, their characters completely changed. Would Africa be any different? She shivered in the evening air, and tried not to think about tomorrow.

Not far away from where Sam was standing in the darkness, a group of men were spending a far less pleasant, though infinitely more rewarding evening. Michael Strong had leopard-crawled some half a kilometre round the main Beira airfield, laying explosive charges in strategic places. Behind him followed four other men, moving just as silently and purposefully.

It was a deadly dangerous business on two counts. Firstly, they might be detected by the Russians at any minute, and secondly, they might accidentally set off one of their charges. Each charge had to be carefully buried beneath the ground along with its linking fuse wire. For complete success, all the charges would have to detonate at exactly the same time, and this would turn the runway into a giant, smoking pile of concrete and tarmac. No plane would ever be able to take off.

Michael desperately wanted a cigarette, but he knew that the red glow of the lighted ash would be almost certain suicide.

For himself, Michael wouldn't have dreamed of sabotaging the runway in this manner with a force he didn't know. It was only because Rayne had hand-picked these men that he was confident they could do the job without detection. Carefully, he attached the wires to another charge.

Night lay over the Indian Ocean. In the spectacular semi-circular lounge of the villa General Vorotnikov had procured for him, Bernard Aschaar rose, drew deeply on his cigar, and then walked out onto the patio overlooking the sea. The General followed him and they both stared thoughtfully into the night.

'General, we have a saying in business: you must always expect the unexpected. You say you are confident – yet you need the weapons you asked me about. In short, you have a serious problem on your hands just at a time when you should be without problems.'

The General was about to interrupt, but Bernard held up his hand.

'I have already made contact with Mr Singh. He informs me that there are two men in Beira who are gun-runners. I have further discovered that they have had dinner this evening with two of your senior officers. This is an odd occurrence that I hope does not indicate a breach of security in your ranks.'

The General smiled, surprising Bernard. 'Mr Aschaar, I was aware of the arrival of those two men in Beira. However, I was not aware of their business. The two officers to whom you have referred are members of the KGB. They are merely attempting to find out a little more about our friends.'

'You have restored my confidence, General. I should think we could arrange a meeting tomorrow with these men. We'll see if we can organise the purchase of the assault rifles you need. If they agree, and are genuine, you should not have to wait long for your delivery.'

Guy and Rayne made it back to the hotel just after midnight. Rayne had the definite impression that their two Russian friends had hoped for rather more information than they'd actually received . . .

The meal had changed everything. Rayne couldn't leave Mozambique now until he had found Sam. The problem was, he hadn't a clue where to find the men who'd taken her away from the Russians. Shit, he thought, sitting down on the bed in the peace of his own room, whoever was looking after her was taking one hell of a risk. And there was no way he could find out more without endangering the whole success of his mission.

He was worried about their cover, his and Guy's. What the hell would happen if the Russians did approach them for guns? That could put them in a very tight spot.

He lay down on the bed and stared at the ceiling. He did not think he was going to enjoy a very restful night's sleep.

Rayne walked slowly up the steps of the Beira yacht club. It was five minutes to ten. At breakfast this morning Fernandes had gleefully passed on General Vorotnikov's request for a meeting and now, with sweating palms, he was keeping the appointment. He'd decided to come without Guy, and had dressed for the occasion. He wore a navy blue double-breasted blazer and immaculately pressed khaki pants. Around his neck was a cravat, and his hair was slicked back. He was going to act hard, like the man on whom his cover had been based.

The General was waiting for him at a table close to the edge of the balcony. Behind him, the Indian Ocean stretched to infinity. Pink clouds lay flat across the water, almost obscuring the horizon. Next to the General sat a giant of a man with long, curling black hair and dark Levantine looks. Rayne had never seen a face that reflected such a concentrated expression of power. The man brought a chill to his body.

He could tell the man was already judging him, carefully sizing him up before the first verbal contact. The man's hands lay calmly on the table, massive wrists covered in a mat of black hair that disappeared into the chalk-white cuffs of an immaculately tailored shirt. The suit was dark blue, of striking double-breasted cut. Wealth and power, that was the over-all impression.

'Good morning, Mr Brand.'

Rayne was wary of the General, especially in combination with this other man. 'General Vorotnikov, it is a pleasure to meet with you.'

'Let me introduce you to my friend and colleague, Bernard Aschaar.'

So this was the man the bank manager had mentioned. One of the most powerful of the Johannesburg mining magnates and an international businessman. What was he doing here? Their eyes locked as they shook hands, two men of similar determination.

'Mr Brand, I spoke to Major Sverdelov very late yesterday evening. He is a friend of yours, I believe?'

So he was right, there had been nothing casual about the dinner. It had been a subtle form of interrogation which they had either passed or failed, depending on the purpose of this morning's meeting.

'I am sorry, General, I only know two Russians in Beira, one called Carl and the other called Ivan.'

'Ah, it is Carl Sverdelov I am referring to. Our senior officers do not openly boast of their rank, it would be a security risk. Well, we meet on common ground.'

'I'm afraid I don't understand you.'

'You are a gun-runner, Mr Brand, and I am a soldier. At this very moment your expertise can solve a problem for me.'

'I'm sure that the Russian army has plenty of its own guns.'

'Mr Brand, I am not trying to trap you. I will be direct. Mr Aschaar is a businessman, he will negotiate for me. I need four thousand assault rifles in ten days' time.'

'Make?'

'AK-47.'

'Calibre?'

'The 7.62mm cartridge, we are not using the AKS-74 in Africa.'

'You want four thousand – that's a big order.'

227

There was no way he could obtain so many weapons so fast. He would have to stall as much as possible. He thought quickly.

'Considering the size of the consignment, a basic fee of five hundred dollars per rifle would be the price. Then I would require a deposit – two million dollars immediately. There might also be transportation charges running to another half a million. The time factor is everything, the weapons would have to be flown in.'

The terms had to be hard, it was his only chance. He was fast getting himself into a very dangerous situation.

'We would give you half a million up front, that's all.'

'I have not yet agreed to supply the arms, Mr Aschaar, do not start defining the terms. Do you have any idea how difficult it is to obtain such weapons? I could only deal with you on the basis of a hundred per cent payment up front. I'm sure that as a businessman you must understand my position.'

'Ridiculous!' Aschaar sneered, one eyebrow raised. 'You'll take the money and disappear.'

'I think that our conversation is at an end.' Rayne got up from the table and began to walk away. He wondered if he'd overplayed his hand. He had half crossed the balcony when he heard Aschaar's voice, as he had expected.

'All right, Mr Brand, I accept your terms. But I need some sort of guarantee.'

Rayne returned to the table and sat down again. Now Aschaar was far more amicable. 'Mr Brand, I apologise. I should have asked you if you would like a drink?'

'Coffee.'

Aschaar gestured to a waiter while the General made polite conversation.

'You like Beira, Mr Brand?'

'No. It is a place for business, not for pleasure.'

Rayne saw the furrow on the General's brow deepen. He said, 'I have a grudging acceptance of the way things operate on this continent, but you must admit this is a desperate place.'

'We have not had an easy time here, Mr Brand. We have given much and received little in return.'

You have given nothing and taken everything, Rayne thought. 'An unrewarding business, General. I like to see results for hard work.'

'In politics the immediate rewards may not seem attractive, but the long-term gains more than make up.'

Rayne felt it was time to cut the chat and get down to business in earnest. The less time he spent in the company of these men, the better.

'I have a proposal, Mr Aschaar. If you have the money here in Beira, then payment can be a relatively simple affair – Mr Singh the banker and I discussed such an arrangement only yesterday. What I suggest is this: you pay the two million dollars into my account, and Mr Singh will only transfer it to an account I have nominated in another country once he is certain the shipment has arrived. If I fail to perform, you get the money and the interest back.'

'And what if you and Mr Singh have concluded a little deal on the side?'

'Knowing your power and influence, Mr Aschaar, I hardly think that Mr Singh would like to cross you – or the Soviet Union. One must always choose one's adversaries with care.'

Rayne sipped his coffee, trying to stop himself from shaking. He wanted to get away. Aschaar spoke again.

'Mr Brand, if this deal goes through successfully, I hope to be able to do more business with you in the future. How do I get hold of you?'

Rayne put down his coffee, reflecting on Aschaar's craftiness. 'We do good business. Unfortunately I have always had a policy of making the first contact. I do not divulge personal details or contact numbers. When you need me again, I will get hold of you.'

'A strange way of doing business!'

'A good way of staying alive, Mr Aschaar.' Rayne got up to leave. 'We will start the moment Mr Singh has the full amount. Two and a half million dollars, Mr Aschaar.'

Aschaar jumped up, knocking his chair backwards. Rayne reacted instantly, ready for action, balanced on his feet like a cat. But Aschaar's hands remained at his side.

'I thought you said the last half million was a ball-park figure depending on the cost of transportation?'

'In the course of our discussion I realised I would have problems with you on that. Two and a half million is my price, take it or leave it.' And Rayne sincerely hoped that Aschaar would leave it.

'This will take time to approve,' the General said angrily.

'Time I have plenty of. Your answer will be the amount deposited with Mr Singh.'

Aschaar sat back. The look in his eyes did not make Rayne feel in the least bit easy. He left the yacht club, earnestly hoping that Aschaar would not come forward with the money.

Unfortunately the answer was in the foyer of the Hotel Beira when he arrived back. Fernandes was waiting for him. 'Mr Singh says you must phone him, it is most urgent.'

Rayne was through to Singh in less than a minute.

'Good morning, Mr Brand. You are already doing very well. I am holding two and a half million dollars. It will be transferred to your Swiss account the moment I have ascertained that the goods have arrived intact.'

'Thank you, Mr Singh. Thank you very much.'

'What do you think, Mr Aschaar?'

'He's a strange character, this Bruce Brand. Not what I had been expecting at all. He's far too tough for my liking. He'll deliver, I'm sure of it, but don't you think it's a bit too much of a coincidence that he should be here just when we want him? Whoever he is, I'd like his background checked out.'

'It has already been done and found to be completely clean. Well, clean is not perhaps the right word, but let us say he lives up to his formidable reputation. Do you not think he asked an outrageous amount for the weapons?'

'Yes. Naturally, he won't be paid, I simply told Singh to lie to him. If he has any sense he'll get out of here fast. I still want him watched as closely as possible, but we must be careful not to upset him – I wouldn't like the supply of the rifles to be affected in any way.'

'The moment I get them we can start full mobilisation of all our ground forces. I hear that the British are even intending to bring out their own policemen to oversee the Rhodesian elections! Mugabe assures me that he will win, but I don't believe him. There is no place in my plans for calculated guesswork; the result I require can only be achieved by an invasion. The new Zimbabwe without the Beira Corridor is worthless.'

'We are of one mind, General. There's nothing to worry about; elections or not, the people are still clamouring for blood.

In a few weeks' time they'll have it – and we shall achieve our objective.'

Rayne sat on the balcony of his room, sipping a beer. He asked himself what the hell the formidable Mr Aschaar was doing in Mozambique? It didn't make sense. Why was he having morning tea with a Russian general? Whatever the answer to these questions might be, there was obviously a larger and more sinister plan in operation than the one John Fry had outlined to him.

As he thought about it, it began to make more and more sense. The Russians would be able to link up the two countries and make them far stronger. The crippled Mozambican economy could be propped up with the Rhodesian one and the latter could use the former's ports. The next stage was predictable: the severing of all ties with South Africa and the declaration of unity with the African National Congress. But where did Bernard Aschaar fit in with that scenario? There must be even more to the whole plan.

Whatever Aschaar had in mind, he wasn't going to get very far. Not if Rayne could help it.

'You fucking bastard! You fucking, fucking bastard!' Lois fell off the side of the chopper into the sand and lay face down, sobbing. There was nothing more he could do. It was over. Captain Gallagher would hate him for ever.

Everything had gone wrong. On the Saturday afternoon he'd taken the chopper for a final test flight. After flying out over the sea he'd been coming in towards the beach when the engine started to cut out. Everything he tried had failed. The engine would appear to pick up, then suddenly lose power again.

Desperately he'd wrestled with the controls, terrified that he was going to smash down into the sand. Somehow, he'd managed to bring the chopper down just above the high-tide mark. He staggered out and rested on the beach for over an hour before he tried to fix the engine.

Lois had thought the malfunction would be easy enough to find. Probably some dirt in the fuel lines, he had told himself. But, as the sun set on Saturday evening, he'd realised it wasn't going to be that simple. Fortunately he had a rat-pack with enough food and water to last him for two days. He hadn't slept that first night. He'd thought about what Captain Gallagher would do when he came to the farmhouse and found it empty. No chopper. No Lois.

That had been two days ago. Due to his own foresight, he had a full set of tools and the workshop manual with him, and he'd worked and worked, dismantling a section of the fuel supply system, and then other parts of the engine. Sand blew constantly over the machine, and combined with the salt spray from the sea to cover the whole thing in a sticky crust of dirt.

Now it was the third day. He knew time was against him, but he would not abandon the chopper. He'd run out of water the day before, and he'd had to get some water this morning by sinking a container into the sand and stretching some plastic sheeting over it, then weighting it in the centre with a stone so that when the early morning dew formed on the inside of the sheet, it rolled down into the container. That had provided half a cup of rather brackish water.

He was sure that the chopper's problem was a blockage somewhere in the fuel supply system; he'd been too hasty in filling the tanks and should have taken more care to double-filter all the fuel. The battery was getting tired now, too. There was nothing more he could try. Anyway, he was all in.

He got up out of the sand, crawled back to the cockpit and searched around in the storage containers inside. Eventually he found what he was looking for. He pulled himself into the pilot's seat with the pistol on his lap.

He watched the waves rolling up the beach, lost in his thoughts for a while. The old, wounding words echoed through his head. 'Bloody faggot, good for nothing.' Then he released the safety and pulled back the pistol slide.

The muzzle of the pistol tasted strange in the roof of his mouth. This was the best, most effective way, he had been told – but he was scared that the explosion might push his head back and cause the bullet to go out of the side of his mouth. He pulled his legs up and rested them against the control panel ahead of him. This, he reasoned, would force him back into the seat and ensure that his body stayed still at the moment of firing. He breathed in, closed his eyes and – pistol at the ready – pushed his legs hard against the panel.

The noise of the chopper engine starting up was deafening. The machine shook violently, and he fell forward, dropping the gun. Then he was at the control panel, hastily grabbing at different switches, making sure that the miracle wasn't lost. His whole body tensed as he lifted the machine off the ground, then he started to laugh hysterically at the irony of it all.

He swooped down low over the sand, scaring a flock of birds on the edge of the sea, then headed for a large tree and pushed the button controlling the two M134 six-barrel 7.62-mm Miniguns. Moving in closer, he opened them up, and the tree exploded into pieces as two thousand rounds of ammunition tore into it in under fifteen seconds. On his second fly-past nothing was left but a tattered stump.

He turned the helicopter quickly to the west and headed inland, keeping as low to the ground as possible. Then he crossed over the place where he knew the camp must be and saw that it was deserted. He pulled away rapidly as a South African Army Land Rover pulled out of the bushes to see who was coming in to land.

Lois approached the farmhouse cautiously. He'd flown in as the sun was setting and had landed a considerable distance away. To move to the building on foot was the best course. If there was anyone waiting for him, he'd be in a better position to surprise them. He reckoned the Army Land Rover at the camp meant one of two things. Either the South African authorities had apprehended Rayne with his men, or they had discovered the site after Rayne had left. The latter was the most likely.

By the time he got to the back corner of the house, Lois was pretty sure there were people about. His senses were hyper-alert, the slightest noise putting him into a crouching stance, ready to fire.

The lights came on as he was about to disappear into the bush. Gunfire erupted around him. In a fraction of a second he had swung round, aiming his rifle very carefully. He hit the floodlight with the first shot and then pivoted slightly and fired at the spot where he had seen a man·with a rifle break from the bushes, heading straight for him.

The man screamed out, and Lois heard him stagger forwards. In the darkness he glimpsed the outline of an R3 assault rifle and quickly picked it up. He could just make out a man in uniform illuminated by the lights inside the house, giving orders.

There was only one choice. Lois switched the firing switch to the single-fire position. Without hesitating, he squeezed the trigger, going for a head shot. As the man crumpled to the ground, Lois aimed his second shot at the light in the house.

First Lieutenant Koos Conradie could hardly believe his eyes. There on the dirt, lying in a pool of blood, was the legendary Major Piet Viljoen – not popular, but still something of a hero amongst the men. He'd said that the army wasn't capable of handling the investigation of the suspicious goings on at the farmhouse on their own. Sadly, he'd just been proved right.

The radio operator ran up to First Lieutenant Koos Conradie and, breathing heavily, waited for permission to speak.

'Yes, Swart. What's the airforce say?'

'Sir. Direct orders from Pretoria, sir. We are to remain here. On no account are we to attempt pursuit. This is a Bureau of State Security matter. The airforce have been told that my previous message about a helicopter was a mistake.'

'Shit. The bastard's just shot two of our men. Now we're supposed just to let him go.'

'The orders came from the highest authority,' Swart stammered nervously.

'All right Swart. Switch the bloody radio off. I'm going to demand an explanation.'

John Fry left the American Embassy in Pretoria just after 9 p.m. Things between him and the American Ambassador had been very tense. He had not expected trouble so early on from Rayne's men, but he had alerted the South African border forces not to act immediately if anything strange happened near the Mozambican border.

The American Ambassador as usual had not wanted to help him. A direct call from the White House had changed his mind and brought him away from the glittering evening function he'd been enjoying. The Ambassador then made the call to the South African Minister of Defence. The Minister was furious: two South African soldiers dead, and some maniac in a helicopter who was to be left alone.

The Ambassador spent ten minutes listening to a tirade against his country's double dealing on the African continent. The American Ambassador then reminded the Minister of the importance of some undercover arms deals between the United States and South Africa.

After a few moments' silence the Ambassador was told that his security representative could make a call to the South African Bureau of State Security. The matter would be treated as top secret and there would be no embarrassing disclosures. The Ambassador apologised for the death of the two South Africans – and at that point the Minister slammed the phone down.

Fry had to admit that he would have behaved in exactly the same way. The US Ambassador, Billy Halliday, vented his wrath on John Fry.

'Heavens, John, you guys are still playing God. I don't know what you're up to, I don't want to know. But if it causes an international incident, I'll personally see to it that you get roasted.'

'I must remind you, Billy, that officially I don't exist. I'm not here. The security of this continent is a top priority with the United States. It's not going to be another Vietnam, you must understand that. And we have no intention of letting the Russians control one of the world's most mineral-rich continents. So we fight our war behind the scenes. People do get killed, but for you it's rather like when you buy meat from the butcher – you just enjoy the taste, you don't have to participate in the killing. Of course I'm sorry those South African soldiers got it, but that's the nature of undercover work. There'll be more deaths before this thing is over, more sacrifices.'

Billy didn't particularly like Fry's simile. 'But you must be careful. The Russians are looking for trouble. We burnt them on that incident in Angola and no doubt they're still smarting. I don't need any embarrassing prisoners trotting out unpleasant details of the activities of the CIA.'

'That's the last thing we have to worry about, Billy. Now, if you will excuse me, I have to talk to my friends down the road.'

John Fry liked Pretoria. It was a pleasant city of wide streets and many trees. Unlike the stark skyscraper ruthlessness of Johannesburg, designed exclusively to promote the getting and spending of money, Pretoria's architecture had a soothing period flavour. Although only twenty minutes by car from Johannesburg, it had a warmer and more pleasant climate too. He walked to his car parked amongst the shadows and drove off casually.

Always he had to watch. You didn't have the luxury of careless-ness when you worked in security. He didn't have far to go, but he took a particularly circuitous route.

Eventually he came to a large British colonial house and parked next to an anonymous-looking Mercedes-Benz in the drive. He went up to the front door, waiting the customary ten minutes before being admitted. He took a deep breath as he stepped over the threshold. He was entering the headquarters of the South African Bureau for State Security.

Sarel van der Spuy was waiting for him. 'Fuck it, Fry, you make things very difficult for me. You certainly get a star grading for intrigue. Do you realise who that lunatic of yours shot? Major "Iron Man" Viljoen. Shot straight in the head.'

Fry decided to act defensively. He had the upper hand anyway, so there was no point in overplaying.

'But I thought he retired a couple of years back,' he said.

'Evidently he met some businessmen who'd seen some strange activities in the St Lucia area. The Major flew over the place to check it out, but by the time he arrived your boys had already flown off. But you see, Viljoen was a detail man, so he checked out the whole area and found this deserted farmhouse. A few strange objects in the workshop were all the evidence he needed to call in the army.

'Anyway, one of your bastards came back. They were waiting for him, but he obviously knew they were there. He came in in a helicopter, but he was clever enough to land it a kilometre away. He killed a private and Viljoen, then got clean away.'

John Fry was troubled – it didn't make sense. Rayne had never said anything about having organised his own air support.

'Sarel, I think we've got our wires crossed. It doesn't sound like one of my guys. They would all have been together, anyway.'

'It's too late to find out now, John. But I can't believe what you're saying. The man in the attack was white. Now what would someone like that be doing in the St Lucia area unless he was one of yours?'

'Could be a poacher.'

'Don't be bloody stupid. Show me a poacher who's able to take on the South African army. That guy was a pro – I've spoken to the guys who were there. He moved like greased lightning and he was armed with an assault rifle. Listen, John, look at what happened to us in the Seychelles, a complete bugger-up. These people you employ are mavericks, they're completely unreliable.'

'No, the man I'm using is different. If it's him there'll be a logical explanation to all of this. What are you going to say in the press?'

'Routine. It was an accident. The Major thought he saw a terrorist and it turned out to be one of our own. They killed each other by accident.'

'Can you trust your men to keep their mouths shut?'

'If they don't they'll have their balls cut off without anaesthetic.'

'One more thing, Sarel. If your men run into anyone in the next week, shoot to kill.'

'And if they're yours?'

'They'll be expendable by then.'

'Remind me never to work for you, John. You're a ruthless shit.'

John Fry left the house and lit a cheroot, his mind in turmoil. Gallagher was obviously a crafty, clever bastard. Major Long had said he was over the edge, a man punch-drunk from too much combat duty. Well, Gallagher didn't seem much like that. He'd turned out to be a cool operator – too good for the job. The chances of success were slim enough, and the chances of getting out alive non-existent. He'd obviously realised that, and organised the helicopter accordingly.

Fry shrugged. No matter what precautions he took, Gallagher wouldn't last long if he returned into South African or Rhodesian air space. All that mattered was that he stopped the Russians.

In the radar tower at Beira Airport, Comrade Asimov lay slumped over the book he had been trying to read. He had drunk far too much the previous evening and bitterly resented the fact that he had had to be on duty by six that morning. There were no exercises planned for that day, and no planes coming in on the blank screen; as he reasoned, his being there was a complete waste of time. After resisting the urge to be sick several times, and trying to keep awake with awful synthetic coffee, he had eventually dropped off to sleep at seven o'clock.

If he had stayed awake he would have seen the tiny dot approaching the airport from the south. At first it would have seemed that the dot's destination was the airport, but then it

237

would have disappeared off the screen while still some kilometres away. Now the radar screen was blank again and there was no evidence that the dot had ever existed.

The sound of footfalls on the steel ladder leading up the control tower woke him. He quickly stuffed the book under the table and took a fast swig of coffee before sweeping his hair back and gazing intently at the radar screen. He could sense that someone was coming through the trapdoor, but pretended to be locked in concentration and unaware of any other sounds.

'Asimov.'

His name was said quietly, so he pretended not to hear.

'Asimov!'

He jumped with fright, half affected and half real. As he did so, he knocked the coffee over the control panel and it dribbled over the edge onto the floor. He stood to attention and saluted his superior. 'Good morning, sir.'

'Asimov, I've told you before, you must keep watching that screen all the time. You haven't seen anything?'

'Nothing out of the ordinary, sir.'

'Idiots, absolute idiots. They don't deserve to run the country, let alone live off it. One of the fools who works in the mess says he saw a giant helicopter flying near here on his way to work. Just the sort of line they like to give you, gets you all worked up for nothing. I'll make sure the fool works hard today. Absolute nonsense, anyway, unless it was one of ours. What the hell would have the range to make it this far? It would be suicide with what we've got on the runway. Bloody Rhodesians aren't that stupid. Anyway, I'd be surprised if they've got any helicopters left.'

Asimov laughed dutifully at the joke. His head was throbbing and all he wanted to do was sit still and not think at all.

'I'll keep a look-out, sir, one can't be too careful.'

'Very good, Asimov. And clean that coffee up and get this place ship-shape. General Vorotnikov is bringing that man who arrived yesterday to see the airport in all its glory. Make sure this room is so clean that I could lie on the floor without dirtying my uniform. Is that understood?'

'Yes, sir.'

'Well, don't just stand there, you idiot. Get on the phone and call someone to clean this mess up.'

*

Getting the truck had been one problem, driving it was another matter. The gearbox didn't appear to be fitted with synchromesh and each change was accompanied by nightmarish howls from the differential. At first Lois had wondered if he'd picked up a dud, but once he'd got used to the noise, the machine was all right.

Taking out the driver of the truck hadn't been easy. He'd used the old trick of putting an obstacle in the road and jumping the vehicle when it slowed down. Then he had climbed along the roof and swung down across the cab, ripping the door open and grabbing the driver by the throat. Holding the steering wheel with one hand as the man fought against him, he'd braked, and then pushed his combat knife in smoothly below the lower ribs.

The man stopped screaming after a few minutes. Lois dragged the body out of the cab and covered it with rocks and earth. He carefully covered his tracks as he returned to the truck.

He had to get more aviation fuel for the chopper, that was all there was to it. Without it he would soon be as dead as the man he'd left carefully hidden under the earth.

The road was good, which partially made up for the dreadful springing on the truck. He bounced along in the darkness till he came to the first road-block and leered down scornfully at the black guard who came up to him. The man spoke to him in Portuguese. 'Where's your pass?'

'Where do you think?'

The guard almost snarled with anger. Lois reached inside his jacket, whipped out his Browning and shot the man in the face. Then he roared off, his back soaked with sweat.

As he had expected, the security on the fuel storage depot was far tighter than at the road-block. He'd parked the truck some distance back and leopard-crawled up near the front entrance. Now he moved in slowly and soundlessly towards the sentry post. He came at the man from behind and held a combat knife to his throat. 'You come with me,' he whispered in Portuguese.

The security guard dropped his weapon and walked in the direction Lois steered him. It took fifteen minutes to reach the truck. The man stank, he'd urinated in his pants with fear.

Lois indicated that he should drive the truck. 'You drive. One wrong move and I slit your throat.'

They drove slowly through the entrance gates and past large

239

storage tanks. They pulled up next to some hundred-litre drums of aviation fuel. Lois needed ten. He knew that the guard wouldn't be able to load the big drums into the back of the truck by himself; he'd have to help him.

They were lifting up the second drum when the man shifted his weight and pushed the container over onto Lois. The next moment he was on him, smashing his fist into Lois' face. Lois brought his left hand up flat and hard into the man's crutch. The man drew back screaming and Lois crashed his knee into his skull. His adversary fell over, dead.

Lois loaded the truck by himself. It was back-breaking work, and by the time he'd got all ten drums on, he was totally exhausted, but at least the engine started easily, and he began to steer the machine towards the entrance gate. Now his progress was slow, the load of fuel on the back weighing the truck down heavily. Another guard was at the entrance. Outside, there were soldiers everywhere. Lois knew if they went for him, he was finished.

To his surprise, the guard lifted the boom and let him out without any fuss.

He took the right fork in the road and headed north. All the details of his exact landing position were accurately stored in his head. He had carefully surveyed the surrounding ground before coming in to land.

About a kilometre further on, he swung off onto a dirt path to the left. Then he stopped and carefully covered up the tracks of the truck tyres. Now he moved very slowly, not wanting to do any damage to the bush at the side of the path. Every fifty metres he stopped and went over the vehicle tracks with a branch. He dropped pieces of dead bush to heighten the impression that no one had been that way for a long time. The sun was rising by the time he made it back to the helicopter.

Larry Preston went through the hardware again very carefully. Everything had to work perfectly when they stormed the bank, the stun grenades especially. They had to knock the guard out before he could sound the alarm. Then it would be straight to the strong-room. If high explosives didn't move the door, they had the rocket-launcher to fall back on. The trouble was, it would make such a noise that the whole town would know the bank was under attack in seconds.

After being cooped up in the store for nearly three days, Larry's nerves were seriously on edge. The town was bristling with soldiers throughout the day, and he'd witnessed passers-by being arrested and interrogated on the spot. One man had been shot dead for being uncooperative. The only thing that kept Larry sane was the thought of the money in the vault. He vowed he was never going to go through this hell again.

He didn't like Mick. The Rhodesian was more interested in the success of the operation than the money – Larry thought he was crazy. Mick had told him a lot about Captain Gallagher, and the more Larry heard, the less he liked his commander. Gallagher wasn't a mercenary in the strict sense of the word, he was doing this job because he believed in it. The man was obviously a maniac, and that meant there was less chance of them all getting out alive. It wouldn't surprise Larry if Gallagher actually intended to return the money they got from the bank to the Rhodesians. Well, in his book that was crazy. He had a few plans of his own.

Larry shifted uneasily, keeping watch through the whited-out windows of the shop. Mick was up on the roof of the hotel, watching the bank. Gallagher was somewhere in town, searching for a bloody woman he'd taken a fancy to. Larry wished they could attack the bank the next day and get the hell out. For all he cared, the Russians could take over the whole of Africa.

A patrol crossed over to the store. They looked directly into the whited-out windows and Larry felt his heart beating faster. God, he would be glad when they got out of this place.

The ballroom of the Grande Hotel was impressive, to say the least. Now, with the huge table at its centre, it looked formidable. A casual observer would have been forgiven for imagining that a vast banquet was about to take place.

The double doors leading into the room opened, and in trooped General Vorotnikov with three of his senior officers. After him came Robert Mugabe, commander of ZANLA; President Samora Machel; and the other ZANLA guerilla leaders. There was one representative of the FRELIMO forces, invited more for form's sake than anything else.

When they were all seated, the General got up to deliver a short opening speech. Reluctantly he spoke in English because that was the one language they all understood.

'President Machel, Mr Mugabe, gentlemen. This is an historic moment. For the first time a black freedom movement will overrun the country it is attacking. This will be no sham victory organised from the West . . .' the audience broke into muffled applause '. . . but a complete take-over. Salisbury is the prize, and it will be yours by the middle of next week. We will provide you with the air support you need, along with the necessary weapons. Victory, I can confidently say, will be easy. What I have invited you all here today to discuss is a subject very close to the heart of our President. That is, what happens after victory?'

A murmur of dissent passed through the audience as the General introduced the subject of the meeting. Mr Robert Mugabe stood up, and the General had to allow him to speak. Mugabe was a big man, verging on the portly; his hair was brushed back, revealing a powerful face, and he wore a pair of large, black-framed glasses.

'I take your point, General, but I cannot understand why we should be discussing what happens after victory. I have learnt the bitter price of defeat and imprisonment – let us throw all our energies into winning this war. We, not the Russians, will decide how we run Zimbabwe when it is ours.'

Enthusiastic applause followed Mugabe's speech and the General began to feel uncomfortable.

'I fully share the sentiments of Mr Mugabe, but experience has taught me that unfortunately the way in which victory is achieved determines what will follow. President Machel, the President of Mozambique and our host, was a victim of the Western conspiracy. After he had attained victory, all the spoils were taken from him . . . I ask you, gentlemen, quite frankly, does Mozambique have a successful economy today?'

The room burst into an uproar, President Machel stared at the General, the anger in his eyes almost electric. This was a crucial moment. The General continued, knowing that if he stopped he might be overwhelmed. 'Yes, but does it? I ask you, would you be so angry if Mozambique had a successful economy?'

President Machel got to his feet, and the General's heart sank. Machel, a thin, intellectual-looking man, was drawn and haggard. He banged his fist against the table and immediately the room became silent. For a few agonising seconds he said nothing.

'Gentlemen, what the General says angers me. And do you

242

know why? Because he speaks the truth. I thought today that Mozambique would be wealthy, the envy of Africa. Instead we are desperately poor, perhaps the poorest country in the world. We took everything when we came to power, and got nothing in the end. You know what happened: the skilled people left our country, so that at one stage there was only a single doctor in the whole of Mozambique. We had no one to advise us but our colonial masters. Now we have been forgotten by the West – as Zimbabwe will be forgotten after your victory. Do you think the sanctions will be lifted? Maybe, but the shortages will continue. The avenues of trade have been cut off. After a bloodbath, all the white people will leave . . .'

Angry shouts cut Machel off in mid-sentence, but he shouted on. 'Don't be fools! We need those people, especially their skills because we do not have such skills ourselves. Robert, you must listen to me or you too will gain nothing except poverty. This must be a victory for the people, and there is no victory and no freedom in a country where young babies die because they do not have enough to eat. Do you know where the principal source of income for my country comes from now? Do you?'

The room was silent, they knew what he was going to say.

'From South Africa. And if they decide to repatriate all the Mozambicans working on their mines tomorrow, we will be devastated. We have no "independence" in the true meaning of the word. Now, let the General continue.'

The Russian did not rise immediately, he wanted the impact of what Machel had said to register fully with the audience. He knew that Mugabe trusted Machel implicitly. They were the commanders of the moment and they had to sell his plans to their own people.

Vorotnikov got up slowly from his chair and paced away from the table. All the eyes around it followed his progress. He came to the map that still hung on the wall, depicting the Portuguese empire at the height of its influence.

'This map should not be here, but I am glad it is. Portugal was a great nation once, the most powerful in the world. And what is it today? A small European state of no significance whatever. The Portuguese empire did not develop overnight, nor did it fall apart quickly. Both processes took a long time. After her first revolution Russia went through terrible hardship and it was only through the great plans of Stalin that Russia gradually became the powerful nation that she is today. Wealth and power, so desirable, so long and difficult to achieve. But I want to offer you both, and in a very short time.'

Robert Mugabe rose to his feet. 'I will listen to what the General has to say. Later we will debate whether we accept it or not.'

'Thank you, Mr Mugabe. Our plan is quite simple. There are key areas in the Rhodesian economy that must continue to function, and the people who run these areas should be kept on, be they black or white. Property must not immediately be expropriated and an impression of stability must be established. I know this is hard, but it will pay dividends in the long term. A western pricing system must be retained and the economy must function as it did before. The power will rest with your own people, but for a transition period the control of the means of production will still rest with the white people. They, however, will have a much smaller share of the profits.'

'And who will be powerful enough to administer and finance this transition period?'

The General was impressed with Mugabe's grasp of the situation. 'I have found a very wealthy international businessman who is prepared to fund the new state. He will require nothing more than a percentage of the profits. He has the experience and the knowledge to create a sophisticated infrastructure, especially in the area of mining.'

'Such a man would become far too powerful.'

'Mr Mugabe, you would rule the country. If you did not like his methods it would be relatively easy to throw him out. He would not want to share political power with you; his aims are merely commercial.' He reached down into his briefcase and pulled out a large document. It was not the one he had been working on with Aschaar for the last year, but a cleverly revised version, and showed the majority benefit from the new regime going to the state. Altogether, the document outlined a very attractive scheme that promised to make the new Zimbabwe a prosperous country. It was his trump card.

Vorotnikov passed the file over to Mugabe. 'A lot of work has gone into this document. It contains the ideas of some of the best business brains in the world, responding to the ultimate opportunity – the creation of a new state from the drawing-board up. Naturally it will take you some time to work your way through the details, and I think it will be best to hold back any further discussion until you and your colleagues have had time to digest it.'

Mugabe stared at him coldly. 'This "grand plan", does it have the stamp of approval of your own government?'

Mugabe had uncanny insight, thought the General. A most perceptive question. '*I* am in charge of my government's activities in this region. These plans are approved by me as the official representative of the Soviet Government in Southern Africa.'

'Very good, General Vorotnikov, but you have evaded my question. What would the Soviet government think if they were to see these plans?'

'They would naturally approve of them. I do not see the point of your questioning.'

'General, if you were to disappear tomorrow and another man were to replace you, I would be most anxious that he should abide by these plans.'

'I see your point. You want a guarantee?'

'Exactly. I could strike a deal with you today, and tomorrow you could be gone.'

'Let me put your mind at ease, Mr Mugabe. This plan is self-perpetuating. Once you introduce these businessmen into the country, they will not leave, they will be driven by the desire to make money.'

'And how will my people feel about that?'

'They will not have empty bellies. They will have steady employment. And you will draw plenty of taxes from them to build up your army and thus strengthen your power-base.'

'You argue very convincingly, General. You realise that your own role in this new country will be purely advisory?'

'I did not expect more, Mr Mugabe.'

'It is human nature to want more. But you must understand my position. I am a staunch supporter of Marxism, but I also respect what you have to say about the failings of the Marxist state. I do not want the new Zimbabwe to suffer as Mozambique has done. On the contrary, Zimbabwe must become very strong, so that the South Africans will fear us, and will come gladly to the negotiating table – the fighting has gone on for too long. Meanwhile, however, we still need you. Only with your assistance will we be able to score an outright military victory over the imperialists.'

This was the sort of talk that Vorotnikov loved to hear – though he had absolutely no intention of encouraging peaceful change in South Africa. For his own purposes, the more violent the struggle the better.

'What you say is true. But I would argue that most of the problem comes from the divisions within your own ranks. If you had managed to combine your efforts with those of Joshua Nkomo, I am sure that you would have achieved victory by now.'

'Nkomo does not think as I do, General. He does not fight the war of the flea, his men seek direct, suicidal engagements. We seek to win the hearts and minds of the people; we wear our enemy down through a war of attrition. In the new government there will be a place for Nkomo, but he will never be head of state. After the take-over there will be no elections for a long, long time. The state must first rebuild itself before the people have the right to vote.'

'Trust me, Mr Mugabe. You will see, when you read the document, that we will take complete control of the means of production the moment the invasion is launched. Then *you* will take control of a going concern, rather than a failing one. The British, of course, will be furious. I would advise you not to apply for membership of the Commonwealth, but rather to come to us for investment funding. After the creation of the new Zimbabwe, the world will no longer say there is no successful black economy.

'The iron is hot. I ask you to study these plans day and night. The less time you take to make a decision, the sooner we will achieve an overwhelming victory.'

As the General finished speaking, Robert Mugabe made his decision. 'Thank you, General. We will see if your fine words are a match for those contained in this document. We will reconvene tomorrow afternoon. My commanders and I have a busy twenty-four hours before us. I congratulate you on being so open with us. However, I will not be pressured into a decision.'

The delegation of black leaders filed out of the room, leaving Vorotnikov and his aides alone. Carl, to his left, was the first to break the silence.

'General, forgive me for asking, but did you strike a deal with Mr Brand?'

'Yes, Carl. A tough man.'

'It is disgraceful. This will be the first time the Soviet Union has ever had to pay to buy its own weapons. The profit should accrue to the people, not a dirty capitalist entrepreneur.'

'You are correct, Carl. But you must understand that the moment I have the weapons I will eliminate Mr Brand, and he will not be paid.'

'Ah. You live up to your reputation, General.'

The man had climbed up to the balcony in the darkness, and now he came into the room. He stank, he was haggard and unshaven. His eyes were black round the sockets and he had a wild look about him – yet Rayne knew him from somewhere. The man came into the centre of the room and stood in front of Rayne's bed, looking at the barrel of the gun pointed directly at him.

'You think I let you down. You have to realise that I got here as soon as I could.'

'Lois!'

Rayne leapt to his feet and embraced him. In a flash he realised the immense courage it must have required for Lois to have flown into Mozambique and then entered Beira to find the hotel.

'This place frightens me, Captain, it's far worse than I expected. I've already had to kill to survive this far. The helicopter's ready, so are the bikes. I managed to get into the fuel depot just outside the town, and I smuggled out enough fuel to get us out of here safely.'

'I don't know how you managed it, Lois. It must have taken a hell of a lot of guts. We've had problems, but mostly we've been lucky. So what happened? I tried to make contact with you, but after I failed we couldn't put off the launch-time.'

'Problems with the bloody helicopter. It was a miracle I got her going again.'

'Still giving problems?'

'She's flying like a dream. The armaments are working perfectly too. You couldn't have a better machine for the job.'

'Did you clear out the farmhouse before you left?'

'No chance. When I came back to the main camp after you'd left, the place was crawling with the SADF.'

'What the hell!'

'I was lucky I didn't land or they would have had me. After that I flew back and landed a kilometre from the farm. By then I was cautious. There was an ambush – well prepared, but I got the jump on them. I killed one soldier and the commanding officer. That caused complete pandemonium and I was able to get out without being located. I flew over the Mozambique border that same night – the last thing I needed was the South African airforce trying to hunt me down. Luckily, as far as I know there was no pursuit. Is everyone here?'

'Guy is with me in the hotel, Larry and Mick are monitoring the bank. Bunty's covering the road to the airport and Michael Strong is busy sabotaging the runways. Now that you've arrived, everything is in place. We'd better speak to Guy; it's time to let him know about our emergency way out.'

Lois saw that there was something else worrying Rayne. 'Captain, you're not telling me everything, are you?'

Rayne focused his eyes directly on Lois. 'Sam's here, Lois. She was abducted by terrs on the border a week ago. Then the Russians got hold of her. For some reason I can't quite understand, she was taken from them and is being hidden somewhere.'

Lois turned and looked out at the darkness. 'Whatever it takes to find her, sir. I'm with you.'

Bernard sat on the balcony of the villa, sipping a whisky and staring out to sea. There was much on his mind and it had to be sorted out very quickly. Always plans and more plans. A lifetime of intrigue and corporate in-fighting had taught him never to rely on one strategy or one man alone.

He looked down at his watch. A quarter past three. His appointment was for four o'clock.

He had read long ago about an American movie mogul who spent at least an hour of every day on his own, thinking about what he was doing. The story had surprised Bernard, because this was something he himself had been doing for a long time. Business was much like a game of chess: make your move too quickly and you'd regret it later; wait too long and you'd give your opponent the advantage.

Well, now the game had changed and he must make new plans. The wily Russian General was more cunning than he'd expected. Now he'd have to cover his bets, act to protect the enormous amount of money he was sinking into the project. He would have to operate as he did in every African state in which he did business, through bribery and negotiation. Well, whatever the outcome, the General would end up paying, he'd make sure of that . . . He felt cut off in this place, away from the phones, teleprinters and screens that kept him in touch with the daily events of the international business world.

In London Jay would be completing negotiations on the purchase of a large office property in the heart of the City – the new headquarters of the Goldcorp Group. Even though British taxes were prohibitive, it was worth the move; in London they'd be able to distance themselves from the South African government, and better position themselves for the transfer of power when it finally came.

Bernard smiled to himself as he imagined the expression that would appear on certain South African faces if it was known that he was shortly to meet a man who was not only a vehement Marxist, but also dedicated to the downfall of the South African government.

For a moment, too, Bernard thought about the problem of Jay and the woman. What was her name again – Helen? It had been stupid, the sort of boy's prank that got one into big trouble. They had far too many enemies to make that sort of mistake comfortably. That was where the old man had always been right. You killed or you were killed.

He intended to prove Max Golden correct. It wasn't going to be long before Max handed over control to Jay, and then Bernard would make his move. The control he had always wanted would be his; the Goldens would be past tense.

Bernard sauntered down the stairs into the garden. As he did so, he carefully moved his hand up behind his back, as if to scratch between his shoulder blades, and felt the familiar form of the thin throwing-knife that hung between them. He never took chances.

He spoke to one of the servants, telling him he was going for a walk on the beach and did not want to be disturbed. The servant bowed obsequiously and disappeared inside the villa. Strange, thought Bernard, how even after independence most men preferred to serve others rather than to be masters of their own fate. He ambled towards the beach through the flowerbeds, his eyes constantly scanning the area around him.

The servant to whom he had spoken watched him fearfully

through the folds of curtaining in the lounge. The big man moved like a cat, the thick, black curly hair of his enormous head partially obscuring the powerful face. Bernard turned round, sensing that he was being watched, and the servant disappeared quickly behind the curtains.

Once he was on the beach, Bernard relaxed. There was no one about – the area round the villa was heavily guarded, and anyone who dared to trespass was savagely beaten up. He could not fault the General on his security arrangements, they were impeccable. He continued along the beach for some five minutes until he came to a path that branched off through trees. Looking behind him again, to make sure that he wasn't being followed, he disappeared into the trees. He walked on through thick vegetation until suddenly he was at the perimeter fence. As promised, there were no guards here, and a black man in combat uniform was waiting for him with a four-wheel-drive vehicle.

This man gestured for Bernard to get into the passenger seat and then blindfolded him. They drove in silence for about ten minutes, then Bernard's eyes were uncovered.

They were parked outside an elegant country house. A short green lawn led up from the drive to a line of imposing Roman pillars that formed the front of the building. Bernard was glad the meeting had been set up in this secluded place. He was without any protection yet he enjoyed the danger.

As he approached the dark green door with the gold handle, he slowed his pace. There appeared to be no one about. Perhaps they had let him down? There was always that risk.

As he came up to the door, it opened to reveal an enormous black man in military uniform with no rank badges visible. Bernard walked cautiously through the door into the white-tiled reception area.

'Mr Aschaar . . .'

The moment the man spoke, Bernard's impression of him changed. The voice was clear and cultivated; this was no ordinary soldier.

'. . . you will have to wait some time. He is deep in discussion. He apologises for your having to wait and informs me that if you are angry another time for a meeting can be arranged.'

If he had been in Johannesburg or any of the world's industrial capitals, Bernard would have got up and left, but not here. He sat down on one of the Edwardian chairs and picked up a copy of *Time* magazine.

Leafing through it, he was not surprised to see a picture of himself in the financial section, and talk of a large-scale take-over by the Goldcorp Group within the South African mining industry. He turned the pages, not wanting to clutter his mind with those problems before his crucial meeting.

He moved to the social pages and listlessly read through an article on Penelope O'Keefe, the film star, and had nearly finished it when he realised that she was the daughter of one of his arch rivals. He remembered trying to have her kidnapped and before that, attempting to bring down the plane she was flying in. The death of Sir George's daughter would surely have destroyed him and made his mines vulnerable to a takeover bid from Goldcorp. She was spectacularly beautiful and he felt bitter, remembering Marisa his wife . . . There was still the anger inside him. She had demanded he have those tests, and he had learned that he would never be able to father a child.

It was true that they could have implanted some of his semen in her body, but already their relationship was doomed. He had seen the contempt in her eyes – contempt for him, Bernard Aschaar, because he could never father a child properly. The bitch! She had always known how to attack him where he was most vulnerable, and now she had at her command the perfect, devastating weapon. One night after they had made love and she had criticised his performance, he had beaten her up.

She almost wanted that – to see him lose control. But she had thought he would stop and he didn't, he carried on till she couldn't scream any more. They had taken her to hospital, and a plastic surgeon had had to fix her face.

He visited her in hospital the next day, her face blue and covered with bruises. She had laughed at him, called him a common thug. He could see the look of contempt on the faces of the doctor and the nurses.

Now she lived independently, continuing to harass him. There were things in his past she knew about. Things he wanted no one else to know . . .

'Mr Aschaar, Mr Aschaar.' The voice intruded upon his unpleasant memories. 'You can go through now, he is ready.'

In the room beyond, the curtains were closed and the lighting was subdued. A man sat hunched over a bare table. His head was hidden in his arms and he did not get up at the sound of Bernard's entry, but spoke from that position.

'Mr Aschaar, I must state now that I both despise and respect you. You have much that I want. I know of your dealings with other black politicians, that you never give anything away, but you do set up factories and provide work – though I am sure those things are of peripheral interest to you.'

He lifted his head and stared at Bernard. 'What is it that you are offering me, Mr Aschaar?' Behind the thick lenses of the spectacles, the black eyes watching him were very much alive. Bernard felt that this man was quite similar to himself. He decided to be straight. He wasn't sure how much this man knew of his dealings with Zambia, Kenya and Angola.

'Soon you will rule a country.'

'That is not for certain. It could be Mr Nkomo, you could well be talking to the wrong man.'

'I never talk to the wrong man. I know from my informants that in a fair election you will sweep the board. I also know that you are an intelligent and well-educated man. Your country is your life, you would not wish to see it descend to the condition of Mozambique. You need power to succeed in your ambitions. Your next target must be South Africa.'

Bernard finished and waited. The man facing him did not say anything for some time, but eventually he spoke. His face had hardened and there was an irritated tone to his voice.

'Firstly, I do not like people who put words in my mouth, though much of what you say is true. I am aware of the difficulties. I have already spoken to some people with far more power than you, Mr Aschaar, in fact I believe that you might even be allied to those people. Your guiding hand was apparent in the document General Vorotnikov handed to me at the end of the conference, was it not? Is this now a double-cross?'

Bernard smiled evilly. 'Suppose the Russians cannot assist you, what then?'

The man pushed back the glasses which had slid down his nose. 'Then I will have little to do with them. I will make my own way.'

'Exactly. This meeting is merely to discuss arrangements if that situation should arise. My company, the Goldcorp Group, would be able to help you to press ahead with the developments you wanted to continue. We would provide extra capital.'

The man looked at him cynically. 'Exactly as you have already described in your document?'

'No, not exactly. You would be able to hang onto more whites, and the governments of the West would feel far more kindly disposed to your new regime. The developments could take place a lot faster.'

'You are advocating that we should not continue with the invasion plan?'

Bernard raised his eyebrows and moved forward, resting his hands on his thighs, his voice now almost a whisper.

'Far from it. I am merely saying what could be done if the invasion plan should not succeed.'

'Covering all your options, Mr Aschaar?'

'There is only one option I wish to cover, which is that I should get the principal mining rights in your new country. That is my only interest in this matter. The more mines my group controls, the more power we have to influence world pricing.'

The man laughed maliciously. 'You get all the control and we take a small cut?'

Bernard leaned back and put his hands behind his head. 'Hardly. You don't have to concern yourself with the running of large mines. You can charge taxes on these industries as well as getting a percentage of the profits. Who else will run those mines for you?'

'The Russians. They have the technology.'

Bernard got up and paced over to the window. He looked away from the man seated at the table.

'Yes, that is true. However, I think you know better than I do the high cost of such expertise. I have no interest in wrecking your country for profit. You might be surprised to know that I hate any form of anarchy. As a capitalist, I am appalled by waste.'

'Industrial waste, of course, Mr Aschaar, not human waste.'

Aschaar turned from the window and stared coldly at the man. 'One learns to be cynical about the value of life in Africa.'

The black man smashed his fist hard onto the desk in front of him. Bernard didn't flinch. He waited for the man to break the silence.

'I do not find your clever comments in the least amusing, Mr Aschaar.'

'Experience has been my teacher. I took a gamble when I

253

came to you – but I can promise you that there will be no gamble for you if you come to me. You need me. You have nothing behind you but the most protracted and unsuccessful guerilla war in recent history.'

The man rested his clenched fists on the table in front of him and glared at Bernard.

'They say that you are a bastard, Mr Aschaar, and I can only agree with them. Your logic is faultless, you are loyal only to opportunity. I agree to do this deal with you, but only on the strict condition that you do not overstep the limit. Then I will reserve the right to expropriate all your mines.'

'I have your word that what we have discussed will not go beyond these four walls?'

'This conversation has been far more dangerous for me than for you, Mr Aschaar. Naturally I do not think General Vorotnikov would be happy if he found out about it, but then it is not in my interest to tell him.'

'I trust you. I would suggest a period of one year at the most to phase in the new operating rules and the new personnel.'

'Just do not forget who will be in control, that is all I ask of you. Now . . . Please, I have much to arrange. I will see you again when this is all over.'

They shook hands, looking into each other's eyes one final time.

Bernard left the room and returned to the jeep where he was again blindfolded for the return journey. Only when he was back on the beach did a smile creep onto his face. It had gone much better than he had expected. The man was no fool, and it had been a good decision to meet him, well worth the risk of Vorotnikov finding out. The prize was just too big to let slip through his fingers. Of course there would be others who would approach Mugabe, but none of them could match Bernard's expertise when it came to the mining industry.

Now he must get out of Beira as soon as possible. His plane wasn't scheduled to leave until Sunday afternoon, but he couldn't move the date forward without attracting undue attention. Tomorrow, Friday, he would visit the bank again and go over his affairs. Tonight he would have dinner with the General.

Robert Mugabe waited until Aschaar had left the room. Then he walked over to the cabinet in the corner next to the window

254

and lifted its lid. Inside, the two large reels of a tape recorder turned slowly round.

He pushed the stop switch and they ceased moving. Then he rewound the tape and played it back. Only after he had heard the entire conversation again was he satisfied.

As he was listening another man had come into the room. When the playback had finished Robert Mugabe said, 'It is the best I could have hoped for. He will drive a hard bargain but we need his expertise. I have more faith in him than in Vorotnikov. The Russians are too hungry.'

'We must be careful, Robert, very careful.'

Jay left the woman's flat at about nine-thirty that morning. There was a continuous drizzle and he dashed across the road, hailing a cab.

'Round House, The Boltons, South Kensington.'

He ignored the cab driver's good-natured banter and stared out at the rain. It had been a good night, but he wouldn't see her again, despite all the promises he had made the previous evening. Jay always prided himself on the detachment he could bring to his relationships with women. Hyde Park flashed past on his right and he checked his watch. Twenty to ten. There was plenty of time.

By the time the cab pulled up outside the imposing residence that dominated The Boltons, the rain was pouring down. A butler ran down from the entrance, holding an umbrella; he paid the cab driver, then opened the cab door for Jay. In the entrance hall he took off Jay's raincoat and showed him into the drawing room. 'He will be ready for you at ten, sir.'

Jay picked up a copy of the *Financial Times* and turned to the share prices. He was pleased to see that the Goldcorp Group was as strong as ever. As anticipated, the shares of Waugh Mining were rising, but this would not deter Goldcorp, they would continue buying through third parties.

He looked up to see the butler staring across at him. 'He will see you in the study, sir.'

Jay went through and knocked on the white double doors before entering. 'Come in.' The deep voice he knew so well growled from behind the panelling.

His father was dressed in white riding breeches, and his mane of white hair cascaded over a black hunting jacket. The brilliant blue eyes flashed as Jay entered the room.

'Sit down.'

Jay walked over to the window seat and sat down. He looked idly round the room at the crowded shelves of books.

'I am impressed with your performance, Jay. If you carry on like this, you will take control of the Group at the end of this year.'

Jay couldn't resist letting a faint smile run across his lips. 'Thank you, sir.'

'And what is your decision on the other matter?' Max Golden sat down behind the desk and pressed his fingers together, looking intently at Jay.

'He's in Mozambique at the moment, following up his plan to finance the Rhodesian revolution with the Russians . . .'

'You have not answered my question, Jay.'

'Patience, sir. On Bernard's return I will tell him of your decision. This will naturally result in his implementing his plans for my downfall. I've discovered his new hiding place for the photographs and I'll have them back before he can do a thing.'

'Your previous attempt was deplorably ham-fisted. Bernard had to call Muller in to sort things out. And now we have Major-General Deon de Wet on our backs.'

'Correction. On *Bernard's* back.'

'Very good, Jay, very good. And Miss Seyton-Waugh?'

'As she has refused to cooperate with us, the photographs of her will be released. Naturally she'll be forced to step down from the CMC, and in the rumpus that follows I will take command. Tony Rudd will sell out when he realises that Sonja is a whore, and I'll make sure his remaining son Robard dies of a drug overdose.'

'And the policeman?'

'De Wet will follow his brother to the grave. I think he can be assassinated by some black extremist.'

Max Golden got up and strode across the room. He pumped Jay's hand warmly. 'I'm proud of you. Aschaar was my final test for you.'

'He's finished.'

'Don't underestimate him, Jay.'

'I've discovered his weak link. Marisa, his wife, has proved most cooperative. She has already borne me a son.'

256

Max Golden grimaced. 'Was that really necessary?'

'Do you think Aschaar would have shown me any compassion?'

'None.'

Sonja said goodbye to Helen and drove slowly back to her hotel. Her second visit had been worth it. She gripped the steering wheel very tightly. Already it had cost her all her strength to go against the blackmail threats from Goldcorp, and each day she dreaded the appearance of the photographs and the subsequent scandal. Only Deon gave her the courage to go on. Even now, in England, she knew she could rely on him.

Helen's story had confirmed her fears. Bernard and Jay would stop at nothing to achieve their ends; she, Sonja, was just a pawn in a larger game.

The moment she got to the hotel she went to her room and phoned Deon.

'There's no legal way of stopping them, Sonja. They have too much power. Muller's on their payroll and he's slowly destroying my credibility in the force. I know he wants me to resign, but they'll have to throw me out.'

'Deon, you must be careful. They know you're involved with me. They've killed Pieter. Now you're in the firing line.'

'I'll worry about me. You must come back here now, and then I'll sort those bastards out once and for all. It's either them or me.'

Colonel Michael Strong stretched out his arms and then recoiled at the sudden smell of his own sweat. It was five days since he had last washed. They had become like animals, living in the dirt round the perimeter of the airport.

Even though his nerves had hardened, the anticipation of the action scared him. One wrong move and they would all be dead. He watched every man closely, always looking for signs of strain or weakness. It would only take one fool to give the game away, and he would have to dispose of any man whose nerves broke now.

He wondered if Rayne was operating under the same strain in Beira. He had last seen Bunty Mulbarton the day before. That was when he realised what he must look like – seeing Bunty so haggard and exhausted. Incredibly, Bunty had been able to mine the road to the airport without being detected.

One thought worried him constantly. What if the escape plane didn't arrive? Had Rayne made some form of contingency plan? He was sure Rayne must have something up his sleeve, but what?

Through the sights of his machine-gun he watched a squad of Russian soldiers move over the tarmac. He calculated that he could have brought each one of them down if necessary. The distance was just three hundred metres, he could do it with one squeeze of the trigger. The figures looked almost like toy soldiers through the shimmering heat haze on the tarmac.

The sweat dripped from his forehead onto the stock of the machine gun. He glanced at his watch and saw that it was just after two in the afternoon. Four bloody hours to go, he thought to himself – as he remembered that he was the one who had started routine watches of six hours on and six hours off. It was painful, but it was the only way of guaranteeing their safety.

The General sat alone at the edge of the yacht club, staring out to sea. Nothing could go wrong, he kept repeating to himself, nothing. The logic of it was overwhelming. The Rhodesians could never stave off an all-out attack on Salisbury, their arrogance would be knocked out of them for good. Only the pilots would know of his private orders, and their battle plans would only be opened after take-off.

The time for questioning would come after the attack. It would be a daylight assault, early in the morning when everyone was at their least alert. First a wave of bombers would destroy the airfields, and fire bombs would then be dropped on the capital to create as much havoc as possible and bring people out of the buildings and into the streets.

Then would come the second wave. Fire at random and destroy all people in view. Vorotnikov smiled as he repeated the order to himself. The planes would strafe everything in sight, there would be a bloodbath of epic proportions. No stupid settlement plans after that, and no danger of any whites sticking around. Aschaar's plan would just have to adjust itself. The executions could begin after twenty-four hours – people's courts would deliver the death sentence.

The West, no doubt, would celebrate the victory and keep

quiet about the carnage. As far as the rest of the world were concerned, the Rhodesians were degenerate racists anyway, and deserved everything they got. The few liberals would be quietly forgotten. Vorotnikov would bury them.

Still, he did need the blonde American journalist. She would tell the official story of the glorious new state; she would interview the white people – who would be so terrified by that stage that they would say anything that was required of them . . .

After that there would be martial law and complete expropriation of all white-owned property: a true people's revolution that would be an inspiration to the USSR. His name would feature in *Pravda*, honours would flood in . . . He dreamed of travelling through the streets of Salisbury to the sound of cheering crowds, the saviour of the oppressed.

He finished his drink and stood up. He must return to the villa and his friend, the South African businessman. Usually he would not have drunk so much, but the tension was getting to him. He would have to be careful.

Sam 2

Sam was scared. They'd moved her to another village, which hadn't made her feel any safer. She wished she was back in America, a child again, with her parents to protect her. She daydreamed sometimes that she was on their ranch and riding her pony up to the foothills of the Sierra Nevada . . . This was all so foreign. She lay down on the hessian hammock in the corner of the hut and dozed off to sleep.

She was woken in the darkness. She lashed out and a strong hand caught her own in a vice-like grip.

'Sam. It's me.'

She felt her pulse quicken. She was pleased to see him, yet she was glad it was dark so that he could not see the warm smile that flooded her face.

'I'm sorry, Tongogara, I've been scared.'

'Relax, they'll never find you even if they come looking.'

'And if they torture the villagers?' She saw his face crease with agitation in the half-light and she wished she had not asked such a stupid question.

'They would remain silent. For me, they would die.'

'I have made you angry. Please forgive me.' She wanted him to like her, not to think that she was just a helpless, vulnerable woman.

'I am not angry with you, just with myself. I have seen strange things, parachutes hidden in the bush near Beira.'

'God! Rhodesians?'

'If it's them, then they must be here because they have found out about the invasion plans. How would they have found out?'

'Perhaps from the South Africans? They have the best intelligence system in Africa. I don't think they could be here in large numbers, you would have seen more evidence of them. What are you going to do?'

'Nothing. Absolutely nothing.'

'You're crazy.'

'Sam, many of my own people are against the idea of the invasion. There has been enough death and devastation in this war. By sacking Salisbury we shall merely confirm what the Rhodesians and South Africans are always asserting in the world media.'

'That you're a bunch of savages.' In the half-light she saw the irritation on his face, but he still managed a smile.

'You put it so eloquently. If we can settle this war peacefully, an example will be set for South Africa. If the Rhodesians interfere here now, it will be more ammunition for us at the United Nations. But I can't believe that the Rhodesians would be so stupid as to launch an attack against Mozambique at this sensitive stage.'

'They might be a crack force, the SAS or the Selous Scouts. Could you locate them?'

She felt a tremor of hope. Perhaps Rayne might be amongst them. She was reminded of her love for him. And yet she needed Tongogara; she couldn't quite come to grips with her feelings for this man who'd saved her life.

'If I found them, they'd kill me or I'd kill them. This is war.' They sat for a long time in the darkness, not saying a word. Sam wished that he would take her in his arms, she wanted him desperately. Wanted to feel the strength of him.

He moved towards her and she felt the electricity tingling through her body. But he only kissed her softly on the cheek, then he got up and left without a word.

Maybe they were watching him now. The war was almost a game for them, while for him it was his soul. Why did they fight so well? That was something that intrigued him. Was it because the Rhodesians were a frontier people? Perhaps they were slightly crazy.

He would keep a low profile if they moved in, and make sure his own men kept out of the way. Let the Russians be the cannon fodder for once, it would teach them a good lesson.

They were not as strong as they thought. An engagement with the Selous Scouts would ruin their yet untested image of strength.

Tongogara walked easily in the darkness, making little noise and always aware of what was happening around him. The war was only the beginning for the black man in Africa. His dream was to establish an Africanist state, neither communist nor capitalist. Tongogara felt deep resentment at the way the foreign governments tried to impose their own political systems on the new black states. Before these white men had come into Africa, his people had had their own political systems; but now, in states like South Africa and Rhodesia, the people had been oppressed for so long that they had forgotten their heritage, lost all their pride.

And then the bitterness came back to him, as fresh as the day he had decided to fight for the cause. The white Rhodesians had so little to lose. If the tide turned against them they would merely retreat back to Britain or across the border to South Africa, with their material wealth substantially intact. And how they would jeer at the mistakes of the new black government – mistakes that were the direct result of their own policies. Of course, men who had no experience of power would abuse it at first, this was inevitable.

The white man loved Africa, the land he had taken from the black man, and he could not stand to see it plucked from his grasp. God, how he wished he had been born in another place, at another time, content to live quietly with his wife and bring up his children!

Tongogara stumbled on through the darkness. Back to his men, back to the war.

After a hot bath and a shave Lois was transformed. Rayne still couldn't believe the sudden turn of events: it was a miracle that Lois had been able to fly the helicopter so close to Beira without being detected by the Russian radar systems at the airport. The bikes and other equipment were already in position, the helicopter hidden under a screen of camouflage mats and foliage.

He gave Lois a complete breakdown of his own battle plan and then went down for dinner with Guy as usual. He realised there was no point in keeping Lois's existence a secret any longer – on the contrary, it was now vital that everyone knew about

Lois, in case anything happened to himself. Everyone must know that they had a second way out if the plane didn't come.

To Rayne's surprise, Guy was not particularly astonished. 'I couldn't believe that such an able commander as yourself would have relied on just one avenue of retreat. We all guessed you had something up your sleeve, but why was it so important for you to go through that charade of dismissing Lois when we were in South Africa?'

'I felt then that secrecy was very important. I couldn't be certain, until we were here, that everyone was completely behind me, and I didn't want anything to jeopardize Lois' side of the operation. As it was, he had a very close shave with the South African army after we left. You don't get any second chances in this business, as you well know. Tomorrow I want to get Lois out of town and back to the helicopter. If the plane does arrive on schedule, he'll make his own way out.'

'But it'll take him a lot longer in the chopper.'

'He knows the risks. I made sure that he was one hundred per cent aware of them. We couldn't have a better back-up man.'

The next morning early, Rayne took Lois up onto the hotel roof to show him exactly how they planned to attack the bank. At nine o'clock a big Mercedes pulled up outside. Rayne recognised Bernard Aschaar. He handed the binoculars to Lois.

'That's Bernard Aschaar, head of Goldcorp, one of the world's most powerful mining companies. He's one of the co-ordinators behind this little show. He's got a small fortune in this bank.'

Lois said nothing but Rayne saw his jaw tighten and his fists clench. It was unlike Lois to show emotion so openly.

'It's him, it's the same bastard. I'd like to strangle him with my bare hands.'

Rayne had never heard Lois talk in this way before. Suddenly he had a new insight into the man, he saw the bitterness that drove Lois on.

'You know Aschaar?'

'It's a long story, and it's not pleasant.' He was silent for a few moments, then spoke again. 'It's a part of my life I'd rather forget. I was working as an aircraft mechanic at the Rand Airport. Times were tough and as usual they were especially tough for me. I was desperate for money, and no doubt someone got to know about it. Anyway, one day I got a phone call and a message to say, was I interested in a special job, a one-off affair that would give me enough to retire on? Of course, I said I was. One thing led to another and eventually I agreed to fix a plane for them.'

'How do you mean "fix a plane"?'

'Sabotage. You fiddle with the controls, it's easy enough, and it can't be detected after the crash. It's a popular way of wiping out businessmen who've become a problem. That's what they told me this was about, fixing the private plane of some bastard who'd taken a lot of people for a lot of money. I couldn't argue with that, so I agreed to do the job. The money was incredible. All I had to do was fix the controls, leave my job and collect the cash. The crafty bastards had lied to me from the beginning.'

'They never paid you?'

'Oh yes, they paid me, but then they tried to wipe me. They were scared of an investigation. They never told me a professional pilot would be on the plane and that there'd be passengers. I'd never have done it then, I swear to you that's the truth.

'There was a whole article about it on the South African TV news. The moment I saw that I knew what was going on. There was this girl on the plane, the daughter of some wealthy financier, and it was her they'd really wanted me to wipe out. Typical big business strategy – hit the bastard where it hurts most and then railroad him. I'm sure the buggers didn't give up after the sabotage effort failed.'

Rayne felt himself going cold but said nothing. Lois's was not the only life that had been affected by the incident. Now Rayne knew exactly who had tried to kill Penelope. He was going to get the bastard, that was for sure. Lois misinterpreted Rayne's clenched jaw.

'Look, I know it was attempted murder, but believe me, I'd never have done it if I'd known there were innocent people involved. They sent a hit-man to get me that evening. He nearly did, but he took me for a sucker, didn't know I had a black belt. I killed him. After that I got the hell out of the country. Now I'm back in hell.'

'So what do you feel about Aschaar now?'

'I'm going to get him. If not here, in Johannesburg or somewhere else, I don't care how long it takes. You see, that's my goal, to hit the bastard back. After I'd fought their hit-man I had to have both of my testicles removed. It's not something you forgive.'

'Lois, if there's any way we can get him after the attack, we will. His plane is still on the airstrip – and if he isn't out by early Sunday afternoon, he won't be going anywhere in a hurry.'

Siva Singh sat in his office for a long time without moving. A small voice inside his head told him to phone the General immediately, but another, more urgent voice told him not to.

He had no doubt that Aschaar would carry out all the threats he had made, and worse. Anyway, perhaps he knew a lot more than Singh. If the invasion succeeded then all would be well and Singh would make a lot of money; but if it was a failure there was now another option, in many ways equally attractive. It was merely business: he had just transferred his interests from the General to Mr Aschaar. He pulled a tissue from one of the drawers in his desk and cleaned the blood off his face.

Then he set about cleaning up the broken articles on the floor. It would never do for the staff to know that he had just been slapped around by one of his important clients.

The afternoon sun was low in the sky as Rayne drove the Peugeot slowly along the dirt road. The road-block had been easy, the guard was beginning to know him well. He gave the man a packet of cigarettes, talked to him for a few minutes and then drove on. The guard would never have believed that there was another man hidden in the boot of the car.

Rayne pulled over at the side of the road and got out of the car, walking straight to the back and opening the boot. Lois emerged, partially covered in dust. He got into the passenger seat and Rayne started the car again. After another kilometre Lois gestured to a tree on the right.

'That's where the first bike is hidden. I've also buried a 9mm beneath it with twenty rounds. A couple of grenades as well.'

Rayne kept on driving, anxious not to waste time. A bit further on Lois gestured to the left and Rayne saw a small rocky outcrop.

'Under a pile of stones, directly behind that lot.'

Rayne nodded and kept the car moving.

'The helicopter is another five kilometres down this road on the left. You have to pass through some very thick bush to get to it. About three hundred metres from the road there are thin lines attached to grenades fixed in the trees. Once you've avoided those, you're safe. You can drop me off here. I don't want to go any closer in the car.'

'Thanks, Lois, for everything. On Sunday you should hear a lot of noise at about five in the afternoon. We should be with you within the hour if our own transportation doesn't come in. I suggest, if we don't pitch up, that you get the hell out of here by six-thirty.'

'I'll wait. They won't find me.'

Rayne slowed the car down, they shook hands and then Lois got out and disappeared into the bushes in seconds. Rayne turned the car round and headed back towards Beira.

Now there was only one day left, and he hadn't seen a sign of Sam anywhere. He kept the car going at a slow pace and tried unsuccessfully to concentrate on anything he might have left out . . . Perhaps there was another clue to her whereabouts that he had missed. He couldn't let the men down, but there was no way he was going to leave till he had found her.

Maybe Lois would agree to stay with him. No, he couldn't ask that, the place would be terrifying after the attack. Everybody white outside the Russian camp would be considered a traitor. People would be hauled off the street and interrogated.

He got back into Beira as the sun was setting and parked the car at the back of the hotel. There was nothing left to do, and he knew the next twenty-four hours was going to pass agonisingly slowly. Fortunately he'd heard nothing more about the arms deal he had arranged with the Russians.

He went up to his room and opened the double doors leading onto the balcony. He would have no more alcohol now, his reflexes had to be at their very best for what was to come. There had been no contact from either Bunty Mulbarton or Michael Strong, but this didn't bother him; keeping silence was far more important than keeping in touch.

Now he had time to think about what Lois had told him. When he got back to South Africa he would tell Penelope's father the whole story. How many other people's lives had this maniac wrecked in his quest for more and more power? But Aschaar was another score to settle, one that would have to be dealt with later.

He reviewed the instructions Fry had given him. To avoid

266

destroying the fuel storage tanks; to take the bank and destroy the contents of the safe-deposit boxes; to hit the airport at the same time and then to get the hell out. Not for the first time, he began to question these commands. The bank was a sensible enough diversion to take the focus of Russian attention away from the airport defences – but why should he waste his time destroying the contents of safe-deposit boxes? And why the hell shouldn't he torch the fuel tanks?

On top of the fear Rayne already felt at being in enemy territory came the new fear of betrayal.

Major Martin Long reached for the bottle of sleeping tablets and poured another two into his hand. He looked at his alarm clock. It was past midnight.

He swore out loud. Samantha Elliot lost in enemy territory, Rayne Gallagher gone on a crazy mission for the CIA . . . They'd been his friends, and what had he given them in return for that friendship?

He picked up the framed photograph of his father and threw it hard against the wall, watching the glass splinter into tiny pieces. It wasn't his fault his father had been a coward, a failure. Yet he'd never been man enough to confront him with the truth, and instead he'd protected his father's lie and betrayed his friends.

He picked up the phone and dialled the emergency number he'd been given. Maybe there was something he could still do.

John Fry looked up at the ceiling reflectively, said goodbye and put down the phone. Major Martin Long's usefulness was definitely over. The panicky call late in the evening had surprised him. Of course he'd reassured the Major that Captain Gallagher would be well looked after.

He picked up a folder lying next to his bed and paged idly through it. The attacks on the bank and the airfield were scheduled to take place on Sunday afternoon. After that he would be able to relax again. With the contents of the safe-deposit box in the bank in Beira destroyed, there would be nothing to worry about. Vorotnikov's career would be finished and his own assured.

As for Gallagher and his men, well, they would indeed be taken care of.

Tongogara

Tongogara sat huddled in an old wool blanket in the lonely
kraal. He was very worried. Usually there was dissension
amongst his men, but now they were quiet. A new feeling
possessed them – a sense of approaching power. They felt in
their bones that the attack on Salisbury would be successful, and
already the anticipation of victory was strong in them. There was
talk of killing, looting and raping. Tongogara knew better than
to argue.

After all the idealistic talk of communism and a people's state,
the years of dreaming how to refashion their country, this was
what they had become – a rabble bent on revenge, whose
savagery would confirm the worst suspicions of the white men.

He had changed. The loss of his wife had changed him, he
knew that. Mnangagwa was also different, maybe because he
had trained as a lawyer. They had talked at great length and
both decided that they would take no active part in this assault.
Instead they would follow behind and try to restore some order.

What would it take to make these men change? It was too late
for them, nothing would change them now. They had only been
educated in handling the AK-47. Would future generations even
appreciate their sacrifice? He prayed that his dream of a free
and prosperous Zimbabwe would not turn into another Angola.
Angola should have been one of the wealthiest countries in
Africa and now it was almost as poor as Mozambique.

Tongogara looked up at the stars that had looked down on
Africa for eternity. Time was running out for black Africa. The
benevolent attitude of the West would change, his people must
earn the right to successful government. While they lived in

chaos they would always be at the mercy of foreign powers. In a previous age they had been slaves, but today they were still fighting for their freedom. And outside Africa, no one wanted the black man. While hundreds of white families left the continent every month, able to relocate with ease, Tongogara and his countrymen had no choice but to stay where they were and fight themselves out of the mess the Europeans had created.

He felt Sam's arms around his shoulders, felt the warmth of her body arousing him. The irony of this moment caught him by surprise. She, the white woman who was only free to come out at night.

In spite of himself, he pulled her close to him. His lips touched hers briefly and he sensed the desire in her body. It frightened him. He had to think of some way to get her out of this place. Any development in their relationship could only be a disaster.

'What are you worried about, Tongogara?'

'The attack the Russians have planned for next week. It will be terrible. It will probably go down as one of the worst massacres in history.'

'There is little you can do about it now.'

Now Sam sat in silence. She thought of all the people she knew who lived in Salisbury, most of them elderly, for the young ones had either left or joined the army. She could imagine what would happen – she had seen American soldiers running riot in Vietnam, civilised men reduced to the level of savages . . . Of course, that was what Tongogara was scared of, the black man living up to his comic-strip image . . .

'You are thinking of the people you know there?'

'Yes . . . And more. You are right, it will be horrifying. And you will win anyway, without this invasion. History will look kindly on you if all that is recorded is the war for independence; but a massacre is different. Is there nothing you can do to stop it?'

'Not without destroying myself in the process.'

'Leave, Tongogara, and take Mnangagwa with you. Get out of here and get away. With a start like this, what sort of a country are you going to have anyway?'

He got up and paced up and down in the darkness. She could tell he was angry, angry at her and at himself.

'Maybe there is a way. If we incapacitated the Russian planes . . . If they did not have the fuel to make the flight to Salisbury,

269

then the attack would not take place. And a big enough explosion would be seen from Rhodesia and give cause for investigation. Yes, it would work, but at what a price? I would be known as the traitor who sold out my own people.'

He stared up at the stars in desperation. Sam rose and came across to him. He wrapped his arms round her and she looked up at his face.

'They would never know it was you. However, the main thing is that you would have prevented one of the worst episodes in African history from ever taking place. It's a decision only you can make, Tongogara. I cannot help you.'

'How I wish that I had never met you!'

She pulled away from him, her eyes flashing with anger in the darkness. 'All I'm doing is reminding you of your responsibility. Don't forget your men captured me in the first place! I'm just a reporter. Let me tell you that your attack on Salisbury would be the news story of the decade, and if I got out of here I could make myself millions by writing a book on it.'

'You would do that?'

'Well, what happens, happens. Why not? Of course, I wouldn't reveal your name. Or I could write another book, in another time and another place, about a man who had the courage of his convictions, who stood up for what he believed was right and avoided something terrible.'

Tongogara reached out and took her hand. She resisted, but he pulled her close again. He spoke, drawing energy from her.

'For a woman you have much power. I cannot ignore the truth of what you are saying. If I do as I plan to, we will make for the border together – I won't be able to live here again afterwards. Then we must go our separate ways. I shall be taking a big risk by trying to sabotage the fuel supply depot, something could well happen to me. You would have to fend for yourself. I don't know if you would survive.'

His voice, which had been loud and angry, was now soft and caring. Sam steeled herself against this new tactic of evasion.

'Don't worry about me. I'm not important – but what you have to do, is. As long as you think it's the best thing for your people. I've survived this far, I'm sure I can make it on my own.'

He smiled. It was almost as if he had wanted to hear this declaration from her.

'Then it is decided. I will have to move quickly now.'

'You'll ask no one to help you? Not even Mnangagwa?'

'Mnangagwa will be my eyes and ears here at the camp. He will explain my absence, he will say that Vorotnikov has sent out a death squad to get me. But I will do this thing alone. If it goes wrong, then I will be the only one that they can blame – I cannot implicate anyone else.'

'When will you do it? You don't have much time.'

'As soon as possible. This Sunday. I cannot risk leaving it for longer. They'll start stepping up security soon, in readiness for the invasion.'

Sam looked at him in the darkness and knew that indeed he would do it, though at terrible cost to himself. She would not interfere any more. Perhaps, instead, she might even try to help him.

The heat of the midday sun was burning down on them, the black soldier and the white journalist. At their feet was an open bolthole, and lying at its entrance an array of arms and ammunition.

'There are thousands of these dumps all over the country. Only a few know of their existence. It's our guarantee of safety – we learnt the hard way about the danger of keeping all our eggs in one basket, the Rhodesians hit our big dumps as easily as a man swats a mosquito bloated with blood. This cache contains arms and ammunition for fifty men, plus supplies of tinned food. I could have got the weapons through my own men, but that might have attracted suspicion. This way it is only you and I who are involved.'

Tongogara spoke softly. He stared at Sam who had dropped down on her haunches, her breasts clearly visible through her sweat-caked bush shirt. No, he told himself, she is not for you. Every day he had felt more and more drawn to her, and the force of this attraction frightened him. It reminded him of how he had felt for his wife when she was alive.

He wanted to maintain the pace they'd kept up since they'd left the kraal, but she seemed exhausted. She looked up at him, guessing his thought.

'Can you keep going like this all day?' she asked.

He took the pack from her back and forced her to sit down. Then he loaded the weapons into his own rucksack. He spoke as he worked.

'It is only through long experience that I have learnt the value of swift movement. You kept up well, though I don't think you would have lasted much longer.'

'Bastard!'

He smiled. He liked her spirit. 'Ah ha. I see that you Americans also fear to hear the truth.'

'Touché.'

He carefully covered the bolthole with leaves and sand. Then he hoisted the massive pack onto his back and helped Sam to her feet. She looked him straight in the eyes. 'Don't worry, Tongogara. I'll keep going.'

Loaded down with the weapons they had acquired, they now moved slowly back the way they had come. Tongogara was also more cautious because they were near the airport and the area was crawling with Russian troops. They kept to the shadows, and moved swiftly over any open ground they had to cross. It was nerve-racking, and frequently they rested in the bush, panting to regain their breath. Sam's reporter's curiosity was awakened. 'Is this always what it's like?'

'It is usually worse because when I am inside Rhodesia I can never relax. The man who feels comfortable is a dead man. Now I move like a disease through my own people, silent and deadly.'

'When will you strike?'

'Tomorrow afternoon.'

'So soon?'

His face hardened. 'The longer I leave it, the more dangerous it will be. Often the more time I have to think about an attack, the more afraid I become. Waiting around for too long is death.'

They got up again and kept moving, skirting the airfield. Eventually they lay down in the tall grass running along the edge of the main runway. Sam stared aghast at the vast array of weapons and the camouflage sheets covering the planes. It would all be completely invisible from the air.

'Bombers and fighters,' she whispered. 'God, there's a fortune sitting there on the tarmac, Tongogara. How do we take that lot on?'

'By not taking it on. All these planes need fuel to launch an attack – and I intend to cut off their supply. Once I've done that, we can come back here, but now we must keep on moving. We have to be in position by tomorrow morning.'

They crawled away from the runway, and only stood up once

they were back in the thicker vegetation on the perimeter. Sam was sweating now with the fear of being so close to the enemy. She moved closer to Tongogara and whispered to him, 'I had no idea it would be this bad. It's crazy to attack them. They'll massacre us.'

'Sam, that is the language of defeat. We have surprise on our side; when we attack they'll have no idea of our numbers. I'll rocket the tanks, which will go up in great sheets of flame – it will take them months to rebuild. I know the security on the fuel tanks is lax, it's their weakest link. We must conserve our energy to get away as quickly as possible.'

Sam dropped her pack and put her arms around him. 'Just hold me for a few seconds.'

Tongogara held her tightly. He could sense the fear she felt but would not admit, and his body shivered with the excitement of her closeness. He closed his eyes. Danger made him acknowledge what up to now he had been forcing himself to deny. Dammit, he said to himself. Yes, dammit, I am in love with her.

It was many minutes before Sam broke the spell. 'Surely we'd be better off getting away in the darkness?'

'You're right. We'll attack the tanks just before sundown. Anyone who looks at the blaze will be dazzled for a long time afterwards. It will be very difficult for them to pursue us.'

They moved very slowly now, keeping to where the vegetation was thickest. The thorns tore at Sam's skin so that soon her face was a mass of bloody streaks, and perspiration poured from her forehead and mingled with the blood. She felt terrible but did not complain. Eventually the enormous shapes of the fuel tanks appeared before them and they sank gratefully into the shade of a huge flame tree.

'Now we must rest. Tonight we can go down to the shore and wash, the salt will be good for the cuts on your body. You did well, Sam, it wasn't an easy advance. Try to lie perfectly still, keep yourself calm with the thought of the water you will bathe in this evening.'

Sam lay down at Tongogara's side, closed her eyes and tried to imagine that she was back in her parents' house, playing with her brothers and sisters. She relaxed in the comfort of this image of her past, blocking out the sounds of the mosquitoes and the terrible heat. Soon she was dreaming.

Her brothers and sisters had taken her favourite toy away

from her and she was desperately searching for it. Eventually she climbed out of a skylight onto the roof of their house, and saw that the teddy bear was lying in the gutter. She edged towards it, conscious of the terrible drop below, and was almost within reach and stretching out for it when the tiles beneath her started to shift, and she began sliding inexorably downwards.

Desperately she clutched the teddy to her breast, and then tumbled over into the void. Now she was flying through the darkness, and it was strange that she did not hit the ground but felt as if she was tumbling down an endless shaft, and the loneliness and oppression of the void pressed in against her so that she pulled the teddy bear closer. Suddenly she struck an object in the darkness, and the teddy was flung from her arms. She started to scream –

She woke to find Tongogara's hand clamped hard across her mouth. Once he was certain that she was no longer going to cry out, he took his hand away.

'A bad dream?'

'I'm sorry, I nearly blew it for you.'

'Once you start apologising for your dreams, you might as well be dead. They are the secret messengers of your soul.'

'You believe that?'

'Of course. Tell me about your dream and I'll tell you what's wrong.'

Sam recounted the dream, the memory of it still vivid in her mind. He listened intently, nodding his head occasionally. When she had finished he was silent for a few moments as he decided what to make of it.

'You realise that a nightmare only comes because you are unhappy or afraid? I thought maybe it was something to do with our present situation, but in fact it has nothing to do with this. There is someone you love, someone you need desperately and who you feel has been torn away from you. With that person gone, you are lost.'

The accuracy of what he said frightened her. He had understood her innermost feelings perfectly.

'Ah. I see the truth of the dream makes you silent. I think that you did not want to know the message. Is there a man you love whom you're scared you've lost? He must be mad, if he is prepared to give you up. But forget about him for the moment, there is nothing you can do about this until you are away from

274

here. Your worries will distract you. This man, I think he will come back to you.'

'I wish I had your confidence. He would never marry me.'

'Do not try to think for him. Think about yourself. There are few women who have your courage, it's a rare quality. I want you to write your story, I want you to be happy. Forget him, he will not forget you so easily.'

'Thank you. I won't disturb you again.'

'I'll wake you when the darkness comes and we can go down to the sea.'

For a long time Tongogara stared into the distance, then he lay down next to Sam and fell into an uneasy sleep.

When twilight came they made their way silently towards the water. Now they were away from the road, the fuel tanks about five kilometres to their left. Sam could see their shapes on the horizon, ugly cylindrical forms that looked out of place in the African landscape. In the cover afforded by the dim light, Tongogara loped along almost casually, far less vigilant than before.

Soon darkness overtook them and Sam started to trip over roots and branches that Tongogara easily avoided. He slowed his pace to allow her to move more carefully. She noticed that his assault rifle was always at the ready. He might seem relaxed to her, but he wasn't taking any chances. She had thought they would reach the water quite quickly, but she must have underestimated the distance; hours seemed to pass, and yet they were still apparently no closer to the shore. It was only at about ten o'clock that the ground started to slope downwards and the fresh smell of sea air assailed her nostrils.

Moments later they were on the sand, the water stretching out in front of them. Sam forgot the war and the purpose of their journey. The place was wonderfully romantic; she could imagine the thrill of the Portuguese navigators who had first ventured into these waters; she could imagine them seeing this verdant coastline for the first time, imagine the desire that must have welled up in them to explore the mysterious interior.

Perhaps she and Tongogara were the first people ever to walk on this particular stretch of beach. No lights were visible in the distance, there were no human sounds. She pulled off her outer clothes and waded out into the salty water. It was marvellously cool as it lapped against her limbs, her cuts stung as the salt worked its way into them. Immediately she felt refreshed.

Tongogara had first to remove the massive pack and all the ammunition he was carrying before he could go into the water. He came in next to her, and she shivered involuntarily. The deep masculine smell of him aroused her senses and she stared at his body. Until now she had always seen him in the familiar dark green camouflage uniform that left only his face and arms exposed. Now he was naked she saw that there was not an ounce of fat on him; his arms were enormous above the elbows and his neck latticed with cords of muscle; there were the marks of old wounds on his stomach; his hips were slim and sinewy. Her eyes dwelt on the area between his legs and the pride of his manhood. He stretched his arms upwards and then sank beneath the water, rising up quickly again as it cascaded off his body.

They did not speak. Instead he drew her close to him, and her arms clasped him instinctively. They kissed for a long time and she reached down with her left hand to guide him inside her.

The next moment her legs were round his torso and her hands dug into his flanks. He was bigger than she expected and she felt the pain as he penetrated deep within her. She hung her head back and sighed with joy; as the tension vanished from her body she knew that all along she had wanted him. She felt his body shudder as she worked herself against him, the orgasms running through her in waves of excitement. Then he climaxed, and she felt the deep, silent sigh within him. He let her down into the water slowly and she swam out, not caring about the risk of sharks. If she died tomorrow, she would die happy.

Now she knew him, and the memory was hers to cherish forever. For the first time in months she felt truly free.

The water became cooler and more refreshing as she pulled away from the shore. After a while she turned, and saw the lights of Beira that had been concealed from the beach. She shuddered, and moved back quickly towards the shore, only happy when she could see the lights no longer. They were an intrusion, and she did not want to know that they were there.

He was standing on the beach, watching her as she came in towards him, and she could see the flash of his pearl-white teeth as she emerged from the water. She guessed that he had been worried because she had gone far out.

He took her hand and they walked back towards the vegetation. They dressed slowly, not wanting the moment to pass. Then they walked some way in from the shore and ate an unappetizing meal of tinned fish. They lay down next to each other.

Tomorrow they would attack the fuel tanks. They were both quiet, knowing that this might well be the last night of their lives. The sounds of the bush took on a special significance, everything that spoke of life to them was treasured. After an hour or so they drifted off into an uneasy sleep.

Rayne and Bernard

The knock on the door of his hotel room startled Rayne. He got out of bed, gun at the ready. His nerves were on edge; Saturday had passed with agonising slowness – he had seen the same tension building in Larry, Mick and Guy, all anxious that nothing should go wrong and well aware of the danger that lay ahead. At least with the helicopter as back-up they were not going to be left high and dry.

He walked carefully to the bedroom door and opened it slowly, surprised to find Bernard Aschaar standing in front of him, alone. Rayne disguised his unease and smiled.

'Mr Aschaar. Come in. I can only offer you whisky but at least it's of a passable standard.'

'Whisky will be fine, Mr Brand. I'm glad to have found you alone.'

Rayne decided to leave the conversation to Aschaar. The man was going to have to make the first move.

'When will the guns arrive?'

'On Monday,' Rayne lied.

'You are too good at your job. You have delivered faster than anyone could have imagined.'

'You stressed the importance of timing on this deal. You've paid for a fast delivery and that's what you've got.'

'What I have come to tell you is that the situation has changed appreciably. I have had certain discussions, and from a business point of view it would be better if the General was not supplied with the weapons he needs right away.'

God, Rayne thought, what's he playing at? He wants to

forestall the invasion date. Immediately he was on his guard; he felt he was being led into a carefully engineered trap.

'I'm afraid the machinery has been set in motion. I have to accept delivery, I have no choice in the matter – I have paid the pilot and chartered a plane. Besides, from my understanding of the situation here, if ZANLA are not supplied with those weapons there's going to be a lot of trouble. I don't want to get involved in that.'

'I am not making myself clear – '

'And what about General Vorotnikov? He wants those weapons. I'm going to let him down if I don't deliver.'

'I'm not talking about a non-delivery. I'm merely asking you to delay delivery. And I realise the difficulties from your point of view, and am therefore advancing you a further million dollars to arrange it.'

Rayne pretended to be unimpressed by the amount. 'You realise that if word gets out, my career will be over? And the Russians are past masters at sorting out people who let them down. How am I protected in this deal?'

'For a million dollars I should think you wouldn't care.'

'A million dollars is chicken-shit to you, Mr Aschaar.'

Rayne saw the anger flare on the man's face. 'You could tell Vorotnikov about our little deal,' said Aschaar. 'He'd be just as happy to eliminate me as he would you.'

'No go, Mr Aschaar. Ten million dollars is the minimum bid on this deal.'

Aschaar rose up like a coiled snake about to strike. Rayne's gun was pointing at his chest in a fraction of a second.

'Try me, Mr Aschaar. Try me.'

Aschaar sat down. 'You're a bastard, Mr Brand.'

'I'm not in your league. Pay me what I want or get out.'

'All right, but . . .'

'No buts. You pay. I do what you want. You shut up.'

Aschaar closed his eyes for a second. Rayne guessed he had rarely been spoken to in this way before.

'You'll get your money, Mr Brand.'

Rayne immediately sensed treachery, but there was little he could do about that now. He said, 'How late do you want the delivery to be?'

'As late as possible. I want you to inform me, in the presence of the General, that there has been a delay. That you are prepared to forfeit the whole deal if necessary because of the late delivery. Of course he will not accept that proposal, he needs the guns desperately.'

'And when do you want me to put this to him?'

'Tomorrow, at lunch at the villa. A car will come to collect you at twelve-thirty.'

'Unfortunately tomorrow I have important business.'

'For ten million dollars you can drop it. It's vital that you inform the General tomorrow when I am present. Just make sure that you arrive for lunch on time, Mr Brand.'

'Don't worry about me, Mr Aschaar.'

'Very good. And it will be best if you are alone. You must appear as distressed as possible, and I'll be very hard on you. I'd like you to leave hastily, and then I'll patch things up with Vorotnikov after you've left. It has to look realistic.'

'Goodnight then, Mr Aschaar. I'll see you at lunch.'

Rayne closed the door, and found that he was shaking.

Even without the prospect of getting the rifles he needed, Vorotnikov would go ahead with the Salisbury attack, Rayne was sure of it. He would have done, in Vorotnikov's position – and the man must have some kind of weapon he could still hand out to his black forces. No commander would let slip the military and political opportunity of a lifetime for want of a bit of hardware. Rayne smiled to himself. It was interesting to know that he and his men would not be the only people happy if his mission succeeded; Aschaar obviously no longer wanted the invasion to succeed either – though for what reason, Rayne hadn't a clue.

Vorotnikov stood on the beach outside his villa, staring out across the waters and watching the moonlight ripple across the waves. He picked up Rhodes and thoughtfully scratched the little mongrel behind the ears, speaking to him softly.

'I am on the verge of achieving my dream. With my own people there is no problem, but with my friend Mr Aschaar . . . I'm not so sure.'

It had occurred to him that there must be other Western businessmen besides Aschaar who would be interested in developing the new Zimbabwe. He had been wrong to involve Aschaar.

Aschaar had to leave Beira by plane. An accident could be

arranged. The Lear jet was the perfect target for a heat-seeking missile, and he had SAM-7 rocket-launchers amongst his armoury. He wished he had the American equivalent, he wasn't particularly happy about the effectiveness of the SAM-7. He remembered the statistics from the Yom Kippur War: over half the A-4 aircraft hit by SAM-7 missiles had managed to return to base. Still, with a light aircraft like a Lear jet the weapon could be effective.

He put Rhodes down and stretched his arms above him. If the invasion was successful and Aschaar was eliminated, he would be safe. With Aschaar dead, the evidence that the General had consorted with capitalists would be gone. Anyway, no one would dare to incriminate a national hero, and he would quickly organise his power-base within the Kremlin to make sure that nothing could go wrong. He didn't want to think about what would happen if the invasion failed.

He turned round and walked back towards the villa, followed by the ever-faithful Rhodes.

Bunty Mulbarton stared down at the eerie glow of his watch and saw that it was just after 2 a.m. The day before had been sheer hell. The heat and the mosquitoes had been terrible, but the worst part was that he couldn't relax for a second. Groups of black soldiers kept joining the road, coming out of the bush from all directions. There was constant risk of discovery and he had to be on the alert all the time. When one of Michael Strong's group had unexpectedly come up to his position to confirm that everything was all right, he'd almost shot him.

Now he wanted the action to start. How he was going to get through the next day was beyond him. Gallagher had certainly been correct when he said that they'd earn their money. Most of the mercenary jobs he'd taken on before involved sitting around at a cushy base camp or in a town. This was different, more like genuine army action.

Bunty thought about his role. His job was to blow up the road when the vehicles retreating from the airport came along it. This would block the road with wreckage, forcing the vehicles behind to make a diversion, and these vehicles would then hit the minefield Bunty had laid on either side of the road and be blown to pieces – if everything went according to plan.

He would then pin the Russians down with sniper fire while

Michael Strong's group made their getaway; then, he'd join up with them and they would make for the lift-off point together. According to his calculations, they should be flying away from Beira by the time darkness fell.

Bunty desperately wanted a cigarette, but knew that it would be disastrous to have one. That single pinprick of red light would be enough to give them away.

On the airfield Michael Strong waited for the next day with grim anticipation. He had no illusions about what was going to happen – he had seen enough planes go up before. It always surprised him how they lit like thatch houses. Aeronautical fuel was highly volatile. He'd advised his men to keep well back when the shooting began, because the waves of flame would be more dangerous than the rifle fire. The worst part would be seeing the Russians running around with flames leaping from their backs. He'd promised himself he'd shoot any man he saw burning to death. To his mind, that was the most horrific way to die.

They'd counted every plane on the airfield, and his express orders were that no man was to retreat until each plane had been destroyed.

He kept on rehearsing the action in his mind, trying to see if there was any point he'd missed. It was a game he always played with himself at times like this. More than once it had saved his life. Try as he might, he couldn't find any loopholes in his strategy.

Bernard arrived back at his villa and went up to his room to catch a few hours' sleep before dawn. It always amazed him how he tired of people the moment they ceased to be of use to him. He had been stupid to get involved with the Russian in the first place. Still, one constantly learned from one's miscalculations.

Tomorrow would be amusing. After that, later in the afternoon, he would leave this place in his private plane and that would be the end of his involvement with the invasion. But before he left, he would have the pleasure of witnessing the sudden, dramatic death of General Vorotnikov after hearing shocking news . . . Yes, he could sleep easy tonight, knowing he had arranged that.

*

The evening air hung heavily over Beira. Then the wind began to blow across the water, gently at first, then harder, whipping the trees along the shoreline into uneven motion. The few boats in the harbour began to tug at their moorings as the water became more disturbed. A full moon cast silvery patches on the tips of the waves, thunder rumbled ominously in the distance. The horizon was thick with water-laden storm clouds, carried towards the port by a strong south-wester.

Then the bad weather struck in earnest. First came stronger winds, tearing at the trees and shrubs. Windows rattled, litter was blown across the streets. Outside the port, small dust storms developed along the dry, untarred sand roads. The wind made strange noises through the trees and any animals that were in the open soon made for whatever cover they could find. The moon disappeared behind a giant cloud, and the eerie landscape below was plunged into blackness.

The first drops of rain came an hour later. They tamed the sandstorms, beat musically on the tin roofs of Beira's shanty town, a strong and steady downpour. It would rain like this for at least the next twelve hours.

The air now smelled sweet and pure, or at least it smelt so to Sam, sleeping under a blanket beneath a big tree with Tongogara snoring noisily beside her.

The universe had changed. She had felt the coming of the storm in her bones and shivered involuntarily. She had pulled the plastic ground-sheet over them as protection from any rain that might pass through the heavy foliage of the branches above. Now she could see the wisdom of Tongogara's choice of sleeping place. They were slightly higher than the surrounding ground, so that any water running down towards the sea would naturally be deflected away from them.

Bad weather had always been a good omen for Sam. It always symbolised a change for the better in her life. She remembered that the day she left school it had rained, and on the day she had become a trainee reporter. She was glad to see that Tongogara was still sleeping quietly.

Silently she moved his pack, ammunition and rifle to a place where they would not get wet. Her father had taught her all he knew about hunting, especially the handling and care of weapons. Once she had put the weapons in a dry place, she moved back to the warmth of the blanket and lay down to sleep again. The rain was falling more heavily now and showed no signs of abating.

She closed her eyes and imagined she was back in her flat in Salisbury, enjoying a bottle of red wine from the Cape and listening to a Miles Davis record. Soon she was asleep, the storm forgotten.

In the first grey light of the overcast morning, the runway looked like burnished black glass, with every plane reflected in it. There was a heaviness in the air, and the steady beat of large raindrops against the hollow metal of the fuselages. Not a human being was in sight, and to a first-time observer the place might have appeared completely deserted.

Michael Strong lifted his binoculars and noticed in the reflection of the eyeglass that his lashes looked as though they had morning dew on them. He shivered again with the cold. His uniform was absolutely sodden, it felt like a straitjacket; the hardy clothing had become as tough as board, and there were even large puddles of water on his back. 'Bloody hell!' He muttered aloud as he tried to reposition himself on the soggy ground.

He stared through the glasses at the pools of water along the edge of the runway and knew instinctively that half the charges they had so carefully laid must be considered inactive. Because it hadn't rained once in the last week, they had ignored the possibility that it could rain at all. Well, they couldn't replace them now, in daylight. They'd just have to hope that enough of them worked to do a decent job.

He looked at the dial of his watch, covered with water droplets like everything else. Half past six. That left another ten and a quarter hours before they were due to strike. He knew that the time was going to pass painfully slowly.

At the other side of the runway, outside the storerooms, Major Conrad, the commander of the Beira air base, was worried. It was obvious that the big pool of water building up against the wall of this particular store indicated an equally big pool of water inside.

He unlocked the padlock on the door and entered. He hadn't

been inside for some months. On his schedule he saw that the contents of this store were listed as canned foodstuffs.

One look at the cases and he realised that there had been an administrative mistake. It was that idiot, the quartermaster, who was now languishing in solitary confinement before he joined the prisoners in the workcamp.

The crates in the storeroom were long and rectangular, and certainly didn't contain tinned food . . . With mounting excitement he began to prise open the top of one of the cases.

Michael Strong picked up his field-glasses and surveyed the runway for the fifth time in as many minutes. He couldn't quite believe what had happened. In less than an hour all the Russian perimeter guards had disappeared. If they stayed away, it would mean that their attack could be far more effective . . . Only a fool would have reduced the guarding levels at such a strategic installation. There must have been a change in command.

The other possibility was that they had been spotted, and the forces around the perimeter had been withdrawn in anticipation of an attack. He watched all the buildings like a hawk, especially the storeroom which had just been rapidly and completely emptied. It was the same one the commander had left in a hurry earlier. What the hell was going on?

General Vorotnikov put down the phone and decided that he would mention the good news at lunch. Now they would not have to cooperate with this rather sinister arms dealer. What fools they were at the airport! He had immediately transferred control to Captain Balashov, who was ordered to make a thorough inspection of all the AK-47 assault rifles in Store 21, and report back.

The plans for the invasion of Rhodesia could now be set in motion. He would call a meeting of all the pilots on Monday morning, and give them a complete battle plan. On Monday afternoon he would hand out the assault rifles to all the black forces, which would instantaneously boost morale, and impress upon them the generosity of the Soviet Union towards the oppressed black peoples of Southern Africa.

Rayne worked with Guy and Larry, hidden from view in the back of the shop. Mick was on the roof of the hotel, watching the bank.

Slowly they dismantled and rebuilt each of their weapons. They would get no second chances once they began the attack, and seconds would make the difference between success or failure. They were all on edge.

It was ten o'clock, and as usual on a Sunday the streets of Beira were almost deserted. The atmosphere was wet and cold. Rayne spoke to Guy and Larry as he worked the action of his rifle.

'I have to meet them for lunch, I've got no choice. If I don't turn up they'll probably come looking for me, and it could blow the whole operation. In the event of my not returning by five o'clock, you must attack the bank under Guy's command.

'As planned, you'll drive down the main street and turn off just past the bank. A couple of stun grenades through the front window will knock the guard out, after that you can use all the explosives you want to blow open the door of the safe.

'I want to get the contents of every single safe-deposit box in the place destroyed. There shouldn't be more than about fifty. You can shoot open each one in a matter of seconds. Don't waste time, and above all don't panic.

'The attack on the airport will begin at exactly the same time. Bunty will blow up the road the moment the Russian forces are mobilised. The Russians probably *will* panic, which will give us an added advantage provided we can stay cool. Planes to pull us out will be coming in at the site of the old airport just before sundown this evening, but if anything goes wrong, Lois will be waiting for us. I'll give each of you a map locating this emergency take-off point. I only have two objectives, and they're to destroy the safe-deposit boxes in the bank and destroy the airport.

'All I can do now is wish you all good luck. I'm happy that conditions are good for the attack.'

Larry and Guy listened, grim-faced. They knew the risks, the odds weren't good.

Rayne walked out of the back door and stood for a moment in the pouring rain. Michael Strong and Bunty Mulbarton would have laid charges all over the place; he just hoped they'd sealed all the connections well enough. Even the slightest drop of moisture would be enough to stop a charge from going off.

The sky was thick with dark, menacing clouds, and already there was a light breeze which promised to strengthen as the day went on. Before, in the sunlight, the town had looked run down but exotic; now, with ugly red puddles dotting the uneven tarmac of the roads and rain spilling off the gutterless roofs, it looked merely squalid. It was almost dark enough to be evening now, and the tarmac was a mass of dancing raindrops, making it impossible to see to the other side of the road.

The torpor of Africa struck Rayne at that moment. What the hell did it all matter, anyway, since Africa would get her own way in the end? No foreign power could seriously upset the natural equilibrium of the Dark Continent, which always took back what anyone tried to take from her, always remained unchangeably herself. At that moment it seemed inconceivable to him that a group of Russian planes could hope to demolish the power structure of an entire African state.

And somewhere in this storm was Samantha. Then he knew why he was sad – because he had so little chance of finding her. He walked up to his room with a heaviness in his legs and in his soul.

Tongogara woke to find himself in a pool of mud, and as he raised himself to his feet, the water ran from his camouflage suit, leaving him freezing cold. Anxiously he glanced around for his pack and the weapons. He heaved a sigh of relief when he saw that Sam had wrapped them in a groundsheet under the tree. She was curled up near the tree, the top of her body dry, but her legs as wet and as muddy as he was. His soul was stirred as the memory of the night before came back to him.

Her eyes opened while he was still looking at her, and she smiled. 'We couldn't have picked a worse day.'

She got up and went over to him, kissing him softly on the lips. She watched as he fought with his emotions. He was silent for a while and then replied, 'You're wrong, Sam. We couldn't have picked a better day. This weather is the best cover we could have asked for, maybe a bit uncomfortable now, but it makes it almost impossible for the guards to patrol the fuel tanks effectively. We must get moving, I want to be in position as soon as possible – there's no telling when this weather may change. And thank you for putting all the equipment under the tree. I was stupid not to have done that. If it had got wet we might as well have given up now.'

Keeping the weapons wrapped in the groundsheet, Tongogara pushed them into his rucksack. He did not carry the assault rifle now, there was no need. Sam followed him as he strode through the bush towards the beach. They didn't speak again until they started making their way up the shoreline towards the fuel storage tanks.

Sam felt at one with him, now she understood the fire that lay behind his cool exterior. She treasured her knowledge, and was determined that she would not let him down.

'We're lucky, Sam. This is going to take us less than an hour. We could never have come along the beach if the weather had been good, we'd have been too easily spotted, but in this downpour no one's going to see us. And we can talk as well.'

They continued up the beach, the rain lashing in gusts against them. It was nearly an hour before Tongogara indicated that they should pull off the beach and move back into the bush. In the distance Sam could see the giant cylindrical shapes of the storage tanks. She looked out to sea. This was where the Pungwe River met the Indian Ocean. They were almost in Beira itself. Her heart skipped a beat. There was no pulling out now, she was committed.

The fuel depot at Munhava in downtown Beira consisted of forty massive tanks dominating the horizon. There were also several outbuildings containing two-hundred-litre fuel drums. Next to the depot was a run-down shanty town. It was through this uninspiring area that they had to pass undetected.

The roads were awash with mud, and there was no one in sight. They moved from building to building, hiding behind each one and checking the way in front of them before they moved on. It didn't take them long to pass through the town. After that they had to sprint from the last buildings across an open stretch of ground and a road, and throw themselves down flat in the mud on the other side. Then they crawled their way to the perimeter fence of the fuel depot two hundred metres away. They lay in the mud as Tongogara took out a pair of pliers and carefully cut the fence along the bottommost level. He whispered to Sam as he gradually made an opening.

'The trick is to create a way in, but to make sure that no one notices the break in the fence. It'll be hard to get through this narrow hole, but there's no danger of it parting wider. Once we're through I'll wire the gap up.'

Minutes later they had slipped through the hole and had crawled behind some low bushes.

Sam wondered whether they would ever get out alive. She realised how lucky they had been with the rain. There was no way they could have got into the high security area that quickly if the visibility had been good. Whenever the rain cleared briefly between squalls, she could see the sentry towers looming ominously above her. Her pulse refused to slow down. Already she could feel the excitement of the risk they were taking.

'We must get ready. We won't be able to hit all the tanks, but from where we are now it shouldn't take long before the whole lot go up. There'll probably be a trigger reaction – once one tank is alight, the fuel vapour from the other tanks will catch easily, provided we puncture each of them successfully. I'll use the rocket-launcher and you can cover me with the machine-gun. Whenever you can, fire directly into the tanks.'

He hauled out the 7.62 mm PKM GPMG, capable of firing rimmed cartridges with over twice the propellant charge of the standard AK-47 assault rifle. The weapon was a brilliant hotchpotch of the best features of several other weapons, including the Kalashnikov rotating bolt, Goryunov cartridge extractor and barrel-change, and the Degtyarev feed-system and trigger.

'I'm sorry, Sam, I don't have the tripod for the machine-gun. You'll have to rest it on top of the pack frame and shoot the best you can. I've only got a limited supply of ammunition, so try to fire in short effective bursts.'

Next he hauled out the SAM-7 Grail missile-launcher. 'This is usually used for shooting down aircraft but it'll also prove very effective on the fuel tanks. It weighs enough on its own without the rockets. I've managed to bring three, which should be quite enough to light this place up. Now we must keep down until after five o'clock.'

Tongogara looked down at his watch. In six hours' time they would be almost dead with cold, but they could not afford to attack earlier – they needed the failing light to get away successfully.

Sam shivered. She was both wet and cold. She had never been in a situation like this, never even imagined it. As a reporter, however close she came to the action, she had always remained separate from it. Now she was directly involved. She realised that there was no longer any point in being afraid. She had persuaded Tongogara to take action and now she must support him, even to the death.

He pulled her close to him and kissed her again. She was powerless in his arms.

At the edge of the airport runway, unknown to Michael Strong or to airport security, two men waited, hidden in the bush. They had a rocket-launcher of the same type Tongogara had just unpacked some three kilometres away.

The senior officer repeated General Vorotnikov's instructions to himself again and again. The weapon was not one hundred per cent accurate, and could only be used on a departing target – for it was only then that the heat source of the plane would be visible. The trick was to zero in on the departing plane's engine and apply partial trigger pressure. Once the missile had locked into the engine's heat source, the light would turn from red to green. After that it was simply a case of applying greater pressure to the trigger.

There would be no danger of anyone seeing a flash from the ground because the boost charge burned away before the rocket even left the barrel. Once the rocket was safely out of the tube, a sustainer would ignite and accelerate the missile to Mach 1.5, fast enough to catch any aircraft in the process of taking off.

It would be a case of hit and run. There would be only one chance at the target and they had been warned about the penalties for failure. The man knew the limitations of the rocket – which was why he kept on rehearsing the precise details of firing the weapon. He was also worried about the rain and its effect on the rocket's guidance system. The chances of making a direct hit did not look good.

He looked at his watch again. He had been told by General Vorotnikov that Aschaar's plane would take off quite late in the afternoon.

The car arrived for him outside the hotel at twelve-thirty precisely. Rayne breathed a sigh of relief; every minute counted now if he was to be back at the hotel by four o'clock that afternoon. The chauffeur dutifully got out of the Mercedes with an umbrella and went to the front entrance of the hotel to escort Rayne back to the car.

They pulled away quickly and Rayne kept wondering what he would do if he didn't make it back in time. He wished he could have taken the Peugeot, but they needed the Peugeot for the attack on the bank.

Rayne's Browning pistol was carefully pushed down into his belt, concealed by his sports jacket. He couldn't risk going out unarmed – he didn't trust Aschaar, and for all he knew, the meeting could be an elaborate double-cross. The more he knew about Aschaar, the more he wanted to help Lois get him. It was all a question of timing, he told himself, as the big car pulled up the long gravel drive leading to Aschaar's villa.

He was impressed by the villa. Revolutions come and go but the wealthy stay wealthy. In twenty years, perhaps the only things that had changed here were the quality of the security and the nature of the occupier's business. He was shown through the main door by a black manservant and escorted to the verandah at the rear.

'Mr Brand, how good to see you.' Aschaar lunged towards him from the shadows. His hand was outstretched and they shook quickly in the uncertain partnership of conspirators. 'Can I get you a drink?'

'A beer would be fine.'

'Not the sort of drink I would choose on a cold day, but then I am a whisky man myself.'

The arrogance never left Aschaar, thought Rayne; the desire always to put the other man down, however trivial the matter. He took the drink and sat down on one of the cane chairs. He was damned if he was going to be intimidated by this man. The rain dripped steadily outside and for a few minutes neither spoke. Aschaar was the first to break the silence.

'You are clear on what you have to say?'

'Perfectly clear.'

'The General is in good spirits today, I don't know why. He will take the information you give him very badly. I'll act as a counterfoil to his anger. In the true sense of the expression, we have him over a barrel!'

Bernard tucked his hands into the narrow pockets of his double-breasted suit. It was not a casual action. His left hand found the deadly drug with which he planned to lace the General's drink. If they accused this Mr Brand of murdering the General, too bad. He disliked the man's aloofness anyway – and he was undoubtedly up to no good. What was his real business in Beira? There were so many rebel groups active in the country, he was probably doing a roaring trade. Probably he sold arms to the Rhodesians as well . . .

At that moment the General walked onto the verandah, followed by a small dog. He did not seem surprised to see Rayne, just displeased. To Rayne he did not look like a man who would be easily unsettled.

The small dog went to Rayne, who put his hand down to scratch behind its ears. 'Rhodes likes you,' said Vorotnikov, smiling reluctantly.

'General, Mr Brand is joining us for lunch.'

Bernard watched the servant who was pouring their drinks. He waited till the General had walked towards the edge of the verandah, then bumped clumsily into the servant carrying the General's whisky. 'I'm sorry!' The glass broke as it hit the floor and the man hurried quickly out of the room for a cloth.

'Let me pour you another, General.'

Bernard went across to the drinks cabinet, carefully taking the vial from his pocket and emptying the contents into a glass. He then poured a generous measure of Scotch, and was pleased to see that the crystals dissolved readily. He was about to taste the drink himself when he remembered that even the slightest amount of the poison would be dangerous. He added the small amount of soda the General liked.

'Mmm. Excellent.'

Bernard breathed a sigh of relief as the General took a large mouthful of whisky. 'I see it's time for us to eat.'

They went through into the dining room, which must have been the most luxurious in the whole of Beira. Solid silver was laid at each of the three place-settings; Waterford crystal glasses for white and red wine stood elegantly next to fine bone china.

While the main course was being served, General Vorotnikov was called away to the phone and Bernard and Rayne were suddenly alone again. Bernard was quick to seize the opportunity.

'I'll wait till we've finished lunch and are back on the verandah for coffee. He'll be furious, but don't worry, there's nothing he can do about it.'

Actually Bernard couldn't have given a damn if the General shot Mr Brand then and there. What he wanted to see was the heart attack that would be brought on by the sudden excitement, and the drug. The more furious the General got, the more quickly he would die.

Bernard glanced down at his watch. He wanted to be away well before five. His bags were packed ready to be placed in the car. Naturally, there would be a certain amount of hysteria when the General's death occurred – he would make sure there was a servant with them while they were having coffee. The responsibility for the death could be laid firmly on Mr Brand. In fact, it might be convenient to have him arrested immediately, on suspicion.

Putting down the phone, the General couldn't have been more pleased with himself. The call had informed him that the AK-47 rifles were now being thoroughly cleaned and repacked into their boxes. He would present them to ZANLA on Monday afternoon, in a special ceremony that could also be used to commemorate the death of Mr Bernard Aschaar . . . He returned to the dining room in a good mood.

Bernard looked up as the General came through the doors. 'Good news, I hope?'

'Excellent news. We will be able to mount the operation next week. And I feel confident of victory.' The General waited expectantly for them to bring up the topic of the guns, but nothing was said, and for the moment he let it pass.

After the meal they went out on the verandah. Rayne was becoming increasingly anxious. Time was running out fast, and if he didn't get away soon, his men would have to launch the attack on the bank without him. To his frustration, Aschaar continued to remain silent while the coffee was being served to them. He was obviously going for maximum shock value. At last he spoke.

'Well, Mr Brand, my arms shipment should be here soon.'

'I am afraid, Mr Aschaar, that I have run into some problems. Things are not going as smoothly as I would have expected.'

'But naturally we can still expect delivery on Monday?'

'Out of the question. It may even be a month before the weapons arrive. There's nothing I can do about it.'

Aschaar's face became dark with anger. Rayne had to admit he was a good actor.

'The terms were for speedy delivery! If you can't deliver on time, you can forget about being paid!'

Bernard kept glancing across at the General. By now the man should have been furious – and the drug only worked effectively if the subject experienced an emotional upset. But the General was quietly sipping at his coffee and appeared quite unruffled. In fact Bernard was sure he could even see a slight smile on the man's face. This profoundly unnerved him. Suddenly, he no longer felt confident. Vorotnikov was getting the edge on him, and that was very, very dangerous.

The General stared at him and then spoke softly. 'Mr Aschaar, Mr Brand has double-crossed us.'

To Rayne's horror, Aschaar smiled. Good God, what was going on?

'Very likely, General. However, you do need the arms. Without them, your plans will come to nothing.'

'Relax, Mr Aschaar. The original consignment of AK-47 rifles that I ordered was found early this morning in a storeroom at the airport, so we have no need of Mr Brand's kind services after all – punctual or otherwise.'

Rayne let his hand work its way beneath his jacket to the butt of the Browning. The General looked at him coldly. 'Tomorrow morning you will repay Mr Aschaar his deposit. Meanwhile, consider yourself under arrest. And you need not think of escaping. I control Beira.'

He yelled out a command in Russian, and before Rayne could react, two of Vorotnikov's bodyguard had rushed into the room, grabbed his arms and taken the pistol from his belt.

'Mr Aschaar, you will get your money back in the morning, I will see to it. There is no need to delay your departure.'

Bernard Aschaar hardly noticed what the General was saying; he was facing the fact that his plan had gone horribly wrong. If Vorotnikov didn't get emotionally worked up during the next twenty-four hours, the effects of the drug would wear off and he would probably survive. This meant that the attack on Rhodesia was now inevitable. It was not the way Bernard had wanted things to go; the agreement he had struck with Mugabe would have been much more profitable than trying to share power with the General. For the moment, however, he would have no choice but to play along with the Russian – and hope that another opportunity to dispose of the man would present itself in the near future.

'Er, thank you, General,' he said. 'I must indeed be on my way.'

Locked in a windowless room in the villa's basement, Rayne smashed his fist again and again into the wall. He'd never get back to the hotel in time now – it was hopeless. They'd have to launch the attack without him. Why had he been so foolish as to trust Bernard Aschaar, even for a moment . . . For the first time he felt himself begin to despair.

And then, at a quarter to five, the door was opened and he was led outside. He was pushed into the front seat of a jeep, next to the driver, while another man sat in the back with his gun pushed hard into the back of Rayne's head. They set off.

As soon as he came out into the open air, Rayne's spirits had lifted. Now it was just a question of creating an opportunity . . .

'Any cigarettes?'

The driver looked at Rayne without interest. Very deliberately, Rayne took off his watch and held it up, pointing, to indicate that he wanted to trade the watch.

'Imbecile,' said the driver scornfully, 'I can speak English.'

Rayne pressed on, ever hopeful. 'This for a cigarette?'

The driver smiled, and said something to the guard. Rayne's heart leapt as he felt the gun barrel removed from his skull. Out of the corner of his eye he saw the guard searching for a packet of cigarettes in his jacket pockets. Rayne shot round, grabbed his lapels with both hands and head-butted him.

The vehicle swerved off the road as Rayne grabbed the guard's gun and pumped two shots into the driver. The guard swung a heavy punch at Rayne, who ducked to avoid it and ripped off a shot which hit his adversary in the shoulder.

The Russian was a hardened fighter and just kept on coming. Rayne blocked another blow, dropping the gun. He rose, delivering a roundhouse kick to the side of the guard's skull in the same movement, and the guard fell sideways, grabbing Rayne so that they both fell out of the vehicle onto the sand road. Now Rayne had the advantage, his reflexes were faster and the extra space gave him the chance to dodge his enormous opponent's blows.

The guard came for him again, and Rayne delivered a hammering karate punch to the side of his forehead, then drove his left foot into the guard's left knee. His opponent toppled back, and Rayne immediately climbed in with three quick punches to the stomach. As the guard fell over backwards, Rayne scrambled back into the jeep.

Just as he was about to pull himself into the driver's seat, he felt his ankles being grabbed and he was wrenched down again onto the ground. The guard was breathing heavily, but his grip on Rayne's ankles didn't slacken. Rayne felt his hand touch something cold. A spanner. He grabbed it, and brought it crashing down onto the guard's head. Suddenly, his ankles were free. He dragged himself back into the jeep, pushed the body of the other Russian from the driver's seat, and put the dead man's gun on the passenger seat beside him. Nothing was going to slow him down now.

The engine started easily and he turned the vehicle round and floored the accelerator pedal. At full throttle, the jeep jumped around the road like a cat on a hot tin roof. Rayne clung to the wheel without using the brake pedal. He cursed out loud when he realised he'd lost his watch. He knew he was late – *how* late was what mattered.

The first buildings of Beira came into view on the road leading into the Avenue Oliveira Salazar. He'd have to go straight to the bank, taking the risk that his men might open fire on him.

He passed an army patrol, flat out, and they stared at him in astonishment as he barrelled along the main road, keeping right in the centre. Next a passenger car loomed into view as he came round a corner. It refused to give way but Rayne went straight for it, and at the last minute the driver lost his nerve, swerving off the road and ploughing into a brick wall. As the engine got hotter Rayne managed to coax the speed up even higher. Nothing mattered but getting to the bank. The streets flashed by.

He thought about Aschaar and how he was going to get even with the bastard . . . The tyres squealed and slid in protest as he nudged the vehicle round the sweeping curves of the road bordering the golf course. Nothing was going to stop him.

The Avenue Massano di Amorium was deserted. It was as if the whole town could sense that it was a place to avoid that miserable, wet Sunday afternoon. The rain fell steadily, leaving giant pools on the uneven road surface. There was no one to notice the vehicle parked in the open area next to the bank, or to hear the sound of breaking glass and the muffled explosion of two stun-grenades.

No one challenged the three men who had broken into the bank. Two of them moved with silent purpose through the desks towards the doors of the main vault, while one remained near the front door, his eyes combing the deserted avenue for the slightest sign of trouble.

Guy was really worried. He'd kept to Rayne's orders, but that didn't make carrying them out any easier. Where the hell had the Captain got to? Maybe he'd been imprisoned. Without him, Guy felt less than confident about their chances of making it out alive.

The pouring rain made it difficult for him to see far into the distance, but he knew that when they blew the vault the time for moving fast would begin. The detonation would wake the whole town. He glanced back inside the bank and saw that Mick and Larry were already applying the plastic explosive to the hinges on the vault door.

Rayne had told them to use more explosive than was necessary, to make sure that no one missed the blast. The question was, would the explosion pull the whole building down on top of them? Guy was wary of explosives, he'd had too many near misses to regard them with anything but respect. He went back to watching the main road.

He saw the jeep as it hit a large puddle and threw up clouds of spray. It was coming fast. Guy tensed, guessing this must be the first reaction to their breaking into the bank. They must have triggered some secret alarm unknowingly. He raised the Galil ARM rifle, pressing the stock firmly into his shoulder, then checked that the standard twenty-five round magazine was firmly in place. He loved the rifle. The Israelis had developed the Galil, naming it after the head of their design team, Israel Galil. In a stroke of brilliance they combined receivers made by Valmet of Finland with rough-turned barrels obtained from Colt Firearms of Hartford, Connecticut. The new Galil was a magnificent weapon with fully forged and milled receivers, chrome-lined bores, chambers and gas blocks; the gas pistons were chrome-plated too. Now Guy turned the selector switch from S to F and fixed the jeep carefully in the 300m peep-sight.

The jeep came nearer, and he fixed his aim in the centre of the driver's sternum and began the slow squeeze on the trigger.

Two shots. That should compensate for any inaccuracy that might be caused by the movement of the vehicle and the difficulty of seeing through the rain.

He was surprised that only one person had responded to the alarm – he would have expected a greater show of force. His finger began to tighten. The man was clearly in view now. It would be an easy shot. He squeezed slowly.

The whole town shook with the magnitude of the explosion. In seconds a black pall of smoke hung over the Pungwe River. Further explosions followed, and gradually the people who had been convinced it was just bad thunder became aware that something serious had happened.

Even in the pouring rain the flames from the giant fuel storage tanks refused to die down. Instead they fanned out, setting light to other tanks, triggering more explosions, creating an inferno of smoke and flames.

Suddenly the sky was filled with flashes as the anti-aircraft gunners let rip. High explosive shells were lobbed into the air and exploded in orange bursts on the horizon. It was like a fireworks display gone mad.

Larry

Rayne was almost at the bank when the first big bang occurred and he swung instinctively off the road. He dropped out of the jeep and crawled underneath the chassis. Looking away from the bank towards the west, the direction from which the noise had come, he saw to his horror huge clouds of smoke billowing into the air above the area where the fuel storage tanks were located. He'd specifically instructed his men that the tanks were not to be attacked. Who the hell had disobeyed his orders?

But then why shouldn't they blow up the tanks? It made sense in more ways than one. After all why not totally destroy the Russian installations around Beira? Again Rayne questioned Fry's orders and began to wonder what Fry's true objectives actually were.

A loud singing sound made him turn suddenly – to see Mick running to the front of the bank building with a spinning reel of wire cable leading back to the front of the vault. Then a bullet impacted into the wall next to him, spraying him with plaster. He looked up to see Guy sighting his rifle on him.

'Guy!'

There was a silence. Rayne dropped flat on the ground behind the jeep. One wrong move, and Guy's next shot would hit him.

'Captain. Is that you?'

'Yes!'

'You can come out.'

Cautiously Rayne raised his head to see that Guy's rifle was no longer trained on him. He sprinted across the road. 'I was held up. Only just made it.'

Guy wiped the sweat off his forehead. God, it had been close.

'I nearly killed you, sir. Thank God, the explosion spoilt my aim.'

'Who the hell blew the tanks?'

'I don't know, but we're blowing the vault now.'

Larry came out of the front door of the bank moments later.

'OK. Everything's set, there's enough plastic on the front of that thing to demolish a bridge. Keep down when I activate the detonator.' He quickly attached the two wires to a small box with a handle on the side.

Rayne watched the rain dripping off the sides of the roof. The explosions at the fuel depot continued to thunder in the distance.

Larry spun the handle around quickly and then lay close in against the wall, gesturing for the others to do the same.

'For God's sake, keep your heads right down.' Then he pushed the plunger down hard.

A sheet of flame shot through the interior of the bank as the high explosive erupted into life. The front windows were blown out and the doors ripped off their hinges. The metal roof ballooned upwards and then mushroomed out, throwing lethal bits of metal in every direction. The windows in the block of flats opposite were shattered to smithereens.

The blast obliterated every other noise, and for a moment it seemed as if the rain had stopped. Then there was the sound of falling masonry and burning wood.

Rayne lifted his head first. His ears were singing. There was another small explosion and he dropped flat again. He wondered if there was anything left of the vault at all. Crawling out, he looked at the charred shell of the Bank of Beira. To his amazement the walls were still standing and much of the roof still hanging in place. He leapt over the wall and into the building, the others following closely.

Rayne was sure the Russians must already be mobilising to move in on the bank. The noise of the fuel tank explosion would have carried to the military base, and now, with the explosion at the bank, the alarm must have been well and truly given. He just hoped it was enough of a diversion to pull some of the troops away from the airport.

He had to admire the professionalism of Larry's work. The safe doors were hanging on their hinges but none of the area behind them was damaged at all. He heard Larry speaking from behind him.

'Move it up, the structural damage is very bad. The whole place could cave in on us.'

They followed Rayne into the main vault, pulling out the large plastic rubbish bags that they had brought with them for storing the bank notes. Rayne said, 'Remember, only take dollars, pounds or foreign currency, the local stuff is worthless.'

Rayne moved into the safe-deposit-box area and quickly saw that most of the boxes were unlocked – only a very few were actually in use. Fry's instruction to destroy everything echoed through his mind. Once he had shot the locks off the boxes, he poured all the contents into a pile, ready to fire it. Even though time was of the essence, he could not help glancing at the documents, some of which were in English, others in Cyrillic script.

Suddenly he caught sight of Aschaar's signature – and almost instinctively he stuffed this group of documents inside his jacket. Maybe this was something he could use . . .

Larry and Mick were stuffing bank notes furiously into their plastic bags while Guy waited outside, ready to warn them the moment anyone showed up. There had been far more foreign currency in the bank than Rayne had expected. He swore silently; the money would be a hindrance. He wished he could just tell them to dump it, but he knew that would be asking too much.

Mick burst out of the doorway after Rayne and they threw the bulging bags into the back of the jeep. Rayne decided to leave the Peugeot behind. He looked down anxiously at Guy's watch. Five-fifteen. He had anticipated being out of the bank by five-ten. They were nearly all set now, but where the hell had Larry got to? A shout to his left informed him, in no uncertain terms.

'Put your hands up, get out of the jeep. Watch it, Guy, I know there's a gun beside you. That's better. Now, get over to the garage.'

Larry walked out of the bank, an Uzi carbine in his hands and an ugly expression on his face. He moved with his back to the road, some two metres from them.

'Larry, you fucking bastard!'

'Shut it, Gallagher.'

Rayne guessed Larry's plan. He shouldn't have given him the map showing him the pick-up point. Larry would lock them in the garage next to the bank, drive out to Lois and tell him they'd all been killed. He was the only one who knew about Lois, because Rayne hadn't yet been able to tell Michael Strong or Bunty about him. Larry would probably fly out of the country with Lois, then kill him and keep the money for himself. It was that simple, and that disgusting.

'Move it to the garage. Don't try anything stupid.'

They moved slowly away from the jeep and towards the open doors of the garage. Now they would be caught by the Russians, and that meant certain death. How could Larry do this to them? It was worse than shooting them in cold blood.

Suddenly there was the noise of a vehicle in the street behind them. Larry turned momentarily, and Mick took the opportunity to go for him. He sprinted forwards, aiming for Larry's back. Mick was almost on him when Larry turned back again. Rayne shouted out in desperation, 'Mick!'

Mick grabbed the muzzle of the Uzi as Larry pulled the trigger. He spun away from the barrel as the bullets hit him in the stomach.

Larry pointed the weapon towards Rayne and Guy. 'Don't try anything, you fuckers, or you'll go the same way.'

Rayne kept his eyes on the Russians who were jumping out of the truck down the road. He saw one of them raise his rifle.

Larry screamed out as the bullets tore into his back. Pockmarked with blood, he fell forwards. Rayne ran to pick up the Uzi. He moved in close behind the wall and pushed the muzzle over the top, letting off a quick burst of fire. There was a scream, and the sound of metal crashing into concrete. When he looked over the wall it was to see one Russian lying in the road clutching his leg and three more running for cover. He aimed again and hit one man before he made it to safety. Then he ducked to avoid the burst of fire that came from the other two. Mick was lying on the ground next to him, holding his stomach and trying desperately to get up.

'Stay down, Mick, they'll cut you to pieces.'

Guy crawled up beside them and lobbed a grenade at the wall their two attackers were hiding behind. They ducked, and waited for the explosion.

Seconds later there was an ear-shattering thump and they all made for the jeep. Guy carried Mick and dumped him in the passenger seat, then he leapt into the driver's seat and started the engine. As they pulled away, the firing started again and

Rayne opened up at the wall. They accelerated up the main street, leaving the bank far behind.

Guy pushed the jeep as hard as the engine would go. Each time the revs reached bursting point he would change gear and the vehicle shot forward. Mick kept on screaming out with pain, but there was nothing they could do.

Rayne slapped a fresh magazine into the Uzi and grabbed another from the floor of the jeep. Now he had two machine-guns, one in each hand, and he braced himself against the back of the jeep, ready to fire the moment they ran into trouble. Mick gradually won his battle against the pain of his bullet wounds and managed to hold a Galil assault rifle in his hands. It wasn't a moment too soon. As they rounded the next corner, they ran straight into an ambush.

A truck had been turned over, blocking their path, and gunfire erupted from both sides of the road. Rayne opened up on the left side and immediately there was a reduction in fire. Mick pumped a couple of carefully positioned shots into the bush on the right as Guy aimed the jeep at the gap between the left side of the road and the roof of the truck. They tore towards it, travelling at over a hundred kilometres per hour.

Rayne kept firing into the bush. Bullets whacked into the side of the jeep. They made it through, immediately running into thick smoke from the burning fuel tanks near the roadside. Gunfire was everywhere, anti-aircraft shells kept on exploding in the sky above them.

The rain lashed down harder and the jeep slewed from side to side as it careered along the dirt road at top speed. Guy fought with the steering wheel, battling to keep the vehicle on a straight course without losing speed.

It was impossible to tell which direction trouble would come from next. They had to get away from the centre of the action as quickly as possible.

Everything had gone horribly wrong.

Major Balashov, first-in-command at Beira airport, watched the Lear jet climb skywards. Visibility was bad, and the plane was almost out of sight although it had only just left the runway.

'What the hell?'

Balashov nearly fell over backwards as he saw an explosion at the rear of the plane. It looked very much as if it had been hit by a ground-to-air missile, but who could have fired it?

He yelled at the radio operator. 'Make immediate contact! They must try to land if it's not already too late!'

The plane plummeted earthwards, smoke pouring from the rear, but the engine did not seem to be on fire. Balashov looked on with grim fascination.

To his surprise, the pilot regained control and the plane began to climb again. The radio crackled into life. 'We have slight rear end damage. Will continue to Nairobi.'

Balashov shrugged his shoulders. If they wanted to live dangerously, then why should he interfere. Now he must find out who had fired the missile at the plane, and why. He headed for the stairs – then fell forwards as the building shook from the force of an enormous explosion.

Bernard was trembling. He'd been afraid before, but never like this. The whole plane had shaken as the missile hit it. At first he'd thought they were finished and he'd gripped the edge of his seat, powerless to do anything.

One name sprang to mind. Vorotnikov. The man was cut from the same cloth as himself, totally ruthless.

He heard the pilot's voice come over the intercom. 'Jolly close shave that, sir, I can tell you. It's a damn good job we didn't try to get back on the ground. Look down out of your port window, the whole place is going up.'

The charges had ripped across the runway, tearing it to pieces. At the same moment, they rocketed ten of the closest planes, then moved forward to fire on more of them. The wave of heat was unbelievable. Michael Strong tried to make a quick mental calculation of the value of the planes exploding around him, but gave up.

The rocket attack on the Lear jet had preceded their assault by seconds. At first he'd been furious because he thought the rocket had been fired by one of the men under his command. However the incident had worked to his advantage because all the Russians in the control tower were looking upwards at the stricken jet when the runway blew up. The sleek white plane had skimmed effortlessly away through the clouds of rain.

Michael Strong wondered if the men inside knew just how lucky they'd been.

The attack on the ground was now going better than he'd expected. The planes were catching light fast; aviation fuel was running out of them, shooting out across the runway in sheets of flame.

It was only now that they were out of Beira, that they could afford to stop. Guy continued the breakneck pace along the main dirt road until he found an innocuous-looking turn-off, and sped down it for some metres before swinging hard into a clump of thick bush and killing the engine.

Mick was far more seriously hurt than Rayne had first thought. They laid him down on a groundsheet and Rayne carefully removed Mick's jacket and undershirt to get a better look at the bullet wounds. He felt sick when he saw the ugly line of holes running across Mick's belly. It was clear the Rhodesian didn't have a chance of surviving, in fact it was nothing short of a miracle that he was still alive.

Mick tried to speak, but dark blood came out of his mouth and he coughed badly. Guy held a water bottle to his lips and he managed to take several deep gulps.

'Dammit, sir,' he whispered, 'I knew Larry was a bad bugger, but I never thought the bastard could shoot me so close up in cold blood.'

His face was white and his body was very cold. His eyes gazed fixedly in the distance, and tears ran down the side of his face, though he wasn't openly crying. Then the pain hit him again and he pulled Rayne towards him, staring at him desperately.

'Don't blame yourself for this, sir. Listen, I've got a little girl, her mother can't stand the sight of me, but Tracey still needs the money. Just . . . just make sure she gets it, will you?'

'I promise, Mick.'

'Just make sure she gets it.'

His eyes closed and his head dropped to one side. Tears started to Rayne's eyes, tears which he made no attempt to hide from Guy. They'd been through so much together. If only he'd obeyed his instincts, he would never have recruited Larry Preston.

He stood with Guy in the pouring rain, not saying anything, the dead man lying between them. In the distance there was continuous rifle fire. Rayne guessed it must be coming from the airport.

The first sally came at them a minute after the explosions began. Fifteen Russian soldiers charged them, all armed with AK-47's. Michael Strong gave the command to fire.

The Russians immediately dived for cover and retaliated. For five minutes bullets lashed into the ground all round Michael. But his men were good, and slowly but surely eliminated every one of the enemy soldiers. After that, no one else tried anything for a while.

Then small pockets of fire began erupting from the area round the control tower, and he gave the command to have it rocketed. The missile smacked into the top of the tower, blowing the roof off and setting the control-room on fire. Men poured out of the bottom door and ran for cover. Another group of Russians was desperately trying to put out one of the planes with a fire-extinguisher, but to no avail.

The Colonel could see that there was complete breakdown of command. Men were running around directionless; officers screamed out orders, but no one obeyed them.

Now would be a good time to detonate the next set of charges. These had been carefully laid next to the supply store, which he was sure contained large numbers of weapons and high explosives. The more devastation he caused, the better.

He pushed the plunger down hard and blew up the barracks.

'You can't blame yourself,' Guy said. 'I would have hired Preston, he was a bloody good soldier, but he was also a greedy man.'

Together they dragged Mick's body over to some boulders, and covered it with earth and stones. They worked in silence, grim-faced, and when they had finished they stood still for a moment, taking a last look at their comrade's grave.

It was as they were moving back to the jeep that Rayne heard the noise. Immediately he gestured for Guy to get down. They each picked up an assault rifle and moved carefully into the bush. Then they crouched down and waited.

For a while all they could hear was the dripping of water in the leaves of the surrounding trees, and the far-off sounds of men at war. With the soldier's instinct they waited patiently, listening for other more distinctive sounds. It was a safe bet that if they had heard men in the bush, then the men would also have heard them. It would be a war of nerves to see who would move first.

At last there was a faint rustle in the bush not ten metres away from them. They saw a shape moving stealthily towards the jeep, and another appeared just behind it. The one in front was definitely carrying a gun. At first Rayne thought they were going to investigate the jeep, but instead they continued past it. He gestured to Guy to start moving in behind them. They kept some twenty metres apart and began to close in.

'Halt! Drop your weapons!'

Rayne shouted the command in Portuguese and prepared to open fire. The two figures stopped dead in their tracks but the one in front still held onto his weapon even though he did not turn round.

'Drop it, or you're dead.'

This was it, thought Rayne, another second and he'd open fire.

The man let the weapon drop to the ground. A desperation seemed to take hold of his frame and Rayne saw his shoulders sag.

'Put your arms on top of your head. Both of you.'

They obeyed the instruction and Guy sprinted forward and picked up the weapon.

'Don't try anything. You're both covered.'

Rayne moved closer, anxious to find out more but still very wary. 'Turn round.'

One of them turned round, the other seemed to hesitate but then followed suit.

Rayne found himself staring at an enormous black man. The face radiated authority. The figure next to him seemed tiny by comparison, a dirty-faced white boy. They both stared at him in horror, and it was only then that he realised he must be covered in Mick's blood. They looked quite desperate, and he realised that whatever they were up to it had little to do with the ordinary military operations conducted in the area.

'We'll have to tie you up and leave you at the roadside.'

Rayne had continued to speak in Portuguese but the black man replied to him in English. 'I don't know who you are, I don't care. But if you leave us by the side of the road they will kill us. We have to get away. Keep me if you have to, but let him go.'

The other figure turned to Rayne. 'We're no threat to you, whoever you are. Let us go.'

Rayne and Sam

To Guy's horror Rayne dropped his rifle and ran forward. The black man moved to block him, but stopped as Guy's rifle came up to his chest; the white man screamed as Rayne moved forward, 'No, no, no! You bastard!'

It was then Guy realised that the man was in fact a woman.

'For God's sake, Sam, it's me!'

The woman stepped back a few paces, looking at Rayne, and then flung her arms round him.

'Rayne, Rayne, I thought you were going to kill me. God, what's happened to you?'

'There's no time to explain. We've got to get out of here.'

He held her tight, still not really able to believe that it was her. Everything had changed. Now he could get the hell out of this place.

Guy saw the black man staring in complete amazement. That makes two of us, he thought to himself. Then he remembered about the woman Rayne had been searching for.

Rayne could not believe his good fortune, could not believe it had happened. He turned to Guy and the black man.

'We need a few minutes alone, I know there's not much time but it's important.'

The black soldier and Guy sidled uneasily back to the jeep. After a bit, Guy put down his Galil and pulled out a packet of cigarettes. He offered them to the black man and then took one for himself. The seconds were ticking by, seconds that could spell the difference between life and death, but Guy knew that whatever Rayne wanted to say to this woman, it was important.

The black man spoke first.

'You're crazy, you'll never get out of here alive. On foot we have a good chance, in a jeep you will be ambushed.'

'We're flying out of here. The rest of our men are attacking the airport. If they fail, we're finished – the Russians will blow us out of the sky.'

Tongogara stared at the blood on Guy's uniform. 'You've been hit?'

'No. One of the men with us in the bank decided he'd like the money for himself. He turned on us.'

'Money always leads to corruption.'

'Where are you going?'

'North, to Malawi. There I will wait till independence comes to Zimbabwe, which will be quickly. Then I will move down into the new Zimbabwe where there will be much work to be done. I want a peaceful life after all these years of war.'

Guy regarded the black man with respect. This was no ordinary soldier.

'It was you who blew up the fuel tanks?'

Tongogara grimaced, then stared at the Frenchman. 'Sam and myself. Once one tank went up, the rest caught very quickly.'

'But how did you get away?'

'I think the Russians thought it was an air attack. They just kept on firing up into the sky.'

'Wasn't the woman a hindrance?'

'No. Sam's a brilliant shot.' Tongogara looked away to where Rayne and Sam were hidden in the trees. 'I think she's just found someone she's been looking for for a long time.'

Guy noted the sadness with which he said this and knew that behind the simple words there was a world of feeling.

Sam stood looking at Rayne in silence, a hundred different emotions coursing through her body. In the surprise of his arrival she hadn't had time to think, but maybe that was good because it meant she had shown exactly how she felt about him – and in the same moment she realised that he had reciprocated.

Now she looked at him, she could see how he had changed in the short time they had been away from each other. He was thinner, and faint lines had begun to appear on his face. She noted that although he was dressed in a smart casual suit, an assault rifle lay in his hands, and his suit was caked with blood.

What the hell was he doing in this awful place and how did he propose to get out of it?

'I wanted to see you desperately but I was ordered to leave immediately.'

'You left the army, you left me. I was furious; bitter too. I couldn't understand how you could drop me so easily.'

'It was important that my cover remained perfect.'

'Important! Fuck you, Rayne Gallagher, aren't I important? What are you doing here, trying to kill a few more blacks for the glory of Rhodesia?'

The next minute she was in his arms sobbing.

'I'm sorry, Rayne, I didn't mean it, really I didn't. When you left without saying anything, it was one of the worst moments of my life.'

Quickly he told her about the mission to stop Vorotnikov's invasion, how he'd discovered that she was in Beira and how he'd been searching for her.

'But how could you hope to stop the whole invasion, just the two of you?'

'There are twenty of us, all hand-picked mercenaries with a precise plan of action. I can assure you that the invasion will never take place.' She could see from the expression on his face that he meant what he was saying.

'We meet on equal ground then, Rayne. Tongogara rescued me from Vorotnikov – and he too decided to play his part in preventing the Salisbury massacre.'

Rayne felt jealousy stirring in his heart for this man who had spent so much time with the woman he loved. He wondered how far their relationship had gone. Then he hated himself for thinking that way.

'And how did you, one black man and one white woman, propose to stop the invasion?'

'We've already done it.'

'You blew up the fuel tanks?'

'Yes. We thought you must be Russian soldiers trying to track us down.' She stared at him intensely. 'I thought you were going to kill us – you know how you automatically expect the worst. It was as if we had made all that effort, and then some divine force had decided to show us how futile it all was.'

'You and Tongogara must fly out with us. We're not going

311

back to South Africa, but up to the north. From there he'll be able to go anywhere he wants.'

He could see that she looked sad, as if she was tearing herself away from something very important.

'I'll come, but I know he'll stay here. I've already asked him a thousand times to get away. You see, he can't, he belongs here. You can't imagine what it took him to blow up the fuel supply depot. He's betrayed his own people.'

Rayne wondered if John Fry would ever believe that he had not been responsible for the destruction of the fuel supply depot. Somehow he doubted it. But then he didn't really care. In his own mind he could see absolutely no logic in Fry's insistence that the fuel tanks should remain intact. When they got out, he would make sure Fry gave him some answers.

'We must move on, Sam, time is running out. I don't even know whether we're going to make it out of here alive.'

He turned to walk back to the jeep, but she called after him.

'Rayne?'

'Yes?'

'I just want you to know that I love you more than any man I've ever known.'

'I feel the same way about you, Sam. I promise you that if we make it through this, I won't leave you again.'

She smiled at him and together they ran back to the jeep.

Guy jumped into the driver's seat and Sam sat next to him. Tongogara and Rayne leapt in the back, submachine-guns at the ready. They pulled away quickly and bounced along the track back towards the dirt road. Every time they hit a puddle they were showered with red mud, and by the time they got back to the main road they were soaking wet.

It was hard to see anything in the poor light and the pouring rain, but they didn't have time to take it easy – they had to make it to the collection area before it became pitch dark. Guy pushed the engine grudgingly up to maximum revs and wrestled with the steering wheel as the vehicle drifted from one side of the road to the other. All his energy was spent in trying to keep them on a straight course. When they ran into the ambush they scarcely knew what was happening . . .

The rocket hit the jeep square in the side and lifted it up and over like a playing card dancing in the wind. After that came a withering hail of gunfire that ricocheted off the vehicle's metal sides. One bullet caught the petrol tank and the jeep erupted in flames. Still the bullets hammered into it, though it was clear that nothing could survive the fire.

One of the attackers got up and moved tentatively forward. The rest followed, looking for the bodies that must have been thrown clear by the explosion. They had almost reached the jeep when a burst of machine-gun fire cut them to pieces. Not a man survived, though one soldier did stagger backwards for a few metres before falling riddled with bullets.

Guy dropped the still smoking machine-gun into the sand at the side of the road. He looked up to find everything was red. There seemed to be no explanation for this and he felt a great weariness overtake him. He had been thrown clear of the jeep and landed hard on his legs. Both his main femurs were broken and his combat trousers were a mass of blood. He tried to crawl forwards, but collapsed.

Guy remembered once when he was a little boy on the streets and had stolen a man's wallet. The man had chased after him and eventually caught him by the scruff of the neck. Guy had shaken with the fear. The man had smiled kindly at him, taken the wallet back, then pulled all the money out and given it to him. Guy tried to hold onto the memory of the man's face, but it began to recede, and he felt as if he was travelling down a long tunnel. At the end was a light that seemed to beckon to him and he knew that was where he had to go.

As Rayne came round, all he could hear was crying. He could see Tongogara in the distance, armed and scouting the area.

He pulled himself up and was relieved to discover he hadn't broken any bones. The crying sound was louder now, and he saw that it was coming from near the charred wreck of the jeep.

Slowly he moved towards it and saw that Sam was crouched over a body lying next to the side of the road. She was holding the head in her hands and he could see that the rest of the body was soaked with blood.

To his horror he realised that it was Guy. He ran forward, thinking that he must still be alive, and Sam turned to look at him, her face contorted with anguish. He could hardly bear to look at her.

'He's dead, can't you see he's dead? Damn you, Rayne!'

313

Rayne felt a strong arm on his shoulder, pulling him away, and he yielded to the pressure. He turned round to see Tongogara, a muddy apparition in the falling rain.

'Leave her. She's had enough.'

They both walked over to the area where the blast had come from and found the rocket-launcher lying in a pool of muddy water. Behind them in the bush was a small truck with the keys still in the ignition. Tongogara got into the cabin and started up the engine. Then he carefully reversed the vehicle out onto the road.

Tongogara's whole body was still shaking from the force of the impact with which he had hit the dirt road, after the blast had thrown him clear of the jeep. Too stunned to move, he had watched terrified as the armed troops moved towards him; then he had seen them cut to pieces by Guy before he died.

Rayne joined Tongogara in the cab and looked at the black man's watch. It was getting late.

John Fry had certainly got his money's worth. Three out of the four of them dead. Rayne wondered if the casualty rate at the airport had been as bad. This was a suicide mission if ever there was one.

Tongogara was the first to speak. 'We can't go far in this truck, it is too obvious a target. I must go on foot now.'

'Come with us, there's a plane waiting. You can go anywhere in the world you want to.'

'There is nowhere in the world that I want to go. My future is here.'

Rayne looked out of the windscreen and along the road that was strewn with dead bodies. Tongogara said, 'I know what you're thinking. I think it too. Death. I don't want the slaughter to carry on, I am sick of the waste. Perhaps by staying I can do a little to stop it. But you must take her away from this; she has been through too much. Take care of her.'

They shook hands, and Rayne watched Tongogara go down the road to Sam and pull her away from Guy's body. He kissed her on the cheek, then lifted Guy's body in his massive arms and disappeared with it into the bush. He did not return.

Sam got into the truck beside Rayne. She was silent. He could feel his heart beating; he sensed that there was a deep bond between Tongogara and Sam, and he had to fight to keep his

314

jealousy under control. After all, he was the one who had left Sam behind.

He pulled away and turned the truck round quickly. There was no sign of Tongogara any longer, and the place seemed lonely and empty. He pushed the vehicle as hard as it would go. Not much further, and they would reach the place where Lois had hidden the scrambler. Sam moved across the seat and held herself close to him, guilty after her earlier outburst.

'He was a good man, that Frenchman, I could tell. I don't know how much more of this I can take.'

'Will Tongogara be all right?'

'He'll be fine. He's like an animal in the bush, they'll never find him.'

'In a minute we're going to stop. We can't carry on in this truck, there's too much distance to cover in such a conspicuous vehicle. Can you handle a ride on the back of a motorbike?'

He slowed down, looking carefully for the place that Lois had shown him earlier in the week. It wasn't easy to find in the half-light and the pouring rain, and he had to get out of the cab and survey the side of the road before he eventually found the hiding place.

The bike was covered in mud, but the pouring rain quickly washed it clean. Rayne got back into the truck with Sam and drove it off the road, far enough into the bush to keep it hidden.

It took him some time to kick-start the bike into life. He handed Sam the Uzi machine-carbine he'd been carrying, and showed her the exact firing sequence. 'Don't hesitate to use it. We won't get a second chance.'

The bike started noisily and Sam jumped onto the back, holding the gun in her right hand and Rayne with her left. Then they were off, flying over the muddy ground at a speed that made Sam keep her eyes closed for the first few minutes.

'Just hold on tight, and whenever I move to one side you follow suit.'

Rayne had to shout these instructions at the top of his voice because the machine was screaming along at maximum revs. His arms ached as he struggled to keep the bike from sliding over in the thick mud. The ambush had proved that the enemy forces had rallied and were taking counter-action, so at every bend he scanned the road ahead to see if there were any signs of another. At least on the bike they would not be so vulnerable because they were a smaller target moving much faster. He felt the wad of paper pressing against his shirt, and was glad that he still had the incriminating document of Bernard Aschaar's that he'd taken from the bank.

He turned to the left and accelerated down another, less frequented dirt road. The map that he and Michael Strong had studied for so long was engraved on his memory.

It had taken quite a bit of research to discover that there had once been a second airport near Beira. Up to the end of the Second World War it had been used by the RAF as part of their navigation training programme, but after that it had fallen into disuse, and independence had finally killed it off. Rayne anticipated that they might have to clear the runway in some places, but that shouldn't be a major problem. He estimated that they were now less than five minutes away, and began to wonder if Michael Strong was there already.

Captain Balashov dialled General Vorotnikov's private number. To his surprise the phone was answered by General Vorotnikov himself. He sounded furious.

'Yes, yes. What the hell is it?'

'Captain Balashov, sir. First-in-command, Beira Airport. We are under full-scale attack. All planes destroyed, runway destroyed. Enemy is closing in and firing from all sides . . .'

'Is Aschaar there?'

This seemed a stupid and irrelevant question to Balashov but he answered it all the same.

'He took off before the attack started, sir. The enemy rocketed his plane, but it didn't come down. He's making for Nairobi.'

To his astonishment Balashov heard the General cursing. He would have thought that at least the news about Aschaar was good.

'Take counter-action immediately, Balashov.'

'But that's suicidal, sir!'

'Take counter-action, Balashov, or consider yourself stripped of command and under arrest from this minute.'

'Understood, sir.'

He put the phone down and staggered outside. There were men running in all directions. He saw one man on fire, screaming his head off, and he pulled out his pistol and cut the man down.

Immediately he was the centre of attention. The men looked at him fearfully.

'Get together. Load your rifles. We have to counter-attack.'

One of the men started to protest, but Balashov lifted his pistol and the complaint was dropped. He scanned the frightened men around him, searching for any other backsliders. He wondered if this was what it had been like in the First World War before the men crossed over the tops of the trenches to almost certain death.

'We will fan out and then advance, is that understood?' There was a dutiful murmur of acknowledgement.

'Forward!'

They moved out beyond the flames and began to advance slowly.

Michael Strong couldn't believe his eyes. He had never seen anything so stupid in his whole life. It must be the same man who had removed the perimeter guards.

He gestured to the men either side of him to hold their fire. Then he quietly murmured his orders.

'Let's not make this a massacre. Single shots only, please. Aim carefully. Maybe if we bring a few of the buggers down, the others will go home.'

The figures continued to advance. Silhouetted against the flames, they made perfect targets. Michael was still counting on their nerve breaking, but nothing of the kind happened. Reluctantly he picked up his rifle and aimed for the leading man.

Captain Balashov had never been so scared in his life. The firing had stopped and he couldn't see the enemy. He got the disturbing feeling that he was being watched.

Perhaps the attacking force had left. The lack of return fire seemed to confirm this. Now that he and his men were almost away from the smoke and flames, he could see a little better through the drizzle – The shots erupted without warning. Three men directly in front of him were cut down and he felt a bullet fly past. There was a sickening thud as it found the man next to him.

He turned to look behind and a bullet tore into his right shoulder. His nerve broke, and he started to run back. Some of his men did not notice this and pressed forward to their deaths, but the rest followed their commanding officer, sprinting back towards the flames.

Balashov was breathing heavily. He'd had a foretaste of death, and that was as far as he wanted it to go. He knew there was no point in phoning General Vorotnikov, the man was crazy and would order him to remain at his post till death.

'Get the trucks!' he shouted. 'We must abandon the airport.'

The men looked at him dumbfounded. Balashov was a fool, moving from one ridiculous tactic to the next.

'Get the trucks!'

Balashov's voice was now a high-pitched scream, and this time the men didn't wait to find out if he would reinforce his orders with his pistol. The V-8 engines of the three GAZ trucks idled noisily as some three hundred and fifty troops and pilots climbed onto them. Balashov jumped into the cab of the leading truck and gave the order to pull off. In a matter of minutes the air base was completely deserted.

The moment the trucks had disappeared, Michael Strong and his men entered the base and started systematically destroying what was left of it. Michael was busy pouring petrol over the floor in the room below the shattered control tower when the phone rang. He picked it up and answered in the politest English.

'Good afternoon, Beira airforce base.'

General Vorotnikov was on the other end of the line. He could not believe Balashov's impertinence and let forth a stream of Russian invective.

'I'm sorry, old boy, but I don't understand your language.'

Vorotnikov switched to English. He would have the man sorted out later. 'Have you made the attack, Balashov?'

'Balashov and his men have left. I am now destroying what is left of your base. Have a nice day.'

Bunty Mulbarton looked down at his watch. They were running out of time. He'd been expecting some sort of Russian relief force to come along the road, but none had appeared. Now to his astonishment he saw a vast convoy of trucks speeding towards him.

Bunty smiled to himself. Michael would be pleased. They had obviously abandoned the airport in a hurry. The first truck was ahead of the others, but fortunately they were all travelling close enough together for his charges to have maximum effect. His hand moved to the electric detonator and pressed the activator switch. Now he had merely to touch the red button on top of the unit to set off the explosive charges hidden beneath the road.

Balashov was beginning to feel quite jubilant. He had, after all, evaded being captured by superior enemy forces. Now they could regroup and counter-attack in the morning. He could confidently tell Vorotnikov that they had tried to attack the enemy and had been mowed down by withering crossfire. There was no way he or his men could have remained at the airport, they would have been mercilessly destroyed by the enemy.

Balashov urged the driver to go faster, anxious to get as far away from the airport as possible. He sweated as he remembered that he had given the order to reduce the number of perimeter guards. Perhaps that order would be forgotten after the afternoon's chaos. He was not so sure that he would come out of a commission of enquiry looking particularly competent.

They rounded a very sharp corner, slowing down considerably.

There was a muffled explosion and the truck was thrown slightly off course.

Balashov looked around worriedly and then turned to the driver.

'Get out of here. As fast as you can!'

Bunty Mulbarton shivered, the charges had obviously been deactivated by the heavy rainfall.

There was a noise behind him and he swung round. Ted Donel jumped down from the bank above and landed squarely on the ground next to him.

'God, Bunty, we're really in a fix.'

'Haven't seen Colonel Strong yet, have you?'

'No, just his handiwork in the distance. Looks like he's blown the whole bang-shoot to smithereens. How long do you think it'll be before reinforcements arrive?'

'I don't want to be around to find out.'

'Exactly my feelings.'

Bunty gestured for Ted to follow him and they made their way up the side of the slope. At a pine tree he had marked when they had first made their way up the bank a week before, Bunty started down towards the road.

319

They moved more cautiously now, making sure there was no one below them. In the distance there was another explosion. By the time they reached the roadside it was getting dark and visibility was not good. All the same, they hoped they wouldn't be stuck too long in such an exposed position.

Siva Singh rushed up to what was left of the bank. He had driven his car here himself, and at incredible speed, wearing only a pair of shorts and a T-shirt – for once his obsession with being dressed for the occasion had been abandoned.

He noticed in panic the bank notes lying all over the street in the pouring rain. Sprinting up the front stairs, he stared aghast at the doors of the vault which were hanging on their hinges. Slowly he moved forwards, praying that only money had been taken, but his worst fears were confirmed when he saw that the floor was scattered with empty safe-deposit boxes. He made his way to the nearest telephone.

'General Vorotnikov. Singh here . . . Yes, I know you have bigger problems . . . The fuel tanks . . . All destroyed? No, I don't believe it. The airport under attack? It must be the Rhodesians . . . Worse, they have hit the bank. Yes, all the documents have been taken. They obviously knew exactly what they were looking for. Yes, the agreements are gone. Your guards should have been here, but instead they were at the fuel supply depot. General, General . . .'

The line went dead. Singh stumbled through the wreckage around him and went back into the vault. Plaster fell from the ceiling, cascading off the top of his head. Perhaps he had been wrong; maybe some of the boxes had been left untouched. Carefully he searched through the rubble, but every box he found had had its lock shot away.

He made his way back through the fallen masonry to the front entrance. Outside in the rain he saw vast black clouds billowing up from the fuel supply depot. Just an hour before, he had been relaxing at home, feeling supremely confident about the future. Now everything had changed. He could hear the frantic reports coming through on the military radio in the jeep nearby. He could hear the shouts and screams of men being injured by gunfire – and suddenly it dawned on him that these reports were not coming from the fuel depot, but from the airport.

Siva Singh raced back to his Mercedes and drove home as

quickly as he could. If there *was* an invading force, then they would only know him as a private citizen, not as a supporter of ZANLA and the armies of the USSR. And nothing on earth was going to persuade him to come outside again today.

Fernandes sat in the bar of the Hotel Beira, drinking neat brandy with a shaking hand. He had just been in the shop next door that he had rented out to Mr Brand. It hadn't been hard to guess what had been stored in it, and he'd also seen signs that men had been living there.

Every time there was another explosion in the distance Fernandes trembled and spilled some more of his drink, but at least he had for reassurance the comforting chill of the Berretta pistol stuffed into the belt of his trousers. There was only one choice left for him, and that was to get out of Beira as fast as he could.

He got up and reached for his car keys behind the desk of the hotel foyer. Once he had them safely in his hands he walked toward the front entrance of the hotel. He froze as he saw who was coming towards him.

Ivan had been ordered to arrest the owner of the hotel by General Vorotnikov. The order had been barked over the telephone at him and he was told in no uncertain terms that he must torture the Portuguese till he squealed like a sucking pig. Ivan despised torturing as an activity so the order was odious to him even though he disliked Fernandes, but he allowed none of this to show in his reply to Vorotnikov.

The Hotel Beira looked completely deserted. He parked the car and entered through the double front doors – immediately bumping into Fernandes, who was on his way out and did not look pleased to see him.

'Going out for a stroll, Fernandes?'

'I have urgent business to attend to.' He attempted to bustle past Ivan, but found his way blocked.

'Don't push me,' he bristled.

'You're under arrest. Direct orders from General Vorotnikov.'

Ivan moved towards him, instinctively reaching for his pistol as Fernandes retreated, desperately searching for an angle of escape. He pointed his Berretta at Ivan. The Russian had cornered him.

'Come on, Fernandes. Put that pea-shooter away. It's time we had a little talk.'

Fernandes looked nervously at the big Russian. To him it was a simple enough equation: kill or be killed. He would be tortured and he knew he couldn't face that.

'You wouldn't do it, Fernandes.'

Fernandes closed his eyes and squeezed the trigger.

When he opened them again, Ivan was lying on the floor screaming, blood pouring from a wound in his side.

'You fucking bastard! You're going to die for this!'

Fernandes shot Ivan a second time in the chest, and the Russian slumped to the ground like a sack of potatoes. But, as Fernandes ran out into the street, Ivan pulled himself up, sighted his pistol and fired two shots before finally collapsing. The bullets hit Fernandes in the centre of the spine and flung him across the tarmac.

The two bodies, both covered in blood, lay quite still in the pouring rain.

Vorotnikov felt his world collapsing around him. The stabbing pains in his chest, which had started earlier in the afternoon, were becoming more pronounced every minute. Was this a heart attack? He tried to stagger towards a chair, but knew he couldn't reach it. The pain, the pain! He fell across the floor. He felt his body start to convulse and he screamed out in agony.

The world went very black. He was being drawn towards a place he did not want to go. The face of the American journalist came into his mind, the long blonde hair, the beautiful husky voice, but every time he tried to fix on her image it began to fade. He knew now that he would never catch her.

Relaxing with a whisky in one of the sumptuous leather-covered seats of his private jet, Bernard Aschaar was beginning to feel rather more philosophical about the whole business. Perhaps, indeed, it had all been a giant mistake from the beginning. Anyway, he would negotiate with Mugabe when he came to power; at least the groundwork had been effectively laid.

He smiled as he looked through the report he had taken from his briefcase. It made pleasant reading. It was an analysis of his plan to gain control of the world's gold mining production. He would step up the pressure on Sonja Seyton-Waugh – he was sure he could break her – then she would sell up, and her mines would give him the edge he needed to acquire world control.

The interior of the cabin was dark and soothing, the only light coming from a spotlight on the ceiling. Bernard's whisky was nearly finished. As he rose to pour himself another Dufftown Glenlivet from the elegant crystal decanter, a sudden, interesting thought crossed his mind. He sat down, and raised the captain on the intercom.

'I want you to make direct contact with Vorotnikov's villa.'

Bernard waited patiently. Eventually the intercom crackled into life. 'I have Vorotnikov's servant on the line, Mr Aschaar, he's not very cooperative.'

'Just make the connection.' Immediately the sound of static dominated all else.

'General Vorotnikov?' There was a lengthy pause and Bernard's pulse began to race furiously.

'I am afraid the General is unavailable at the moment.'

Bernard recognised the routine stalling tactics. He said, 'The General and I had agreed to speak to each other at this precise time. Please connect me, this is irritating.'

'My apologies, sir, but you will not be able to speak to General Vorotnikov.'

'Why the hell not!'

'He died of a heart attack late this afternoon. You will have to . . .'

Bernard switched off the transmission, then walked over to pour himself another Scotch. His hands were rock steady and his face sported the biggest smile it had worn for a considerable time.

Almost at the rendezvous point, they saw a Russian patrol coming in the opposite direction. Rayne screamed at Sam to hang on as he accelerated off the road and pulled the bike down.

Trembling, they lay in the foliage as vehicle after vehicle rumbled by. If they were spotted, they wouldn't have stood a chance.

The moment the patrol had passed Rayne dragged the bike back into the road. Sam leapt on the back and Rayne accelerated off, pushing the machine as fast as it would go.

Everything was a blur. The bike was running rough. A knocking sound from the engine indicated that there was something seriously wrong. Ahead, through the trees, he could see the flat stretch of ground that was the old airport. Languid palms ran along the sides of the grass runway and an air of foreboding hung over the place.

The engine seized moments later, pitching them both forward onto the road.

Rayne was winded by the force of the impact and for a few minutes he couldn't move. He was terrified that they had been followed – that a truckload of Soviet soldiers would come around the corner at any minute and open fire on them.

At last he staggered over to where Sam lay silent on the ground.

She opened her eyes as he bent down and managed a smile. 'Next time I go for a bike ride, I'll make sure it's with someone who knows what they're doing.'

He helped her to her feet and they walked towards the runway. If John Fry kept his promises, the plane circling above would land as soon as he released the flare to indicate that they were all in place.

'This is the six o'clock news. Reports have just been received that a large Soviet invasion force, based in Beira, has been attacked and destroyed. Both the United States and Great Britain have voiced their dissatisfaction with the Soviet Union's tactics at this delicate stage of the Rhodesian Independence negotiations . . .'

John Fry listened to the BBC World Service report with satisfaction. He imagined the consternation it would cause in Moscow. Now he would wait eagerly for his agent in Beira to report back on the extent of the damage and the effectiveness of Gallagher's attack.

He was in black tie, ready to attend a ball at the American Embassy in Pretoria. In his hand was a glass of neat whisky and in the elegant glass ashtray on his desk lay a smoking Hauptmann cigar.

John Fry never regretted the loss of life that was the inevitable by-product of his profession. During his twenty-five-year career in espionage he had learnt to distance himself from people and events – a necessary form of self-preservation, for otherwise he would have found orders like the one he was about to give, almost intolerable. But to John Fry agents were simply pieces of vital equipment, to be used tactically at the right time. They did not have families, or souls.

Sometimes he remembered the time when he had fallen in love with a woman agent. She had been expertly briefed and was quite convinced that the information she was carrying was of vital importance to the Soviet Union. Only he and a few other top officials knew that she had been fed a story to tell her Soviet captors once she had been arrested. He had almost cracked, almost broken the rules and gone over to get her. Betty.

That was when it had all started, the complex web that he had spun over so many years. He had never slept with any women except prostitutes since that time. He hadn't married. He was more successful than ever at his job, but somehow something was missing.

The monitor above his desk crackled into life and he heard the unemotional tones of the radio operator who sat in the basement four floors below him. This innocuous building, at the heart of Pretoria, was to all outside appearances the head office of a large American import and export company. Only a few top people in the South African National Intelligence Service knew that it was the headquarters of the CIA's Southern Africa section. In the basement was a labyrinth of electronic listening equipment that monitored broadcasts from agents operating throughout the African continent.

Intelligence that Fry had gathered here over the past year had pointed to the existence of a frightening Soviet strategy: the Russians were infiltrating the government of every single African country. Though Fry kept much of this information to himself, his directive from the US government was clear: to thwart Soviet expansionism in every conceivable way without letting the situation develop into another Vietnam.

It was a tough assignment, especially now that Rhodesia was on the verge of getting a new government. Gallagher's attack on Beira, for example, would have to appear to have been the work of the Rhodesians, and this he would engineer over the next few days. The Soviet government must never know that the true instigator was John Fry of the CIA.

The voice of his agent in Beira came through on the speaker, and Fry pushed the red button on the intercom to open the conversation.

'This is Lynx. Please give me your account of the weather.'

'Affirmative, this is Cub. The business is good and the weather excellent. Gallagher is performing up to expectation. Everything is as it should be, apart from one major difficulty.'

John Fry tensed. What the hell was wrong? He had not calculated on Captain Gallagher making any mistakes.

'The eagle has died.'

John Fry went white. He had given Rayne no instructions to kill General Vorotnikov. Perhaps he had heard incorrectly.

'Cub. Is the eagle the king of the birds?'

'Affirmative.'

He could be recalled to Washington for this, it was a major catastrophe. Vorotnikov had been a man they could out-guess; his replacement might be a different animal altogether.

John had chosen Rayne carefully on Martin Long's advice; he'd been certain that he would be reliable. Why had he killed Vorotnikov? Whatever the answer to that question, one thing was certain: Gallagher knew far more about what was going on than was good for him – and that John Fry could not tolerate.

Though the outside world might still be persuaded to believe that it was the Rhodesians who had attacked Beira, Fry knew that the Soviet government would never buy that story now. The death of Vorotnikov would be a big issue. There could well be reprisals. There would definitely be investigations.

'Lynx. It is past my bedtime.'

The transmissions were always kept short so that there was no possibility of their being traced. Already this one had gone on beyond the recognised time limit.

'End report Cub.' The silence that followed was one of the nastiest John Fry had experienced.

He made another radio transmission.

'This is Lynx.' The distortion from the other end was horrendous. 'Affirmative, this is Swallow.'

'Cancel collection.'

'Are you fucking crazy?'

Fry exploded. The pilot had broken the code sequence. 'Abort collection, Swallow.'

There was a grim silence. Then, 'It's your party, Lynx.'

'You will abort collection?'

326

'Affirmative.'

Fry switched off the receiver and smiled. If the Soviets caught Rayne they might just make him talk – but perhaps he didn't need to worry. It was far more likely that they'd just shoot him on sight.

He walked over to the drinks cabinet in the corner of his office, took some ice out of the concealed fridge and dropped the cubes into his glass. He poured himself another generous whisky.

He wondered how Rayne would react when the plane did not land. He knew they wouldn't last long in Mozambique. Of course, he'd made quite sure they wouldn't by ordering his agent in Beira to make certain that the Russian military knew where the collection point was. With a bit of luck they'd just gun the lot of them down without taking any prisoners. After that Soviet high command could guess all they liked, they'd never find out the truth.

Now he would have to concentrate on Mugabe. The man was an intellectual and a Marxist. He might present problems, and then again he might not.

Restlessly pacing up and down the room, John Fry happened to glance down at a young couple in the street below, laughing, with their arms round each other. The thought crossed his mind that it might be nice to have someone to go home to, someone that he could talk to. But of course, everything he handled was classified, and the way he operated there was no one he *could* talk to.

He sipped meditatively at his drink. What had persuaded Rayne to disobey orders? The question bothered him, he had not expected this. It crossed his mind that Rayne might be involved with the magnate Aschaar. Fry was aware of Aschaar's activities, knowledge which he kept to himself. Aschaar might be useful to him in the future. But if Gallagher and Aschaar somehow knew about *his* activities, what then?

He walked over to the filing cabinet and pulled out the file on Vorotnikov. Years of intelligence work, carefully analysed to build up an accurate picture of the man; now it was all wasted, they would have to start again on his successor. Fry must contact his agent in Maputo in the morning and begin to find out who that successor might be. He sat down at the desk again and pushed another set of buttons on the intercom.

'Control, get me London Section Six. Use code X12GTT, category Urgent. I want immediate clearance.'

'Yes, sir.'

It would take about ten minutes for the contact to be made. As he fed Vorotnikov's file into the shredder next to his desk, he wondered again how Rayne and his men would feel when the plane did not land. Naturally they wouldn't expect anyone to know where the pick-up point was, so that would come as a surprise too. The more he thought about it, the more he was sure that the Soviets wouldn't take prisoners. They'd be bitter, and bitter men never thought straight. It would be over a day before a senior Soviet officer took the reins, and by then it would be too late.

An orange light flashed on the intercom, indicating that the link-up had been made.

'This is Lynx, who is my quarry?'

'Badger, old chap. Bit late for you, eh?'

Bugger the Brits, he thought to himself, they always made fun of the CIA jargon. He tried to curb the irritation that was creeping into his voice.

'Operation Troy is complete. The elections can proceed, no need for any heavy metal.'

'Affirmative, Lynx. The kites were sent down just for a show of strength, if you follow my drift.'

'Understood, Badger. Task force has been abandoned as planned. Survival chances nil.'

'You'd better hope so, Lynx. Anything else?'

John Fry didn't want to continue but knew he had to pass on the information he had just received. 'The eagle has been killed.'

'I say, Lynx, you're going to be in hot water over that one. Who's the replacement?'

'Don't know yet, Badger.'

'Naughty, you're going to get your knuckles rapped.'

'Mugabe will be the favourite now. Can you handle the situation?'

'Mugabe won't win. We'll be bringing in policemen to control the polling.'

John smiled to himself. The absolute arseholes! Did they really think that British bobbies were going to control the intimidators?

'OK, Badger, you can return to your lair.'

'Good hunting, Lynx.'

He was alone again. What was worse was that he was conscious of it – a bad sign. Being on his own usually didn't bother him.

He looked down at his silver-faced Piaget and saw that it was getting on. He was over half an hour late for the ball, and lack of punctuality always irritated him.

Rayne stared up at the sky in horror. The plane had ceased circling the runway and had disappeared into the clouds.

Sam clung to his side. 'What's happened?'

'The bastard's not coming in.'

Major Navrativlova was so tired that he was having difficulty keeping his eyes open. Even the endless cups of black coffee were failing in their usual stimulatory effect. He lit another cigarette and surveyed the ashtray full of butts on the table in front of him. The truth was, he was afraid of what would happen when General Vorotnikov's replacement arrived. For the moment, *he* was in command of Beira, and with the port under attack it was an unenviable position.

Someone came into the room and he turned to see who it was.

'Ah, Carl. You come in like a stinking jackal, ready to eat your prey when the killing has been done.'

Navrativlova hated the men from the KGB and their formidable power. He believed that the army came first and intelligence second. He also suspected they had something to do with Vorotnikov's death – it was known that the General and the KGB did not see eye to eye.

'I have some intelligence information which may make you a little more relaxed.'

Major Navrativlova stubbed out his cigarette. 'Don't play games with me. Tell me what you know, Carl.'

'This enemy force. They've a rendezvous, now, at the site of the old airport.'

A smile lit up Major Navrativlova's face. He ignored Carl Sverdelov's warning – 'Be careful. They're obviously a crack unit' – and jumped to his feet and ran for the door.

Carl gazed after Navrativlova's departing back. The man was a fool. He hadn't even bothered to ask how Carl knew where the rendezvous was. Not that Carl would have told him the truth. And anyway, no one in the Russian military would ever have heard of John Fry.

Rayne turned round with a start. The rain had stopped. Then he heard the sound that had scared him, the heavy roar of approaching trucks. He pulled Sam down, ran into the trees at the side of the runway and looked down the road. Was it Michael Strong with Bunty and the rest of the men?

The trucks moved onto the centre of the runway. Even if the plane did come back, it could not possibly land now. Now he could see the troops sitting in the back of one of the trucks, the barrels of their rifles glinting ominously.

No one had known about the pick-up point beside himself, Bunty, Mike and John Fry. And even if Mike or Bunty had already been captured, they would never have talked so quickly under interrogation. He heard the engines being switched off, and saw the Russians leap out of the trucks and run into the trees. It was an ambush. His worst fears were confirmed.

Rayne's mind raced as he racked his brains for a solution. Sam had crawled up next to him.

'What the hell's going on?'

'Double-cross. The Russians must have been told about the rendezvous. I don't know how the hell to warn the guys.' He gave her a kiss on the lips. 'If I don't make it, just remember that I love you.'

'If you die I'll never forgive you.'

Not bothering to silence their movements, they moved quickly through the trees in the direction from which the trucks had come.

Another truck came tearing along the road and turned onto the runway. To his horror, Rayne saw that Ted Donnel was driving.

'Ted! It's a trap!' He screamed the words out of his lungs, but Ted didn't hear him.

A rocket, fired by the Russian troops in the trees, hit the front of the lorry, killing Ted instantly. The vehicle burst into flames. Michael Strong and the rest of the men dived out of the back into a withering hail of gunfire.

'Oh, my God!'

Rayne grabbed Sam and pulled her down as she cried out in

horror. A bullet passed through the air where her head had been.

Then Rayne opened fire on the Russians.

Navrativlova screamed out in agony as a bullet ripped through his right buttock and flung him to the ground. He lay in the dirt, biting it with pain, clawing for something to grip onto.

Carl Sverdelov had been right. This was the rendezvous-point all right. But these men were very good. Already they were returning fire.

All round him there were explosions and screams. His men were dropping all the time. The enemy fire was now coming from two directions at once, although he had only seen one truck.

After ten minutes the firing stopped, and Navrativlova could hear the screams of wounded men in the failing light. He pulled himself to a standing position, and another bullet slapped into his back and flung him face down on the dirt.

Michael Strong lay on his back, his rifle held hard against his chest. The attack had come as a complete surprise; they'd been a sitting duck for the rocket as they drove onto the runway, and then the machine-gun fire had caught them as they bailed out at the back. He knew the enemy must have been told exactly where to find them – but he couldn't believe that Rayne would have double-crossed them.

The man next to him lifted himself up and started to run. Bullets tore into his body and he collapsed to the ground. Another man raised himself and a bullet smacked into his head, covering Michael with blood and bone.

Now it was do or die. He had no idea how many soldiers had ambushed them; all he could do was retaliate whenever someone fired. Every time he fired, he gave away his position and had to move on.

The screaming of the wounded turned the whole thing into a nightmare. In the growing darkness Michael glanced at the luminous dial of his watch and saw that it was six-thirty. He wondered if he would ever see daylight again.

Rayne whispered to Sam to keep down. Then he eased the paper-thin combat knife out of his waistband and dragged himself forward. It would be a grim business, but he could think of no other way of getting to his men. He had to cross the runway. The enemy were moving in under cover of darkness, and he knew he would have to be careful he didn't bump into them.

He came across the first shape in the darkness, and slowed down. There was a slight movement, and he could see the form of a man holding his rifle, lying face-down on the ground.

He leapt on top of him, made instant identification, and shoved the blade in hard below the lower ribs. The Russian's head fell forward, and Rayne waited for all movement to cease before crawling on again. Sam followed behind him, horrified at the loss of life. Bodies were strewn around the truck.

Rayne moved more cautiously now, knowing he was in the area where his own men should have been. Sure enough, he found three of their bodies. He felt the bile rise in his throat. To have gone through so much, and then to be cut down by an act of treachery . . .

In front of him he saw another still body, but he was wary. The man was holding a rifle close to his stomach – like himself, he was alive, and hyper-aware. Sudden tension gripped him. He remembered back to the ambush of months before, the horror of having killed his own men.

Very softly, in English, he said, 'Please identify yourself.'

There was no movement. Rayne swallowed, moved closer and spoke again.

The shape moved – and at once Rayne was poised like a cat, hand tensed round his knife-handle, ready to leap forward onto the body. The man put the rifle down and turned over.

'It's Michael, Rayne. There's hardly anyone left alive. Where the hell have you been?'

'We had problems. That bastard Larry turned on us and then we got ambushed. I'm the only one left, except for someone I found along the way.'

'And what's going on here?'

'It's the bloody Russians. Someone's double-crossed us.'

Their conversation was interrupted by a burst of machine-gun fire and a high-pitched scream. After that there was a deathly silence. Rayne gazed into the impenetrable darkness that surrounded them.

'Did you get all the planes?'

'Yes, and the runway. No one will use that place for weeks. The Russians actually retreated.'

'Moving around now is pretty suicidal. I got one of them further back.'

'Dammit, Rayne, we can't sit this out, it's over ten hours till it gets light. We have to get out of here.'

'OK. You can follow me and Sam back the way we came.'

Before he could say another word, gunfire erupted from the trees. They all dropped flat. Shaking, Rayne felt for Sam's hand. She was crying, 'We're finished! We're finished!' He didn't say anything.

'Rayne . . .'

It was Michael Strong's voice, barely audible. Rayne left Sam and crawled over in the darkness to where he guessed Michael to be. The big man was covered with blood.

'I've let you down, Rayne. I wish I could have . . .'

Blood trickled down from the corner of his mouth. Rayne gripped his head in his hands.

'Michael, fight it! You're not finished yet!'

'It's the way I wanted to die.'

His eyes closed. Rayne felt for his pulse, but there was nothing.

For Michael Strong, life was over.

He didn't need to say anything to Sam. He crawled back to her, and for a moment they lay together on the cold ground, not speaking, not touching. All round him in the dark he could hear movement, the soft and stealthy rustle of the Russian troops slowly closing in on them. He put out a hand to touch Sam's face, and looked into her eyes.

'They won't be taking any prisoners, Sam.'

He pulled the pistol out of his waistband and removed the safety. He put the barrel of the pistol to her head.

'Forgive me?'

She kissed him on the lips. 'Rayne, without you . . .'

The silence was suddenly shattered by the roar of an approaching vehicle. In seconds it was on the runway, headlights blazing, and even as Rayne's finger faltered on the trigger it drew up beside them and an enormous black man leant out of the cab and bellowed. 'Get in! For God's sake, get in!'

Tongogara! Rayne and Sam pulled themselves into the back of the jeep, and while Mnangagwa, smiling grimly, floored the accelerator pedal, Tongogara opened up with the machine-gun, raking the Russian troops before they had a chance to return fire.

Rayne felt faint. He had never been so close to death. He stared at Tongogara, who fired off another fusillade of shots and then sat down in the passenger seat. His deep voice said, 'You were betrayed. The KGB knew about your operation.'

'How?'

'Do not ask questions, Captain Gallagher.'

Rayne was silent for a moment. Then he said, 'I have another way out of here.'

Tongogara turned round to face him, his eyes flashing. 'You live up to your reputation. Where is this way out?'

Rayne told him where the helicopter was waiting for them.

'That is good. But our only way to this helicopter is along the main road, and reinforcements will be coming fast.' He reached down and picked up two Russian camouflage jackets from the floor of the cab. 'Here. Maybe we can fool them.' Then, Mnangagwa put a metal helmet on his head, as did Tongogara. Rayne had to admit that they looked pretty convincing.

Tongogara slapped Mnangagwa on the back. 'If you see anyone coming, just keep going, and we'll keep down.'

A set of lights glowed eerily ahead in the darkness. Rayne slammed another clip of ammunition into the Uzi and passed it to Sam. Tongogara pulled his own Uzi carbine onto his lap and Rayne drew out his pistol. They kept very quiet, each trying to work out what the vehicle ahead of them was. The closer they got, the more it looked like a road-block. Tongogara decided they had only one choice.

'Keep going right up to it, stop next to them. Don't say a bloody word. When I whistle, open fire. And Mnangagwa, you must drive like mad to get us through.'

'And if they've got a machine-gun placement?'

'Don't even think about it.'

Mnangagwa slowed down, his pulse quickening as he realised it *was* a road-block. One truck was parked across the road, another was at the side, facing him, with its engine running and its lights on full beam.

He aimed for the left-hand side of the road, where there was a gap between the truck and the roadside. A spotlight shone directly in his face as he pulled to a halt, and a man screamed at him in Russian. He raised his hand in a salute.

Tongogara got the impression that the road-block had only just been set up, so that their chances of getting through were better than he'd expected. The Russian yelled again and he tightened his grip round the Uzi. The spotlight and the lights of the truck would be his first hit. After that he'd fire wild. The Russian guard came up to the side and looked in. Evidently he was fooled by their disguise because he smiled and said something else in Russian.

Tongogara whipped up the Uzi. The bullets massacred the spotlight, and the lights of the truck a millisecond later. At the same moment Rayne and Sam started firing, while Mnangagwa accelerated forward, praying that there was enough room for him to make it past the trucks. Bullets ricocheted off the bodywork and he could hear screams of Russian invective behind him.

The side of the jeep scraped against the truck, producing a hideous shrieking sound, and Tongogara lobbed a grenade into the back of it as they went past – the explosion nearly knocked the jeep over. Rayne aimed the Uzi out of the back of the jeep. As he had expected, the second truck swung round and followed them. As the lights began to bear down on them, he carefully sighted the Uzi, then shouted for Mnangagwa to apply the brakes; the moment the other truck came nearer, he opened fire. He knocked out the lights with his second burst, then Mnangagwa accelerated again.

Flashes of gunfire erupted from their pursuers and Rayne lay flat to avoid being hit. Tongogara eased another grenade out of his waistband and pulled out the pin. Carefully he counted up to five and then lobbed it into the centre of the road. It exploded five seconds later in front of the truck, shattering the radiator, shrapnel hitting the driver in the face. The big truck skidded off the road and burst into flames.

Mnangagwa shouted above the roar of the engine, 'How much further to the helicopter?'

'Another four kilometres. Just keep the lights on bright so I can see where we are.'

They thundered and bounced along the dirt road, terrified of every blind bend ahead. Rayne prayed silently that Lois had stayed put. If he'd gone, they were finished. The roadside became familiar and he gestured for Mnangagwa to slow down. 'OK, we can get out along here.'

Mnangagwa aimed the jeep along a storm drainage ditch curving off the side of the road. He wanted it to be out of sight of any soldiers who might be pursuing them.

'Jump off!'

Mnangagwa screamed the command as the vehicle started to bounce around out of control. Rayne and Sam leaped out, followed by the others, – and the jeep smashed into rocks with a terrible sound of tearing metal.

They ran across the road and then dived into the bushes for cover. Rayne led the way, the thorn bushes tearing at him as he pushed his way deeper and deeper into the bush. They were just beginning to feel secure when there was an explosion in the distance. The jeep had gone up.

Tongogara looked grimly back at the flames. 'Dammit. That's told them exactly where we are.'

Heeding Tongogara's words, Rayne moved faster up the slope. The moment the ground levelled off he headed to the left, towards the rocky outcrop where he hoped that Lois was still waiting for them with the helicopter. In the distance they could hear trucks drawing up, orders being yelled in Russian. Shots were fired in their direction.

As they got to the rocks, Rayne turned round. The veld where the truck had exploded was burning steadily, and fanned by the wind that had come up after the rain, the fire was advancing rapidly along the side of the road. Silhouetted against the flames he could see the shapes of soldiers, marching steadily towards them. More shots exploded against the rocks above them.

Now the flames danced round a big tree that stood about one hundred metres behind them. Its topmost branches caught fire, creating a bizarre firework display against the black horizon. Rayne could hear the crackle of the wood as the tongues of flame devoured the entire tree. He stood transfixed until Tongogara tugged at his arm, urging him on.

He led them through the dark shadows that fell over the rocks, leaping from boulder to boulder towards the ridge bordering the clearing where he knew the helicopter to be. Mnangagwa and Tongogara kept pace easily, helping Sam whenever she fell.

*

Lois, sitting on a high rock, saw four figures emerge into the clearing below him and he raised his rifle ready to fire. One was a woman, the other three were men with automatic weapons. He waited, his finger on the trigger.

'I don't know where the hell he is. I hope he's all right.'

Lois recognised Rayne's voice at once. 'Rayne. Here!'

Rayne spun round and looked up to see a figure on the rock above him. He breathed an immense sigh of relief, and watched as Lois scrambled down from his perch and ran up to them.

'So where are the rest of the men?' Lois looked round anxiously.

It was only then that the full extent of what had happened dawned on Rayne. 'Someone tipped off the Russians,' he said.

'Just you four?' He couldn't believe it. Rayne said nothing.

Sam looked back. To her horror she saw that the whole sky behind the ridge they had just descended was a blaze of fiery light, and all along the top of the ridge, black figures against the glow, were Russian soldiers.

'Move it! They're coming right for us!'

She sprinted towards the helicopter as Lois jumped into the cockpit. While gunfire erupted all around them, Tongogara lifted her up and hoisted her in after him. Rayne stood his ground, firing the Uzi.

Tongogara shouted, 'Get out of here!' But Rayne, blazing away at the advancing troops, yelled, 'Tell Lois to take off with Sam. We've got to pin down their fire!'

It was then that Tongogara moved up behind Rayne and hit him across the back of the skull with his rifle butt. Sam screamed out in horror – and then was silent as Tongogara carried the unconscious Rayne to the helicopter and bundled him inside the hold. He gestured to Lois. 'Take off! Get the hell out!'

Again Sam screamed as she was carried upwards, away from Tongogara and Mnangagwa, who fired continuously into the men now sprinting through the flames towards them.

Sam stared down. Back to back, the two half-brothers fired into the ranks of the enemy. She saw them move apart, saw Tongogara hold up his rifle in a gesture of defiance as Mnangagwa desperately slapped another magazine into his weapon, and then they were together again, firing back to back, in a last heroic stand.

And then, almost simultaneously, Mnangagwa tumbled forwards and his brother staggered and fell, clutching at his chest. Sam screamed out, and Tongogara rose up again, staring into the darkness.

'Live for me.'

Did she hear the words, or did she only imagine them? The noise of the helicopter blades roared in her ears as she saw the body of the black man rise up on a burst of machine-gun fire, then fall for ever from her sight.

Lois flew close to the ground, following the road that led towards Beira. He knew he had to reach the shoreline fast. Flying inland would be disastrous – he had no points to navigate by, and they could easily go in the wrong direction, wasting both valuable fuel and time. The gauges below him glowed eerily, and he scanned them anxiously to make sure that everything on board the chopper was functioning as it should.

Rayne came round and pulled the giant hatch closed so that he and Sam were enclosed in the dark fuselage. He could hardly believe that it was all over. It felt strange – to be safe.

'Where's Tongogara?'

'Dead.' Sam's face was streaming with tears. 'He knocked you out and then threw you in the hold. He and Mnangagwa stayed on the ground, drawing off the Russian fire so that we could get away. Oh Rayne!' She put her arms round him and buried her head in his chest, clasping him tightly. He saw at once that she had been in love with Tongogara. And Tongogara had saved their lives.

It was now, when he should have felt relief, the satisfaction of a job well done, that the rage and the bitterness really welled up in him. How many good men had been lost tonight? How many acts of heroism had gone unrewarded – except by agony and death? They had died by treachery.

Sitting there in the throbbing darkness, holding Sam's hand, Rayne thought of John Fry. He thought of Bernard Aschaar too. There was no way he was going to leave the score unsettled.

Rayne and John

The crowd of black fighters were gathered together in the wet Mozambican darkness. There was none of the happy anticipation that usually characterised such meetings, the laughter, the singing. They all knew why they had been summoned.

In the distance, torches flamed as their leader appeared. They saw the glint of light on his glasses. He climbed onto the roof of a truck and stood above them. There was utter silence. The rain fell steadily.

Mugabe began, 'The war is over for us. The Rhodesians have struck yet again. The forces of Western imperialism again threaten the independence of the peoples of Africa.'

A murmur of assent rose from the crowd.

'Our Russian friends have failed us. We needed major air support to launch the attack on Salisbury. The Russians, who claimed they were omnipotent with their modern fighters, were easily outwitted by our enemies. Every Russian plane has been destroyed. There will be no attack on Salisbury.'

A stunned silence descended on the crowd. Unmoved, Mugabe went on.

'This, I say, is a good thing. As Africans we must stand aloof from that kind of aid. It is the foreigners who have always held us in subjugation, it is the foreigners who made us poor and powerless in our own lands. They must be defeated!'

The applause that greeted this command was tumultuous.

'I know that you are sick of fighting, but you must forget your sickness. We must fight on. And though for the time being you must lay down your rifles and return to the land of your birth for the forthcoming elections, remember that the elections, too, are a contest, a battle that we must win. The Matabele dogs to the west must never rule over the Shona peoples. Our victory must be complete and overwhelming. You must make sure that the people vote for the people. If the Russians want our friendship after such a victory, they must bring us food before guns and treaties!'

The crowd was screaming now with excitement.

'What happened tonight was a victory for the people. We will never have an obligation to these Russians. Now each man will have his own land, his own house, his own vote, and his children will be able to stand proud in his memory. Long live Zimbabwe!'

The applause was overwhelming, and Robert Mugabe climbed off the car into the arms of his supporters.

Lois put the chopper gently down on the undulating runway and watched the grass flatten under the force of the rotor blades. The moment they were down, he killed the engine and began shouting instructions for hiding the machine. He had landed as close to the trees as possible. Now it was a matter of taking the rope he had in the fuselage and winching the machine under the branches. It would have been impossible for them on their own, but Lois had brought along a giant ratchet used by lumberjacks for hauling logs up a slope. They attached it to a tree and began to lever in the helicopter, clearing away the lower branches as it disappeared under the leafy canopy.

By the time they had finished, they were completely exhausted. They had crossed the South African border at dawn that morning, and stopped briefly to refuel in the green wilds of Tongaland. Now they were in the Transkei, not far from Port St Johns, at a deserted airfield Rayne knew of from his Selous Scout days. The place was perfectly situated in the middle of nowhere.

Rayne led them down the winding path towards the house. Nothing had changed since he had been there years ago, the key was hidden exactly where he remembered. Lois and Sam were too shattered to make it to the bedroom and curled up at once on the main carpet. In a matter of minutes they were both fast asleep.

Rayne willed himself to stay awake. He moved out onto the balcony and the sea air went some way towards reviving him. He was sure they would come looking, and he wanted to prove his suspicion correct. It was just a question of how long he would have to wait.

Two hours later his patience was rewarded. The giant Mirage jet appeared on the horizon like a magical silver bird. It was criss-crossing the sky, moving slowly down the coastline. He shivered as it came towards him and when he heard its engines at last, he instinctively ducked for cover – but not before he had clearly identified the livery of the South African Defence Force.

He need not have worried. All the pilot saw below him was a deserted house and a particularly attractive deserted beach.

When she first came down to the beach, he could tell she was unaware of his presence. It was typical of her that she had found her way down there without knowing that there was a way at all.

Her long blonde hair blew in the wind, exposing the strong jaw, the high cheekbones and wide sensuous mouth. Her eyes were fixed on the waves, and she tore off her clothes as he had done and bounded towards the white, thunderous surf.

He felt himself aroused by her nakedness, the full firm breasts, the legs that seemed to go on forever. The appetite that had remained dormant for so long woke, hungry, and he sprinted into the waves after her, strong and erect with anticipation. She swung round with surprise. Then there was the coming-together, the embrace in the fresh blue water of the Indian Ocean.

He led her across the beach and into the dense leafy forest that surrounded it.

Under the shadows of the trees he pressed himself against her naked body.

Her hands gripped his buttocks, kneading, and pulled him into her. There was to be no slow foreplay, only the satisfaction of a long, smouldering desire. His toes gripped the leafy soil and she straddled him and wrapped her long legs around his torso. He could hear her screaming with excitement and his own body moved in rhythm to her own.

He came once, and then again. All the while he could feel the multiple orgasms that rippled through her body like the endless succession of waves smashing against the sand of the beach. It was the fulfilment of all they felt for each other, the long-hidden desires that now cried for release.

*

341

When they walked up from the beach together, hand in hand, Lois was lying straddled over his silver bird. He'd let the big helicopter down from its hiding place in the trees, and there was green paint lying all over the ground as he worked feverishly with a flat spatula, peeling long lengths of it from the fuselage. He was stripped down to a pair of shorts, and soaked in sweat.

'This stuff works like a dream, man, I've nearly finished. All I'll need to do is paint on some false civilian numbers and we'll be fine. I can repaint some parts of the fuselage with whatever's left in that storeroom where you found the paint-stripper.'

Rayne saw the guns and the rocket-launchers lying on the ground. The helicopter looked completely different without them.

'Do you think we'll be able to fly out tomorrow?'

'Definitely. We can fill up with the fuel that's left here and we should make Johannesburg easily, if that's where you want to go.'

'Yes, but I don't want to be seen.'

'I know a private landing strip where, if you've got money, no questions are asked.'

'Then we're on for tomorrow.'

John Fry sat in his office in the Pretoria headquarters of CIA Southern Africa. He had an untasted cup of coffee at his elbow, and he was sweating. He couldn't remember ever feeling like this before – terrified, desperate, and powerless. The last twelve hours had been a slow descent into nightmare.

They had begun well enough – exceptionally well, in fact. He'd started the day by reading the *Rand Daily Mail* account of the Beira assault. 'When Will The Killing Stop? Mercenary Force Wipes Out Beira' the headline ran, and it had been an innocuous little article, referring merely to a 'sophisticated military action' by an unnamed power. The 7 a.m. news on the SABC's English Service hadn't been nearly so coy. 'After yesterday afternoon's raid on Beira the British Foreign Office handed out a tersely worded statement condemning the action as foolish and irresponsible. Lord Haversham said that it was about time the Rhodesians learnt that the rule of the gun was over in their part of Africa . . .'

He'd enjoyed that hugely – it was just as he might have written it himself! Of course, the Rhodesians would be furious with him for conning them into believing that the action *wouldn't* be seen as theirs – but what could they do about it now? As it was, he'd nicely pulled off his own private show, efficiently eliminated all personnel, and above all, got those safe-deposit boxes destroyed. Now he was safe. Now the evidence of his involvement with the KGB was gone for good, and he could easily carry on with his career as their most effective double agent. He'd smiled to himself, considering the Russian situation now. Vorotnikov's bid for power in the Soviet government was over. No doubt the KGB would now move in and establish its own links with the new Zimbabwe government.

And so it was in a happy and relaxed frame of mind that he'd sat down an hour later to listen to the recorded report of his operative in Beira.

'Time, 8 a.m., Beira station,' the cold voice declared. 'Report two men and one woman escaped in Bell-Huey gunship. Probable destination South Africa. ZANLA third-in-command Joshua Tongogara enabled escape of Captain Rayne Gallagher and captured American journalist Samantha Elliot. Identity of helicopter pilot unknown.'

That was when the nightmare had begun.

His first move – he'd put his hand to the phone even before the report was finished – was to ring Sarel van der Spuy, head of South African Intelligence, and spin him a cock-and-bull story about a Bell Huey helicopter – the very one implicated in the killing of 'Iron Man' Viljoen – being seen near the Mozambique border; according to his intelligence reports, Fry told him, the helicopter was in the hands of Russian agents. Van der Spuy had fallen for it hook, line and sinker. 'We'll get the bastards!' he'd bellowed down the phone. 'Don't you worry, John!'

Smiling grimly, John Fry had put the phone down and sat back to consider the position in more detail.

It was that incompetent Martin Long who had recommended Gallagher to him . . . And Gallagher was now a serious threat. He'd had the foresight to organise his own escape, and he'd got out alive with first-hand evidence of the whole operation, including his force's final betrayal. What if he came looking for revenge? Captain Gallagher was just the sort of man who would want to avenge his friends. He was the sort of man who did what he thought was right, and never mind the consequences; the sort of man you couldn't rely on to obey orders . . . suppose he hadn't obeyed the order to destroy the safe-deposit boxes, so that those vital documents were lying around in Beira for anyone to find? Or supposing Gallagher himself had taken the documents?

But it was when Fry started investigating Samantha Elliot that the anxiety really began to get to him. She was that journalist, wasn't she, the one whose photographs had helped to bugger up the public reaction to Vietnam? Surely they had a file on her downstairs?

In the giant sub-basement room that was also a nuclear shelter, he indexed in the code for Samantha Elliot and watched the information come up on the computer. Student activities . . . Activities in Vietnam . . . Activities in Rhodesia . . . Published photographs in *Time*, in *Stern*, in *Tribune* . . . Suspected political sympathies . . . Suspected political affiliations . . . Lovers . . . John Fry saw the name of Rayne Gallagher staring up at him.

It was a disaster. With the help of Samantha Elliot, Rayne Gallagher could blow his story round the world. Pray God van der Spuy had got the gunship and killed them both – and the pilot too!

After that, it had been a question of waiting. He'd sat at his desk, reading reports, signing letters, making phone calls, and all the time waiting, waiting.

At last the call had come. Van der Spuy had to announce the failure of aerial reconnaissance. No Bell Huey had been seen on the Mozambique border. John Fry had to face the almost certain possibility that Gallagher and Elliot had got across the border undetected and were now in hiding in South Africa, possessed of information that could destroy him utterly.

They parked the helicopter at the private airstrip without incident, and arrived at the Daytona Motel on foot, just after two o'clock. It was a seedy-looking place, and the clientele looked seedy too.

Sam giggled. 'This is obviously a lunchtime rendezvous for businessmen and their mistresses. They'll probably think we're out of work, looking for a job.'

Rayne saw what she meant. The three of them were still in the same grubby clothes they'd been wearing when they got out of Mozambique.

'Maybe we should choose somewhere else,' said Sam.

'Rubbish, this is exactly the sort of place we should stay. No one asks any questions and everyone looks the other way.' He glanced at Lois. 'You've got our money, safe, haven't you?'

'Sure thing. I've hung onto it through thick and thin.'

The hotel manager, sitting in reception with an open bottle of beer and the *Star* newspaper in front of him, and a cigarette drooping from his bottom lip, managed to look even sleazier than his establishment.

'Whaddya want?' The tone indicated that he did not see Rayne as a potential customer.

When Rayne said nothing, the man got up, took the cigarette from his mouth and had another swig from his bottle of beer. 'Look, china, I'm trying to relax.'

'Listen. I want two rooms and I want them clean. We intend to stay at this establishment for some weeks so I want them away from the busy area.'

The man swept a greasy lock of black hair from his forehead. 'Well, sir, the standard rate's twenty per person per night, and the deluxe rate's twenty-six. In the deluxe you get a lounge area and your own fridge. You also get a colour TV and colour-coordinated wallpaper and curtains.'

'OK. Two deluxe rooms – one for my friend here, and one for the lady and myself. And we'd like them next to each other.'

'My pleasure, sir.' He leered knowingly. 'I'll get your keys right away.'

Rayne woke up at six the next morning. He resisted the temptation to stay in bed beside Sam, who was still sleeping soundly, but got up and made some coffee. Then he dressed and went out for the morning paper.

He enjoyed the *Rand Daily Mail*, a paper which did its best to fight the restrictions of the South African government. He was pleased to see that there was no mention of the helicopter, and read with interest an editorial on the attack on Beira, which declared that it was obviously an attempt by the Rhodesian government to weaken Robert Mugabe.

He turned idly to the business section. To his surprise, a picture of Bernard Aschaar completely dominated the first page. His mining consortium, the Goldcorp Group, was evidently set on acquiring even more mines, and Aschaar argued that this consolidation of interests would bring about a reduction in the cost of producing gold. Rayne was sure that was the last thing Aschaar intended to happen.

He handed the paper over to Sam and poured coffee.

'That's interesting, Rayne.'

'What, the editorial on the raid?'

'No, this article that says a new Russian general has arrived to take over Soviet interests in Mozambique.'

'But what about Vorotnikov?'

'According to the article he died of a heart attack on the day of the assault.'

'What a coincidence!'

'You don't think his death was an accident?'

'I doubt it. You know Aschaar was with him or had just left him at the time?'

'Foul play?'

'Exactly.'

Rayne started thinking. Aschaar's power was awesome; he had been naive to think it would be easy to get his revenge. Perhaps he needed help from someone else, someone who knew Aschaar well, had access to him, and could help put him away. There must be many others who felt about Aschaar as Lois and he did.

Rayne had two things on Aschaar: his involvement in the invasion of Rhodesia, and his having paid Lois to sabotage that plane all those years ago. Penelope had been in that plane – and he'd seen in the paper today that she was spending a couple of weeks in Johannesburg. She could put him in touch with her father, Sir George, who was on the CMC and must know Aschaar intimately.

Rayne cleared the papers from the bed, pulled Sam down next to him and held her close. He needed her, he loved her and he wished that they could go away together, just to have some time alone. But he had to get John Fry and Bernard Aschaar.

'Sam. Two things. What I want us to do today is, I want to tell you in detail, from first to last, everything about the assault on Beira, and I want you to write it down, and then we'll see if we can find a typewriter anywhere in this dump, and maybe you could type it up. I'm not sure what I want to do with it yet, but I think we have to make a detailed account of everything that happened – if only for insurance purposes. Are you with me?'

Sam nodded.

'And then this evening I want to go and see Penelope O'Keefe. I want to talk to her about Bernard Aschaar. I've told you about her, haven't I? There's nothing between us now, I swear it.'

'All right, Rayne. I believe you!'

They put the finishing touches to the account late that afternoon. Rayne had added an appendix listing every character involved in the operation.

'Rayne, any editor in the world would give a year of his life to be able to print this story. It's incredible!'

'You'll have to hold your horses on that. I'm sure it will be published in the end, but let's see how we go, take things step by step.'

'What are your plans for John Fry, Rayne? You haven't said anything yet about him. How are you going to make contact?'

Rayne smiled grimly. 'I'm still working on it. But I think I know someone who might be useful.'

That evening, before Rayne went out, they drank a toast and then sat still for a few minutes, thinking of those who had not made it out of Mozambique alive. Sam thought about Tongogara. One day she would write a book about him, to make sure his story did not die.

The outside bar at the Sunnyside Park Hotel was one of Johannesburg's favourite watering-holes, and as Rayne drove past he could see that the area round the pool was filled with late-night revellers. The hotel that lay behind, however, was far more exclusive. It had once been the official residence of Lord Milner, the governor of the Transvaal after the British victory in the Boer War. Rayne parked among the Mercedes and the BMWs, thinking how much of the atmosphere of that time the building still retained.

Rayne knew that someone like Penelope would not receive uninvited visitors, so he waited till the man at the reception desk turned his back to take a phone call, then spun the visitors' book quickly towards himself. Penelope O'Keefe had the sixth floor to herself. He headed for the stairs – a better bet than the lift, which he suspected might not go as far as the exclusive sixth floor without the use of a special key.

The sixth floor was dimly lit. Facing him across the landing was a majestic set of double doors. Rayne was halfway across the carpet when a dark form intercepted him, and he found

347

himself staring straight into the eyes of a typical strong-arm – unintelligent but vicious.

'I suggest you get out of here, mate.' The accent was surly and the words were spat out in his face.

'I've come to visit Miss O'Keefe. I have an appointment.'

'I don't think so. She didn't tell me she was expecting anyone.'

'Let me see her!'

The next moment the man took a well-aimed swing at him with his right fist. Rayne neatly side-stepped, grabbing the arm as it zipped past his ear and twisting it expertly up and back behind the man's back. Then he rammed the man's face into the wall, and he fell unconscious to the floor.

Rayne pulled off the man's tie and bound his hands behind his back. Then he slipped off the belt from the man's trousers and tightly bound his legs together. He carried the inert body to the bannister above the stairwell and, double-checking the strength of the knot round his feet, hung the man face-down into the void. This done, he walked back to the double doors and rapped on them sharply.

He heard her voice from the next room. 'I told you I was not to be disturbed.'

Rayne walked through and saw the woman he had loved many years before lying in a silk dressing-gown on a chaise-longue, watching the television. She was more beautiful even than he remembered – almost too perfect. She turned and stared at him uncomprehendingly.

'Who the hell are you? And how did you get past Max?' Her accent had an American twang to it.

He sat down on an easy chair facing her and crossed his legs. 'He's big, slow and as thick as they come.'

'That's true. Don't I know you from somewhere . . . ?'

She got up from the couch and walked towards him with a slow, sensuous movement that was entirely natural to her. She took his face in her hands.

'God, Rayne, you've changed. I'd heard you were dead. You never wrote, never stayed in touch.' She stared at him. 'And what have you become, Rayne? You who had the most talent out of anyone I knew?' He was silent. She said, 'How did you know I was here?'

'I saw the article in the paper and put two and two together. You always loved this hotel.'

'And you know all about me?'

'I've seen your films, they were on circuit in Rhodesia. You're a brilliant actress, a star. I always knew you'd do it.'

'Yes, I've got it all – fame, wealth and beauty. What more could I want?'

'You don't fool me with that kind of sarcasm, Penelope. You like what you've got. I think you've turned yourself into the sort of person you always dreamed of becoming.'

'And what's wrong with that?'

'Nothing. Now how does one get a drink round here?'

'That cabinet in the corner. You can get me a whisky while you're about it. Just ice.'

Rayne poured and handed Penelope her glass. 'To our youth.'

'You've got someone else, of course, you bastard. Tell me, what's she like?'

Suddenly he wished he hadn't come. He would have preferred to remember the old Penelope. She was even more attractive now, but she was hard – as hard as fame and fortune could make her.

'She's an American, a journalist. A very strong independent woman like yourself.'

'Spare me the compliments. Is she attractive?'

'Yes, she is attractive.'

'The bitch, I hate her.'

'Come off it Penelope, d'you know how many women must hate you? You can have any man you want.'

'The only men I want I can't have. Everything else I get. Fate has been cruel to me, Rayne.'

He could hardly believe what he was hearing. Her bitterness was bizarre.

'Don't look so astonished, Rayne. You're one of the few men I can be honest with. You come to me like a thief, so you might as well steal my secrets. By the way, where is my so-called bodyguard?'

'Hanging upside down from the stair-rail.'

Penelope ran out of the room to see for herself. She came back laughing and called the manager to have the man cut free.

'His face has gone purple!' she said, pouring herself another Scotch. 'I don't know how you did it!'

It was her third drink since he'd arrived. Rayne wondered if alcoholism had been one of the other perks of her success.

'Don't look at me like that, I can drink Scotch just like my father. There's far worse than this to get addicted to in Hollywood.' She looked him up and down, then smiled mischievously. 'If you walk round Johannesburg dressed as you are, people will think you're an out-of-work game ranger.' She smiled at him. 'But I know better. Oh yes, don't look so surprised. I've followed your career quite closely. Actually, I always thought you'd go into politics in support of the black people, not devote yourself to shooting them down.'

The anger flared through Rayne like a sudden whirlwind. He picked her up by her wrists and held her close to his face. 'You bitch!'

Suddenly he was kissing her uncontrollably and her arms were round his back. She aroused the same responses in him as she always had; and the passion was still strong in her too. When he pushed her gently away, she started to cry and sat down on the couch next to him.

'What's wrong with me, Rayne, why don't you want me?'

He could feel how vulnerable to her charms he still was, and he got up from the couch and walked to the balcony. He looked down at the people far below. It wasn't worth it. If he betrayed Sam, he would lose her. He heard Penelope's voice behind him, echoing his thoughts. 'You want to keep her, don't you? Well, that's your decision. You can stay my friend at least.'

He turned back to face her, more in control of himself now. She sat on the couch, looking at him, her legs drawn up close to her body, her arms hugging her knees.

'Why did you come here, Rayne?'

'I had to see you. I've found out about a few things that happened to us long ago. You remember the air crash?'

'I still have nightmares about it.'

'Well, it was no accident, it was organised – killing you was to be a way of destroying your father. The man behind it went to great lengths to cover the whole thing up, but now the secret's out and I mean to get him. And I think you might be able to help me.'

'Who was it?'

'A man by the name of Bernard Aschaar, acting head of the Goldcorp Group.'

Penelope looked aghast. She turned to the window. 'It can't

be! I had dinner with him the other evening. He's such a pleasant, worldly man.'

'Yes, very worldly. You should have asked him what he was up to last week.'

She sat down on the couch and looked up at him. 'I did. He said he was up in Kenya, looking over some mines.'

'He was in Mozambique, in conference with a Russian general. I saw him with my own eyes.'

He saw the disquiet grow on Penelope's face. She leaned forward anxiously.

'He's just about to sign a major deal with my father. Daddy has been against selling his mines for years, but this time the offer was too good to refuse.'

'All Aschaar wants is power. And he'll do anything to get it. He's a madman. Whatever deal your father does with him, I can assure you there'll be problems.'

Penelope finished her whisky and stood up. 'You must speak to my father, Rayne. You must tell him what you've told me.'

Rayne stared into her eyes. He had to be sure that she would not run to Aschaar.

'All this must remain between us, Penelope. I have a score to settle with Bernard Aschaar. If he has any idea of who I am or that I'm still alive, I'll be in great danger. No one knows that I'm back here except for you, and I want it to stay that way.'

She tossed her head back, her eyes flashing. 'Don't you think you can trust me, Captain Gallagher?'

Yes, he could trust her. There was a core of true steel inside Penelope, always had been. 'I trust you,' he said.

She smiled. 'I think it's a good idea to talk to my father. He's one of the most powerful men in the mining business. He sits on the CMC, you know, and he's in contact with Aschaar on an almost daily basis. If you're looking for revenge, I'm sure my father can tell you the best way to get to him.'

'All right. Can you reach him tonight?'

Penelope got up. 'I'll phone him now.'

While she was telephoning from the next room, Rayne walked over to the balcony and gazed down at the people arriving at the hotel for dinner, ready for an enjoyable Friday evening. What the hell am I doing? he asked himself. I should have taken the first plane out of the country with Samantha and forgotten the whole business.

351

But then he thought of the men who were lying dead on an old landing strip in Beira. His face hardened and he turned away.

Penelope came back into the room. 'He'll be here soon.' She pulled her silk gown tight around her waist and grinned mischievously. 'While we're waiting for him, you and I can have a nice chat about old times!'

Rayne was surprised at how old Sir George looked, but his presence, his air of authority, were the same as ever.

'God, Rayne, I hardly recognised you. I believe, from the little I've heard, you've seen quite a bit of action in the last few years? Now, what's this you want to talk to me about?'

Rayne told him the whole story about Aschaar and the plane. Sir George's face grew longer and longer as he listened, and when Rayne moved on to the subject of Mozambique, he asked Penelope for a second whisky. Clearly, he could hardly believe what he was hearing. After Rayne had finished, he was silent for some time.

'It all makes sense,' he said at last. 'I can see now that the bastard's been trying to put the screws on me for years – and I've never realised it! Obviously he's decided to start buying me out. That Mozambique business is a real eye-opener. He should be put away for life! He's nothing less than a cold-blooded murderer. My mining company, together with those other mines he already owns in Rhodesia – that will give him enormous power. But what can anyone do to stop him?

'Sonja Seyton-Waugh's been taking on the Goldcorp Group recently, but it's a tough battle, I can tell you. I don't know how you could catch a man like Aschaar out. He's too wily to find himself in a court of law.'

He took out one of his cards and handed it to Rayne.

'That's my private number. I'll give you any support you need. If you're in trouble, just call me. Needless to say, my own deal with Aschaar will be off. From what you've told me, I've escaped very lightly.'

Rayne weighed his next words very carefully.

'Sir George. I have a proposition for you. You tell Aschaar that the deal is still on, but that you've brought in an expert to structure your side of the deal. You raise the purchase price of your mining utilities to an exorbitant amount, and you tell

Aschaar that your new expert advised you to do this, and say that if he wants to negotiate he must deal directly with him.'

'And you will be that expert?'

'Precisely.'

'You'll be playing with fire, Rayne.'

'There's no other way I can get into Aschaar's headquarters without raising his suspicions. I know the risks, Sir George. Once I'm in there, I can put my own plans into action. You ring him tomorrow and tell him about the new deal.'

'All right, you're on. I'll set the ball rolling with a call to Aschaar in the morning.'

When Sir George had gone, Rayne took Penelope's hand and kissed her on the cheek. 'Thanks, Penelope. Thank you for everything.'

'Business is over, so it's back to the little woman?'

'Maybe if you met her, you'd hate her less.'

She looked at him tauntingly. It took all the strength he could muster to give her one more chaste kiss upon the lips, and then walk slowly away.

Sam was lying on the bed when he got back, face-down and fully clothed. As he approached her, she turned over and stared up at him, and he could see at once that she must have been crying for a long time.

'So did you enjoy yourself, Rayne? It must have felt good after all these years. You bastard.'

He bent over the bed and tried to pull her towards him – and she rained blows at his face. One struck him so hard that his nose started to bleed. 'Take your hands off me!' she cried.

'Pull yourself together, Sam. Penelope means nothing to me.'

'Don't lie to me, for God's sake. Spare me that!'

'Sam, nothing happened between Penelope and me. Perhaps something would have happened if I didn't have you – but I do have you, and it didn't.'

Sam looked up at him and started crying again. This time he held her very close to him, and gradually he felt her begin to relax. After a little while she went to get a towel, and even managed to smile as she gently cleaned his bloody nose. When she had finished, she lay down next to him on the bed.

'I'm sorry, Rayne. I couldn't stop you from going. I knew I mustn't do that, but I couldn't stop myself from worrying either.

She's very, very beautiful. Most men would commit murder just to spend an evening out with her.'

Rayne looked up at the cheaply painted ceiling and thought how lonely Penelope was, despite her fame and her looks. 'Sam, you must learn to trust me,' he said. 'If you can't do that, then we're never going to make it together.'

'It sounds so easy.' She sighed. 'But emotions aren't things that just go on and off at the click of a switch. All I can do is try.'

'That's fine, that's all that really matters.'

'So what happened?'

He told her briefly.

'Good,' she said, when he had finished. 'But now listen, because I've got some interesting information as well. You know you spoke of needing someone to help you get Aschaar, and that it would have to be someone you could trust?'

'Sir George fits the bill all right.'

'I think there's someone even better.'

She handed Rayne some magazine clippings, all showing the same tall, beautiful woman. Rayne looked at Sam, intrigued.

'Sonja Seyton-Waugh,' she said. 'Have you heard of her?'

'Sir George mentioned her name.'

'She runs a mining group that most men would be scared to handle. She's a woman of enormous ability – and from these reports you'll see she's gunning for the Goldcorp Group. I happen to know she also hates Bernard Aschaar. And I know her personally – I interviewed her some years back in the States.'

'That's excellent, Sam! She sounds just the person we need. Why don't you get on the phone to her right away.'

Grinning, Sam shook her head. 'First of all, it's too late for social calls. And second I'm now going to make love to you so passionately that you'll never want to think about Penelope O'Keefe ever again.'

Sonja

Rayne knew the number by heart. It rang for a long time before it was answered.

'Major Long speaking.'

'It's Rayne Gallagher.'

There was a lengthy silence.

'Rayne. I thought you hadn't made it. I thought . . . I have bad news for you.'

'Sam's with me, Martin. She's safe.'

Another silence.

'Good God, man. I have to see you. There's so much to explain.'

'Like the plane that didn't come to pick us up? Eighteen men dead?'

'Rayne, it wasn't me. I didn't know.'

'Why, Martin? You knew most of those men. I trusted you as a friend.'

'Where are you?'

'Not so fast. You'll send Fry in to kill me, no doubt.'

'You bastard!' The voice on the line cracked with rage and despair. There was something that sounded almost like a sob. Then Martin Long said, 'Give me a chance. I'll prove you wrong, lad.'

'All right. Here's what I want you to do . . .'

Samantha arrived at the Waugh building early in the morning, smartly dressed in a dark blue suit she'd bought the previous day. She crossed the marble entrance hall and took the old-fashioned lift with its gleaming brass fittings to the top floor.

'Good morning madam, can I help you?' A young man in tortoiseshell glasses looked up from his desk in the foyer.

'Yes, I'd like to see Sonja Seyton-Waugh.'

'Do you have an appointment, Mrs . . . ?'

'Samantha Elliot. No, I don't have an appointment, but I did an interview with Sonja some years ago in New York and I was wondering if she'd grant me another?'

'She's very busy this morning, but I'm sure that if you're prepared to wait, she'll see you. Please sit down. This morning's papers are on the table.'

Moments later the young man returned. 'Miss Seyton-Waugh would be delighted to see you, Miss Elliot. She won't be long.'

While she waited Sam once again read through the account of the Mozambique assault that she and Rayne had composed the previous day. She wondered if she was making a fool of herself. For all she knew, Sonja might not be in the least bit interested. She had also brought with her the documents and articles Rayne had taken from the safe-deposit boxes, but the trouble was, they were in Russian . . .

A woman had come in through the door and was staring at her. Sonja Seyton-Waugh was as attractive as ever, but there was also a gentle quality about her that hadn't been there the previous time Sam had met her.

'Samantha Elliot. What a nice surprise! Please come through, it's so long since I saw you.'

Sam smiled warmly. She felt that it would be all right after all.

The spacious office was furnished with antiques, and the floor was strewn with Persian rugs. The view from the window was breathtaking. Sonja said, 'I've read your articles on Rhodesia. They're great! And I believe you want an interview?'

Sam looked at Sonja again. This woman must know a great deal about Bernard Aschaar, and Sam was sure that she wouldn't approve of his activities. She could be a valuable ally.

'Sonja, it's a long story I've come to tell you. In fact it's so long and complicated that I've brought a written account of it for you to read later, if you will. But let me just give you a brief account of it now, myself . . .'

Sonja listened intently as Sam quickly went through her own and Rayne's experiences in Mozambique. The moment she mentioned the name Aschaar, Sonja's attention quickened, and by the time she had finished, her listener was staring at her as if hypnotized.

'What are you going to do, Samantha?'

'Rayne has two objectives. The first is to find John Fry, the American who made sure that he and his men would not get out of Mozambique alive. The second is to put a stop to Bernard Aschaar once and for all.'

'You mean, kill him?'

'To see him brought to justice.'

Sonja got up and walked to the window. 'I've known Bernard Aschaar for a long, long time. I have strong personal cause to hate him, and I hate him for what he's doing to the mining industry. I'd like to see him brought to justice too.' She turned. 'But, Samantha, I also understand enough to know that bringing Bernard Aschaar to justice will be virtually impossible. And you must realize how dangerous he is. If Aschaar comes to suspect that you're out to get him, you're as good as dead.'

'Rayne took these documents which Fry told him to destroy. They were kept in the bank in Beira. One of them has Bernard Aschaar's signature – look. But as you can see, they're all in Russian.'

'That's not a problem, I have a friend who's a lecturer in Russian at the university. Let me have them – if you trust me – and I'll get them translated.'

'Thank you, Sonja. And will you meet Rayne, talk to him?'

Sonja nodded, and touched Sam's shoulder. 'Fate has brought us together again. There's someone I'd like you to meet too – someone with his own particular reason for hating Bernard Aschaar, and able, perhaps, to help you bring him to justice.'

Major Martin Long drove the hire car up to the doors of the deserted warehouse. Looking into the rear-view mirror, he saw the vehicle behind him pull well over to the right. Fine, they were in position. He looked down at his watch to check the time, then felt beneath the folds of his dark green anorak and touched the butt of his gun. He shivered. No backing out now.

Rayne looked over at Lois who sat quietly in the passenger seat, the submachine-gun in his hands covered by a piece of sacking. Lois was utterly dependable. There was no one he'd rather have with him in a tight spot than Lois.

'Well,' he said, 'Major Martin Long may have sold me short, but he's repaying his debt threefold now – Fry's a deadly animal.'

'A KGB agent working for the CIA,' Lois said. 'I'd hate to think how many people he's had killed.'

Through the windscreen Rayne saw Martin Long striding up to the distant warehouse.

'Martin's out of his car and moving into the warehouse on foot. Let's go!'

Martin peered through the gloom. Shafts of early morning sunlight filtered down through the skylights and lit up boxes of machine parts as if they were actors on a stage. He felt uneasy and glanced down at his watch again. Fry was late.

'Very good, Major. Now please walk into the centre of the building.'

Martin looked round for Fry, but the voice was the only evidence of the American's presence. He began to walk very slowly forward.

'Major Long, please. I haven't all morning to waste. You came here to talk, I understand, so please move into the centre. And remember there's a rifle trained on you.'

Martin moved into the middle of the warehouse. 'It's over, Mr Fry,' he said. 'You're exposed. You're a bloody communist agent. A traitor and a killer.'

Fry appeared from behind a packing case. 'What are you talking about, Major?' There was an unsettled expression on the American's face.

'Captain Gallagher has the documents you asked him to destroy. The documents that prove you're an agent of the KGB.' He pulled the gun out of his anorak. 'You killed eighteen fine men, Fry.'

'Put that gun away, Long. You're surrounded.'

Coldly, Martin Long pulled the trigger.

Fry lunged towards him. The bullet found its mark but Fry kept coming, seized the gun and pressed the muzzle against Martin's skull.

'One word out of you, you son of a bitch, and I'll blow your fucking brains out.'

Martin wanted to vomit.

He glimpsed the bulletproof vest beneath Fry's jacket. The American had outguessed him.

'Where are they, Long?'

'You won't get out of here alive.'

Fry raised up the gun butt and brought it down against Martin's skull. He rolled over unconscious.

Rayne looked across at Lois.

It was five minutes after they'd heard the single shot ring out from inside the warehouse.

'Is Long admiring his handiwork?'

Lois pulled the sacking from the machine gun. 'I'm going inside. I think something's gone wrong.'

Rayne whipped out his pistol and darted in through the door.

Inside the warehouse was deathly quiet. They moved quickly along the sides, ducking behind packing cases. It was Rayne who saw Long stagger to his feet. Desperately he looked around for Fry's corpse. There was no sign of it.

'He was wearing a bulletproof vest . . .' Martin looked into Rayne's eyes.

'I told him you know he's a KGB agent. He got away . . .'

Christ, Martin thought, I've buggered up again.

They met, the five of them, at six in the evening in Sonja's beautiful sitting room – Sonja, Deon, Rayne, Lois and Sam. After Sonja had made the introductions, she poured them all a drink and they sat on her leather couches looking at each other rather uncertainly.

'Since I'm the hostess,' said Sonja with one of her most glamorous smiles, 'let me start the ball rolling. Both Deon and I have now read your account of what happened in Beira, and I've also had the documents you gave me, Sam, translated by my university friend.'

Rayne thought Sonja was one of the most elegant women he had ever seen. He also liked the look of Deon de Wet; the big man's face spoke of both suffering and strength, a powerful combination that Rayne understood only too well.

Deon said, 'The agreements are almost identical. They're about the setting up of a Marxist state in Rhodesia–Zimbabwe. The earlier agreement is between a KGB agent, John Fry, and the leaders of ZANLA. The later one is between Bernard

Aschaar, General Vorotnikov, and the same ZANLA leaders. Is that what you expected, Captain Gallagher?'

Rayne smiled. 'It's Rayne, please. Can't we all be on first-name terms?' There was a general murmur of assent. 'Yes,' he went on, 'it's exactly what we anticipated, isn't it?' He looked round at Sam and Lois. 'That first agreement proves John Fry is a double agent – it shows he was actually working for the KGB, negotiating with ZANLA for a KGB-backed invasion of Rhodesia. Then, when the Russian military came on the scene in the shape of General Vorotnikov, the KGB got cold feet and asked Fry to abort the whole thing. So, with his CIA hat on, he recruited us to do it – making sure that we, and all the evidence of his KGB activities, were destroyed in the process.'

'Only things went wrong for him,' said Deon, smiling grimly, 'and you three got out alive, bringing these documents with you. And being the sort of man you are, Rayne, you're no doubt going to avenge the deaths of those eighteen good men left behind in Mozambique.'

It was Rayne's turn to look grim. 'We tried – and we failed. Didn't we, Lois?' Stern-faced, Lois nodded.

Rayne lifted his head and looked Deon straight in the eyes. 'But don't imagine we've finished trying. I'll get him yet. There are more copies of our Beira story than the one you're holding, and I think they could be put to good use . . .' He smiled. 'But Deon – and Sonja – it's not really John Fry that we've come here to talk to you about, it's Bernard Aschaar. This second agreement here makes it plain that he's an extremely dangerous and devious operator, but we have far more evidence of his corrupt and evil doings than this – and I gather from Sam that you've suffered severely at his hands too?'

Deon and Sonja looked at each other. Sam saw their hands meet, and Deon give Sonja's a gentle squeeze. It was obvious that they were very much in love – no need to wonder any longer about the reason for Sonja's new gentle glow of happiness.

'It won't be easy for either of us to talk about it,' said Deon. 'The damage the bastard has done to both our lives is immense. But we want to see him put away where he can't do anyone any more harm, so if you want to hear about what he did to us – what do you think, Sonja?'

Sonja nodded, her eyes bright. 'Let me get everyone another drink before we begin.'

And so they told the story of their involvement with Aschaar. Deon recounted his investigation of the burglary at Aschaar's house and how it had led him to Sonja. He told of Aschaar's obvious partnership with his police boss, General Muller, and how, following Muller's murder of a suspect in the cells, his marriage had been destroyed and his police career sabotaged in order to intimidate him into keeping silent. He told briefly, with suppressed emotion, of the murder of his brother Pieter. Then Sonja told them about herself, and about Helen, and what Aschaar and Jay Golden had done to them. Finally she talked about Bernard's ruthless and megalomaniac plans for the South African mining industry.

When they had finished, there was a long silence. Then Lois said, 'It doesn't sound much after what you've been through, but I've had dealings with Mr Bernard Aschaar too,' and he told them how he had been bribed to sabotage the plane carrying Penelope O'Keefe, and of the dreadful consequences.

'What an appalling catalogue of evil,' said Sam at last. 'And think how many others must also have suffered at his hands!'

'The thing is,' said Rayne, 'what are we going to do about him? What I want to know first is, are you two with me?'

'You hardly need to ask the question,' said Sonja, smiling. 'Of course we are.'

'Good. Next question: what sort of action shall we take?'

'I'm in favour of a straight assassination,' said Deon. 'High-powered rifle with a telescopic sight. I'll do it. Probably go for a night shot, just as he's going into his house.'

'Cold-blooded.'

'After what he's done, I think it's a pretty painless way to go, Rayne.'

'And it means descending to his level.'

'That's true.'

'I want to see the bastard publicly humiliated and brought to justice.' Rayne leaned forward. 'Listen, here's my plan. I've arranged with Sir George O'Keefe, the mining magnate, to play the part of his negotiator, and I've got an appointment to see Bernard Aschaar at eight o'clock tomorrow evening. I'm taking Lois with me, and I want you to come too, Deon – and then I want all three of us to confront Bernard Aschaar with his crimes, and you, Deon, to make a legal arrest.'

'How do we get past security?'

Rayne grinned. 'Surely between us we've had enough experience of skulduggery to be able to get past a few security men.'

'Are we armed?' asked Lois.

Rayne thought for a moment. 'I think we have to be. I don't want to use force – it's to be a last resort – but Bernard Aschaar's the sort of man I just don't want to confront without a pistol in my belt.'

Sam cleared her throat. 'May I ask a question?'

'Go ahead.'

'What about us?'

'What do you mean, what about us?'

Sam said, 'I mean, there's no way that Sonja and I are going to be left out of this, is there, Sonja?'

'No chance,' said Sonja. She looked at Deon. 'You know I have to come,' she said. 'You know I have to confront him.'

'OK,' said Rayne. 'All right. Change of plan. Deon, Sonja and I go up to the meeting with Aschaar. Lois, you and Sam wait downstairs for us in reception, just in case we need a bit of back-up.'

'Just a minute,' said Lois, 'I don't know that I like that.'

'Lois, you're the best back-up I ever had. Now don't quarrel with it.'

'All right. Whatever you say.'

There was a small pause. 'That's it, then,' said Deon. 'We're all set.'

'I'll get some wine,' said Sonja, 'and we'll drink to the destruction of Bernard Aschaar and all his works.'

There would be no sunset in Johannesburg that evening. At six o'clock the sky was packed with dark cloud, the air was hot and heavy. City workers, making their way home, looked up now and then in the expectation of rain, but the threatening storm obstinately refused to break.

In his office at the top of the Goldcorp Building, Bernard Aschaar felt uneasy, he didn't know why. Perhaps it was the weather. Perhaps it was because he had come so close to death in the plane when he left Beira. But he had genuine cause to worry, as he well knew. His sources in Mozambique had informed him that the attack on the airport and the fuel depot could not have been mounted from Rhodesia – so who was behind it? His sources had also told him about the raid on the

Beira bank and the disappearance of the agreement he had signed with Vorotnikov . . . He had the uncomfortable sense of another force, a power he did not know about, working behind the scenes, and he did not like it at all. He would have to be on his guard.

A tall blonde woman in a skin-tight dress walked into the room. 'Will there be anything else, Mr Aschaar?'

Bernard ran his eyes over her for the twentieth time that day. Jay had said she was 'a good lay'. 'No thank you, Rae. You can go now. And you're clear about your duties next week, aren't you?'

'I think so, Mr Aschaar. May I wish you a pleasant trip?' She gave him the full benefit of her smile.

'Indeed you may. Good night.'

This evening, Bernard was going to London for a week. As soon as he'd seen O'Keefe's agent, the helicopter would pick him up from the roof of the building and take him to the airport in time for the nine-thirty flight.

Alone again, Bernard got up and walked to the window. Below him Johannesburg was bathed in the lurid light of the approaching storm. He wanted control of this city – control of it through its most precious and revered property, gold, the yellow metal that had fascinated men for centuries. If it had been just a question of money, he would have bought control years ago – but certain people refused to be bought. Here perhaps was another source of his unease: Sonja Seyton-Waugh and her association with Major-General Deon de Wet.

Aschaar had sensed de Wet was trouble from the moment he started investigating the theft of the photographs from his house. According to Muller, he was an honest cop on a moral crusade – nothing more dangerous. After he'd had Pieter de Wet murdered, Deon had seemed to get the message for a time, and stayed quiet. But it hadn't lasted long. He'd been harassing the Goldcorp Group in general, and Bernard in particular, whenever there was the least opportunity; and Bernard was sure that it was Deon who was giving Sonja the courage to resist his blackmail threats. It was all thoroughly unsettling.

Bernard turned restlessly from the window and walked back to his desk. He'd ring General Muller, have a word with him about stepping up security. He'd been meaning to do it for some time, anyway. He picked up the phone and dialled the General's home number.

'Hallo, Piet, it's Bernard here. How are things . . . ? I want to talk to you about security, Piet. I'm going away tonight, for a week or so, and I'd like to have a word with you before I go. Can you come here, about eight-fifteen this evening?'

Bernard paused, to let Muller tell him at some length that most unfortunately he had a prior engagement. 'No, Piet,' said Bernard when he had finished, 'I'm quite sure that in fact you will be able to come, and I shall look forward to seeing you in a couple of hours' time.'

There was a short silence on the other end of the line, then Muller said shortly that he'd be there. Bernard put the phone down with a smile. He had enough dirt on the General to make him dance to any tune he chose.

Through the big plate-glass windows the sky now had a bruised and angry look. Bernard viewed the worsening weather with concern.

There was a knock on the door, and a man in pilot's uniform entered. 'Mr Aschaar, I just came to tell you that I'll be ready for take-off from eight-thirty onwards.'

'What about the storm?'

'Naturally, if the rain's very heavy I'll wait a bit before take-off. But it shouldn't trouble us otherwise, sir.'

'Good. I'll see you later, then.'

When the pilot had left the room, Bernard went to the wall and pushed a button concealed at the side of one of the panels. Immediately a large safe was revealed. He typed in the electronic combination number and the door was open within seconds. He counted out R500,000 in used notes.

That, he thought, would be more than enough to bring Sir George's lackey round to his own way of thinking. He closed the safe and the panel, placing the money in an antique silver box on a side-table. Then he sat down at his desk and opened the file on the take-over of Sir George's mining interests. Pleasant to contemplate the further expansion of his empire; there could be no happier way of passing the next couple of hours.

Outside the windows of his office, the storm clouds continued to gather, but still it did not rain.

On the very top floor of the Goldcorp Building, the Goldens, father and son, faced each other.

Jay said, 'What I want, Father, is that you should sack Bernard Aschaar.'

Max Golden stared across the desk at his son. He said nothing.

Jay swallowed hard. He was still standing in front of the desk – his father had not asked him to sit down. He went on, 'When we met in London, Father, you said you'd think of handing the company over to me at the end of the year as long as I didn't make any mistakes. Well – ' he paused, and stared defiantly at the man across the desk – 'I think I've done pretty well, and now I think it's time I had my reward.'

An evil smile crossed Max Golden's face, and he gestured for Jay to sit down. The stormy red light, reflected in the office's huge windows, cast an eerie glow across the old man's face.

'Forgive me if I'm wrong,' he said, 'but didn't you tell me then, when I saw you in London, that Sonja Seyton-Waugh was as good as finished?'

'Well, yes, Father, but – '

'I don't see any sign of her being finished, Jay, do you? Have you got those photographs from Bernard, as you promised me you would?'

'I haven't yet, but – '

'And that policeman who's on our backs all the time – de Wet, isn't it? Major-General de Wet? – didn't you tell me then that it was only a matter of days before you had him eliminated?'

'Father – '

'And has he been eliminated, Jay, or is he still making all our lives a misery?'

'But – '

'And finally, Jay, what of Bernard himself? In London you told me he was finished. Your very words. But he isn't finished, is he? Far from it.'

Jay's face was haggard. He said nothing.

'You see,' said Max Golden, 'I'm afraid I think very highly of Bernard's abilities. I think, dear son of mine, that he'd run this company very well.'

Jay shuddered, and rose unsteadily to his feet. 'I see I have to act,' he said.

Max Golden walked to the window, looking across at the thunderclouds. 'The day of reckoning, Jay,' he said. 'The day of reckoning.'

Everyone

They entered the front entrance of the Goldcorp Building and stopped at the front security desk for clearance.

'I'm afraid I only have clearance for one person from Sir George O'Keefe,' said the security man.

Rayne said, 'These two friends of mine would like to wait in reception, please – ' indicating Sam and Lois – 'the other three of us are going up.'

The security man looked at the little group in front of him. He knew the type – tough men, beautiful women, expensive cars, expensive tastes. They often came to the upper level offices in the evening – no doubt they'd be going out on the town with Mr Aschaar and young Mr Golden when they'd finished their business. Mr Aschaar hated being troubled unnecessarily; it might be more than his job was worth if he made a fuss.

He said half-heartedly, 'I told you, I only have clearance for one.'

Rayne came back sharply. 'Put me through to Mr Aschaar, then.'

The security man gave in. 'All right, sir, the three of you can go up. Just remember to tell Mr Aschaar that you were registered as a group, if he should ask.'

They got into the private lift and Deon pushed the button for level 2.

'Isn't Aschaar on the top floor?' said Rayne.

'No, that's reserved for old man Golden. Aschaar's the next rung down. Still, he can't complain, he has most of the second level to himself.'

'Is there any other way out of the building?'

'Just the fire escape.'

The lift stopped at the second level and they all walked out into the white-tiled reception area. Through the huge windows Rayne stared out at the storm that was just beginning to erupt. The lightning flashes were more frequent now, and the skyline was thrown into relief with every burst of silver light. Water droplets crowded on the giant sheet of glass, smeared across it by the strength of the wind. At forty-six floors they were higher up than any other office building in Johannesburg.

They walked into the reception area and waited for Aschaar to appear. At precisely eight o'clock he walked through the door. Deon he did not know, but he recognised Rayne and Sonja instantly. He stood his ground, legs apart, smiling.

'You. What are you doing here? I have a business appointment. Get out of this building, Mr Brand, or I'll have to call the police.'

Aschaar's use of the pseudonym immediately brought memories of Beira flooding back to Rayne. He remembered especially how Aschaar had looked on calmly while Vorotnikov ordered his arrest. He spoke harshly, making the strength of his determination clear.

'Your meeting is with me, Mr Aschaar. The name Brand was a cover while I was operating in Mozambique. I'm Captain Rayne Gallagher, and I'm representing Sir George O'Keefe. Let me introduce my two associates. Miss Seyton-Waugh, who I think you know, and Major-General Deon de Wet.'

Aschaar stared at them coldly. The reality of Aschaar, here, was as frightening as it had been in Beira. Rayne felt a growing sense of unease. The plan had seemed so simple when he outlined it in the comfortable confines of Sonja's house. Now they were here, on Aschaar's territory, and he did not feel that they were completely in control of the situation.

'Come through to my office,' Bernard said quietly. He turned his back on them and headed down a passage, and they followed him into a spacious room, sumptuously furnished.

Aschaar sat down at his desk and looked at them. What were Sonja Seyton-Waugh and Deon de Wet doing with this Rayne Gallagher? And how the hell had Gallagher got out of the hands of the Russians? He did not believe for a moment that what they were going to discuss had anything to do with the O'Keefe deal. He'd been set up.

367

Sonja looked round her at the opulent decor. She hated it – she hated being here. They should not be meeting Aschaar on his own ground – it was a mistake to come. She looked anxiously across at Deon.

Bernard saw Sonja's discomfiture and smiled. He was secure. He had them, so to speak, at his mercy.

'Mr Aschaar,' Rayne said. 'When you met me in Beira I was working for the CIA, putting an end to your carefully orchestrated invasion plans. But our relationship goes further back than that. I expect you've forgotten the time you had Sir George O'Keefe's plane sabotaged in an attempt to kill his daughter. I happened to be on board too. And the engineer you bribed to do the job is prepared to testify to your complicity.'

Momentarily disconcerted, Bernard recovered his wits and smiled again. He couldn't quite believe their stupidity. What were they expecting him to do? Hand himself over to the police?

'Mere supposition. I expect you bought the engineer as easily as I'm supposed to have done.' Bernard gave a dismissive flourish of his hands.

Deon stepped forward, his hatred of Aschaar rising to the surface. 'You are a traitor to this country. Rayne has the document you signed with Vorotnikov from the bank in Beira – is that bought testimony, Mr Aschaar? I'd call it treason, and I can tell you, so would any South African court of law.'

Rayne could see that Aschaar was suddenly trembling with rage. 'Get out of my office,' he said through clenched teeth.

'There's more, and we're not going anywhere.' Deon said icily. 'For example, Mr Aschaar. I investigated a robbery at your house. The safe in the main bedroom was still open and I found certain articles there.'

'And you took them away and are guilty of robbery, Major-General. I should think you were in enough trouble already without admitting to that.' It was amazing how swiftly Bernard had regained control of his emotions.

'I should think you wouldn't want the films and pictures I found in your safe used as evidence in court.'

Bernard raised his eyebrows. 'Why? Am I in these pictures you planted in my safe?'

'No. But Sonja is, and she saw you taking them.'

Bernard looked at Sonja with contempt in his eyes. 'Am I

supposed to object if some woman insists on taking her clothes off in front of me?'

Sonja stared at him without fear. 'Don't try that on me, Bernard. You and Jay are the lowest class of humankind. You're finished.'

Deon pressed on. 'Miss Seyton-Waugh was your victim. Then you did the same thing to your secretary, Helen. We have Helen, Mr Aschaar. She'll take a long time to recover from the drugs you pumped into her, but she'll testify against you and Jay in court.'

'So it was you who wrote that blackmail note?' Bernard said softly.

'Correct.' Deon paused. 'And there's one more thing. You had my brother murdered.'

Bernard allowed a faint expression of reproach to cross his face. 'Oh, you're wrong there, de Wet, I do assure you.'

Deon's control snapped. He whipped forward and hammered his fist into Aschaar's face. As the blood slowly began to trickle down his top lip, Deon ground out, 'And now I'm going to put you where you belong, Mr Aschaar. You're under arrest.'

Bernard lay back in his chair as if overcome. Before they could react, he had pushed backwards against the desk with his feet and, still sitting, shot through the doors behind him.

As Sonja, Rayne and Deon charged after him, he was on his feet and opening a cupboard in the wall of the next office. He pulled out a pump shotgun, and before they could draw their own weapons, he had them covered. Then he moved forward and grabbed Sonja, forcing the barrel of the shotgun into her jaw.

'Put your guns down or the lady dies.'

As Rayne and Deon, very quiet now, threw their weapons onto the marble floor, there was a sudden noise behind them. Bernard turned Sonja round, forcing the metal barrel so hard into her jaw that tears ran from her eyes.

Jay walked into the room. He stared at them.

'What the hell's going on!'

'Why don't you act out your little part, Jay?'

'What do you mean?'

'The discussion your father had with you an hour ago. D'you think I don't know everything that goes on in these offices? Now, over there with the rest of them.'

Running, Jay made for the door. The explosion from the shotgun was deafening. He lay on the floor, his left leg a mass of blood and bone.

'Jesus, Bernard!'

'One more move and I'll blow your head off!'

Rayne felt the sweat trickling down his forehead. The speed of Bernard's reactions, the ease with which he handled his weapon, were frightening. Deon had been right: this was a man to be reckoned with.

Bernard flashed another smile at his enemies.

'Now you have all had your say about me, I'd like to tell you a few home truths. What a pathetic show you'd make in the witness box, wouldn't you? A cop with a predilection for pornographic pictures' – his eyes went to Deon – 'who's divorced his wife and is having an affair with a nymphomaniac. And you, Rayne Gallagher, a soulless mercenary who is also a gun-runner.'

He tightened his grip on Sonja's arm so that she screamed out in agony. Then he gestured for Rayne and Deon to kneel on the floor while he sat down on the edge of a desk, Sonja still clamped firmly in the crook of his left arm.

'I know more about you two than you know about yourselves. Who shall I start with? Yes, Deon de Wet. Your father was a successful attorney, wasn't he, Major-General? He made a lot of money and your family lived in the lap of luxury. Then things went wrong, but you never knew why, did you, de Wet. Well, now I'll tell you. Your father made the stupid mistake of having an affair with Mr Golden's mistress – and Max Golden doesn't like interference in his private concerns any more than I do, and so he broke your father as easily as a little boy snaps a twig. Remember being turned down for that law bursary at Witwaters-rand, de Wet? That was what finally got to your father, wasn't it? Did you know that of all the applicants you had the highest marks and the best academic record? But of course that hardly counted when Mr Golden was head of the board of governors and turned you down personally.'

Deon felt his spirit crushed. In the end he had come to believe their lies, believe his own father guilty of dishonesty and fraud.

'Your father knew the truth, de Wet. That's why he shot himself. Not a strong man. – No, don't be so stupid as to try anything or I'll remove part of your lady friend's face.'

Bernard pushed the shotgun into Sonja's mouth so that a trickle of blood ran down her jaw. Ignoring Jay, who was clutching his leg in agony, he bent his gaze on Rayne.

'And you, Rayne Gallagher, the man who turned his back on a successful career as an advocate. Why was that? Because you killed a man in a rugby match, wasn't it? What a tragedy! Shall I tell you what really happened? As you perhaps know, the man you killed was Tom Rudd, second son of Tony Rudd, the mining magnate. Goldcorp has long-term plans for taking over the Rudd empire, Captain Gallagher. We turned the first son into a drug addict, but we didn't want the second son to inherit either, so when it was discovered that Tom Rudd had a serious congenital weakness of the upper spine, we blackmailed the consultant into silence and he let the silly bugger carry on playing rugby. It was only a matter of time before the inevitable happened, and Tom Rudd broke his neck. Clever, don't you think?'

Rayne could not believe what he was hearing. Aschaar had almost destroyed him; Aschaar had ruled his life, had been the puppet-master pulling his strings. He felt a cold, quiet hatred burning within him. The man was evil, rotten through and through. They had been fools to think of arresting him. He was beyond the reach of law. Justice was too good for him.

Bernard was enjoying the expression on Rayne's face.

'Yes, Captain Gallagher. And there is nothing you can do about it, nothing at all. And yes, I do remember the business of that plane you and Miss O'Keefe were supposed to die in. Lois Kruger – wasn't that the name of the engineer who was so cooperative? A homosexual, I recall. I believe we still have those pictures of him and his lover somewhere.'

Bernard got up, the shotgun barrel against Sonja's bleeding lips.

'But enough of these sordid revelations, ladies and gentlemen. We must be on our way. Yes, we are all going on a little trip. You will not be completing the journey, but I'm sure you'll enjoy the flight, and especially the landing.'

Over in the corner, Jay tried to raise himself up from the floor. 'You think you've got it all, Bernard.' He was forcing the words out against the excruciating pain. 'But you've got everything except a child. That's why you left Marisa – because she knew you couldn't father a child.'

Rayne saw the tip of the shotgun barrel drop momentarily

from Sonja's lips, and moved forward – but Bernard saw him, and he had to back away.

Jay said, 'Don't worry, though, Bernard. Marisa's got a child now. It's mine.'

In one swift movement Bernard threw Sonja to the floor and swung the butt of the shotgun hard down into Jay's skull.

Down on the ground floor, General Muller burst panting through the entrance doors and made straight for the lifts. There'd been a snarl-up on the bloody motorway and he was late for his appointment with Bernard. He hated doing the least thing to upset Bernard; he was afraid of him.

'Hey!' said the security man. 'Where d'you think you're going?'

'Come on, man. You know me, you've seen me a hundred times. I'm going up to see Mr Aschaar.'

'Oh yes, sir. Sorry, General Muller. Go right ahead.'

As the General was carried upwards in the lift, the security man sat back and looked at his watch. His relief was late again – that bastard Bert never did bother to get here on time. He glanced across at the couple sitting in the waiting area. The man was reading a magazine and the woman was taking a keen interest in the rubber plant . . . They wouldn't be any trouble. He'd just nip into the office, get his coat and tidy up, so that when Bert did decide to arrive he could get off home at once.

'Shall we?' said Sam in a whisper.

'I think we'd better.' Lois nodded. 'I didn't like the look of that chap who just went up. I think maybe Bernard Aschaar is getting himself some reinforcements.'

'OK then. Quick, now, while the guard's powdering his nose.'

They moved stealthily across to the lifts. Noiselessly the lift floated down to them. Its doors slid open on oiled wheels to receive them, slid silently closed behind them, and they were carried up to level 3.

Jay felt almost at peace now, lying alone on the floor of Bernard's office. There had been a time – how long ago? – when he had been in terrible pain. Pain in his head, pain in his leg – but now all that had gone, and he could be quiet. There had been a time, too, when it had seemed vital to reach the intercom on Bernard's desk, somehow to drag his body to the intercom, press the button, tell someone that . . .

But all that desperation had vanished too, now, along with the pain. There was nothing he needed to do, nothing more, ever. He could let the darkness carry him away.

They were herded up a spiral staircase and into a square, glass-walled office set on top of the roof – Rayne, Deon and Sonja; Sonja with the barrel of the shotgun pressed into the small of her back, and her left arm gripped in Bernard's. They saw the helicopter perched on the concrete outside, its rotors already spinning in the pouring rain. Deon and Rayne exchanged glances. It was obvious what Aschaar intended to do – carry them up in the helicopter and then push them out of the door over the mine dumps.

Aschaar shepherded them out into the rain. The wind was suddenly fresh and strong in their faces. All around them was sky, and below them, a long drop to death. There was absolutely nothing they could do.

General Muller sprinted, puffing, up the spiral staircase, drawing his pistol as he went. In Bernard's office he'd found Jay Golden dead on the floor in a pool of blood. My God, what the hell was going on?

He hadn't been on the roof before. He came out into a sort of glass office, and saw beyond it a strange man about to step into the hold of a helicopter, and Bernard Aschaar standing by with a shotgun. He crouched down behind the glass and took aim.

Bernard, hearing a noise, spun round. All he could see, through the pouring rain and the wet glass, was a menacing figure with a gun aimed directly at him. Without even thinking about it, he leapt into the office doorway and pumped a shot into the crouching figure.

Muller collapsed in a pool of blood, his face blown away – and even as Bernard turned back to the helicopter, Rayne was on him, wrestling with him for the gun. Lois and Sam, emerging at that moment from the spiral staircase, saw the two of them locked together – and the helicopter hovering a metre above the roof, with Deon and Sonja staring desperately from the hold.

Instinctively, Lois made for the helicopter. He sprinted across the wet concrete and grabbed the lower landing struts with both hands. As the pilot accelerated, and the helicopter engines screamed, Lois looked down at the drop below him, his arms already beginning to fail.

Sam, crouched just inside the office doorway, shut her eyes.

They struggled desperately for possession of the gun. Aschaar got it, and Rayne dived down as a shot exploded above him. Aschaar crouched to fire again, but slipped and dropped the shotgun in a pool of water.

Running forward, Rayne kicked the gun away from him, and then the two of them were lashing viciously at one another; Aschaar brought his head down towards Rayne's skull but Rayne dodged the blow and caught Aschaar's jaw with a strong right hook. Bernard staggered back and then shot forward, hitting Rayne hard in the pit of the stomach. As Rayne doubled up, Aschaar retrieved the shotgun and took aim.

There was a dull click as he squeezed the trigger. The water had got into the cartridges.

The next moment, Rayne was hurtling forward in a flying rugby tackle. But he was too late.

'Don't move, Captain Gallagher,' said Bernard Aschaar. 'Just stay there, lying on the concrete. That'll do nicely.'

Looking up, Rayne saw to his horror that Bernard was holding the shotgun to Sam's head.

In the air above them, Lois, still hanging on to the helicopter's landing struts, knew he was almost finished. Then he heard Deon's voice.

'Hold on!'

Looking up, he saw to his amazement that Deon had forced open the door of the hold and had made his way out onto the flimsy struts. His left hand locked onto the edge of the door, he stretched his right hand down towards Lois's left wrist.

'I can't reach you!'

Summoning all his courage, Lois let go with his left hand and pulled up with his right. For a moment he was certain that Deon's grip wasn't strong enough, that he was going to fall . . . And then, little by little, he felt himself being hauled upwards.

'My God! My God!' Lois collapsed onto the floor of the hold. He had been so close to death – but he had made it. He looked at the two white faces above him, and struggled upright. 'Come on. We've got to get control of this thing.'

'The pilot's armed, Lois. I'll go first.'

Very, very slowly, Deon turned the handle of the door into the cockpit. Then he flung the door open, and rushed in.

Quick off the mark, the pilot was already halfway to the shotgun lying beside him on the floor of the cockpit. Deon grabbed it, but the pilot still held on. A shot exploded through the side glass. Deon heaved the man upwards, then shoved his elbow hard into his ribs and wrenched the gun from him.

Now Lois was already at the controls, fighting to get the helicopter back on course. Lightning had begun to flash around them ominously. All the time, the cloud base had been dropping steadily, and visibility was now very bad indeed. Struggling to see the Goldcorp building through the gathering gloom, Lois was scared they might run into it. Then, without warning, it appeared in the darkness, ablaze with lights.

He made out three figures on the roof.

Another lightning flash lit up the scene, and he cautiously prepared to land.

Lying face-down on the concrete, Rayne saw another man emerge onto the roof – a man he did not recognise, with long silver hair. In his arms he held a machine-gun. Rayne could see that his face was contorted by some strong emotion – grief, hate? He looked almost mad.

'Why did you do it, Bernard?' the silver-haired man cried. 'It was all yours, everything. You knew that. Why did you have to kill him?'

Bernard, still holding Sam by the hair, shrugged. 'I'm sorry, Max, old man, but that's just how it happened. He's dead, and there you are. No good crying over spilt milk.'

The machine-gun in the old man's arms spoke. Bernard Aschaar spun round, his body a mass of red holes. Blood and glass splinters exploded everywhere.

Bernard staggered to his feet. He grasped the thin-bladed throwing knife from between his shoulder blades. It sang through the air. Max Golden span round to avoid it, but it landed in the back of his neck. Screaming in anguish, he sank to the ground.

No one

John Fry merged into the crowds at Charles de Gaulle airport. He had a rendezvous with a senior member of the KGB; he was to be briefed on his next assignment. He did not see the man who followed him, an umbrella in his hand.

'Sorry, old chap.'

The tip of the man's brolly had accidentally caught him on the left buttock. John felt a slight stinging sensation. But when he turned round, the man had disappeared.

The cramps in his chest started seconds later. He guessed what was happening, guessed that Gallagher must have spoken to someone at the Pentagon, so that now, for him, the game was over.

He fell on his side, people clustering around him. He died of a heart attack in an ambulance some fifteen minutes later.

The man on the wheelchair was pushed out through the front doors of the hospital by a nurse.

The surgeon followed them.

The surgeon thought how different Max Golden looked with his long silver hair shorn off. He had waited till this moment to tell his patient the truth.

'Mr Golden.'

The intense, blazing blue eyes caught his own. He was afraid of this man in the wheelchair.

'The extent of your injuries was more extensive than we realised. At your age I'm afraid there will be no chance of recovery. You will be completely paralysed from the neck downwards for the rest of your life.'

Max Golden did not say anything. But the look in his eyes made the surgeon recoil.

It was a look that spoke of the most savage revenge.

Rayne sat at his desk in the window, reading the text book. He was so absorbed that he hardly noticed when Sam came in with the paper.

'Rayne.' He looked up, blinking. 'Rayne, there's something here I think you should read.'

The headline was, 'Sudden Death of American Diplomat in Paris.' 'Mr John Fry,' the article ran, 'former economic adviser to the American Embassy in South Africa, died suddenly last week in Paris. A statement from the American Embassy here maintains that foul play is not suspected. Evidently Mr Fry had been ill for some time.'

Rayne folded up the paper and looked at Sam. 'At least it's a small measure of vindication for Michael Strong and all the others who died.'

'I thought you'd be pleased.'

Rayne looked across at the postcard on the corner of his desk. It was from Deon and Sonja, on honeymoon in the Seychelles. He knew the news would please them too.

'Sam, I'm going to take a walk.'

'It's raining . . .' But she didn't continue her protest, and smiling, watched him go.

She loved this house in the Magaliesburg Mountains outside Johannesburg. She was here as Bruce Gallagher's guest – welcome to stay here with Rayne for as long as she liked. She got on well with Bruce Gallagher, and was glad that he seemed to understand what his son was going through.

She remembered Deon and Sonja's wedding ceremony a week before. How she had wished that it could be her and Rayne. She'd never wanted children before, but now she wanted them desperately.

Sam watched Rayne's straight back as he walked up the slope towards the top of the hill. She looked down at the books on his desk. She had no doubt that he would achieve his goal, that he would one day become the brilliant advocate he so longed to be. But there were other things that she was more concerned about. She knew that he was still in conflict with his past.

She stared after him, praying that he might find some peace within himself, might finally understand that life was for living.

As he neared the summit, the rain pelted down and lightning crashed round him. Storm clouds filled the horizon, and the parched lands beneath drank up the rain. There was nothing up here except himself and the elements, and he was reminded again of the violence on the roof of the Goldcorp Building.

Slowly a faint smile spread across his face. It was Fry who had died, not him. Aschaar who had died, not him.

He thought again of those last terrible moments with Aschaar; of Mozambique, and the men who would never return. He thought of the day – so long ago it seemed now – when he had killed his own men in the bush. All his adult life had been spent gathering knowledge of death and war, a knowledge not worth having.

Now he wanted to become a part of his own country again, to fight for a future free of violence and corruption. He would spend the rest of his life fighting injustice.

Rayne stood for a long time on the summit of the hill. Then he started to walk back to the house.

Now, at last, he knew that he was at peace with himself. The violence was a part of his past. He had a duty to the men who had died, a duty to live.

It was time to tell Sam how much he loved her.

The walk turned into a run.